REFLECT

RUMORED WOMAN

REFLECT

BOOK ONE

MORGAN MAGAURAN

Publisher's note: This is a work of fiction. Names, characters, places, and incidents
either are the product of the author's imagination or are used fictitiously. Any resemblance to actual events, locales, or persons, living or dead, is entirely coincidental.
However, there is a blend of nonfiction for which references to authors, poets,
musicians, thought leaders, and nonprofits are true and links have been provided.
Scan the QR code below for downloadable pdf to these resources. Ultimately,
it's up to the readers to discern what is real and what to believe in.

Morgan Magauran does not have any control over, or responsibility for, any
third-party websites referred to in this book. All internet addresses give in
this book were correct at the time of going to press. The author regrets any
inconvenience caused if addresses have changed or sites have ceased to exist,
but can accept no responsibility for any such change.

Copies can be purchased at RumoredWoman.com

Lyrics to "Lean In" used with permission from Rising Appalachia.

Edited by Kristen Corrects, Inc.
Cover design by The Book Designers
Cover art by Connor Ryan

Paperback ISBN 979-8-9866903-0-8
Ebook ISBN 979-8-9866903-1-5
Library of Congress Control Number: 2022917941

1. Women Inner Life– Fiction
2. Psychological– Fiction
3.Visionary & Metaphysical – Fiction

First edition published 2022

To my readers,
May the light within you be visible to you
and guide your choices in life.
May you experience the surround of the Great Mystery
and how your light melds with it.

TABLE OF CONTENTS

DRAFT BLESSING

"May the tempo of my life, allow my heart, mind, body and spirit to move at the same pace, the pace of embodied presence.

May my breathing and pausing be a reminder to surrender and receive guidance throughout my day, to soften and melt with breath.

May each day unfold with a priority on creative expression, sensing the deeper currents and stalking the sacred.

May I become patient with uncertainty, welcoming mystery into my life as my beloved dance partner, letting go of expectations, even with disappointment, to honor what is authentic in the moment.

May my connection with the elements re-source my days, cultivating courage, faith and my sense of belonging, be-longing.

May a sense of humor be a source of laughter in my days for enjoying life more fully.

May I be willing to be lost, to venture into the terra incognita, letting go of my need to know, my need to figure it out to be safe, trusting life and experiencing the wonder of renewal.

May I live in the inquiry of what if, maybe.

May I tend to myself, others and our environment from a connection with myself, offering kindness, compassion, and spacious witnessing.

May my listening be an invitation, an integration.

May I dwell in the place of infinite capacity, my heart, offering LOVE.

May my experience be one of reciprocity with all my relations.

May my presence be enough."

CHAPTER I

IMPOSSIBLE

THAT SATURDAY THE IMPROBABLE—and what others would say impossible—undeniably occurred. By nightfall I even had a witness. Ian, my partner, finally met my doppelgänger, and together we observed this apparition of myself arrive through our bedroom mirror. The veil had thinned.

It was an unusually balmy morning for May first in New England. Ian had already departed for a seven a.m. tee time. Our rented home was deliciously all mine to start my day. The window over our small altar in our bedroom was cracked open to bring in a cross-breeze. Just as I was about to light the candle and incense, as I did each morning, I was surprised to see that my cream-colored queen chess piece had been moved. It normally sat on the periphery. Now she sat at the center. Ian and I had an unwritten rule that our sacred objects were off limits; touching them was taboo. *Why would he do it? The queen of all pieces is symbolic of sovereignty.*

Our altar was a small two-by-two-foot cherry table, nested beside the waist-high, overstacked bookshelf. On it were various rocks from our hikes, Ian's crystal pyramid, a Red-tailed hawk feather, a hand-blown blue glass perfume bottle with Kauai ocean water inside, my mother's silver filigree butterfly pin, and a major arcana tarot card, the Tower.

For years I'd been drawn to the archetypes and guidance of tarot. My preferred deck was Thoth, by Aleister Crowley. The Tower was my growth symbol for the year, when my birthday and current calendar year added up to the number sixteen. The image of a toppling tower symbolized change. The colors of the card were predominantly orange and black— the element of fire destroys the old to make room for the new. It represented a year when I could wake up to who I really was, a year I could have a mystical experience. It indicated I'd dismantle anything artificial within my personality, restoring only what was authentic and true. The four figures falling out of the crumbling, burning tower represented my outmoded emotional, mental, intuitive, and physical ways of expressing myself. The Eye of Horus on the top of the card was an Egyptian symbol of perception, seeing the world as it really is. The snake surrounded by a halo implied rebirth, the dove with an olive branch signified hope—hope that eventually I would be at peace as I reclaimed my authentic self.

Beside our altar, crumpled in a heap, was an oatmeal-colored organic cotton baby blanket. I'd bought it for myself years ago when I learned I was pregnant. It never swaddled my infant, nor did I ever hold her in my arms. Instead of returning it, I repurposed it to be my prayer blanket. Kneeling upon it reminded me to surrender my will to the greater Will. I pinched the edge of its crochet ribbing, lifted it up to refold it in half, then laid its rectangular shape out before our shared altar. It was just wide enough for me to sit on and long enough to hold me in an outstretched yogic child's pose.

As I knelt before it, I stared at the new location of my queen. *What if neither Ian nor I moved it?* It was yet another unexplainable occurrence in my life lately. Except, before today, these odd events hadn't happened within the walls of our home.

I draped my red fox pelt over my lap, giving in to the urge to stroke her silky fur. A moment later, I had to strike the two-inch matchstick several times before it hissed and lit. The tiny flame ignited the wick of my beeswax tealight candle but nearly burned my nail before the incense stick caught fire. I blew them both out. A hint of sulfur was soon replaced by the smell of jasmine and sandalwood. The smoke spiraled up and disappeared into the air, conjuring to mind images of the previous appearances and disappearances of my doppelgänger. *Will she make herself known again?*

What I didn't know then was that she would show herself to me three times that Saturday. On her final visit she would cast an invitation for me to leave with her. I'd never had a chance to speak with her before; she never lingered long enough for a conversation. Ian had nicknamed her Rumored Woman because he was never around when she revealed herself. He, like most of us, required his own direct experience to believe something was true. I could tell he wasn't convinced she existed, to him she was more like hearsay, a rumor that doesn't always prove out. I had my doubts as well.

Could Rumored Woman have moved my queen? How did she know where we lived? I'd only ever seen her in public before today. As the day unfolded it became obvious she knew more about me than where I lived.

I never associated my attraction to the veil between the seen and unseen worlds as part of my Celtic heritage. I never imagined my ancestral past had any influence on my life. Like many immigrant families, my parents didn't identify being Irish. Our Celtic culture was discarded in the Atlantic, before my great grandparents came ashore in Boston Harbor. It didn't visibly influence how I was raised, despite the full-blooded lines they passed on to me. However, we did proudly wear green on St. Patty's day. My parents, like the general public, celebrated with an abundance of libations. Even though I didn't grow up being told stories of faerie folk and elfin rings, my mother did tell me I had a vivid imagination. *Is Rumored Woman real or just my imagination playing tricks on me?*

My mind was editing the old adage *be careful what you ask for, you may surely get it.* I sensed it needed a postscript, something like *it just might not be the way you imagined it,* or *be prepared to leave the familiar behind,* or maybe even *be prepared to make sacrifices.* I didn't want to make sacrifices. The Tower tarot card intimidated me. I didn't want to burn my life to the ground. I'd had the feeling for weeks that I was approaching a fork in the road. *What had I set in motion by wanting to partner with the invisible field?* By all aspects I had a good life, but outward appearances can be misleading.

Ian kept hinting he planned to propose. I suspected he hesitated because he feared my answer might not be yes. He was right, at least not yet. I'd been married before and I no longer trusted my judgment in men, nor my ability to commit again. The whole construct of marriage—that two people are capable of living authentically together for their whole adult lives—felt like a fantasy to me. I certainly didn't witness it in my upbringing. At times I thought it was just me, that other couples had it figured out. That was until another one of those allegedly happy marriages in my community filed for divorce.

I wanted to bow before our altar and empty my mind until there was a clear field to speak my blessing. I knelt on my prayer blanket and pressed my palms together at my chest for a few breaths. Breathing deeply, I reached my hands in front, touching both index fingers to the ground just beyond my bent knees. I said, "Amidst it all, I carve out sacred time and sacred space to bow to the Great Mystery," as I simultaneously traced an outward arc on either side of me, forming an invisible oval around me that ended at the soles of my feet.

I bowed my forehead to the floor, arms outstretched in front of me, in surrender. With the weight of my head on the ground, my sinuses started to drain. On my exhales I released the tension created by my need to figure everything out. I let my worries about the future seep into the earth and my tendency to take on too much responsibility slip off from my shoulders. I rested there until I felt at peace and grounded in my own skin. My contact with the earth under my palms, knees, shins, and the tops of my feet reminded me that I am held. *I'm never alone.*

Lastly, I said my blessing. I wrote it for myself and knew it by heart. Somedays I spoke my blessing with my head to the ground, somedays I sat back up, cross-legged, and spoke it upright. That day I kept my forehead to the ground, my mind below my heart, in submission.

"May the tempo of my life
allow my heart, mind, body, and spirit to move at the same pace,
the pace of embodied presence.

May my breathing and pausing be a reminder to surrender and
receive guidance throughout my day, to soften and melt with breath.

May each day unfold with a priority on creative expression,
sensing the deeper currents and stalking the sacred.

May I become patient with uncertainty,
welcoming mystery into my life as my beloved dance partner,
letting go of expectations, even with disappointment,
to honor what is authentic in the moment.

May my connection with the elements re-source my days,
cultivating courage, faith, and my sense of belonging, be-longing.

May a sense of humor be a source of laughter in my days
for enjoying life more fully.

May I be willing to be lost, to venture into the terra incognita,
letting go of my need to know, my need to figure it out to be safe,
trusting life and experiencing the wonder of renewal.

May I live in the inquiry of what if, maybe.

May I tend to myself, others, and our environment from a connection
with myself, offering kindness, compassion, and spacious witnessing.

May my listening be an invitation, an integration.

May I dwell in the place of infinite capacity, my heart, offering love.

May my experience be one of reciprocity with all my relations.

May my presence be enough."

I'd been looking forward to my plans for Saturday all week. I was meeting my three closest friends in Newburyport, twenty miles north from where I lived in Manchester by the Sea, Massachusetts. Veena, Jocelyn, and Maggie knew me better than my blood family ever did, sometimes better than I knew myself and thankfully they didn't hesitate to challenge me, especially when my passionate opinions were preachy. They were my chosen family. As an only child, I was the last one standing now that both my parents were ancestors. Oddly, their deaths improved my rapport with them. Who would have thought?

As friends, we ran the gamut on relationships. Veena was divorced but I wasn't sure we could count that as a strike against the institution of marriage since hers was arranged. Jocelyn was about to celebrate her twentieth wedding anniversary, with two teenage kids, a thriving consulting career, a fifteen-year-old Labrador, and as many years left on her mortgage. Maggie was still flying solo, married to her childcare business; she flipped through men like magazines, unwilling to subscribe to any one. She appreciated her pick of the stand, for one or maybe two nights.

When I looked in the refrigerator to size up my options for breakfast I heard my inner voice say, *This is my life. I wake, I eat breakfast, I work, I eat lunch, I work, I eat dinner, I sleep, rinse and repeat till the weekend rolls around and I socialize between or during meals. Is this all there is?*

I didn't know what I wanted for breakfast—nor my life, for that matter. I closed the refrigerator door and sat on the barstool. On the back of an envelope was a note to me.

Sarah, we're out of eggs
— *Ian.*

Well I won't have eggs then. I rested my elbows on the island counter, cupping my chin and cheeks while my middle fingers massaged my temples. I hadn't been able to shake the nagging feeling I was missing my life, the one only I could lead. *Am I settling for what I'm supposed to want, for the script? Do I want what Jocelyn has: a marriage, career, children, white picket fence around a hefty mortgage? Oh, and let's not forget the dog. That way the act of visibly cleaning up shit can be daily.* If that was the scorecard, I could only tick off one of the five boxes. Even my choice of career as an English teacher was questionable. I probably would have been happier teaching philosophy but that wasn't offered in high school, so I taught it anyway. I admired Socrates. On the first day of school my students were greeted by his quote written in fluorescent green chalk on the blackboard: *The unexamined life is not worth living.*

Sometimes I cross-examined myself. There was a time when I doubted I'd be a good mother. I'd been pregnant twice but never blessed, for different reasons, to hold the miracle of life in my arms. Now I wasn't so sure I still wanted to bring children into this world. The interrelated crises of climate change and systemic racism were enough to give me pause. Having finally woken to these issues, it was hard to go back to sleep—or to sleep at all, for that matter. The temptation to be an ostrich and stick my head in the sand was undeniably present. As a privileged white woman, I had the illusion of the luxury of denial, at least around racism.

Am I doing enough? This question plagued me. I realized it wasn't always about doing, it was about being. *Life is a journey, not a destination. Yeah, yeah, yeah, I sound like a fucking bumper sticker.* I'd read enough self-help books in my attempts to avoid therapy to know all the catchphrases, although since Veena was a therapist, I occasionally got unsolicited advice.

I took out the ingredients for a kale, banana, and frozen blueberry smoothie. I knew later I wouldn't be able to resist a jelly donut when we all met at the Changing Tides Cafe & Donut Shop in Newburyport. Jocelyn's daughter, Sam, was part of a demonstration that Saturday with Extinction Rebellion (XR), a global organization that believed we were in the midst of a climate emergency and that we had the moral duty to take action, whatever our politics. Sam had been increasingly active in the XR's Massachusetts chapter.[1] After hearing her enthusiasm for their work I'd checked out their rebel training video and was impressed with their nonviolent approach: Tell the Truth, Act Now, and Go Beyond Politics.[2]

Likely going beyond politics appealed to Sam given she had the full political spectrum in her parents. Jocelyn was a liberal Democrat and her father, Jim, was a staunch Republican.

Apparently much of my beloved Newburyport and the surrounding coastline was on pace to be submerged in the near future due to climate change. XR Mass had organized a "tidal tour" around downtown with postcards and letters of how the historical sites would be underwater. Jocelyn had helped Sam make postcards and sew her costume. Demonstrators dressed up as ocean people in blue and green, while others were part of the Polar Bear Brigade. I arrived early to see it all for myself. It turned out to be a clever way to use art and imagination to raise

---

[1] Extinction Rebellion, https://rebellion.global/.
[2] Extinction Rebellion, "Heading for Extinctions and What to do About It."
July 24, 2022, Training Video, 23.53, https://rebellion.global/.

awareness through a protest. They won over new members that day. I was ready to join.

Sam, short for Samantha, had surpassed her mum in height. She made a towering polar bear. Maggie could empathize with Sam. She had looked down at all the boys in high school, hence none of them ever wanted to date her. However, Maggie had clearly made up for lost time. Sam had an example that everything has its season, even though at sixteen being statuesque can be hard to carry off. Maggie didn't hide her height with flats. The only thing that was short on her was her pixie haircut. She insisted it was the only way to tame her curls. Someday I'd like to see her grow it out, so she could embrace her even wilder side.

The café's front glass window offered a full view of fresh donuts in the making, an excellent marketing strategy. *Just plant the thought of a warm donut and see what happens.*

As we were out in public, we altered our starting ritual of lighting a candle and sitting in silence until one of us offered a gesture. After a few moments of silence we each reached for our respective sweet or caffeine. Jocelyn asked, "So did you all watch the movie? I felt like my own family dynamics were on display. The teenage boy in the film could have easily been Jeremy. He's attached at the hip to his phone. I'm horrified by the number of hours he spends on it. What is it doing to his brain? I swear he is more distracted than ever." She looked at Veena, who had powdered sugar on her upper lip and pointed to her own lip.

Veena took a napkin to her face. "Is it gone?" We all nodded. "I have several young men who are addicted to their phones in therapy with me. They're sleep deprived. It's not just affecting their attention span, it's inhibiting their ability to form healthy relationships and socialize with friends. Texting is their default communication pattern."

Maggie's phone had dinged. She was typing a response as she spoke. "Texting has been a godsend. It's better than being caught in a long conversation with my mum when I just need to ask a question." We all exchanged glances while Maggie's head was down. Jocelyn was biting her lip. She had a hair trigger for phones being on while we were together. I said, "Hey, Mag, away with that thing, it's circle time."

Maggie looked up. "Yeah, okay, busted. I'm turning it off." She silenced it and dropped it in her leather bag. We all reached for our donut or coffee.

Veena broke the awkward silence. "Sure it's convenient, but it's no substitute for having an eye-to-eye conversation or a call. How else do we learn not to interrupt, to read body language, to empathize?"

"Empathy is in short supply." I looked at Maggie, checking to see if she was still with us. "How are your parents?" Normally we'd assume Maggie was tending to work issues, but since it was the weekend and her closest friends were with her, it had to be a family issue.

"Becoming more and more dependent on my sister. I'm not sure how much longer they will be able to live on their own. Luckily she still lives nearby." Maggie pulled apart a twist of her cinnamon cruller. "I didn't anticipate how this stage of their life would feel living on separate continents." She rolled her eyes as she took her bite. We knew that signal meant a new topic of conversation, please.

Jocelyn obliged. "Did you track the time you were on your phone last week?"

She had taught us how to select the feature in our settings. I had. "I was shocked to see I'm averaging four and a half hours a day on my phone. I'm not on Facebook, Instagram, or Twitter. Although, I'm still a Google hound for information."

Maggie asked, "Don't you use Pandora for your music and listen to podcasts?"

I replied, "Yeah, my phone is now my entertainment source and camera, which admittedly is convenient. Not to mention I text regularly to stay in touch with friends."

"Indra's grandparents have been more a part of her life then I thought possible. With FaceTime they've been able to watch her grow up even though they are halfway around the world." Veena looked wistful. "It's been too long since we've returned to India; her life is so full now it's harder to pull her away from it for a few weeks."

Jocelyn added, "I get that it's not all bad; I appreciate having information at my fingertips. It's hard to believe I grew up with encyclopedias. My kids only know Wikipedia and Uncle Google."

"I find myself wondering what we did with those five hours before there were cell phones?" No one replied. "How many hours is Jeremy on his phone? Is he in the double digits?"

Jocelyn had finished her donut and was using her finger to press up the remaining crumbs and put them in her mouth. "I'm afraid to tell you he is." She pushed her clean plate away. "Did you watch the credits on the film where the business executives leading the tech companies admitted they're fanatical about keeping their kids off screens? I mean seriously, how hypocritical is that?"

At our last gathering Jocelyn had encouraged us to watch *The Social Dilemma* on Netflix, the documentary by the Center for Humane Technology.[3] It was sounding the alarm on the power of social media in our lives; while it could be a force for good, it isn't always. They are shedding light on how it's invisibly outsmarting us, addicting and polarizing our society with its amoral algorithms. I watched it with Ian and found their systemic analysis both spot on and disturbing. The attention economy was a powerful concept as was the notion of tech's impact on us to downgrade our attention spans.

Maggie held the last bite of her cruller in her fingers. "Jeremy probably has his phone out during class." She took the bite and licked the cinnamon off of her index finger and thumb. "God that was good, I'm tempted to get another."

"Talk about distractions!" My voice went up an octave. "Phones in classrooms are a pet peeve of mine."

"So what do you do about it?" asked Veena.

I got on my soapbox. "On the first day I let my students know my expectation is they keep their devices either off or on mute and put away during my class. If I catch anyone using it, there is no warning. I take it and drop it in the basket by the door. I write their name on a corner of the blackboard and they have to leave it in the basket for the next week while they are in my class. If I catch more than three students in a week on their device then the whole class has to put their devices in the basket when they enter class for the remainder of that week and the next week. I want them to know their actions have consequences, not just for them but for their classmates."

Maggie smiled. "Nice try, but how many of your students are just throwing old phones in the basket or using their Apple Watch to play Solitaire?"

---

[3] Center for Humane Technology, https://www.humanetech.com/.

"Ugh, you're killing me Maggie. Sadly you're probably right, I'm being duped." I only half-jokingly yanked my hair out from my head with both hands, mouthing a scream. "I don't want to compete for my students' attention with a screen. Even on my best day I'm not that enthralling."

Veena laughed. "I wouldn't want to be you. I get that surveillance of device use isn't your job. There's a bigger question here: What's going on inside for your students? How is our educational system not meeting them? I hear them complain that at eighteen they can legally vote or go to war but they can't drink. They are waking up to how the world doesn't make sense and many don't want to participate in it. A little or a lot of distraction is the escape they want and no one is going to stop them."

Jocelyn said, "Sam has found groups online she identifies with she wouldn't necessarily have met at school, like XR. She doesn't spend time gaming like Jeremy, she does listen incessantly to true crime podcasts like *My Favorite Murder*.[4]

"Indra too, she listens to MFM. I heard a few episodes," Veena said, "but I wouldn't call myself a Murderino."

"A what?" Maggie and I asked simultaneously.

Veena explained, "It's how they identify themselves. Indra wears her T-shirt and inevitably gets comments from her tribe. MFM covers crimes and often unsolved murders. Many of them are about women or people of color who've disappeared or been killed and the police barely bothered to investigate. I know it sounds like an odd fascination but you're going to love this Maggie, one of the central messages is 'fuck politeness.'"

Maggie broke into a smile and nodded. "You're right, I'd wear a T-shirt that said that."

---

[4] My Favorite Murder, https://myfavoritemurder.com/episodes.

Veena continued, "It's not a get out of jail free card for being rude when there is a difference of opinion. It's more about not overriding your instincts when your body is telling you something is unsafe. Women are conditioned to not make waves, to be polite and take care of others' feelings. Perpetrators consistently take advantage of this tendency to dismiss our inner warning alarms."

"My inner alarm bells went off when I was watching that film. The line, 'If you're not paying for the product then you *are* the product' still haunts me." Jocelyn added, "Nothing is ever truly free. They are monetizing our eyes and attention with advertising dollars."

Veena shuddered. "I couldn't stomach the quote that flashed on the screen, something like the only businesses that refer to their customers as 'users' are illegal drugs and software. The business model is blatantly designed to create addiction—time on screen."

"Speaking of haunting lines," Maggie said, "I read this article in Fast Company that quoted Reed Hastings, the CEO of Netflix, who said sleep is their competition."[5]

"Oh mercy." Veena folded up her napkin and put it on her empty plate. "Binge watching, another source of sleep deprivation."

"I don't want to find another series I like." Jocelyn bunched up her napkin and stuffed it in her empty coffee cup. She started gathering up our empty plates. "It's hard to tell my kids to stay off their screen when they see me on it at night. I tell myself I'm folding laundry or making meals so it's okay. But it's not."

I'd just finished my jelly donut. My fingers were still sticky

---

[5] Rina Raphael, Fast Company, "Netflix CEO Reed Hasting: Sleep is our Competition", November 6, 2017, https://www.fastcompany.com/40491939/netflix-ceo-reed-hastings-sleep-is-our-competition.

even though I'd done my best to lick them clean. I'd been waiting to use the bathroom, but there was still a line. The crowds from the demonstration had filtered into the cafe for a coffee and a sweet. "I think multitasking is a curse. I hate how it prevents me from really devoting my attention to the present moment."

Veena quipped, "It's a survival skill for working mothers, especially single working moms."

Maggie and I were sitting facing the glass windows. She directed our attention with her finger pointing outside. Jocelyn and Veena pivoted around. "There's a perfect example."

We all saw a mother pushing a stroller, while she walked her dog and spoke on her phone with a coffee cup balanced in the cup holder.

"The sad thing is"—Jocelyn turned back towards Maggie and me—"she probably doesn't even recognize it as multitasking, it's just a way of life."

While their attention was on the multitasking mom, I noticed my doppelgänger walk past her. She turned to look straight at me as if she knew I was there. She smiled. I smiled back but furrowed my eyebrows. *How is this possible?*

I sat up straighter in my chair and uttered, "Holy shit, there she is again. Did you see her?" I didn't wait for a response. *Now is my moment.* I pushed my chair back and stood to go. "I'll be back in a minute."

I dashed for the exit but was stuck behind an oversized man in a navy jogging suit with a full cardboard tray of specialty coffees. He attempted to navigate the door but when he let go of the corner of the cardboard, it threatened to fall. He needed another hand. *Multitasking, clearly not his strength.* I held the door, my feet shuffling in place. I tried to remember what my

16

doppelgänger was wearing. *Why didn't I pay better attention to her clothing?* I didn't know what color I was looking for amidst the sea of blue and green demonstrators that still milled around. When I finally got out the door, a polar bear handed me a postcard. I said "Thanks" and quickly took it, so as not to be completely rude, but didn't stay to hear the spiel. I jogged along the sidewalk dodging between people, heading in the same direction she had been walking when I first glimpsed her from inside the cafe. Up ahead was the four-way intersection. *Which path did she take? Should I turn or cross over?*

As I reached the crosswalk the pedestrian signal was counting down from 7, 6, 5... I dashed across. There were only a few folks now on the sidewalks. I scanned their heads to see if I could recognize hers. No luck. She could have ducked in any number of shops or restaurants.

I'd lost her, again. *Damn it.*

At my feet was another postcard. I bent to pick it up. The pull of my friends waiting for me in the cafe caused me to turn around and walk back.

When I returned, Veena asked, "What happened, why did you disappear so fast?"

I hadn't mentioned Rumored Woman to them yet. "I saw someone I've been trying to reconnect with but I don't have her contact information."

"Did you catch her?"

"No, I lost track of her." What I didn't say was "again." Had I known she was planning to track me down later that day, I wouldn't have chased after her.

Sam had come and sat in my chair while I was gone. "Come on Mom, it's time to go, I still have homework."

It was nearly four o'clock. We'd monopolized a table long enough. We all stood up and exchanged hugs. I'd never hugged a polar bear before. "Sam, you've got a great costume for Halloween."

Veena and I chatted for a few more minutes in the parking lot. I privately asked her for a recommendation for a couples' therapist. Living with Ian was turning me into a nag. He resisted picking up after himself and I hated seeing his clutter or fighting about it so I begrudgingly did it. Inside I was fuming with a predictably short fuse. When I flared, he made it about my reaction and not about his behavior.

There was no sign of Ian upon my return home and a part of me was relieved I had the house to myself. After fixing a cup of tea I sat with my back up against our overstuffed, purple twill couch. We'd found it in the secondhand store. My journal rested open on my lap, the mug of Good Earth tea warmed my hands, hints of cinnamon and clove in the air. Although our furniture was comfortable enough, my desire was to sit close to the ground. The orange, wooly mohair afghan draped across my bare legs kept the chill at bay. I'd worn shorts on a day meant for jeans. My optimism for the sun to make a stronger appearance had materialized only briefly with the high of seventy-two degrees Fahrenheit. I had tried to rush the season and failed.

Across from me was a wall of windows; to the right was our screen porch door. The sunlight streamed in and illuminated everything it touched with a golden hue. I referred to it as the hour of dust, because there was no denying my house had a layer of it.

I felt like a cat as I caught the last of the day's warmth in my sun patch on the floor. My eyes took longer to open after each blink; the undertow of sleep was strong. Drowsily, I put the remains of my tea on the floor beside me and closed my eyes.

Images came to mind layering themselves before me like a collage: an old stone bridge arched across a verdant valley with a river rushing below, an owl perched on a leafless tree at dusk, a red fox curled up with her nose tucked into her back haunches, a chess board at the conclusion of the game, the white queen piece on the side having been taken.

When I was a child, just before sleep, I'd see these kinds of collages, filled with images I'd not seen during the day. I never spoke of it to anyone. I thought it was normal. I don't recall when they stopped happening or even missing them until today.

I was enjoying the picture show when I heard the sound of footsteps on the porch. I partially opened my eyes expecting to see Ian as he attempted to sneak through the screen door. He prided himself on being able to catch me in a rare nap. I often faded at this hour but rarely gave into it, typically I just pushed through. I couldn't see him but I was sure I wasn't alone. The sounds were too substantive to be a creature.

I called out, "Hey Ian, I know you're there, just come out."

I saw movement off to the right. The back of a woman with long dark hair billowing in the breeze as she stepped off the porch. My impulse was to get up, but my legs were leaden.

I called out, "Who's there?" as I scrambled to stand. My journal collided with my mug, spraying the remains of my tea all over the carpet. "Shit!"

I had a feeling that it was going to be spilled, just not like this. By the time I crossed the room and pushed open the screen door, she was gone. I walked out onto the porch and called again, "Hey, come back, let's talk, don't keep running away from me."

I turned to go back inside but lingered barefoot on the

threshold for a few more minutes. *Am I hearing and seeing things now? Was this just another figment of my imagination, one more image in my afternoon collage? Besides, how does Rumored Woman know where I live? Could she have followed me home today?* My skin had goosebumps.

CHAPTER 2

THE MIRROR

I WANTED TO IGNORE the spill and wrap myself back up in the afghan. Instead, I fetched some paper towels from the kitchen and mopped up the mess. When the tea stain was adequately blotted, I curled up into the corner of the couch to feel its pressure against me.

I must have drifted off to sleep. When I opened my eyes, Ian was above me smiling. The windows were dark.

"Hello, sleeping beauty. You weren't supposed to wake up till I gave you my magic kiss." He bent down and kissed me gently on my forehead.

I gazed into his blue eyes and said, "Again." As he bent back down, I tipped my head back and caught his lips on mine. "Gotcha!"

Ian's eyes echoed the smile across his closed lips.

"Hey, where did you hide my seven dwarfs?" I hooked my finger on his jeans' belt loop. "Any chance they are in the kitchen trying their hands at dinner? I'm starved."

Ian replied, "Me too, what's for dinner?"

The melted butter softness of my slumber vanished, replaced with a layer of prickly cactus that bristled towards Ian. We had only been living together for a few months and his habit of asking me what was for dinner, like I was supposed to tend to our meals, annoyed me. I snapped, "I don't know, you figure it out."

"Are we a little fussy after our nap?" Ian asked as he towered over me.

Unhooking my finger, I said, "No, *we* aren't a little fussy." I sat up from the couch. His use of the plural pronoun 'we' when he really meant me irritated me. My jaw was set now and I contemplated standing up so we would be eye to eye but I didn't want to leave the warmth of the couch. "I'm a lot fussy. Dinner is a meal we both eat and we are both capable of planning, fixing, and cleaning up after it. So I resent being asked what's for dinner like I should have something in mind."

The truth was I had already thought about it when I debated with myself earlier in the day if I needed to go to the grocery store on the way home. I knew there was chicken in the freezer and we could have it with pasta or rice. If we scrounged well enough in the crisper we could make a modest salad.

Ian was silent.

"I'm tired of being the one who plans dinners and gets it started. Just once I would like you to give it some thought before we are both starved! What did you do for dinner before you moved in with me?"

Ian turned his back to me as he walked away towards the kitchen. "I ate out a lot. Listen, it's no big deal. I didn't mean you had to fix it. You're overreacting. I'll take care of it if you want me to. What do we have?"

I should have been grateful for his offer. I wasn't. Inside

I was growling. I heard my voice rise to another decibel and it wasn't just because he was farther away. "Taking care of it means figuring that out for yourself." *Asshole.* "Call me when it's close to ready and I'll set the table." I also hated it when he told me I was overreacting. I wanted to say, *That wasn't overreacting. Here, let me show you what overreacting really looks like!* He had no idea how much I contained my own anger. I rarely screamed or slammed doors, though I would have liked to.

As I put pen to page, my wrath washed out of me into my journal. It was clear I was fussy, but not just at Ian. I was disappointed that my encounters with Rumored Woman this afternoon were so fleeting. I wanted more. I wanted extended time with her. I wanted to know who she was, where she lived, how she spent her days. I speculated that even though she looked like me, she likely moved through the world differently. *What if it takes two people to live a full life? I'm likely the one obsessed with being productive, teaching and redesigning my curriculum each year. She's probably the relaxed, creative one. What if we could be friends?* I loved the ways my friends who were different from me offered me a fluidity, the freedom at times to imagine being someone different, to move through my own stuck places and engage with the world from a new perspective.

My circle of female friends was a blessing. I was the youngest by nearly twenty years and had benefited from their life experiences. Veena was the oldest, warm-hearted and generous, despite the setbacks life had dealt her. She immigrated to the states from Rajasthan, India soon after her arranged marriage. Her fertility issues drained them of finances and strained their connection. The only surprise on their adopted daughter's first birthday was on her. Her husband announced he was divorcing her to marry his pregnant mistress. Her husband was an ass. Whenever I saw Veena in a sari, I recalled the grace and fluidity with which she moved through life; she rarely came undone. Her resting face was a smile, whereas my lips were often pursed. When she flashed it at me with her soft-throated chuckle, she prompted me to join her and stop taking myself so seriously. I wished I had a better sense of humor.

Ian had put on Pandora. The song "Home" by Edward Sharpe & The Magnetic Zeros was playing.[6] The refrain, speaking about home as a place we share, became my cue to join him. I disliked the tension between us. *How could I have handled Ian's question about dinner with more grace?* If I had a do-over, what would I say to his question of *What's for dinner?* In my back pocket I had two possible responses: *Good question, what do you have in mind?* or simply *I don't know, what do we have in the fridge?* I didn't have to be responsible. I did want to respond with care and connection. Feeling responsible was yet another tripwire for me, a place I often stumbled.

Ian called out, "Dinner's nearly ready."

When I came into the kitchen, he was at the sink straining pasta. He stood two inches taller than my height of 5'7". His dirty blond hair lightened in the summer months. I wrapped my arms around his athletic frame from behind; his girth allowed my hands to easily overlap as I clasped my wrist over his stomach.

"I'm sorry I snapped at you. I want to talk more about our habits around meals without attacking you and see if we can sort out what works for both of us."

He continued his task. His body was like a wall. There was no squeezing of his arms in response to my holding his waist, nor leaning into me with his cheek as my chin rested on his shoulder. He just said, "Fine."

---

[6] Edward Sharpe & The Magnetic Zeros, "Home," co-director Ryan Gall, May 17, 2010, Official Music Video, 5:06, https://youtu.be/DHEOF_rcND8.

We both knew that was code for *I'm still pissed*. Our pattern was for me to apologize again and try to draw him out into a better mood, then become angry when he didn't acknowledge the effort I was making or do anything to indicate his willingness to meet me halfway. I'd traveled this road enough to make a different turn tonight. I didn't have the desire nor the energy to drift into another bad habit. I hated how this pervasive tension over the little things ruined our nights and we separately hid in our books or a Netflix series. I knew we were both hungry. I hoped a rise in blood sugars would boost the atmosphere between us. I opted for silence instead of the cat and mouse game.

Ian had sautéed the chicken with pesto; the smell of garlic and basil laced the air. He'd found enough romaine and parmesan for a Caesar salad. I noticed he had opened a bottle of Tait, Ball Buster shiraz. He enjoyed choosing themed wines and his message wasn't lost on me.

"Thanks for cooking tonight, it smells great." I went about setting our round cherry table, with red wine glasses and a beeswax pillar candle at the center. *Can we still salvage this night, despite the rough beginning?*

The next song that played was "Lean In" from one of my favorite groups, Rising Appalachia.[7] Singing the words along with them I couldn't help but hear their advice:

> Lean in
> Let's begin again
> Bow down
> Try this soft hearted...

---

[7] Rising Appalachia, "Lean In," August 31, 2020, Music Video, 3:38, https://youtu.be/TlS8yAf5ZDI.

Slow down...
Crossed borders, swam waters
Now I need you by my side...

Bow down, surrender. I needed to remain soft myself. I took a deep breath, letting the exhale release any lingering fuss. I wanted to find a way through these impasses. I wanted to mention seeing Rumored Woman again but I held my tongue. Maybe during dinner I would speak of it when the tenor between us had shifted.

We sat down, Ian on my left. I lit the candle, and he poured the wine. I reached for his hand to say a blessing and he gave me an extra squeeze. Ian was a man of many codes and this was one of them. I interpreted the gesture as a way of signaling he was back, no longer hiding out or brooding. I returned the squeeze as I began our blessing. "We are thankful for this meal, our well-being, and the opportunity to share our love with each other as we learn to be in a relationship that nurtures us both. May we remain open to the mystery as it unfolds in our lives."

A smile filled Ian's face, complete with the dimples that always won me over. I eased into the conversation. "How are you feeling about your offsite this week?" I knew he was flying out on Monday.

He said, "A bit daunted. George Floyd's murder at the knee of the police made visible the racism that has never stopped plaguing our country and the blatant disregard for Black lives. The prior work my client had been engaged with around diversity and inclusion has taken a step change. Now they are considering what it means to become an anti-racist organization. We're all reading Ibram X. Kendi's book, *How to Be An Antiracist*, which speaks more to the journey from an individual perspective and what has to happen societally in terms of institutional reform."[8] He paused to take a bite. "We've been grappling with what it looks like as an organization. We know it means examining policies and mindsets, that everyone's individual behavior and how they communicate will need to evolve. It's a major cultural transformation. The key question is what is the path that takes them there?"

I wrangled a large piece of lettuce into my mouth, crunching a garlic crouton. "It sounds like uncharted waters. We both know that training and education is only as valuable as what you put into practice."

Ian started speaking while he was still chewing. "Exactly. The challenge is that conversations have a tendency to get polarized quickly and people are posturing to prove that they aren't racist." He took another bite and continued. "The brilliance of Kendi's work is his recognition of this dynamic, how the attention gets swept up in denial rather than addressing the root causes. He points out the opposite of racist isn't not racist, it's anti-racist."

I could hear my mother's voice: "Don't speak with your mouth full." But if I corrected him I'd ruin the night for sure. I didn't stray off topic. "Wait, what's the difference between not racist and anti-racist?"

"Essentially he establishes there is no neutral in the struggle against racism, eliminating the space of 'not racist.'" Ian paused from eating and speaking to take a sip of wine. "People can either endorse the idea of a racial hierarchy as a racist or actively work to dismantle it as an anti-racist. Being called a racist has become a slur people defend against. It's not the point, it's a distraction. He wants us to focus on power not people, on policies instead of groups of people. Racist and anti-racist are not fixed identities, we are all

---

[8] Ibram X. Kendi, *How to be an Antiracist*, London, England: Bodley Head, 2019.

both in any given day, ideally striving to be more often anti-racist in our speech and actions."

"Really, all of us? Does he include Black people as being racist too, not just prejudiced?"

"It comes down to a definition of terms. I know where you're going regarding who holds the power, who benefits and the presumption that Black people don't have power. He's taken heat on this point. It raises the issue if reverse racism is possible. Again, I think it's a distraction. If an action or system is designed to oppress, if it upholds an inherent superiority I'd call it racist." Ian stood to have seconds.

A familiar weight descended on me as I pondered how I'd been complicit in perpetuating racism by being blind to where it operated. Lost in my own thoughts, I leaned back in my chair. "I struggle with what to do about it that can make a difference. I don't want to feel impotent nor do I want to ignore it." I refilled my wine glass, craving something sweet, something to soothe my growing sense of anxiety about the future. "Do we have any cookies?" I pushed back from the table and went in search of them in the cabinet.

"Yeah, I just bought some."

I noted he treated my other concerns as rhetorical as my attempts to open the bag of Pepperidge Farms Brussels cookies were ineffective. *I will not be deterred.* The crisp butter cookie with dark chocolate centers were a more sophisticated Oreo than I'd grown up nibbling on. Persistence rewarded. I reached in for a cookie and put the bag between us to share. "Sam has the right approach volunteering with Extinction Rebellion; climate change is going to turn me into an activist. I'm fed up with being part of the silent majority. I need to feel like I'm doing something that matters." I nibbled the edges first.

"Sarah, your teaching matters. Don't sell yourself short."

"I know it does; I'm not planning to quit my job. It's more like I see teaching as necessary and insufficient. I hate feeling the paralysis that sets in when I read the newspaper. I want to know I didn't turn a blind eye, that my actions are part of the solution, not perpetuating the problem." I'd finished my cookie and reached for another.

"There's a reason it's primarily youth at these demonstrations; they don't have a full-time job and financial obligations." Ian pushed his plate aside and slipped two cookies from the bag. "Just get to the end of school; you can join Sam this summer at her protests. After all, there is only one of you teaching and grading papers and only so many hours in the day."

He offered me the perfect segue to update him on the recent appearance of my doppelgänger.

"I saw Rumored Woman twice today, first in Newburyport and later here on our porch." I waited to start my cookie until after I had told him what happened. When I finished, he was silent. I'd eaten my entire cookie wondering what he was thinking. "Well, a penny for your thoughts?" I tossed the bag of cookies out of my reach to resist any further temptation.

Ian was uncharacteristically quiet. Finally he said, "I don't know what to make of it. You obviously experienced something, it's just odd that's all. How does she know where you live?"

My hands were fidgeting with my napkin in my lap. I balled it up and put it on the table. I'd been sitting on the edge of my seat and intentionally eased back in our Parsons chair, bringing my feet up to sit cross-legged. "I think it's odd too. I don't want to dismiss it, yet I can't find a way of letting it rest as just another day. I feel a kind of momentum building, but towards what I don't know." I shook my left hand in front of my chest. "Even speaking about it makes the energy up here in my chest all jittery like I've had a cup of coffee. All the other times I've seen her we were in public. Today was different, she came to our home. There's no denying there is an intentional connection between us. Before I tried to write it off as just a coincidence, but not anymore, not after this afternoon."

We both got up to do the dishes, as if clearing the table might make the unresolved conversation dissipate too. Ian asked, "How is it none of your friends saw her?"

"I don't know, maybe only I can see her."

Ian poured another glass of wine and pumped the wine bottle. His little vacuum sealing device literally sucked the oxygen out of the bottle, preventing it from oxidizing further and preserving the flavor, like freezing it in time. I stared out at the porch. I wished I could freeze the moment when Rumored Woman appeared or at least slow it down. I longed for a chance to meet her, to get to know her. I turned out the lights and turned towards the bedroom.

To my surprise Ian wasn't reading when I walked into the bedroom, he was rearranging the clutter of books, journals, and jewelry on my bedside table. He lit the candle hidden there to signal his desire for a sensual evening. It would have been a fire hazard if the tealight wasn't enclosed in the glass lotus holder. I scanned to see if he put the massage oil out but it wasn't on either of our nightstands.

"Would you like a massage? I can go get the oil."

He said, "No, I have other plans in mind."

I purred inside in anticipation, jettisoning my clothes. Our old cotton sheets rivaled silk as I slipped between them. Ian lit the pillar candles on the dresser just past the foot of our bed and another on his nightstand. The triangle of firelight was enough to illuminate the room.

He yanked off his green *YES* T-shirt with the snake on the front. He locked his eyes on me as he unbuckled his belt, unbuttoned and unzipped his jeans. He stepped out of them and pulled his boxers off in one swift movement. Lying on my left side, I timed raising the sheets to welcome him into our cocoon. The draft was temporary. Now skin to skin, our temperature was on the rise.

When I leaned in to kiss him he surprised me by taking his left index finger lightly to my lips. He traced his finger down my chin and neck, along the centerline of my body. Goosebumps rose on my skin for the second time today. His finger passed between my breasts, down my ribcage, across my belly button. When he arrived at his intended destination, he rotated his wrist and firmly cupped me, his fingers engulfing me.

The heat of his palm sent a tremor to my hips; my lower back began to arch, my legs relaxed open. I wrapped my right arm around his shoulders, pulling him as I rolled from my side to my back, signaling him to lay on top of me.

He slid his hand away with just the right pressure to leave me wanting more. His lips nibbled on my neck. "Better than cookies," he whispered. "Mmm, I want more."

Ian knew I craved the weight of him on me just as we started to make love. He rested on his elbow so I wasn't crushed under his 165 pounds and could breathe freely. It helped me settle into my skin. My hands were free to caress his shoulder blades, sides, and sculpted ass, and my fingers traversed the curves of his butt dents. This time when I tilted my chin towards him for a kiss he opened his lips to me. The taste of red wine and hints of basil lingered in his mouth.

As our hips moved in sync with one another, a pulse throbbed stronger between my legs. I looked forward to a night of slowly kindling our passions for each other till the sparks caught fire, except our plans were interrupted by the pounce of a cat on our bed near my right shoulder.

Ian rolled off the top of me and said, "Well hello puss puss, what are you doing here?"

I immediately sat up against the backboard to distance my face from any possible contact with the cat. "Can you get her out of here?"

"Sure, she's a beauty."

If we had owned the cat I would have happily ignored her or pushed her off the bed. However, I was allergic to cats. *How is it that cats always know who is allergic to them?* Her presence wasn't so easily dismissed. I waved her off with my hands in the air, careful not to touch her.

"How the hell did she get in and who does she belong to?" I wanted to avoid the inevitable eye itching frenzy any physical contact with her hair would create. She didn't have a collar or the look of a stray cat—her belly was round, well fed and her long black fur was well groomed. Her persistent meows demanded our attention.

Ian used his affectionate name for all cats. "Come here, schmutt." He reached across me to scoop her up but she dodged him. First she scampered to the foot of our bed, then leapt impressively to the top of our dresser.

I still wanted her outside. But before I could reiterate my demand, I was startled by the image of Rumored Woman, visible in the round antique mirror I'd inherited from my grandmother. Her reflection indicated she was standing in the doorway of the room, across from the mirror. I turned to see her at the threshold, except she wasn't there. I jerked my head back—she was still in the mirror.

My chest fluttered and my voice almost failed me as I uttered, "Ian, it's her. Rumored Woman, she's here in our bedroom."

CHAPTER 3

THE MEETING

IAN'S HEAD PIVOTED on his shoulders as he scanned the room. "Where?"

She was invisible in the room. I pointed towards the mirror that rested on top of our dresser. "Look in the mirror!"

Its tilt was perfect to capture Rumored Woman's entire upper torso and face. Her long auburn hair rested above her right breast, revealing a slender sweeping neckline. Her collar bones were pronounced, and below the hollow of her throat hung a pendant. The shape was like an incomplete infinity sign, or the letter S, and the bottom resembled a hook. Intersecting the S was a set of mountains or the letter M. My eyes were drawn to it as if it held a secret for me. The longer I looked at it, the more I saw. A crescent moon hung above.

I heard Ian's short intake of breath followed by "Holy shit!" He instinctively looked to the doorway then his head snapped back to the mirror.

My eyes were locked on her. I didn't dare look away again. I'd regained my voice enough to say to him, "Now do you believe me? Just don't move, I don't want to startle her."

Ian said, "Startle her? My heart is about to leap out of my chest!"

We both sat completely still and silent, mesmerized by Rumored Woman's image, wondering how long it would last. My heart raced. Every muscle in my body was constricted on red alert. The cat perched on the dresser; the round of her back met the curve of her neck as she glanced up at Rumored Woman. We were all staring at her. The cat's purring was all we heard in the room.

I'd been holding my breath as well as my tongue. As I exhaled and found my voice. "Who are you? Better still, what are you and why can't we see you in the room?"

She spoke, her voice deeper than I expected. "I've come here for you. You've been summoning me lately. I've held back, waiting to see if you are serious, testing if you really want to see and be seen. I wasn't sure you were ready until today."

I tried to listen but found myself distracted by her slow appearance in the room, at first just a shimmer of an outline that took on more substance as she spoke.

When she had fully materialized she stood at the corner of our bed, no longer a mere reflection. She was, as I suspected, completely naked before us. Her skin was pale and luminescent, like it had never seen the sun but had a healthy, almost otherworldly glow of its own. Her body was slender, her hip bones were obvious. Her shoulders and upper arm muscles could have been rendered in a Da Vinci sketch. She had the musculature of a dancer; even her knee caps had definition. Mine tended to just sag between my thighs and shins.

My glance returned to her dark chocolate-colored eyes. "Can you repeat that? You're telling me I've *conjured* you?"

The cat jumped off the dresser with a thud, landing in front of Rumored Woman, bowing in a long, slow stretch. "Yes, it was your doing," she said as she bent to stroke its fur from head to tail. The cat arched her back up against her hand. Their contact was graceful and familiar.

Her ease with being naked before us kept me from offering her a robe or towel, although I reached to pull the sheets up over our bodies. "How exactly did I summon you?"

She stood back up, letting her arms rest by her sides. "What do you remember from the last time we were together?"

I kept my gaze on her face. "What do you mean together? I've only seen you from a distance, sometimes only for an instant before you run off. I was beginning to think you were just part of my overactive imagination."

She sat on the corner of the bed, twisting her body to face us, her bare shoulder on one side, the other obscured by her hair. "I don't mean recently. I mean when you were young. You would speak with me every day for hours, right up until you started school. Then you stopped rather abruptly." She turned away to look around our room. Her eyes paused on our altar. She looked back and continued, "Our connection has weakened to dream time." The cat was rubbing up against her legs.

Hmm. I sifted through her words for memories. Her voice was familiar now. "I don't recall much of my childhood. I was teased about having an imaginary friend. Are you implying that it was you?"

She patted the bed next to her thigh in an invitation. The cat leapt up and moved directly onto her lap. "Yes, I assure you I was no more imaginary than this cat. Although people have to be willing to see me for me to appear real to them. Ask Ian if he can see me."

I could tell he could see her by his rapt attention. I wondered if he could hear her, too. I turned to him to confirm my suspicion. "Are you tracking all this?"

He had been silent to this point as I'd requested earlier. "Oh yeah, I most certainly can, though I confess"—his hand moved under the sheets—"I've pinched my thigh a few times just to test if I'm awake. I'm doing my best to not completely freak out over here. I don't want to mess up this twilight zone encounter for you." He turned away from her for the first time and looked at me. "We can talk about it later. Besides, methinks she's a good witch." Ian's attempt at humor was enough to bring a smile to both our faces as we looked back at her.

Yeah, good witch but evasive. "Let's get back to the part you've yet to answer: How have I summoned you now?"

Her fingers scratched under the cat's raised chin as if she'd found a switch to keep her motor purring. "Sarah, your morning routine these last few months has changed. You added the practice of speaking aloud the blessing you wrote for yourself after you bow. Your writing it down was the first step. Your willingness to give voice to it, daily, has more power than you know. I've been watching and listening to you for years. Until now, you hadn't invited me back into the conversation. I am, as Ian said, 'a good witch,' which means I follow the rules of not initiating nor imposing myself on you. I must be invited, seriously invited."

It's true. I had been intentionally invoking a relationship with the unseen. I wrote my blessing to instill a different quality to my days, to my life. It all started last year with my gesture of bowing every morning—well, most mornings. I missed it when I didn't. When old habits of checking emails or tackling my to-do list hijacked my attention. Those mornings I got swept up in decluttering the space because I hated coming home to a mess but I neglected my inner landscape. It was habituated for me to simply go from one thing to the next, striving for efficiency and multitasking. While I got a shit load done, I wouldn't describe it as a particularly good day, I just got through it. My days were so much better when I started it before my altar, on my prayer blanket. The phrase *be careful what you ask for, you may surely get it* came back to mind, the one I awoke wanting to edit this morning. So apparently, I did invoke her.

I turned to Ian and asked, "My queen chess piece, did you move it?"

Ian drew his head back. "What? No. I'd never reposition it. You know that."

I turned to Rumored Woman, who was smiling and nodded. "Yes, it was me."

This isn't the first time she has been in our house, in our bedroom. I grabbed the pillow from behind my back and clutched it in front of me, leaning against the headboard. "What now? You're welcome to stay in our spare bedroom. I'm sure I have clothes that will fit you." My mind shifted gears into planning and hostessing. How would I explain her to the neighbors? *Would she come to circle time?* "Can other people see you like Ian can?"

She interrupted my thoughts and stated definitively, "I'm not staying."

I squinted back at her. My nose scrunched up. "You only just got here. How are we to have a relationship if you leave so quickly?"

In the same tone, she said, "You're coming with me."

"Ha, really? Coming where?" I couldn't hide my disbelief any longer. A nervous laugh escaped my mouth.

Her tone shifted to what Maggie affectionately referred to

as *cheeky*. "Consider it the *terra incognita*. It's time for you to be willing to be lost, to venture into unknown territory, letting go of your need to know."

She was offering me back the lines from my blessing. *Did I really ask for* this? The pillared candles Ian had lit on the dresser started to flicker with a breeze and nearly went out.

She continued, but her voice softened just a shade as she cast the invitation I sensed was inevitable. "Are you ready to come with me?"

My hands clutched the pillow closer to my chest. What I heard was *Don't answer me lightly*. "What does that even mean, go with you?"

She stopped stroking the cat but it was having none of it; it meowed louder for attention. The cat knew what she wanted and she wasn't shy about asking for it. "Think of it as inhabiting your blessing, your life, all that you've been asking for."

My blessing was intentionally a working draft. It wasn't destined to be framed or unalterable. It was meant to be alive, to evolve. I hadn't thought of it as a vellum invitation that would summon my doppelgänger. I never imagined it came with an inner landscape to adventure within. I closed my eyes to listen inside my body, asking myself what it would feel like if I said no. *Would I have regrets if she left this time without me?* My hands had the urge to make the gesture of *come back*.

When I was a toddler, whenever my father left on his month-long trips overseas my mother would drive him to the airport. She held me in her arms and we would both wave goodbye, but not the traditional wave, palm out, left to right. We cupped our hands, knuckles towards him, our fingers bent towards us. Our fingers curled back and forth towards our palms, beckoning him to return, to come towards us again.

My eyes flew back open to be sure she was still there. I'd been holding my breath again and exhaled when I saw her petting the cat. She nodded slightly. Did she know I'd already grown attached to her presence? She felt as vital to my well-being as my lungs.

. I assumed if I let her leave without me, she wouldn't be back. She would leave with a part of me that I'd been longing to come to know.

Sometimes I had what I termed a "postcard moment." When I heard a voice in my head say, *I wish you were here.* These postcard moments happened when I was physically occupying a space but my mind and heart were nowhere to be found. *Maybe leaving now is what it will take to actually be here.*

I closed my eyes again and imagined myself with her. I exhaled. My fingers loosened their grip on the pillow. I felt lighter, almost buoyant in her company. My body was at ease. *I trust her even if my mind is flailing at the irrational nature of tonight.*

I opened my eyes and she was staring into them. She was strangely familiar even if I couldn't recall her fully. I marveled at conjuring her. *Why did I summon her now? Why tonight? Why just before Ian and I were about to make love?*

Ian cleared his throat. He was repositioning himself on the bed. I turned to look at him. His brows were furrowed, his head tilted to the left like a puppy upon hearing an odd sound. If I was reading his body language right it was him saying, *Well, what's it going to be?* I reached for his hand, squeezing it gently. I turned back towards Rumored Woman and said, with more confidence than I felt, "Yes I'm ready to leave with you."

His grip strengthened around my hand as he blurted out, "Hey, wait Sarah, what do you mean you're going? You can't just leave. This is ridiculous!"

I turned back to him, stacking my other hand on top of his.

He kept clutching my bottom hand tightly. "What if I can? I want to try. I don't want to let her go without me."

He let go of my hand and pulled back from me, being the first to create a distance between us. "So you're going to go traipsing off to god knows where? With her?" He looked over at Rumored Woman, sizing her up as he would a competitor. "This is beyond absurd. You can't do that."

I reached for his forearm instead of his hand. "I know it's crazy, seemingly impossible, but here she is. What if I can go with her? I have to try or I'll regret it."

He reached for my hand again. His tone softened as he asked, "But how will I know you're okay?" He looked past me towards Rumored Woman, conceding defeat. He flippantly asked, "Can I count on an occasional call or text?"

Rumored Woman replied in her matter-of-fact voice, "You won't be hearing from us. However, the cat will be with you. Don't worry, as long as the cat is okay, all is well. She's very independent, so it's normal if she disappears occasionally. Do your best to care for her. When in doubt, pray."

Ian said, "Oh great, seriously?" He looked back at me, his clutch firm. "You're just going to leave and I'm not going to hear from you until you return? How long will you be gone?"

I wanted to say, *How am I supposed to know?* But I held my tongue and hoped Rumored Woman would answer both of our questions.

Her thumb and index finger spanned her collar bones, coming together and moving apart as she said, "I don't know. I can't tell you that. It depends."

Ian was fond of saying "It depends," but not fond of hearing it said back to him. His whole face sagged, the edges of his eyes and mouth turned down; he'd become a forlorn puppy, no longer curious. I knew nothing I could say would help. I started to waver at the thought of leaving. The pressure of his hand on mine was like a tether. The internal voices I'd been holding at bay were about to assert themselves, ready to second-guess my decision. I let go of the pillow, putting it aside, and turned fully towards him, reaching with my free arm to embrace him. His chest against mine created a pull to stay, to linger. *This is not the night we expected.*

The line of my blessing offered itself to me in a question. *Am I willing to let go of expectations, even with disappointment, to honor what is authentic in the moment?* I could smell Ian's nervous sweat. I took his chin in the cup of my hands and kissed his unyielding lips. When I opened my eyes he was staring at me. While he didn't actually say "Don't go," his magnets were in full force binding me to him. The flutter in my chest was increasing.

I wished the cat had given us more time tonight. I ached to feel again the weight of his full body on mine. Instead I drank in his loving eyes. I flashed on all the times I had missed these moments out of anger or other things I thought I needed to get done. *How many times have I listened to the demands within me to be productive and neglected my desires?* These palpable regrets took me by surprise. I sensed it was time to go but I wasn't ready to let go of the familiar for the unknown. For a moment longer I let my mind indulge in the illusion of safety his arms provided.

Slowly, I started to release him, and his arms opened in response. As I turned away from him, I glanced at the floor and saw my discarded clothes in a heap by the foot of our bed. *How do I pack for this kind of journey? What should I wear?*

Before I had a chance to ask, she said, "Nothing, come as you are."

Feeling the chill of the night air, I asked, "Not even a wrap?"

She shook her head.

Reluctantly, I emerged from the chrysalis of our bed. Standing, I compared her natural beauty to mine; I felt myself grow small. She may have been 5'7" like me, yet her presence took up so much more space in the room.

She reached for my hands and I took hers. I watched the skin on my arms become luminescent. A tremor moved through my body, not unlike an orgasm, that was immensely pleasurable and almost too much to bear.

I heard the urgency in Ian's voice when he said, "Wait, you're fading! You never said when you are coming back! Sarah, goddamn it, when are you coming back? Answer me!"

~⊙~

The outline of Sarah's skin completely disappeared—she vanished. Ian heard no response to his questions, just silence, deafening silence. He waited in desperation for more guidance. "What the fuck! How was that possible?"

Then he heard an owl's call. It was off in a distant tree. He listened to try to determine what kind of owl, grateful for the distraction to occupy his mind. He had to wait a minute before he heard it again. Soft, deep hoots with a stuttering rhythm, "Hoo-h'HOO-hoo-hoo," again followed by silence. He imagined it was a male, a Great Horned owl sounding his territorial calls.

He said, "Your warning is a little late. She's already gone."

Ian turned his attention to the cat. She was back on the bed curled up with her head resting near her paws looking more relaxed than he felt. His mind raced with questions no one could answer for him. *Where did she go? Would she be all right? Would she ever return? Why*

did I suddenly become the caretaker of this cat and why is she so at home in our bed?
Is this just a dream and everything will be as it was when I wake?

He was mesmerized by the way she gracefully swept her tail from side to side. He didn't know how long he'd been watching it. When he checked the clock on his phone, it was well past midnight. Even the owl he had been listening to had flown off.

His mind kept replaying the sightings Sarah had told him about. He hadn't believed her, but he'd been polite. The first time she was downtown, stopped in her car at a four-cornered intersection. She instinctively felt someone was staring at her. She turned to see a woman who could have been her identical twin looking back at her. When the car behind her honked and startled her, she looked away to drive forward. She circled the blocks in a futile search for her. The resemblance between them was uncanny, but something ineffable was distinctly different.

Then there was the sighting at the Newburyport beach, during one of her early-morning walks. Sarah liked to catch the sunrise from there. He slept through it. She returned that morning buzzing. She said she saw a woman at a distance, taking off her clothes to go for a swim. However, before she entered she had deliberately looked back at Sarah and held her gaze. Rumored Woman didn't wait for her to come closer before she swam out into the frigid Atlantic Ocean. He was incredulous that anyone would swim at this time of year. He rarely went in the ocean, even in the summer. Sarah said she had waited by her clothes in the sand until she lost sight of her in the waves. It all sounded too crazy to him. *Would tonight have unfolded differently if I believed her sooner? Could I have accompanied her instead of being left behind as a non-believer? Will she return to me?*

Still the cat lay there beating a steady rhythm with her tail. He admitted defeat. He was beyond sleep tonight. He wanted some relief from the endless loop of questions playing in his mind. His bass sat in the corner of their bedroom, beckoning to him. Earlier in the day while he was golfing he had a baseline come to him. Maybe if he held the instrument in his hand it would return, and he could translate it.

As he got up to move, the cat followed.

CHAPTER 4

WAKING DREAM

W E EMERGED STANDING before a large stone bridge that arched over a lush river valley. My bare feet were on a carpet of moss. Birds excitedly chattered in the trees above as if disturbed by our sudden presence. The sky had the hue of twilight, with lavender clouds. The air was warm, with a gentle, tropical breeze. I turned around to see a knoll of wild grasses and stone outcroppings. The masonry of the bridge reminded me of the old stone walls I had admired throughout Ireland's landscape. Being naked I was grateful there were no other humans in sight. My modesty wanted this to be a private journey. My wish would not be granted.

The reality of my decision to leave with Rumored Woman was front and center. *What have I done?* While I believed I'd summoned her, I was at a loss to know what this journey was to be about. I wanted her guidance, some direction as to what to do next, some sense of what was to come.

She read my unspoken thoughts and suggested, "Let your mind rest awhile and simply feel. It is time for you to trust, time for you to reinhabit your body. There is nothing you have to figure out. You're safe here. Relax."

My arms were crossed around my chest. "Relax, easier said than done. My mind is so hungry for answers you have to at least feed me an appetizer if not the main meal to quell the beast. For starters, I don't even know what to call you. Rumored Woman was our nickname for you but now that you're standing here with me, you're clearly not a rumor anymore."

She put her hands on my shoulders, looking squarely at me. My skin tingled from her touch. "It's up to you if I become more than a rumor. You've had a sense of me for years. You've summoned me and now left with me. But don't be fooled, we are not separate. I, like everyone you will meet on this journey, am an aspect of yourself. The choice is yours who you want to integrate. Your consciousness is your most powerful resource; tap into it and re-source yourself." She let her hands drop.

My peripheral vision saw a flash of something. I tilted my head to see my left shoulder glimmered briefly with phosphorescence. I watched the iridescent greens and blues fade back to my pale skin. I dropped my hands to my sides and wiggled my spine. I felt like Dorothy. *We're not in Kansas anymore. Will there be lions and tigers and bears and a yellow brick road?* Ian was right, she was the good witch. *Except, I can't call her that.*

She smiled. "I don't have a name. I've been called many things by many people and all are true. You can call me Faith."

She had an uncanny way of reading my mind. I smiled and exhaled more deeply at the thought of Faith as my guide in this otherworld. *Faith is definitely called for now.* If this journey was about me claiming my relationship to Faith as no longer a rumor, rather an integral part of my life, then game on.

I had an impulse to cross the bridge. I looked briefly at Faith and she nodded slightly in encouragement. I guessed she was telepathic. Riding horses had taught me not all communication required words.

Glancing down, I chose to walk on the largest stones. They were cooler than the air and smooth on the arches of my feet. I heard the water rushing below and peered over the edge to gauge the height. Looking down made my stomach lurch followed by a wave of nausea. I stepped back and stood still with my eyes closed waiting until I felt steady within.

My morning blessing came to mind. *May the tempo of my life allow my heart, mind, body, and spirit to move at the same pace, the pace of embodied presence. May I become patient with uncertainty, welcoming mystery into my life as my beloved dance partner. Now is the time to embody my blessing. Let mystery be my beloved dance partner, not resist it or cross-examine it.* But how? I flashed on horseback riding. When I asked a horse to canter, I had to receive his movements in my body. My hands followed the movement of his head. My pelvis was fluid with the rhythm of his stride.

I opened my eyes to see her gaze focused on me as a witness. She anchored me while I felt adrift. Her spine was straight, her legs and feet blended into the earth as if they had grown roots. She was holding me true to my intention, no more distractions permitted, no more wavering. If her eyes could talk, I imagined they were saying, *You've got this.* I hoped I would discover that same level of faith in myself.

I continued walking to the other side of the bridge. I paused when my feet reached the cushy mosses that covered the ground.

Where to go from here? I heard a faint rhythm that sounded like ocean waves meeting the shore. *If I keep walking, will I arrive at the beach?* When I closed my eyes to focus on the sound, it grew louder. *That doesn't make any sense—I'm standing still.* I waited. Then it came to me. *This is not any outer landscape, this is my own inner landscape. I'm hearing the sound of my own heart beating.*

My attention landed on my heart. I knew it pulsed as a muscle to pump blood through my veins. I didn't give it much attention until now. I placed my right hand over my heart and listened with my palm. My skin felt silky smooth; this spot rarely saw the sun. The soles of my feet had a pulse as well. *Is it mine or coming from the earth?* I wiggled my toes, bent my knees, and dropped my arm to my side. I started to twist my shoulders from side to side letting my hands gently swing. The tension flowed from my shoulders and arms. My feet were solidly on the ground; my upper body became more fluid. *I am both solid and fluid.* All the times I had recited to myself, in tense moments, "I'm an ocean, I am going with the flow." It felt truer in this moment than I ever imagined.

Faith smiled at my discovery. "Why not follow your own advice?"

I opened my eyes to see her still on the other side of the bridge. Her assurance flooded into me. *I do have this. I can drop into my practice of Authentic Movement; simply move with Faith as my witness.*[9] I held her gaze for a moment, then closed my eyes and stood still. The faint pulse of my body had its own drum beat. *My body is an instrument. What if I learned to play it, to listen to it?* I swayed again, just slightly at first shifting my weight from foot

---

[9] Lee Fuller and Lynn Fuller, "About Authentic Movement and Witnessing", July 25, 2022, http://leeandlynnfuller.com/about-authentic-movement-and-witnessing.

to foot, bending my knees, until my hips wanted to follow in the movement. Soon my rib cage and shoulders were surrendering to the pull. As my neck yielded to the rhythm, tension ebbed out of me. My body felt like a long strand of sea kelp rippling in the ocean currents. A breeze blew my hair away from the edges of my face.

My hands floated up from my sides, elbows bent, palms turned towards one another. I detected a slight pressure, a tingling sensation on my fingers and palms as if an invisible ball of energy had emerged between them. My wrists softened as my hands caressed this ball, one hand above the other. My hands naturally followed the movement of my hips, slightly at first, straying a few inches on either side of my navel. As the tingling sensation built up in my hands, I moved them farther apart until they could have held a small melon.

As my hands flowed back and forth across my midline, my elbows became more fluid, my shoulders dropped down and back, my chest opened. My hands wanted to move differently, while still holding the ball of energy. The bottom hand seamlessly rotated towards the top when it was time to turn back to the center. With my eyes closed, I envisioned a golden light in the wake of my hands that traced an elongated figure eight. What began as a faint strand grew more substantive in depth and dimension. The path my hands followed became a braided golden cord in the shape of infinity.

Periodically I felt a clunk or heard a pop as one of my joints—knees, hips, or a vertebra in my spine—released its tension. The movement had a momentum all its own and I effortlessly followed it.

I kept my eyes closed, giving my body over to this easy

rhythm. My mind, which had been remarkably quiet, began to stir. It named the opposing forces my hands wove between. I sensed the emotions of love and fear, the archetypal energies of the feminine and masculine, the ways of knowing—intuitive and rational. The continuum of opposites were endless: day—night, short—long, esoteric—exoteric. My movement invited me to mingle among them with neither attraction or repulsion.

I'd choreographed the dance of my life, a dance of my hidden wholeness. I longed to inhabit these aspects of my life more intimately, to welcome my invisible holiness. As I moved through time—my past, my future—my attention landed on the crossover center point, the present. A rainbow of colors like the surface of a bubble pulsed between my hands.

Out of nowhere I heard a voice say, "Wow!"

Startled, my hands jerked wider. The rainbow of light disappeared as I opened my eyes to see another woman standing a few feet from me. I could have easily taken a step towards her and reached out my hand to shake hers but I didn't. Her hands held a leather-bound journal and purple fountain pen. She wore khaki shorts with lots of pockets, an untucked white V-neck and flip flops. As I stood there naked and barefoot, a wave of self-consciousness rushed up my body, as my neck and face flushed red. I resisted the urge to cover my private parts. I kept my hands by my sides.

Her head was on a swivel as she took in her surroundings. The clouds in the sky were lit up in hues of pinks and oranges. "Holy moly, what's this all about?" Her auburn hair was pulled back in a bouncy ponytail that swished as she turned. Her gaze came to rest on my face. "Where am I?" Her question ended with a slightly higher tone; her questions were my questions.

I replied, "No idea." She mirrored my curiosity about this adventure.

I turned towards Faith who still stood at the opposite end of the bridge to see if she might answer us. Faith's lips smiled as she spoke, "In time, yes, the answers will reveal themselves. For now you simply have to learn to live with your questions and wonder a while longer."

The woman who had given voice to my questions was already writing in her journal where she stood. She was left-handed like me. I asked, "Who are you?"

She looked up as she replaced the top of her pen and closed her journal. "I'm Curiosity," she replied. "I'm a part of you, your curious side."

I shook my head in a double take and looked back to Faith who only nodded in agreement. I turned towards Curiosity. The resemblance was undeniable. *Another doppelgänger?* "A part of me—how many of me are there?"

She shrugged. "I don't know but I'd like to find out and meet them. Wouldn't you?"

I was still perplexed by my capacity to incarnate different states of my own consciousness into living form. *This is too weird. Unbelievable. What is this place where my inner life is now inhabiting my outer landscape?*

She read my mind and replied. "It is wild, a true odyssey."

My mouth hung slightly open as I gawked at her. *She did it again.* She echoed my thoughts. She was telepathic, like Faith.

Curiosity continued asking my questions. "Have I always had this capacity and just never known it? Can other people come to know themselves this way too?"

Each time she asked a question, her eyes widened a bit.

Curiosity stepped aside and sat on the ground; her knees became a desk while she wrote in her journal.

Another woman appeared swiftly in front of my face. I took a step back. She wore blue jeans and a black tank top. Her pixie haircut was shorn so close to her skull I doubted she even needed to comb it. Her weight was on her back foot, the other slightly in front. My eyes fixated for a moment on her cowboy boot as it continuously tapped a beat on the ground. I couldn't help but admire her taste in shoes—the stitching was clearly handcrafted. I looked up at her when she started fluttering her hands back and forth, as if trying to rush her red fingernail polish to dry. Under her breath I could hear her saying, "Come on, come on." I turned to see Curiosity fading from sight.

I didn't offer to shake her hand either. I hesitantly said hello to this version of me. *Who is she?*

Still in constant motion she asked, "How long is this gonna take?"

I recognized her tone and the absence of a simple courtesy to say hello back, the way she launched right in. She was all too familiar to me, with her need to get going. I'd conjured Impatience. "I'm lost here, what do you mean, how long is what going—"

"The answers to our questions, exactly how long is the 'in time' Faith referred to?" she asked, interrupting me. Her hands were still waving in tighter, faster circles.

I felt a tension build in my shoulders and reached across my chest to rub my trapezius muscles. I started to say, "I don't really—"

She cut me off again. "Seriously, what are we doing here?" Impatience's hands halted.

Impatience's tone had not improved. Each time I paused, she attempted to finish my sentence. I opted instead to ask questions and let her do the talking. "What are you so impatient about?"

Her foot continued to tap. "I hate wasting time. Time is a precious gift and should only be spent in the most valuable and efficient way."

"How do you know what is the most valuable and efficient use of your—I mean our—time?"

She answered, "If there is a faster way of doing something, it's a waste of time to do it another way."

I noticed she didn't address the point of what was most valuable. I realized it was a matter of personal opinion, one we might not agree on anyway. I sensed she was ready to move on. I was certainly ready to be rid of her. "Thank you for—"

But before I could get another word out she had turned and walked away. I was going to say "for coming" but instead I just said, "Goodbye." *Good riddance is more like it.*

I had no regrets seeing the back of her. I wished Curiosity had lingered instead. *Did she leave because Impatience arrived? Is Curiosity inherently patient? My blessing invokes patience with uncertainty. Clearly I have work to do to shift my relationship to time.*

I took a deep breath and shook out my arms and hands. She had offered me a hint. *Impatience arises when I want to do something other than what I'm doing, to be somewhere else, to hear something else. Impatience is at odds with being in the moment. Impatience is born out of having expectations about time which conflict with real time.* I wished I had Curiosity's journal. I hoped she made note of that.

Not knowing who to call next but feeling the hangover influence of Impatience, I was antsy. My shoulders were still tight.

Faith had remained on the opposite side of the bridge. *Why did I cross it? Should I turn back?* I looked ahead for clues. *Where are the damn signs that indicate what happens if I turn left or right? If I'm supposed to know where to go, I don't.*

I paced. *Impatience is contagious.* It was getting darker out. I turned back for guidance only to see my view of Faith blocked by another woman striding over the bridge towards me. I didn't think I'd invited anyone else. I wanted to move on. She was dressed in a black short-sleeve jumpsuit, black flats, and a black fedora hat; her hair was invisible. Her face was tense. The little lines that I always thought appeared over my eyebrows from squinting in the sunlight were etched in her forehead. There was no reason to be squinting in this light. Her lips were pursed too. *Well that explains why those same lines are appearing around my upper lip. My resting face is so not a smile.*

She started speaking before she arrived. "Precisely, you get frustrated when you think there is a right way of going about something. I'm closely tied to Impatience. We go hand in hand so to speak." She extended her hand towards me and I shook it. Her grip was firm. "The bridge we share is called expectation. You have expectations about what should occur and then when it doesn't follow your plan, I appear as I did now." Her eyes were stern. All my attention was drawn to her face, as if the rest of her body didn't matter as much. Her brows were dark and her body was stiff with her arms crossed in front.

Clueless and feeling more irritated at myself for being stuck, I asked, "What am I to learn from my Frustration?" I continued to pace for a few strides while I looked down at the ground.

Frustration replied, "This may be suicidal on my part, but since you asked, you could stand to learn a little flexibility.

Remember there's always another way to go about things. Life rarely goes as planned. It's simply not worth getting worked up about everything that doesn't meet with your expectations."

I stopped and looked at her. "I don't mean to be ungrateful, it's just that you're not telling me anything I don't already know. I find I have a hard time embodying what I know and when I don't live by it I get frustrated with myself."

She nodded. "Yeah, well you need to meet my parents next. When Criticism and Judgment get together they inevitably produce more kids like me."

I decided she presented a perfect opportunity for me to practice my flexibility. "Okay, let's conjure them both up." I tried not to lock my knees for their arrival.

Criticism and Judgment materialized on my side of the bridge. They took another step into my personal space. My body shuddered and leaned away from them. Their weight was thrown over to opposing hips. Their gestures mirrored one another like bookends. Each had an arm across their middle, the other elbow rested on the wrist, their free hand obscured their mouth. They muttered something between themselves I couldn't understand. One pointed her index finger at me, the other bit the nail of her thumb. They surveyed me from head to toe.

I flashed back to the church steps, after mass, watching my mother and her best friend speaking quietly to one another. They didn't point; it wasn't polite. On the drive home I'd hear my mother's critique of what other women had worn to church. "She looked like a long drip of water in that coat, she's too short to carry that look off well" or "Her new hair color is too harsh for her complexion. She needs to change hairdressers, they're not doing her any favors."

I decided I didn't want to engage with them after all. I felt like I'd listened to them most of my life. I only wanted to ask one question: "What would it take to silence the two of you?"

They immediately responded in chorus. "What a bad idea silencing us. Why would you want to do that? Besides, you would never be strong enough to do that!"

They kept rattling on about all my inadequacies and then I heard a clue in the pattern of what they said: "I would never be —— enough." That was their central message. Together they had the power to make me believe I wasn't enough, good enough, smart enough, fast enough, old enough, pretty enough, the list goes on. *What if I am enough—not perfect, simply enough?*

"Did I hear my name?"

A voice from behind me had me spin around. *Oh my god, not another one.* She was dressed to the nines, as my mum would say. Her blue linen shirt dress was impossibly free of wrinkles, accessorized with a chocolate brown belt, a matching leather clutch and high heeled pumps. Her shoulder-length hair was side parted and coiffed with big wide curls, Marilyn Monroe style. It must have been hairsprayed in place, no strands dared move in the breeze.

She asked, "Did you want to see me now?"

My head involuntarily shook no. "You must be Perfect."

"Yes, I am, couldn't you tell? Not only is my appearance flawless, so are my thoughts and actions." Her complexion was enviable.

"Well, I guess that does make you Perfect. Tell me, are you also human?"

"No, I told you I'm Perfect, no human can be perfect," replied Perfection.

"I thought so, well it's been helpful to clear that matter up once and for all. Actually, I don't believe I called for you. I was focusing on being enough, not perfect."

She vanished.

Criticism and Judgment had witnessed the whole interaction. They quietly backed away.

I was ready to be alone; it was practically dark. *This is enough for now.* With that thought they both turned and walked back over the bridge as Faith strode towards me.

The infinite sense of energy that fueled me while I danced between opposing forces had dissipated with each successive encounter. I wanted to collapse on the mosses near the bridge.

Faith came alongside me and said, "Here is not the best place to rest. Exploring your consciousness can be exhausting. This was a good start. Your instincts around what is enough is important to listen to and cultivate."

The damp, cool evening air chilled me. I heard the call of a distant owl— "Hoo-h'HOO-hoo-hoo"—but no response from their mate. Ian would have known what species it was; he was a fountain of knowledge. The thought of him had me wanting to curl up with him, to crawl into my own bed and declare this all a dream, to wake tucked into my spot under his arm, to listen to his heart, even his pesky stomach growling.

Instead my eyes had adjusted in the moonlight enough to see Faith walking in front of me. I followed in her footsteps. The smell of night jasmine wafted in the air.

We approached a one-story octagonal wooden structure. The triangular roof panels came to a crest in the center. The walls I could see held massive windows. Faith led me through a wide-open doorway. As I stepped in she slid the door closed behind us. I heard it click shut.

A collection of five pillar candles in varying heights were lit on the center of the floor. They barely illuminated the space and offered a hint of vanilla to the air. The ceiling was fifteen or more feet high. Extra-long drapes hung along each wall, their cloth sprawled along the floor as if no one bothered to hem them to fit. I reached out to finger the fabric; it was soft and substantial to touch, like muslin. The folds of cloth created a soft bedding effect along the edges of the room. Darkness and quiet prevailed. It was perfect for sleeping.

A slight mist rolled in from below the door, swirling around our ankles in a wispy, cloudy layer. It obscured my feet and the floor from view. The ground felt plush and cushy, more natural than a rug.

Faith handed me an ivory linen shift. "Here, put this on."

The feel of a well-worn tea towel easily bunched up in my hands. When I slipped it over my head, it softly brushed my cheeks. It immediately trapped the last of my body heat, offering a thin layer of warmth. It hung loosely over me, one size fits all. The hem stopped above my knees. I noted Faith adorned herself in one too, except hers was floor length. She took a few steps towards the center of the room and lay down amid the clouded mists near the floor. I followed her lead.

The mysterious bedding enveloped me. I fell asleep within moments of closing my eyes.

～◯～

When Ian awoke, he didn't feel particularly rested. He rolled over to cuddle up with Sarah, but her side of the bed was empty. He recalled last night's appearance of Rumored Woman, her disappearance with Sarah. *Did I dream it or did it actually happen?* He rubbed his eyes. "That was one hell of a dream." He returned to his side of the bed and swung his legs over the edge. His right foot partially stepped on the boxers he wore yesterday. He separated them from his jeans and pulled them on again, neglecting the morning chill. He was eager to find Sarah to prove his dream theory. He had finally seen Rumored Woman, even if it was his imagination.

"Sarah," he called out as he walked into the hallway, but there was no response. She wasn't at her writing desk, nor answering his call. He was shivering and alone. When he turned to go back to his bedroom, he caught a glimpse of the cat from his dream. It was sitting in the garden watching the bird bath attentively. "Crap, it wasn't a dream."

The events of the night were so beyond his comprehension. He clung to the hope that Sarah was out for a walk along the beach, that he was seeing the neighbor's cat. Even though he wanted his robe, he detoured towards the garage door. In the jumble of shoes, her sneakers were still there mixed in with his but her Tivas were missing. Relief eased back into his mind. *Thank god she's just out for her beach walk.*

He was about to take a step towards their bedroom, towards his robe and warmth when a little voice inside his head said, *Check the car.* Sarah had a habit of driving barefoot and leaving her shoes in the car on the return home. She had no need to put them back on to walk into the house. More than once he tossed them in the garage before he drove off.

When his bare feet reached the cold cement, a chill went up his spine. He held his breath along with his flimsy shred of hope as he opened the driver side door to their white Subaru Outback. *Damn.* His hope went up in smoke. There were her Tivas, tucked up near the driver's seat. He pulled them out and hurled them on the floor.

She really did disappear. He hustled back to their bedroom and clipped his shoulder on the hall corner. "Damn it!"

The cat looked up at him from where she laid against Sarah's pillow.

How did she get in, again? Ian sat on the edge of the bed. "What now?"

Reality, if you could call it that, was settling in. *She's gone. This doesn't feel real at all; it feels more like madness.* A wave of panic started to rise from the pit of his stomach. His eyes began to tear and he choked them back.

He stood up and walked to the bathroom to pee. His reflection in the mirror greeted him. He touched it. It was solid; his fingers met his own. He grunted.

Ian grabbed his robe from the hook and wrapped himself up more tightly than usual. He paced around the house, talking out loud to himself. "Who can I talk to about this? Who would believe me? I don't even want to believe me." He looked at the cat and demanded, "Where is she?"

The cat began purring in response. *What did Rumored Woman say about the cat?* That he wasn't to worry as long as the cat was okay. *Why is the cat's well-being bound to Sarah's?* Well, the cat looked quite comfortable and relaxed, like she owned the bed. He, on the other hand, was distraught.

He stopped pacing before their altar and stared at the Tower tarot card. He and Sarah had joked about it portending a mystical experience for her this year. The joke was on him now. He sat upon his meditation cushion, leaning forward to light the candle and incense called Night Queen. Sarah insisted on using beeswax so their air wasn't polluted with paraffin soot. Her fox pelt was beside him, and he took it into his lap, fondling the silky fur. *This is as close as she is coming to join me.* A lump swelled in his throat again. He closed his eyes and gave in, letting his tears spill down his cheeks.

He didn't want to give into the fear that was rising from the pit of his stomach. In an attempt to hold it at bay, he exhaled more forcefully. The scent of sandalwood infused his inhale. He brought his focus to the contact of his thighs on the cushion and the weight of his arms as they hung by his side. The constriction in his chest slowly eased. Eventually, he settled into his meditation.

Ian wanted to feel connected to Sarah even if they were apart. He knew physical proximity didn't necessarily assure connection. He's shared the same room with her before, talking and even touching but could sense she was miles away. *What if the opposite is true? What if, even with the distance between us, our connection could be vital?*

Now that they were worlds apart, he didn't want to lose her. He needed her to find a way back to him. With each inhale he visualized a golden thread of light between them, strengthening. When he opened his eyes again, he realized his meditation had outlasted the incense. His stomach growled loudly. This was one hunger he could satisfy.

As he stood to leave, the cat purred again. He looked back and said, "What? Are you hungry too?" He realized Rumored Woman never mentioned the cat's name. What would he call her? For that matter, what would he feed her? She looked like she could handle a long name, one that was easy to shorten. "How about Persephone, Per for short, since you never stop purring." She was black except for her two front paws, which looked like they'd been dipped in white paint. Her face had a white marking between her eyes that started at her third eye and dripped down along her nose.

Sarah had a fascination with the goddess Persephone, particularly with being able to pass between the worlds. *Is this what she did last night, finally managed to access a portal? Did this mean she will be gone a third of every year? If so, her timing is off.* She wasn't supposed to descend till winter and this was the end of spring. *What about her classes? Will she be back in time for her students' high school graduation?* That was only a week away. He'd cross that bridge later, if he arrived at it.

"Come on Per, let's make some breakfast." Ian was looking forward to her company. He had a habit of talking out loud to himself and he could indulge in the illusion he was now talking to the cat.

Per didn't budge, as if she knew there wasn't likely to be any breakfast that interested her. It was uncanny how this mirrored his morning pattern with Sarah. She tended to stay in bed on weekends until she was ready to greet the day. She hated being rushed on Saturday and Sunday. She often restrained him when he wanted to get up, pleading for just a few more minutes of cuddling. She'd tuck up under his right arm, her head on his chest. She called it her spot. He loved her resting there and often indulged until the roar of his stomach asserted itself. Sarah nicknamed his morning appetite for breakfast: enemy number 1. It was a constant battle to see who would win, morning cuddling or breakfast preparations. Without her insisting on lingering, he regrettably listened to his stomach as he arrived at the kitchen, alone.

CHAPTER 5

ELSEWHERE

IAN PUT DOWN his espresso. The familiar smell of French roast calmed him. Sarah and he had planned to tackle the garden today, but now he would begin it on his own, clearing out the mat of dead leaves. The pruning he had done on her roses, despite her protests that he was cutting off too much, had proven effective. Tightly wrapped maroon leaves were budding, indicative of new growth. There was a wild shoot he had missed; he would have to cut it off. If Sarah was here, they would have argued about it. She thought he was too eager to prune; he thought she was unwilling to make the necessary cuts in her life. She was loyal to a fault. He thought she stayed with her former husband long after she should have left him, but he wasn't exactly objective about that assessment.

His phone buzzed with a text.

Courts at 11:00? Ready to get beat? Jim, Jocelyn's husband, was his golf and tennis partner.

He texted back, *11:00 yes, beat—no.* He almost wrote *In your dreams* but that was too close to home at the moment. *The garden can wait*, he thought. Ian needed to hit something, work off the pent-up energy buzzing under his skin. Jim and he tended to volley more than tennis balls over the net. They inhabited opposite sides of the political spectrum and weren't shy when it came to debating politics. Having a small yellow object to whack kept them civil. Ian relished landing a deep corner shot Jim couldn't return when he was losing an argument.

His phone buzzed again. It was Jim. *Dinner for 6 at 6:00?*

Ian typed, *Just me tonight. I promise to eat for two if you're cooking.*

Jim could have been a chef rather than a lawyer; it was how he unwound from a tough case. Ian never said no to an invitation to join their dinner table; it was the best restaurant in town and the debates were always lively.

He texted, *Menu?* There was an unspoken agreement: Jim cooked and Ian brought the wine to pair with it.

Roast chicken.

Ian sighed. *Hmm, comfort food.* He had an Ojai Pinot Noir he would pull out of his cellar. His enthusiasm about dinner was tempered by the need to come up with an explanation of where Sarah went. He could bluff easily enough for the week, saying it was an unexpected trip. He was going to be gone as well; with any luck he would return home to her. He knew he was being wildly optimistic but it was in his nature to believe everything would be fine. It was also in his nature to procrastinate facing what wasn't going well.

Her friends often knew her plans before he did. He entertained telling the truth for less than a minute. *They'll never believe me.* They'd ask, "What are you on?" If only this was a bad trip. Ian had used a fair amount of drugs when he was younger; now he favored wine, buying it, reading about it, and for sure—drinking it.

He changed into his tennis gear and Per intercepted him on his way out the door. "Right, you need food too." He barely had time for a grocery run before tennis. Being responsible for the cat was slowly dawning on him. He was flying out tomorrow for the week. *Shit, who will take care of Per?* He planned to ask Sam at dinner. She was the more responsible of Jocelyn and Jim's kids and she was older. *What is it about young men and their frontal lobes taking till twenty-five to fully develop?* Sarah teased him that his brain still hadn't fully developed. *She might be right.*

He returned shortly to Per meowing the moment he opened the door. She began rubbing up against his leg. "Were you lonely without me? I know how you feel." He put the grocery bag filled with a two-week supply of canned cat food on the counter. *How long will Sarah be gone?* "Or are you just hungry? What will it be, wild salmon or flaked chicken and trout?"

Per quieted and sat down. He opened the can on top—salmon, the fishy odor was unappealing. He found a small bowl as a dish and remembered he hadn't put out any water yet either. By the time he had returned from tennis, the food was gone as was nearly all the water. He needed a glass himself; he had forgotten his water bottle. Ian was grateful Jim hadn't asked about Sarah; he hadn't prepared his answer yet. *Jocelyn wouldn't be as disinterested.*

By six, when he knocked on their door with two bottles of red in hand, he was ready for his first glass of vino. Jocelyn answered the door and asked, "Hey, welcome Ian. Say, where's Sarah gone? We expected her today at Authentic Movement but she never showed up and didn't answer any of our texts. It's not like her to be out of touch."

Boom. Not even two steps in the house. At least Jocelyn is predictable. Ian said, "It was a last-minute trip." He tried to dodge naming where she was since he had no idea. "Jim, dinner smells amazing."

Jim was standing at the counter carving the golden-brown roast chicken. "It smells ready, let's sit down. I skipped lunch today." The salad was on the table and the plates were by the stove where a pan of roasted carrots, onions, and potatoes awaited. The smell of garlic and rosemary made his mouth water. Jim carved the breast meat and put it with the legs on the platter.

Ian didn't have to be asked twice. He started opening the wine. Jeremy was standing in the way, on his phone; he hadn't said hello.

"Hey Ian." Sam swatted her brother on the back. "Move! If only your ears worked as well as your texting fingers—it's dinner time."

Jocelyn handed Ian a plate and he offered her the first glass of wine he had poured. "You never mentioned where she went?"

He took the plate and poured two more glasses of wine. "Ah, didn't I?" Ian stalled with a sip of wine to fortify himself. "To the West Coast, a childhood friend needed her."

"Huh, so she won't be teaching this week?" Jocelyn persisted.

"Not likely. With any luck she won't be gone long. Besides, graduation is just around the corner. She would hate to miss that." Ian hoped he sounded credible. He used what Sarah called his professional voice to be beyond reproach.

Jocelyn handed the next plate to Jeremy. But he hadn't looked up to take it. She glared at her son while she put the plate as a screen between his eyes and his phone. "I'll text her later, because cell phones don't belong at the dinner table and it's time to eat." Everyone but Jeremy recognized that comment was directed at him. He had perfected oblivion at an early age.

The subject of Sam's choice for her final paper dominated the dinner conversation. She was debating between the role of mainstream media in defining stereotypical family life or how it reinforced false narratives about minority groups.

"Which decades are you including, Sam?" Ian asked. "I'd love to watch *Father Knows Best* with you if it's in your research; we have our own Jim Anderson here."

Jim only smiled in response.

"I haven't decided yet what to include." Sam continued, "The current era of reality programming of *Survivor* or *Keeping Up with the Kardashians* is quite the contrast. Though the point I want to make is none of it is real. Even what we call 'reality programming.' However our reality does get programmed by it. People imitate what they see and hear and if they hear it frequently enough, they believe it. It's crazy."

Jocelyn added, "I can remember growing up with the Bunkers, *All in the Family* with Archie's blatant bigotry, and the dismissive nickname of his wife Edith, dingbat. Though she was often the wisest one on the show. It always made me laugh and the acting was incredible. I recall being shocked years ago when Oprah Winfrey included a clip from it in her Super Soul Sunday, during her weekly 'breathing space' as it raised the question of our souls. I'm going to see if I can find it."[10]

"Really Mom, you're going to break the no devices at the table rule?" Jeremy goaded her.

Sam stepped in. "No matter what I decide, I know I want to include that show. I recently read this article, 'Racism Isn't Funny, So Why Does Archie Bunker Make Me Laugh?' It made me want to binge watch all nine seasons."[11]

---

[10] Breathing Space, "Archie Bunker Answers Life's Big Questions",Oprah's SuperSoul Sunday, OWN, 2:35, July 25, 2020,https://youtu.be/nfZzBMcArFo.

[11] Jeremy Helligar, "Racism Isn't Funny-- So Why Does Archie Bunker Make Me Laugh?", LEVEL, November 30, 2018. https://level.medium.com/falling-in-love-with-a-racist-7ee-9c3ee11fb.

After the meal was over, Ian split the last of the wine between their three glasses. He raised his glass. "Compliments to the chef. Your Sunday night roast chicken was divine."

Jocelyn, Jim, and Ian moved into the next room but they were not out of earshot of the sibling rivalry in the kitchen.

Jeremy said, "I washed last time, you do it."

"No. I always have to wash, besides I already cleared the strainer and the table and you haven't done anything." Sam picked up the dish towel and started to twirl it. "I'll dry." She snapped it at his back pocket on the bulge of his cell phone. Sam knew the only thing that would prevent him from taking out his phone was having wet hands.

Jocelyn yelled towards the kitchen, "Enough you two, just clean up and stop bickering." She turned to Ian. "Honestly, think twice before you and Sarah have kids, and if you do, one is a good number."

"You're ahead of me, Jocelyn; she still has the pause button on my proposal to her. I have the ring ready." Ian resettled himself in his chair and reached for his wine.

Jocelyn had been tucking the same strand of hair behind her ear all dinner; it resisted staying put. "Don't worry, it's only a matter of time, you two will sort it out. She's a bit gun shy from her divorce. You've been dating for a few years and just moved in together, isn't that going well?"

"Yeah, we're good." Ian thought of their bickering before last night's dinner. In truth, every day had some kind of fuss they had to navigate. They argued over the simplest things, the big stuff they aligned on. He knew Sarah wanted to have children, at least one. As an only child she often wished she had a brother or sister, contrary to Jocelyn's advice. It may have been easier on the parents to have one but Sarah thought it was better for the child to have a sibling. She would say, "They won't have any family when we die." Both her parents were now dead and she was a bit adrift.

Jocelyn mentioned, "Veena asked Sarah the other day if you two had considered therapy."

"What did Sarah say?" This was news to Ian. He wanted to know the context. His wine glass was only a quarter full and he nearly drained it.

"She said she thought it might be a good idea and asked Veena for a recommendation."

"Really, hmm." Ian was taken back. He'd have to ask Sarah about it later. *When, later is the question.* His wine glass still in hand, he finished it. "Does anyone else need some water?" He walked into the kitchen to Sam wiping down the counters. Jeremy had his AirPods in his ears. That explained the silence. "Hey Sam, can I hire you to cat sit for me this week? We picked up a stray and I have to travel for work."

"Sure, you don't have to pay me." Sam added, "I love cats. I can do my homework over there and have some time to myself. Girl or boy cat?"

"Girl. I named her Persephone, Per for short, but she doesn't answer to it yet. I'll leave her food on the kitchen counter. Her kitty litter box is in the utility room." What he didn't say was *See if you can train her to use it.* "I think it's best for her to stay indoors this week till I'm back. I'll leave you a check. You can spend it or donate it, it's up to you. Thanks for helping me out."

Jocelyn was in the doorway. "Did you say you picked up a stray cat? Sarah is allergic to cats. Why are you keeping her?"

"Sarah is up for the experiment; it may just be temporary." He knew she was bound to ask another question he couldn't

69

answer. He finished his water and made his way to the front door. "Gotta get my beauty rest, thanks again for dinner." Ian walked out before Jocelyn asked her next questions. He knew her radar was up. Hopefully Sarah would return soon and answer both their questions about her whereabouts.

When he opened his front door, Per was underfoot, whining to go out. He scooped her up and walked to check the kitty litter box. It was empty. He put her down inside as he said, "Do you know how to shit in the box?" She dashed out of it, spraying kitty litter on the floor. "Shit." Ian ignored the mess.

Per kept pacing and whining at the front door.

"If I let you out at this hour, you might get lost or eaten." He wasn't going to open the door, it was his job to take care of her, keep her safe. Eventually, she had to sort out that this was her home.

She never gave in, she persisted in crying at the door to be let out. Ian put in his fluorescent orange ear plugs and, deaf to her pleas, he promptly fell asleep. In the morning he discovered cat shit at the door. He picked it up and put it in the kitty litter box. Per looked up at him smugly. He looked back at her saying, "Can you take a hint?"

After finishing his cereal and espresso, he fed Per before heading out for a short run. As he closed her in the house he told her, "Be good."

When he returned it was clear their definitions of being good were radically different. His running shoe slid on something in the entryway, giving off a rank smell. "Oh shit, not good Per." She didn't linger for the reprimand but took advantage of his delay in closing the door. "Goddamn it, Per, get back here."

He knew even as he was saying it, it was pointless. She was long gone, like Sarah. Two fiercely independent females that prized their freedom above all else. He walked back outside and removed his shoes, grateful he wasn't in his socks when he walked in. His house smelled foul now. He went in search of paper towels to eliminate the mess. *Maybe Sam will have more luck. I should leave her a note and warn her to enter cautiously.* Of course, by that time it would be too late. He'd text her.

While Ian packed, he heard Sarah's cell phone going off in the next room. He picked it up and noticed all the missed texts from her friends. He turned her phone off. After zipping up his suitcase, he propped open the front door with his running shoe in case Per returned while he napped. He had set his alarm as a precaution even though his internal body clock knew after decades of napping when twenty minutes had elapsed. He also had a built-in GPS, something Sarah wasn't blessed with. *How will she find her way home? Will Rumored Woman deliver her back or is part of this adventure finding her way back?*

Ian awoke to Per at the foot of their bed. When he went to retrieve his running shoes, he discovered a dead mouse on the porch. *Is this a peace offering?* He preferred dead mice to shit. Apparently they were making some progress bonding.

Last night in an effort to switch the subject from Sarah's abrupt departure he asked Jocelyn for her reading list on addressing racism. He'd briefly touched on how his client was considering taking a stand to be an anti-racist organization. Most of her recommendations were books he couldn't immediately lay his hands on, with the exception of the "CEO Blueprint for Racial Equity" produced by the Corporate Racial Equity Alliance (CRE).[12] Jocelyn said it offered compelling

---

[12] "2021 CEO Blueprint for Racial Equity", Corporate Racial Equity Alliance, July 25, 2022. https://corporateracialequityalliance.org/2021-blueprint.

guidance aimed at transformation, not lip service. They all reflected on how in the wake of George Floyd's murder, people took to the streets in demonstrations, while companies donated money and made pledges around purchasing from Black-led businesses and hiring more Black people. Their shared concern was whether these promises would lead to real change or if they would be hollow given there was no real accountability. He had pulled up the CRE's website and downloaded the report knowing internet service on the plane was unreliable. When he started reading it he didn't want to stop, but he knew traffic to Logan was unpredictable.

He made it to his gate just five minutes before they closed it, being the last to board the plane. As they accelerated down the runway and became airborne, Ian watched the ground grow further away. Despite his understanding of the physics of flight, he always marveled at the feat. Once they were at elevation he took out his computer and set it on his tray table. No movie today, he dove back into the "CEO Blueprint for Racial Equity."

The blueprint's introduction laid out a roadmap of actions within three domains of corporate influence: the walls of the company, the community and society. Ian inferred it also meant doing one's own personal work. He had been questioning how he could be most effective as a white male dismantling the institutional racism that was designed to privilege him. He wasn't comfortable not having answers or knowing his next moves.

~⟲~

When I awoke, Faith lay by my side. The soft light in the room came from above. In the center of the ceiling, triangular windows offered a view of dirty white clouds that blanketed the sky. When I focused on a patch of gray there was just a hint of movement. The pillar candles below had been blown out, and the mists of the night before had evaporated, revealing a sea of tiny ferns covering the floor with the color of early spring green. The drapes in the room were a similar shade as the sky, creating a seamless effect. My eye was drawn to the dark wooden door we entered through last night. I noted it was carved with astrological and planetary symbols, including the signs of my birth, Pisces and Neptune. Above the doorway was a quote by Novalis:

"The seat of the soul is there, where the outer and inner worlds meet."

Faith sat up, signaling she was awake too. I turned to see her smiling down at me. She gently stroked my hair, untangling the sleeping knots with her fingers. My mind was not engaged; for once it wasn't trying to figure out what I was supposed to be doing or what was going to happen next. I was content to just lie there.

Time felt slow and expansive, not the customary compression of me strategizing what I needed to accomplish. I rolled over onto my stomach, resting my chin on my hands to stare at my bed of minute ferns and mosses, as a mini lush world revealed itself to me. The inside of my bare forearms welcomed their velvet touch as if each cell of my body could soak up their respite, like parched ground welcomes rain.

I rolled to my side and drifted off to sleep again. The next time I opened my eyes, a tray of prepared fruits was beside me. Slices of ruby orange papaya and creamy white pear with green skins were beautifully arranged on a platter whose outer rim was sprinkled with crimson pomegranate seeds. Beside the platter was a cutting board with a sharp knife. Another bowl held the cracked-open pomegranate half, a curvaceous pear, and a papaya. It looked like the kind of tray Veena would prepare for us. A pang of missing them took me by surprise. I'd left without saying goodbye; I wished I'd explained Rumored Woman to them when I had the chance at circle time in Newburyport.

We affectionately called our monthly gatherings *circle time*; it was distinct from social time. This was when we consciously explored the deeper questions in our lives. Our conversational threads wove in and out of our personal lives, our relationships with partners, our night or day dreams. Inevitably we also covered the territory of our professional lives or societal concerns. Circle time offered us different perspectives, a chance to crawl or leap out of the set stories that have defined our lives. We dropped below appearances, releasing our certainties to linger in our questions with one another.

Our inspiration came from a multigenerational circle of women that one of Maggie's friends had been a part of for over twenty years. They called their circle Chakra. Veena, who immigrated from India, told us it actually meant "circle" in Hindi. We watched a documentary about Chakra that stated there was no one way nor right way to convene a circle. They gathered quarterly for a long weekend at someone's home, making meals together, sleeping and waking together. Chakra had an elder, Anne, who quoted Nelle Morton; she believed circles were about "hearing one another into speech."[13]

[13] Dr. Elaine Graham, "Our Task: 'hearing one another to speech'", Church Times, January 3, 2007. https://www.churchtimes.co.uk/articles/2007/5-january/comment/our-task-hearing-one-another-to-speech.

I loved their ritual of bed tea, a tradition pervasive in South Asia. Everyone, still in pajamas and morning hair, piled into the same bed to enjoy tea and share their night dreams. Maggie, who grew up in London, said she and her mum and sister often had bed tea together on Sunday mornings. As an only child, I missed the companionship of siblings. Given I was outnumbered by adults, the expectation was I would act like one. My theory was that I grew up too quickly. My parents weren't particularly great at having fun and now I wasn't either.

We also read Christina Baldwin's book, *Calling the Circle: The First and Future Culture*.[14] When we realized we were trying to create our circle "right" we decided to just experiment with it our own way. Since we lived at a distance from one another, we picked different locations each month, mostly our homes, sometimes coffee shops. Occasionally we landed at a wine bar, but then we added a sleepover at the nearest home and had bed tea the next morning. We talked about going away for a long weekend together once a year but had yet to do it. Ian nicknamed them my modern-day coven. I knew the circle had power, a kind of magic that invited us to be our best selves.

I picked up a pomegranate seed to start, savoring the mix of tart juice and solid kernel. My appetite was faint. My limbs still felt weighted down, almost leaden. I alternated between nibbling on the fruits and drifting back off to sleep. Sometimes I lingered longer quietly awake. The mists rolling through swept me up in a dreamy timeless space. I felt as though my past, my future, and my present lay before me like the fruit on the tray; I could choose any one to imbibe.

[14] Christina Baldwin, Calling the Circle: The First and Future Culture, Bantam Books 1998.

When the impossible became possible. I turned towards Faith. "I've missed you. I'm sorry I stopped talking with you, listening to you. I'm grateful for this second chance."

She smiled. "You have had more than a second chance." Her tone was kind.

Propping myself up on an elbow, I asked, "What do you mean?"

"As a child, I was your imaginary friend. You saw me and we spoke for hours; we played together gathering dandelion globes and blowing their seeds. Later when you stopped seeing me, I still came to you with images before you fell asleep, your picture show. When you stopped watching it, I spoke to you in sentences, such as *things are not what they seem*, do you recall?"

"Oh god, all of that was you?"

"Yes, you aren't the only clever one; there is more than one way to communicate to those who are open. Luckily you've continued to pay attention to your dreams, keeping this channel open between us." She gently tucked a loose strand of hair behind my ear. "For whatever reason, the material world has captured people's imagination. It hijacks them. They think that it's all there is and have become blind to what's before them. If only they had the eyes to see or the ears to hear a different kind of communication, one often cultivated by indigenous cultures."

I thought about all the ways I dismissed these messages and risked missing my life. My eyes returned again to the quote above the door, Novalis:

> *"The seat of the soul is there, where the outer and inner worlds meet."*

"I've had a sense lately that there is more to life than what I'm experiencing. A longing I've not been able to put into words—it's more of a felt sense of belonging to something larger but my access to it feels fleeting. In your presence I feel a portal to it is opening."

"Trust this sensing, follow it. Sarah, you've been blessed with a swift mind, but it's a curse too if you let it dominate your life. You're more than your mind. Let your soul and body speak to you; listen more deeply to the invitation they offer. This is where your true power resides, for it connects you to everything your mind can't fathom." Her hand made a sweeping gesture of a figure eight. "On the bridge, you began to listen to this impulse and moved in sync with a deeper current. Can you recall how it felt?"

"Yes, I became more spacious inside my skin."

"Exactly, you were more able to greet yourself and receive what the world has to offer. How else did it feel?"

I closed my eyes briefly in remembrance, returning to the dance of opposites. "I tapped into an infinite source of energy; I could have kept it up for hours had Curiosity not startled me out of it." The luminescent ball of energy pulsed before my mind's eye. I wanted a chance to feel it again in my palms but it evaded me. I opened my eyes to see Faith holding my gaze. "I'm grateful you never gave up on me—that I'm here with you now. I want to make room for you in my life." I sat up so we were eye to eye and reached for her hand.

She held my hand in her lap and said, "I'm glad you invited me back. We make a good team. Now it's up to you where we go from here, what you are willing to see and hear, who you are willing to become. I'm merely your guide. Your blessing is a powerful invocation, it's time to embody it." She squeezed my hand lightly. "Let's return to listening to the impulses in your body. Close your eyes and give yourself your full attention."

Whenever a part of my body signaled with the slightest ache or pain I responded by bringing my hands to the place that was speaking to me. The quiet of the room and our stillness had removed all other distractions that would have drowned out my body's subtle requests. It reminded me of my retreats with Authentic Movement, when time both slowed down and opened up, inviting me to simply listen to myself. There was movement, even in stillness, if I paid close enough attention.

I massaged my hands, kneading the muscles of my palms and fingers till they tingled. Faith rubbed my feet, putting pressure on places that sent shivers up my back. I rolled my neck and shoulders in slow steady circles, unwinding the coiled snake that wound around my spine. I repositioned myself on all fours, in the cat's pose arching and curving my spine letting my head follow with my breath. When I became aware of an ache or tightness, I gently stretched in opposing movements.

Most of these sensations left with some deliberate conscious attention. All but two. I'd come to normalize the ache in my lower right back as my constant companion. It didn't prevent me from walking, bending, or moving. The other was a heavy weight over my chest. Again, not so oppressive as to impinge on my breathing, yet not so subtle as to be able to ignore its ever-present pressure. There was no way to get out from under it, to escape it. *How long have I been living with it and never noticed?*

Faith replied, "A long time."

Her tone had turned serious. I brought my right hand to rest on the center of my chest. There was an ache within, not like any muscle aches I felt from over-exercising that ice, heat, or stretching could address. More like the dull chronic ache that's grown with years of sustained neglect. *What lies here, just below the surface of my skin, just beyond my awareness? What did these persistent aches have to tell me now? Is there another woman here? If only I knew her name I could summon her to speak with me.*

With these thoughts, the aches intensified. Whatever was pressing heavily on my chest, clutching at my back, knew it had my attention. What I needed was an interpreter. After years of ignoring my body, we didn't speak a common language. My limited vocabulary consisted of about four words: hunger, thirst, sleep, and pain. Regrettably, I managed to ignore even these minimal communications on too many occasions. I was no stranger to urinary tract infections, not finding time to pee between classes. *No wonder my body remains a stranger to me. I have yet to prove trustworthy with my most basic needs. How could I possibly carry on a more nuanced or subtle conversation? How could I learn to be more fluent in the language of my body?*

I heard someone clearing their throat and looked to see if Faith wanted my attention. She wasn't looking at me, but rather across the room. I followed her gaze to see a woman who wasn't there before. She was lying on her side not far from where we rested. She rose and sauntered towards us, her dusty rose silk spaghetti strap nightgown swishing along the floor, making a whispering sound. She had an aura of softness surrounding her that I thought was created by the cloudy mists that lingered around her. Yet as she stood before me, the languid look stayed with her. Her hair was down, long and dark, in natural waves around her shoulders. Her eyes were brown and wide, with the sensitivity that belonged to a doe. Her movements exuded the grace of a ballerina, even as her arms hung peacefully by her sides. The scent of gardenias accompanied her.

"How come you look so welcoming?" I asked.

There was a tone of compassion in her voice. "Everywhere I look I find another being to love; with each loving embrace, my heart grows even larger. My heart has grown so vast that now it no longer lies hidden within my chest. Now I walk within my heart's expanse so when I meet another, this is what they touch first."

The image she spoke of matched my impressions of her. *No wonder her presence is so comforting, the effect is like being wrapped in a lush cashmere shawl.*

She sat down beside me. "I've never come in contact with another being I couldn't embrace. My heart knows no boundaries." She paused as if to let her words sink even deeper within me. I recognized her as my Compassion. "You have access to me whenever you want; you only have to ask for me with your heart." She gently laid the palm of her right hand over her heart. "Today I appeared because you asked for a translator. I am one of sorts." Her left hand gestured, palm up as if she was offering me something invisible within it. "I prefer to think of myself as a gateway to understanding all that is foreign to us. If you will create the space for me with an open heart, I can introduce you to many aspects of yourself that you have long since neglected. They are only foreign to you because of the distance you've created. It's true, they want your attention; they are knocking at the door the best way they know how."

These aches within my body were asking me to answer the door to be open to them. I laid my hand over my chest, asking Compassion, "Do you know who is knocking here, in my chest? The weight is starting to feel unbearable."

She nodded with her head and her eyes in a single, slow blink. "There is more than one, as you know. I will tell them you are ready for a relationship."

Within moments a woman scuffled slowly out from behind the curtains, a hunch to her back, each step a strained effort. I

expected to see a cane but she had no support. Witnessing her
the ache in my lower back intensified. I imagined the feeling I
had in my chest pervaded her whole being, as if she was being
pulled down by invisible weights. Her head looked towards the
ground, her shoulders caved inward. Her left arm hung limply
by her side and her right arm was bent, her hand holding her
lower back, right where I ached. I half expected to see her collapse at any moment.

When she looked briefly up at me, her face was crumpled,
her mouth turned downward, then her eyes cast back to the
floor. I wanted to pretend she was a stranger to me, yet I recognized her immediately. I kept her well hidden from others.
Her eyes were red and swollen from crying.

Seeing her now, a sharp knife stuck in my throat. I knew
from years of experience that if I swallowed hard, several times,
I could control the tears that were now pressing from the back
of my eyes to be let out. But there was no reason to choke them
off. Not now. It was safe to feel them. I let them continue to
rise, until they filled my eyes and spilled forth, leaving their
trail down my cheeks, continuously dripping off my chin.

I stood up for the first time. My legs were shaky and
weak from inactivity. I slowly walked towards her, opening my
arms to her just as I welcomed the release of my tears. In our
embrace, I felt the full weight she was carrying and finally gave
in to the pressure to drop to the ground.

We wept together like the way heavy clouds release in a
slow, steady rain. I cried for all the times I wanted love and
didn't believe I could have it, didn't believe I deserved it. I
cried for all the times I believed things would be different,
only to be disappointed again and pretend I didn't care. I

cried for the vows I made and broke and the shattering of the dreams that occurred thereafter. I wept for the two children I had conceived but never held in my arms. I wept for all the wounds that had scarred me and scared me from letting myself be vulnerable again. I wept for the unfulfilled longing in me to touch into the sacred. The more I wept, the less I felt the weight in my chest, the lighter my heart became, but the ache in my back intensified.

I knew her well and called her by her name. "Grief, will you tell me your story? I'm ready to listen."

She looked up at me before she spoke. "I will tell you of your own story; even now you believe these feelings lie somewhere outside yourself. For too long now, I have watched you search for what must first be found within yourself so you have a place to receive what comes from another. For years you have looked to another for the love that will sustain you and missed the love that awaits you within. Only in the presence of this love from within can you find nourishment in what is offered from another."

As I listened my lips began to quiver and my eyes flooded with tears all over again. My chin vibrated along with my jaw; my teeth were chattering uncontrollably as the sobs came on stronger. I hadn't given myself over to tears in this way since I was a young child, when I would hyperventilate. My father often told me I was overreacting and I learned to weep silently.

Grief continued, "For too long now, you have longed to be seen and heard, acknowledged by others as their equal. Yet no amount of their love or encouragement will ever be enough to fill the emptiness you feel within—from not loving and acknowledging yourself. You ache from this endless search outside yourself for what, in your heart of hearts, you know can only be found from within. This is your despair. How long will you go on denying what you know to be true?"

I knew all too well of the truth she spoke, my journals were filled with this very wisdom. I struggled in the gap between knowing it and not knowing how to embody it. I spent countless hours in tears, face down in my pillow, in my childhood bedroom, my college dorm, my flat in London, my house on the Cape, and lately in our house in Manchester by the Sea. Weeping with her now, I felt the despair of knowing what I most needed I couldn't give myself.

~◯~

Ian's hands were holding the book, but his eyes and mind were elsewhere. "This is useless." He needed to listen to his body.

Had Sarah been here, right about now she would have been calling him from the next room asking if he was talking to her. Despite her requests, he hadn't been able to break his habit of talking out loud to himself; it must have come from all the years of living alone. He knew she thought that sometimes he just liked to hear himself talk. She was probably right, but he didn't plan to admit it.

His body felt like a pinball machine; as if someone was pumping the levers back and forth to send a ball inside him ricocheting. A run was essential to find a release for this pent-up energy. As he walked into the bedroom for some socks he called out, "Here Per, here kitty kitty, here schmutt."

He half expected to find her on Sarah's side of the bed. This morning she looked like she had taken up residence there. He guessed she was out exploring the new neighborhood; so far she had always come back. Apparently, she had a better sense of direction than Sarah.

Sarah often joked he had a built-in compass, whereas she must have been missing when they handed them out. Occasionally, her instincts surprised them both, contradicting what he thought was the correct way to go and she would be right. He knew these were sweet victories for her and he would exclaim her as a directional beacon. He wanted to believe she would find her way back home soon. Every time he left the house he held on to a sliver of hope that he would return to her and this ordeal would all be behind them. Her persistent absence deflated him.

He set off in the direction of the beach. He was having trouble finding his rhythm. It wasn't till he reached the waterfront that his breath had synchronized with his pace. If he hadn't noticed a cat that looked like Per, he would have kept going. It piqued his curiosity to see her perched on the sand dune left from the high tide. This cat was acting more and more like Sarah, a Pisces through and through—water was her element.

As he came closer he called her name. "Persephone, Per, Per." She just ignored him. He stood by her now as she sat mesmerized by the tidal pool below her. For as long as he stared into the pool, nothing stirred. If there had been a fish he could have understood this behavior as a huntress.

"Persephone, what are you looking at? What's in there?" He saw the outline of a cat and a man. "Are you being mesmerized by your own reflection?" Again she ignored him, never flinching from her concentration. "Felines, they have a mind of their own, far be it from me to understand them." He started running again. The ocean mists were rolling in and the air felt heavy with moisture.

After Ian's run he returned home to another dead mouse on the front stoop with Per beside it. He let her in and left her gift behind. "How thoughtful." He headed straight for the bathroom while Per leapt up on their bed, kneading the blankets into a perfect nest. He showered but skipped shaving; he had no one who would appreciate his smooth cheeks. The weeds in the garden were his next date.

Without Sarah, he had his work cut out for him. The rains and sunny weather had pressed the spring grow button and he needed to make a dent in the weed overgrowth this weekend. His goal was three barrels full. While he weeded, instead of listening to music, he was eager to hear an interview with Resmaa Menakem on *The Breakfast Club* talking about his work.[15] Ian's day job as an organizational consultant and executive coach was often focused on culture change. His professional reading delved into the latest theories about what makes for lasting change at the societal, organizational, and individual levels. Now that both Sarah and Jocelyn had recommended he read Resmaa's book, *My Grandmother's Hands*, it was next on his list.[16]

He recalled a Sunday morning when he and Sarah were both reading in bed. She was almost finished with his book when she became animated. She uncharacteristically said out loud, "Exactly," as she underlined a passage. He asked, "Exactly what?"

She said, "I don't know why I didn't make this connection before after all these years of Authentic Movement." She proceeded to read the passage to him that highlighted Resmaa's belief that the leverage for change wasn't in trying to change people's minds, it was in changing their bodies. At the time they hadn't spoken much about it; they both went back to reading.

---

[15] Breakfast Club, "Resmaa Menakem Breaks Down Deep Rooted Trauma Linked to Racism, Healing Practices + More, Producer Daniel Greene, 1:02:51, August 26, 2021, https://youtu.be/omyzEvVvjog.

[16] Resmaa Menakem, My Grandmother's Hands, Las Vegas, NV: Central Recovery Press, 2017.

Now he heard Resmaa articulating his theory of change, how addressing the unacknowledged trauma in our bodies and collective bodies was the critical path to healing racism in our culture. He reiterated in the interview the importance of slowing down to sense what was happening in the body. Ian saw that as an uphill battle—most people ignored their bodies, spending the majority of their time in their head. While he welcomed the notion of life at a slower pace, it felt like everything was speeding up. Sarah and her coven were unusual in that the body was the basis of their shared spiritual practice, Authentic Movement. His body longed to have her body here now.

Ian noticed a patch of poison ivy growing along the fence line; his neighbor tended to neglect his garden and this intrusion was common. Ian became particularly attentive to see how far it had spread. He went back inside and put on long sleeves and thicker gloves to wrestle it out of the ground. He dug in deeper, raking through to find the feeder roots that had come from below the fence. He would offer to help his neighbor remove it, as poison ivy paid no attention to fence lines.

Resmaa echoed Ibram X. Kendi's message, there was no middle ground, either you were a devoted racist or a complicit racist. He called out white liberals' behavior on wanting to be seen as one of the "good ones," while still operating from the "savior" orientation. Ian reflected that in his line of work, "diagnosing and fixing," he had a tendency to take on the savior archetype. Inherent in this model is "the other" is wrong and there was a right way, but he was seeing how his definitions of right were built from his "white" mindset, which often forced others to act white to be acceptable, to be "correct."

Resmaa advocated for shifting the attention off individual goodness or kindness to building culture. He encouraged white people getting together with other white bodies to address their own trauma, what they experience in their guts, their face, and body when issues of racism surfaced. Ian now understood Resmaa's point, why good intentions aren't enough, why we have to understand the impact of our actions on other people's bodies and take responsibility for that, and become curious as to why people either recoil or lean into conversations.

It is easy to hide behind good intentions and look to be absolved for the impact of our actions, Ian thought. Sarah often tried to point this out to him and he dodged it. She accused him of being beyond reproach and their conversation devolved from there or she became coldly silent. The question stayed with him, though: *What can we do together to build structures of trust?* At least where Sarah was concerned, he realized he had to be more open to her point of view, especially when it differed from his opinion of himself. He defended himself against anything he felt was unjustified, interrupting her before she had a chance to finish her thought. In those moments, the connection between them snapped. Even though he knew better when he was triggered he couldn't stop himself.

~⟳~

As I held Grief, our tears had somehow formed a significant pool of water beside where we lay. I touched my index finger to the surface and brought it up to my tongue. *Salty.* The tiny ripple my finger made radiated in larger circles. Letting go of Grief, I peered down into the water. I spied a mermaid circling below, coming nearer to the surface with each spiral. My mind was screaming, *Not possible!* But before my eyes she propelled herself up out of the water and perched on the rim of the tear pool.

I adored mermaids and they adorned my house in pictures, carvings, and coat hooks. I'd even tried my hand at sketching them. Recently, I imagined creating a water fountain with a mermaid perched on the side of the falls just as she sat now, on the side of the tear pool. Her fin occasionally flipped in the water, sending a ripple across the surface, reminding me she was here, now, not an inanimate creation of my imagination on paper or made of clay.

Her scales, which began at her waist, were luminescent with hints of purple, turquoise, and sea green. These colors had appeared in my wardrobe as I worked more and more with the imagery of mermaids. Her hands laid open in her lap as if she was cradling an invisible creature. Her eyes moved from what laid undetectable in her hands to my eyes and back to her hands. I followed her invitation to take a closer look but there was nothing there, they were empty. I looked back at Faith for a clue.

"This is Forgiveness. Please welcome her here."

Faith and Compassion had come to stand beside us. Grief lay curled on her side on the floor.

I stammered, "W-w-welcome. I am at a loss for words."

She said nothing, but patted the space beside her as an invitation to come sit. As I moved away from Grief, I could see her exchange a knowing glance with Faith. Compassion was the first to sit beside her, laying her palm across her forehead, cradling her head in her other hand. As Faith joined them I saw a holy trinity.

Faith said, "Remember to follow your instincts. Now is a time for diving in and letting go."

What did she mean?

As I sat beside Forgiveness, she spoke for the first time. "I am here to help you accept your past, not forget it." I watched the water droplets cascade from her hair and land on her lap. She continued, "My blessings come from acknowledging the pains, regrets, and wrongdoings of the past on your part as well as others. By accepting life for what it is, it can become part of the past rather than continue to live on as resentment." She paused, waiting for me to look into her eyes. "Do you want help in coming to terms with what lives unresolved in your heart?"

I was still at a loss for words, so I nodded.

She waited in silence before she added, "Let's begin then, it's time to tend to what haunts you."

I noticed her hands had returned to her lap; they cupped something invisible. She had paused again in her speech and looked down at them. As she spoke she raised them slightly. "Remember, acceptance is the gateway to a healthy relation-ship with yourself and others."

I found my voice to ask Forgiveness, "Is this what you hold in your hands?"

She nodded. She lifted her cupped hands to me as if offer-ing me a gift. I looked down at my own hands, still clutching the side of the pool.

Forgiveness said, "First you must let go."

As I released my grip on the edge, I brought my hands before me, my palms upward, fingers open, outstretched. Uncurling my stiff fingers took concentration. At first my ten fingers splayed wide, the roadmap of lines on my palms con-necting my past and future to reveal a story I couldn't interpret.

Forgiveness suggested, "Rest your hands in your lap, relax your fingers so they naturally curl upward. It takes less effort than you think."

I followed her advice. Now my hands mirrored hers. *Could acceptance really be this simple?*

She heard my unasked question and said, "There is more, but this is the beginning. In the beginning you must look to your own hands for the release. For it is by your own actions that you have been caught in the first place."

I was lost in her metaphor. The confusion must have been written on my face.

Forgiveness said, "There has been enough talk for now. Are you ready to dive in with me? To remember."

My hands returned to grip the edge of the pool at the thought of diving into these tears with the mermaid who beckoned me. She just stared at my clenched hands. I turned away from her to see Faith now lying near Compassion, who held Grief. I wanted to stay with them. *Am I to journey on without my guide?*

Faith said, "I am not your only guide. Know that I am always with you whether you see me or not."

I heard a splash and turned to see the mermaid was already in the water, waiting for me to join her. I wanted to ask, *If we are to swim underwater for any length of time, how will I breathe?* But, I was afraid of her answer.

She answered my silent question anyway.

"Just as I do."

CHAPTER 6

TEAR POOL

S TARING AT MY tear pool, my love of saltwater temporarily left me. The weight of grief had returned to my chest like an anchor, dragging me down. Inhaling fully was challenging. *Breathing on land is hard enough. If I move into this ocean of tears, I will surely drown.*

Only Forgiveness's head was above the surface. She looked at me as she suddenly propelled herself from the water. Her head and shoulders popped up like a dolphin before her body arched and dove back underneath. The last I saw of her was a flick of her fin. She created a slight wake that splashed up against me.

I remembered my attempts as a child to imitate the movements of a dolphin in the shallow end of the pool. I knew if I dove in now I wouldn't be able to touch the ground. I was entering the deep end. Normally that wouldn't bother me. Normally I loved the water, it was my element. But there was nothing normal about this moment. I had a paralyzing fear of what awaited me even though I had no clue what the cause could be. I promised myself by the time I reached the count of three I'd end my debate and dive in.

I stood up and pulled off my sheath, letting it fall to the ground, and looked back at Faith for assurance. Her face was calm. She tipped her head up once, as if to say, *Go on.*

I started the count: One, two, and splash.

The water's temperature was almost indiscernible from my own, the only aspect of it that was inviting. My feet searched for a ledge or any form of solid ground; even the edge I'd been sitting on had disappeared. My tear pool was bottomless and boundless as I'd feared. I was treading water. My mermaid companion was nowhere in sight. My breaths were shallow and short. I felt for the first time the terror others might feel in the water, growing more and more uneasy.

I'll only look once for her beneath the surface, I vowed to myself. Then I'd try to get out. I exhaled all my breath then filled my lungs fully and dove under.

When I opened my eyes underwater, I could see her waiting far below me. She waved to have me join her and I shook my head in disagreement. Her invitation held no allure. She started swimming back up towards me and I turned upwards too. I expected to break the surface within a stroke. I could already feel my lungs screaming for breath.

The surface wasn't near. Somehow I'd drifted far deeper than I'd imagined, as if I'd been sinking.

Adrenaline rushed through my muscles. I pulled my arms in strong, long strokes, reaching for the surface, kicking as hard and fast as I could. My right hand splashed into the air. *The surface!*

Immediately something grabbed my left ankle, pulling me back. My hand submerged. I fiercely kicked to free myself, struggling with my arms to reach the surface again. Whatever it was, it was stronger than me and yanked me farther back down. The distance to the surface was increasing. I was beyond panic. A single bubble escaped my nose and traveled up away from me. I looked around to see if Forgiveness could help me and discovered she was the one dragging me with her. *What the fuck, is she trying to kill me for god's sake!* I wanted to yell. *I'm not a mermaid! I walk on land! I breathe air!* But I was afraid to open my mouth. My lungs were on fire. *This is not the guidance I expected. Since when did Forgiveness have a vicious streak?*

I heard the words, "*Surrender to it.*"

It wasn't like I had any other option.

Out of sheer exhaustion I gave up. Bubbles fled from my mouth and nose towards the surface I longed for. I watched them rise. *I'm going to die.*

Meanwhile my body had other plans and automatically inhaled for air. I felt a silky smooth sensation rushing in my nose and down my throat. I expected to choke but it never happened. It was unclear how the water moved through me. *Where did it find its release?* My mind had no explanations. Things weren't what they seemed. For the moment, my relief to be alive surpassed my need to know how or where I'd managed to grow gills.

I looked around for Forgiveness, who was floating just below me, waiting, looking almost smug. She tilted her head and waved to me to join her again. There was a debate team forming in my head filled with various opinions and questions. *What if I pretended to follow her and then swam for the surface? Will she chase me down again and prevent me from getting away? If I try to breathe air now, could I? Does Forgiveness really have my best interest at heart? Do I trust her to be my guide?*

She beckoned me again to follow her with a nod of her head, and this time she turned away without waiting for my response. She swam deeper with her arms and hands relaxed by her side. Her body moved in a continuous wave with her tail flicking up and down. She was nearly out of sight and hadn't looked back.

Indecision is a decision. I stopped treading water and turned down to follow Forgiveness. My hands and arms were busy with a breaststroke while my legs kicked as strongly as I could to make up the distance between us. Now that I'd reluctantly decided to join her I didn't want to lose her.

To my relief, I saw her circling below me. My progress was slow. I had nearly reached her when she set off again. I doubted I was going to be able to keep up with Forgiveness; my arms were already tired. I let them rest for a moment at my side like she swam.

She is going to have to wait for me. She had to know she was far swifter in the water. Instead of kicking with my feet separated, I tried the butterfly stroke kick. My legs were together, bending at the knees and flicking my feet through the water. It surprised me how much more propulsion it gave me. When I returned to using my arms in the breaststroke, they were jamming up against the water rather than pulling me. They couldn't keep up with my speed.

Since the distance between us was closing, I left my hands by my side. Perhaps she had slowed down because within moments I had caught up to her.

I'd been trying to imitate her motion with my body as I swam. She moved like a sine curve through the water. When I looked to see if my body rippled like a wave as I swam, what I saw was my legs had merged into one. I froze. There was a fin where my feet had been. *Oh my God!* My hands raced to touch the scales on my hips and fused legs. They were rough and slippery all at the same time. I marveled at how they nested, one over the other, like a fish or a snakeskin. Even though they tightly bound me, they also allowed me to bend my knees, to twist and turn at will. Half of me wanted to remain still and study my transformation, while the other half simply wanted to experience the thrill of swimming as a mermaid. *Holy shit. This is beyond belief. How will I ever explain it to Ian? He'll never believe me!* I reined myself in. *Don't ruin it, Sarah, by overthinking it. Just go with the flow.* I returned to my mantra. *I am an ocean and I'm going with the flow.*

While I swam, I enjoyed the rush of water through my hair and the smoothness of it against my skin. Now that my focus was no longer directed at keeping up with Forgiveness, I began to take in my surroundings. My eyes softened. I feasted on the underwater world of brightly colored fish: skinny yellow fish with black stripes, oval orange fish with white stripes, long blue fish with patches of orange. I swam within rainbows of colors as schools of fish cruised past me, mesmerized by how they turned in unison. *How did they know? Did someone say "Hey, hang a left" and they all did?* Sometimes they parted down the middle and joined up again, as if avoiding something invisible.

Occasionally, something flickered, giving off a sparkle of light that caught my attention. I felt a strange attraction to the way it dangled and danced in the water, as if flashing an invitation. Yet, Forgiveness ignored them, so I tried to do the same.

Then we came upon something that wasn't dangling, but still. It was thick metal, like stainless steel. The light glinted off of it. We both stopped swimming to take a closer look. My eyes recognized its curved form as a hook. That must have been what I was seeing flashing in the distance, hooks. No wonder she ignored them. This one was embedded in a patch of coral. Forgiveness reached up her hand and traced a nearly invisible line with her index finger, showing me where it was attached to the hook.

I tried speaking for the first time. "Should we remove it?" Why my mouth didn't fill with water or how words were understandable were beyond me—this whole world was beyond me, another realm I'd never found before.

She shook her head. "No, not yet. First we must understand how it came to be there. So that we can take the power it has to return away with it or you will find yourself impaled again and again."

Bewildered, I asked, "How can we know its origins or understand that since we came upon it after it was already embedded?"

Forgiveness swam around it slowly in a circle. I thought she was ignoring my question. She chose a flatter surface on the reef shelf nearby and lay down. As she settled in she said, "I know this journey you are on can be disorienting at times. It's easy to assume this hook is in the reef, outside of you. It's not. This hook is in you. Be still and listen to the story it has to tell you."

Up until now I believed there was some sense in her nonsense. However, now my impatience was taking over along with my need to help. If this hook was in me, I definitely wanted to get it out. My impulse was to fix first, understand later. I suggested, "Let's listen to its story after we take it out. If it's in me, I say it doesn't belong here, I'm sure it's a source of pain."

Forgiveness held firm. "Indeed, there is pain here. Best not to ignore it. Let it speak to you and let it guide your actions."

I hadn't followed her example yet and settled; I was bobbing in place. Nor was I eager to follow her advice. "How am I to let pain guide my actions?"

"You need to start by listening. When you are still, you will feel the truth of my words; surrender to it."

This was the second time she advised me to surrender. The last time her strength forced me to relent. I wasn't up for another power struggle. Though I had to fight with myself to become still. I lay down on the reef; it wasn't as pokey as I had expected. My hands gingerly gripped the edges. I closed my eyes and let my focus move inward.

Eventually I felt a familiar pain in the lower left side of my abdomen. I'd described this pain as a hook before during shadow work with Maggie, Jocelyn, and Veena. The image was drawn on my journal pages. The sensation was one I massaged in the early mornings and late nights while lying in bed looking for some relief. I recognized it, but I clearly didn't know it. Despite what Forgiveness had said, I wanted to believe it was lodged in someone else.

What is the story here? Where has it come from? Why did I swallow it? What will it take to release its hold on me? The relief I had found before was only ever temporary. *If I actually listen to its story, my story, what can it tell me that I don't already know? It's my life, after all. This hook, is it part of my past? Is it something I've yet to let go? Is that why Forgiveness has led me to it? Is there something to be laid to rest here?*

I remembered the pain started when I was fairly young. I often missed school because my stomach hurt so badly I couldn't concentrate on anything else. My mum finally took me to a doctor because the ache persisted in the same place. His diagnosis, after examining me, was that there was nothing wrong. He said they were phantom pains and I would outgrow them. The pain persisted, especially when I was in emotional distress. *Could this be when the story of this hook began?* So much had happened since then I couldn't even recall; to tell that story would take a very long time. Besides, I wanted to move on, my life had changed since then, I'd changed.

I felt the gentle squeeze of her hand on mine. My eyes opened to see Forgiveness staring back at me. Her eyes offered a depth of understanding. She knew how reluctant I was to feel the story of this hook, how much I wanted to move on yet I was continually pulled back into it. This part of my past was like a wound that wouldn't heal. I'd gone over it again and again in my mind. I looked at it from every possible perspective. I knew the places where I had no choice, where there was no one to blame and yet I still felt guilty. I also knew the places where I had made a choice that was hurtful, deadly even, and over these decisions I felt even more guilt.

She squeezed my hand again, and this time she spoke. "Your mind is very quick and clear, yet your mind alone will not be able to remove this hook. You must listen with your heart. Let your heart and mind weave the story of your release. Remember to feel, for only acceptance that is born of both the mind and the heart can lead to lasting forgiveness. When you have been able to give this to yourself, the hook will no longer find a place in you."

At night, Ian occupied himself with basketball season or reading. Sarah had loaned Resmaa's book to Veena so he worked down his reading list. He had just finished Ta-Nehisi Coates's book, *Between the World and Me*, giving him a visceral, rare window into what it was like to inhabit a Black body, especially in relation to the police whom Ian had always thought of as a source of protection.[17] He had no idea the daily risks Black men and their sons lived under, the threat police posed to their lives. His first reaction was that it was for no reason, then he corrected himself. The reason was racism, for no justifiable reason, literally no justice.

His lie of Sarah visiting a friend on the West Coast had become suspect. He couldn't fend off Jocelyn's scrutiny so he stopped accepting dinner invitations to their house. He took on more client work to keep his weekdays occupied, but weekends were undeniably lonely, especially sleeping, waking, and eating by himself.

He looked forward to tennis today with Jim, trusting he wouldn't ask about Sarah. Ian drove up behind Jim's green Porsche 911 Turbo at the light where they both turned towards the high school. It was a 1976 classic and never got old to look at. The lot was crowded for a Saturday, but thankfully there was one tennis court open. Not their favorite because it had a large crack that ran through it. Inevitably a ball would land on it and bounce awry, requiring a do-over. If only relationships had do-overs, Ian would have proposed before Sarah left.

He parked beside the passenger door of Jim's Porsche, careful to leave enough space between them. *No man likes dings on his door.*

"Morning, Ian," Jim said as he extracted his six-foot-frame from the car. "I got my timing wrong today, no dice on

[17] Ta-Nehisi Coates, *Between the World and Me*, Melbourne, VIC, Australia: Text Publishing Company, 2015. https://ta-nehisicoates.com/books/between-the-world-and-me/.

a match. I forgot Jeremy's soccer game starts at noon and I'm supposed to bring the refreshments and help set up the tent."

"No problem, we'll get more exercise this way. Where's the game?" Ian was tempted to watch it himself.

Jim closed his car door. "Luckily it's a home game, right here. I need to go back out, though, and buy a case of Gatorade and some oranges."

Ian reached in the back seat for his racket and a new can of balls. "Hey, I'd love to join you. Why don't we go to the store now? With any luck, when we return a different court will open up."

"Sure, get in. I'll drive us." Jim folded himself back into the car like a piece of origami.

Ian opened the passenger side door. He thought the only thing better than looking at his Porsche was riding in it. "She's a beauty, how's she running?"

"She needs some love." He patted the dashboard.

Jim had put himself through law school restoring and selling Porsches; there was very little he couldn't do well. Sadly, Jeremy showed no interest in learning from his father. There was a tension between the two of them that Ian didn't understand. Ian would have given his right arm to have a father who wanted to teach him to restore classic cars, or anything for that matter. Ian's dad left when he was six and after a few sporadic birthday cards he never heard from him again.

Despite the twenty minutes it took to run their errand, they returned to the same parking space and the cracked court was the only one available. Their conversation about gerrymandering was getting heated. Ian attempted to diffuse it with humor as he unzipped his racket from its covers. "Fun fact. Where did the name gerrymandering come from?"

"I give, where?" Jim was bouncing a tennis ball on the top side of his racquet, warming up his wrist and the strings.

Ian stuffed the last ball in his pocket as he walked to the opposite side of the court. He raised his voice. "Here in Massachusetts, back in 1812, Governor Elbridge Gerry signed into law a state senate map that consolidated the Federalist Party vote in a few districts." Where the lines were drawn, who was included and excluded was critical to the upcoming elections. *Who gets to decide—it's all about power and control.*

Jim was bouncing the ball with his left hand in front of him, about to serve. "You should have been a lawyer, you store useless knowledge like the best of them. Ready?" Jim tossed the ball in the air and came down over it with too much slice, it went straight into the net. He made a slight adjustment and his placement was perfect; it landed deep into the service box, then veered. He caught Ian flat-footed and smiled, noting he didn't even get a piece of it.

Ian started to bounce on his toes. "Again, nice serve." It was true, Ian was filled with facts. He prided himself on being informed. He was a twenty-four-hour news cycle hound; he hated being one-upped on the courts or in a conversation. It was rare for him to admit he didn't know something.

He was off his game today, grateful they weren't keeping score, as he would have been handily beaten. During the first quarter of Jeremy's soccer game he couldn't help but notice the sidelines were populated with parents. The prospect of watching his own son or daughter on the field felt too far away; it left his heart heavy.

My resistance to remembering, to beginning this story, lasted for days, perhaps weeks; time was a blur. I was in an underwater wonderland and there was plenty of beauty to explore. At first, I distracted myself by studying the magnificence of my scales. I hadn't had time to appreciate my transformation while we were swimming. Their coloring was like the inside of an abalone shell, iridescent blues and greens. There were countless tiny scales, perfectly nested in one another binding together my legs yet miraculously caused no sense of constriction. The fin that had replaced my feet was shaped like a whale's tail. Each side of the fin was identical, an underwater wing of sorts, and flapping it was more effective than any pair of snorkeling fins I'd ever worn. The sheer power of it to propel me through the water thrilled me.

Sometimes I took myself out for joy rides, flying through the water with just a few flicks of my tail, accelerating into my corners instead of slowing down. I finally understood the fascination men had for fast cars. I felt a powerful rush inside these scales, more than I'd ever known inside my skin.

Forgiveness rarely left my side. At times she raced with me, at other times she led me on more leisurely excursions where we found sustenance. We always returned to the hook. The hook didn't go anywhere. I had stared at it, expecting it to begin the story for me. I heard nothing. Nothing came to mind that could adequately explain the presence of this persistent pain in my side. Forgiveness, I came to realize, was a mermaid of few words. She simply held the silent vigil with me, lending me her quiet strength.

One day while I was staring at the hook I reached out my right hand and touched it for the first time with my index finger and thumb. It was smooth; no barnacles had dared form on it. I was careful not to tug on it while I lightly grasped it with my whole hand. The metal was cool against my palm. I slowly slid my hand down the length of it to where it disappeared into vibrant purple coral that branched out in several directions.[18] I placed my thumb on the last visible section and stretched my fingers out in an attempt to measure how big the hook was. It was longer than the span of my hand. The visible part of this hook was well over four inches. *How much more is inside me I can't see? How deep does it reach? Pulling it out could rip me apart.*

The words of my blessing arose: *May I live in the inquiry of what if, maybe.*

What if I don't have to pull it out? What if I could dissolve it? I wanted this to be more than wishful thinking. I'd been doing my best crab imitation for weeks, coming up close to examine it and scurrying off. I'd reached my limit on this approach-avoidance dance. The desire to understand the source of this hook and be able to remove it had finally outweighed my fear of the pain it would reawaken.

Forgiveness had offered me a hint, to engage both my mind and my heart, to hear its story. I needed to hear the hook's voice. Another line from my blessing arose. "May my listening be an invitation, an integration." *What if the release depends on my invitation to listen to the hook's voice, to hear its story, I mean my story?*

Bubbles started to form on the surface of the metal. A few peeled off and floated up towards the surface. In all the weeks I had stared at it, I had never witnessed any visible changes. *Mercy, something is finally happening.* A steady stream of bubbles was now releasing

---

[18] David Waldstein, "When Coral's Colorful Show is a Sign That It's Sick", The New Your TImes, May 22, 2020. https://www.nytimes.com/2020/05/22/science/coral-color-bleaching.html.

from the hook and flowing upward in reverse rain.

A gravelly voice said, "We have waited a long time to be heard by you."

Who is "we"?

The Hooks replied, "If there is an opening now, we want to speak with you. If you will listen, your questions are welcome. We are in no hurry; waiting a little longer will make no difference."

I looked to Forgiveness. "I am ready to listen; however, before you begin I do have a question to ask of you. Why do you speak as if there were more than one of you?"

"There are many of us, although we only appear to you on the outside as one. We exist in layers. When we began we were hardly noticeable, like molecules. However, over time, with each layer, we have gained momentum and our thickness increased exponentially. After a certain point, we become like a magnet and our growth continues unchecked until we gain the attention we seek."

As the Hooks paused, I tried to estimate how many hooks were layered within over an inch of steel.

"Do not be discouraged. You will not need to hear from all of us, as we are all related; many hooks have been accumulated off the same theme. Generations. If you can listen to understand the themes we have to share with you, all will feel heard."

When the Hooks said "themes," I thought of archetypes. Overarching patterns of behavior, that even though the players, the place, and time may change, the action and outcomes remained the same. Like my knee-jerk need to fix and solve problems, sometimes before I even understood them. The savior mentality had an inner voice that told me, *Don't just sit there, do something.* The same part of me that wanted to remove the hooks as soon as I saw them.

"Yes, archetypes. There are more than a few. If you are comfortable, we will begin."

I glanced up at Forgiveness who was resting a few feet beyond me in the reef. Her hair flowed sideways away from her to reveal the invisible currents of our underwater world. Her hands were free and repeated the gesture of gently cupping something, as if their emptiness was a gift she offered. "Remember to listen with both your heart and your mind, listen from a place of acceptance, listen to understand. There is no need to defend yourself here, you are safe."

I rested my hands open on my lap, palms up, hoping the embodied gesture Forgiveness taught me would translate into some emotional competency.

Again a few bubbles preceded the steel Hooks' deep, gravelly voice beginning my story. "It's hard to say how old you were when we first arrived. No one has escaped childhood without the wounds inflicted by hooks. We are often referred to as 'being bought, hook, line, and sinker,' when someone believes a lie. In a sense we are consumed, literally swallowed. You've heard that expression before, being 'taken in' by a lie."

I nodded in agreement.

The Hooks continued. "At first, it's easy to be lulled in because the price paid for accepting the lie is negligible in exchange for the comfort the lie offers. In the end however, you pay dearly. Hopefully you will recognize the price of false belonging is not worth the consequences. Our story is one of lies, of unfolding the layers and layers of lies that you have been told and bought, that you have wanted to believe and have begun to retell them to yourself as if they were true."

I resettled in the reef; my stomach started to knot. I concentrated on keeping my hands open in my lap, resisting the urge to fold my arms in front of me.

"When *you* start to become the voice of these lies, *this* is when the seeds grow roots and take hold. When you parrot them, it means you have incorporated them into the fabric of your beliefs and have begun to live your life as if these lies are true. It is then that our layers grow the fastest; their growth becomes exponential."

I'd been thinking of how a sapling became a tree, each year thickening with a new ring of growth. Except these hooks were more like weeds. I didn't want to inhabit a forest of colossal weeds.

CHAPTER 7

THE HOOKS

"LET US BEGIN with the theme of lies that 'you are too sensitive.'" A steady stream of bubbles traveled towards the surface. The Hooks continued, "Along with the message 'you want to trust everybody but the world isn't like that, the world is not safe.' Do you recognize these?"

I swished my fin, slowly creating a current that made the bubbles disperse horizontally before returning to their vertical ascent. "Yes, definitely. I had to wrestle down that last one to even embark on this journey with Faith."

"It's not important who told these to you. Many of these lies are embedded in our culture; we hear them from our grandparents, parents, teachers, friends, employers—the list goes on. It's very hard to ignore these messages. The people who speak them do not deserve your anger. Please offer them your compassion; they suffer just as you have from the lies."

I looked down at the gesture my hands still offered. My stomach had indigestion. I burped and a single bubble escaped from my mouth. I tilted my head up and watched it until it merged with the others.

"These lies became dangerous when you began to distrust and ignore your own feelings, when you started to believe that how you felt was wrong. Wanting to be right, you turned your attention outward, towards those around you. You let them become the authority. Your keen sensitivity enabled you to hear what they weren't even saying."

I'd returned my gaze towards the sea floor when I saw the sand move. A wide flat fish was hovering near the bottom, gliding along. My guess was a flounder; its skin was the perfect pattern of tan and white flecks that blended into its surroundings. I wouldn't have known it was there if it hadn't moved. When it flicked its fins more forcefully, a cloud of sand exploded temporarily, completely blowing its cover.

The Hooks said, "There is an art to camouflage, to blending in, or in some cases, hiding out."

Is that what I've done, hide out so well that I've hidden even from myself?

The bubbles preceded their voice. "That is for you to decide. We will say that at times you've listened more to the feelings of others or their lack of emotions, rather than tuning into your own body and heart's yearning. By doing this, your own instincts were stifled. When this happens, you become disconnected from the inner guide that will never steer you wrong, but only if you believe in it, if you are willing to listen. This is why it is hard for you to know what you want."

I arched my back, taking my hands to the back of my neck, elbows bent towards the surface as I looked up at the distant bubbles. I started to tilt backwards and lost my balance. "Yeah, it makes me compliant or accommodating at first, but later resentful when I finally wake up to the fact I'm doing something I don't want. It's tricky though—being clear about what I don't want doesn't necessarily mean I have a clearer picture of what I do want."

The Hooks chimed in quickly. "Exactly, the picture you walk around with—the picture that you have based so many life choices off of—is one that was given to you from outside yourself, not one that you painted from within. It doesn't reflect your inner landscape. Instead it is built upon what you think you should want, what others want for you, or what they want for themselves."

I heard the checklist: marriage, mortgage, career, kids, and dog, just not necessarily in that order.

One big bubble was released. "Yes, the checklist." More bubbles followed. "Sometimes this list coincides with what you would have chosen anyway and those are the times when you are happiest, but many times you've found the mainstream picture unsatisfying."

Ugh, why is happiness such an elusive feeling? Things are not what they seem. I watched as fish swam through the clouds of bubbles rising above me, dispersing them. Some collided and merged with one another on impact. "The outward portrayal of people's lives and inward experience can be worlds apart. It's part of why I resist social media—too much if it is another form of camouflage: endless posed photos of the best meals, vacations, and parties. I don't trust that it's real, it feels staged. Even real experiences like birthdays are filled with people taking videos to post. Why not simply enjoy it in the moment, not miss the moment by trying to capture it?"

"What is real is a good question. Don't lose sight of it." The Hooks continued, "You are right, things are not what they seem at times."

I recognized the sentence Faith had admitted to sending me. *Things aren't what they seem*, then *can't get there from here*. I wondered why they stopped. Had I stopped listening? They echoed throughout my days until the next sentence replaced it. I spent a lot of time considering what they meant.

Another school of fish had swum by. "Except with animals, I suspect there isn't the same level of deception. I find four-legged creatures more congruent. Maybe that's why I relax my radar when I'm with them."

"Your radar for what?" asked the Hooks.

"For the incongruencies between what is said and what is done. My radar for what is real or trustworthy, for authenticity."

"Hmm, more good questions, what is real, trustworthy, and authentic? Let's listen for the answers, but start with rest, as rest is essential. Where do you rest?" asked the Hooks.

I thought for a moment. "One of my favorite places to rest and reflect on my life was the deck of my former house on Cape Cod. It overlooked the neighbor's fenced pasture where a pair of Arabian horses ran free. Arabs are highly-spirited, with distinctly chiseled faces; I grew up riding one. They were gorgeous to watch as they broke out into a gallop; their erect tails created a tassel-like cascade of hair billowing in the wind. They often whinnied as they chased each other in short bursts, coming to an arbitrary halt or spinning around, tossing their heads to dash off again. Witnessing their unbridled movements, a rare sense of freedom and power arose in me. Sitting on that deck was where I first admitted to myself I felt trapped."

"Trapped how?"

"Trapped in a life of my own making, in the life I was supposed to want. My former husband and I had bought a beautiful, light-filled contemporary craftsman home on Cape Cod. I enjoyed biking and windsurfing with him on weekends. We grilled wonderful local fish and vegetables for our meals. I remember telling myself I should be happy, but I wasn't. I was living what others would consider a dream, but for me it held little fulfillment or meaning. I was hungry for something else but I never knew what." I noted I hadn't had that feeling since I departed with Faith. My life had become an unpredictable adventure.

The Hooks said, "You are not alone. In our society many people think they can find happiness in things or going places, shopping, or dining out, only to find it unsatisfying in the end. Our consumption patterns follow these lies. You know from your travels that people all around the world who have 'nothing' by Western standards of living are often happier than any member of your family, friends, or colleagues."

A piece of seagrass floated by and I grabbed it. I began wrapping and unwrapping it around my finger; it was slick and flexible. "Yeah, I remember backpacking through Europe with a childhood friend. We went to Ireland to visit her relatives. She had never even met them before and they were so welcoming and genuinely happy to see us. We sat by the peat fire and the matriarch of the family served us tea and homemade scones with mouthwatering strawberry jam. Their lives appeared sparse and simple. Their home had just three rooms: a kitchen area, den, and bedroom. Even though they had so little, they still insisted on gifting us placemats they had woven themselves, dying the wool from plants. I was very touched by their generosity and hospitality. Regrettably, I left those mats behind in the divorce. I left everything."

The Hooks inquired, "Even though you divorced, have you really left it behind? Were you ever happy in your marriage?"

I ignored their first question. "In the beginning of our relationship I thought I was happy. Within a few months we were spending most of our time together on evenings and weekends. When I look back I know we moved in together too swiftly. He convinced me it made good financial sense. He argued, why should we both pay rent when we could be spending it on something else? Economics, hardly the basis for living together. I never appreciated the price of my freedom, the importance of my own space so that I could listen to how I felt. I guess it's a prime example of how I tend to let others' desires, expressed or unexpressed, drown out my own." I started to feel nauseous just thinking about it. "Even when I'm not hungry, if it's meal time I somehow feel responsible to get it started and stop my reading or writing. I accept social engagements to go out to eat or join a friend for a walk when what I really need is time to myself. God, I hate this about myself. I'm still doing it."

"Yes, a habit that has taken a lifetime to cultivate will not disappear overnight. You have been making great strides over the last year. Your choice to leave your marriage was the first of many times you honored what you wanted, despite what others wanted or what they might think of you."

I let the seaweed loosen and drift off my finger with the currents. "I remember how awful I felt then; my stomach bothered me every day. I'd had surgery six months prior and I'd begun to fear that they left something in my belly. My digestion was always off, feeling bloated, as if I couldn't metabolize my meals anymore. I lost interest in food and the routines of our day.

"I wanted a different kind of connection with life, with myself, with my husband," I continued. "I started to feel bereft by how little communion I felt in my marriage. We couldn't inhabit a shared silence together comfortably. He always filled it with small talk. We rarely talked about our inner lives. Mostly we played together. We had been in therapy for months to try to address it. I recall when the therapist asked him if he could see I was changing, that I wasn't the woman he married—that I was asking for something else now. He didn't understand the question. I attempted to clarify it. I told him I wanted something more than sharing our outer lives with one another. I wanted to know what was unresolved in his heart, to share my own questions about life and the meaning of it all. I craved a different kind of conversation between us but I couldn't access it. At times I would read excerpts of my journal to him to try to start the conversation but it fell on deaf ears."

I was picking at my fingernails. "Given we both loved the ocean, one time I read him a passage from *Gifts from the Sea*.[19] My mother had given me this book when I left for college.

---

[19] Debbie Elliot, "Anne Morrow Lindbergh's Long-Lasting 'Gift'", All Things Considered, NPR, February 26, 2006. https://www.npr.org/2006/02/26/5232208/anne-morrow-lindberghs-long-lasting-gift.

113

It was one of the few items besides clothes I packed for my semester in London. I even backpacked around Europe with it. I've read it countless times, dog-earing pages, underlining passages, memorizing others. I thought it would help him understand how the sea had become my teacher, why I walked beside it asking the questions unresolved in my heart. Her advice was to be empty and choiceless as a beach. I wasn't capable yet of that kind of patience and faith." I rubbed my hands across my face, resting my cheeks momentarily in the palms of my hand.

"My attempts to spark a different kind of conversation inevitably fell flat. His one-word response would be something to the effect of 'that's nice' then ask what I wanted for dinner or if I wanted to watch a movie. He preferred to eat while watching a screen. I wanted to talk." I stopped picking at my fingernails but I couldn't leave my hands still so I massaged my palms.

Two half-dollar-size bubbles emerged from the Hooks. "So how did you cope?" They floated further apart as they rose.

"I explored my inner life with my female friends; they knew me better than my own husband. He became jealous of the time I spent with them. I was at an impasse. It's why I wanted us in therapy. Our therapist reiterated the question I had been asking for months. She directly asked, 'Do you want to be married to this Sarah, before you, who is different from the Sarah you married? Are you in love with her and who she is becoming?' I distinctly recall he said, 'Being married is what makes me happy.'" I shook my head and pressed harder with my thumb on the heel of my other hand.

"What was your response?"

My shoulders rounded towards my ears and I rolled them

back. I pressed my palms together more forcefully. "I was indignant at first. He completely ignored the point of being married to *me*. But my flare-up was more like a firecracker—I burned out. What little passion I had left for our marriage fizzled. I was done. I felt like he was married to the idea of being married and I was irrelevant, invisible. I finally started to make sense of why I didn't feel met or understood. He could be married to anyone as long as they were a fun companion. While fun was nice, I wanted something sacred. It was becoming clearer to me I hadn't written that into our vows because I hadn't admitted to myself I wanted it when we married. I realized I was alone in my longing for something more." I wrapped my arms in front of me, holding my elbows and putting a pressure on my stomach to ease the ache; it was in full force now on my backside and belly.

"That night we started sleeping in separate bedrooms. I agonized over his answer and the growing disparity between us. I'd walk the beach, sometimes twice a day. My journal pages were filled with my inner debate: to stay and try to work it out or to admit it might be impossible to reconcile our differences." Thinking about it again gave me heartburn. I resettled on the reefs and laid my hands open in my lap again. *I didn't need to defend myself or my decision. I needed to accept them.*

"I remember the late night I sat out on our porch under the star-strewn sky. I searched the vast cosmos for answers to my endless confusion. There were as many questions floating around in me as stars in the sky. Nothing offered me any compass points for navigation. Did I really have the courage to leave the marriage? If I stayed, would I regret my life in five years? If I left would I really ever find happiness within myself or with another? Is happiness just an illusion? Leaving meant causing so much pain for my husband and myself. Would my heart withstand inflicting this pain?

"That night I asked the stars to hold my heart in safe-keeping, to help guide me through the darkness of the days ahead. I awoke the next morning with a story ready to spill out of me. That story was a turning point. I wrote it down. I returned to it several times when I felt bereft. I can see now how that story has brought me here." I felt a lump rise in my throat and a burning sensation in my nose as I choked back the tears that threatened to spill from my eyes. My diaphragm contracted involuntarily.

The Hooks' voice softened as they spoke. "This is the story we are waiting for; please share it with us."

I shook my head. "I can't. I don't have it memorized, despite the number of times I have reread it. Even though I know I wrote it, I think sometimes it came from someone else, the stars perhaps or whoever lives up there. The guidance it offered me was so clear, a clarity that had eluded me. I know that sounds odd."

The Hooks said, "Not odd to us. Read it for us."

Over my shoulder I recognized the cover of my journal: imitation marble, earth tones with a solid dark brown binding. As I twisted further back to see Forgiveness's hand deliver it to me, I wanted to say, *How is that possible? How can you be handing me my journal? How are the pages not disintegrating in water?* But before I even uttered my incredulity, another inner voice countered, *Really? You're lying underwater as a mermaid talking to hooks and now you want to quibble over the appearance of your journal? Let it ride.*

Forgiveness leaned back with her arms crossed under her head, looking up towards the surface. With no further delays than the time it took me to find the page it began on, I gave voice to my story for Forgiveness and the Hooks to hear.

She dreamt of another world where she could swim free; she longed for the sensation inside and out. Where she grew up there were invisible walls. She would get involved in her life, doing what she loved and inadvertently smack up against one. The impact hurt. Although the bruises never lasted on the outside, on the inside they lingered. The collective memory they created caused the world she swam in to shrink. Restless, she swam in smaller and smaller circles, not realizing how small she was becoming, trying to fit inside these invisible walls.

After many years of feeling trapped, she thought she found a way out, a bridge to another world she longed for. Yet, strangely it required her to go against her nature; the fish in her had to stop swimming. The mermaid took on her human form and tried to cross the bridge with her mind. Except she found herself walking endlessly and never arriving. A clear voice echoed in her mind the words: "Can't get there from here. Things are not what they seem."

The sound of water called her so strongly she found a new home beside it with her companion and settled. This must be all there is, *she told herself, content to only walk by the ocean, windsurf in favorable onshore breezes, or swim in the summers. She had married a man who walked on land and loved the sea.*

One day while playing in the waves with her he came up

behind her and wrapped his arms around her exclaiming, "I caught a mermaid!" Something in her stirred; she felt that truer words were never spoken. The feeling ran so deep it disturbed her sleep, her waking hours. Soon after the pains in her belly returned, preventing her from eating; her appetite diminished.

The old feeling of being trapped, unable to swim free was back, even stronger than before; the invisible walls had closed in again. It was most prevalent when she felt presented with false choices, either this or that when neither was what she longed for, nor offered the nourishment she craved. She couldn't figure a way out; she sensed there was a third choice but her mind couldn't solve it. She felt like she had become prey to something larger, a predator that was caging her. She prayed to the divine for help.

"I'm out of my element," she cried.

A clear voice replied. "Sit still. Be quiet, let us speak to you, there is much to be learned. You've run away your whole life from your dreams; you've let your fears decide; in doing so, your ability to swim has been taken away. If you want to swim again, you must dive in and remember no one can tell you from shore where you are pacing now, if you will be okay. You must believe. Have faith. Dive in. Go deep. Where you come up, will be close to freedom. Remember these words. You're nearly there. Use your whole body and let the water carry you. If you need to rest again, do it in water, not on land. This is your element, this is your world."

She protested in fear. "But there are invisible walls."

The voice responded, "There are invisible windows too. Look for them with your heart, not your eyes. Let your body *feel the current that's not contained within you. Listen deeply to feel the current that you can give and receive fully—let that love guide you to open waters; you will not be led astray, this current you can trust."*

I closed my journal. In the silence that followed I couldn't help look around and see myself in my element. *I've become a mermaid. Did I have a sense back then of this future?*

Forgiveness reached for what I thought was my journal, so I handed it to her. She took it and put it behind her head. It vanished. She reached out her hand again and realized she was offering to hold mine. Instead I hooked my arm in hers. I wanted her closer, to feel her by my side.

The bubbles peeled off the Hooks in sets. "We remember that time. You left your relationship shortly thereafter, a step towards the spaciousness you craved, but instead of trusting the emptiness, you filled all your time with work, with commitments to your students and colleagues."

I felt the need to defend myself. "Yes, I've always had a strong work ethic, a compulsion to be productive and to make a difference in the world. I realize I can become too driven, logging too many hours trying to fulfill an inner image I have about what is possible. However, I've found when I am focused on the task at hand, I'm also less susceptible to all the unspoken feelings of others around me. It's not like I consciously ignore them; it's more that work creates a barrier for me so the feelings don't overwhelm me. Instead I let myself be consumed by the task at hand." I felt restless and started massaging my hands again.

The Hooks asked, "So work is your drug of choice?"

"In a way, yes. There's a certain freedom and power I feel when I apply myself with laser focus to work. When I slow down, too many feelings rush in and I get overwhelmed to the point of drowning. I don't understand how other people tune out the suffering in the world, how they still function after watching or listening to the news. I find myself in tears when I learn about the misfortune and oppression of others. I've tried reading the paper instead so I can be more selective about my exposure because I want to be informed. The news hangover that comes after hearing everything that is going wrong in the world incapacitates me. It makes it so I don't want to get out of bed in the morning. When I feel the pain of those less privileged than me I feel impotent. I guess unconsciously I've opted not to feel; it's easier to be numb." I was spinning my sapphire ring around my finger. "So yes, my drug of choice is work. At least when I am working I feel like I am accomplishing something, even if it's never enough."

"Hmm." A tiny line of bubbles began. "When you are working, are you also retreating to your mind? Perhaps this is how you turn your sensitivity to the world off, no longer inhabiting your body or your heart because you don't know what to 'do' with all these feelings? Remember, there's no such thing as being 'too sensitive'; this is a lie."

Ian's work had become ever more complicated. He was on his own edge as a white, male consultant with a client who was increasingly committed to becoming an anti-racist organization. When he debriefed with his client after the meeting, he recommended they work with another consulting firm that specialized in addressing issues of equity, diversity, and inclusion. His reading of Ibram X. Kendi and Ta-Nehisi Coates continued to open his eyes to an unfamiliar history, illuminating the invisible privileges he continually benefited from while the prevailing culture of white supremacy inhibited Black, Indigenous, and people of other skin tones.

For Ian, consulting had always been about diagnosing and resolving organizational cultural challenges. His focus had been on "change management" and helping foster more innovation and learning within the culture; he had no direct experience addressing racism and society's ills. He believed the approach of education on unconscious bias, intersectionality, and microaggressions was necessary but it would be wholly insufficient. If the work was biased to changing minds over engaging hearts and bodies, it inevitably fell short. The change that was required wasn't only "out there," it had to reside within. Change was ultimately an inside job.

Jocelyn and he had spoken about this before, wishing their clients were willing to do their own shadow work. They were also in agreement that a cultivation of empathy and emotional intelligence was essential. Without genuine care it was impossible to expand the circle of compassion towards inclusion. Neither of them considered this particularly new, just detrimentally left out. Sarah often said empathy was in short supply, though for her she was empathetic to the exclusion of herself. How to find the right balance?

The differences between them were often a source of tension: he was more objective while she was subjective; he was the extrovert while she was the introvert. He tended to be the optimist while she was anticipating what could go wrong. Lately, Ian's optimism hadn't borne out. Sarah wasn't waiting for him when he returned home last spring. He stopped writing notes after she missed her students' graduation. Per, however, continued to leave him dead mice on the front porch the day he was due home. Sam half-jokingly complained that Per never brought her "gifts." Ian wasn't grateful. *How does Per know when I'm coming home, when to be a huntress? Does she also know Sarah's whereabouts and return date?*

On his prior return trip there were extra gifts waiting for him in their kitchen. On the counter was a bag with Resmaa Menakem's book, *My Grandmother's Hands* and a note from Veena: *Sorry for taking so long to finish it, enjoy the keema.* She knew it was one of his favorite dishes, ground turkey with whole spices of cardamom, clove, cinnamon, and cumin. Sarah and he had tried to make it themselves but they never got the proportions of garam masala and turmeric right. Veena didn't cook with a recipe, she blended by feel. He looked in the fridge for it but it was gone. For a moment he feared Sam had finished it, but his search in the freezer uncovered a new yogurt container with her handwriting on the top. His mouth watered just thinking about it.

He had brought the book with him and was already over halfway through it. He was looking forward to talking with Jocelyn about it. Resmaa Menakem's theory of change for addressing racism was that the leverage lived in our bodies: Black bodies, white bodies, and blue bodies (the police body). He named past trauma as "dirty pain" if it has not been processed, advocating we all need to start by learning to work through our dirty pain, to transform it to clean pain and stop passing it on to each other and through generations. He renamed *white supremacy culture* to *white-body supremacy*. Jocelyn referenced some of his practices as reminding her of her own Authentic Movement practice, the way it invited her to surface what had been unconsciously held in her body. He knew from his own shadow work that deeply personal work was often universal: his demons were not unique to him.

Resmaa's statement that trauma was not invented in 1619 with the first slave ships had escaped Ian's awareness. Of course it was true; his ancestors were Protestants and had fled to America because of persecution. Being "other" hadn't been safe. For the first time he began to try and imagine how bad it must have been for them to leave their homeland. This aspect of his lineage was unfamiliar.

Ian had grown up feeling safe, living in a predominately white town. There were a few Black students in school that he played basketball and football with but he never visited them in their homes. He couldn't recall a time in his life when he had been the minority, nor the only white body surrounded by Black bodies. He didn't have intimate friends that were Black. He had no idea what they endured nor the extent of the trauma that had been passed on to them from the hands of white bodies. The body practice at the end of chapter six asked him to imagine being invited to a Black friend's wedding and walking into discover he was the only non-Black person in a hall of three hundred guests. Just imagining it caused his body to involuntarily contract, to sense if he was safe.

I was distracted by a cyclone of darker fish whirling towards the surface. Amid them was a whiter, brighter fish of the same shape. It stood out from the crowd that swarmed it until the waters started to turn white and cloudy, till the fish were mostly obscured. I was about to look away when I saw a massive whale shark slowly snaking towards us. This one had its enormous mouth held open amid the white clouds. The fish had dispersed, leaving milky waters that matched the underside of the shark, which was huge, bigger than a city bus. I pulled my arms towards my sides.

"It's okay, you're safe." Forgiveness said, "We can go swim alongside it if you want; it's feeding on fish eggs. It's not interested in you or me." She unhooked her arm from me. "Remember, things are not what they seem."

My curiosity outweighed my fear. I trusted Forgiveness and followed her towards the surface as she swam alongside the shark. Her body was smaller than the distance from its mouth to its side fin. It was beyond immense, easily four times her size. My view from above revealed its topside was gray with a mesmerizing pattern of white dots, almost like a star-filled sky but less random. Its body ended at the head in a wide, blunt rectangular shape. Its mouth was a four-foot-long crease that opened and closed slowly as it swam. I couldn't see any teeth, and for this I was grateful.

It swam unfazed by us, slowly swaying its back fin from side to side. We followed it for a while, marveling at its majesty before Forgiveness turned to lead us back to the Hooks. My heart was still racing at the thrill of our close encounter. I didn't return to the reef; I was too excited to be still. My mind was blank; I'd forgotten what we had been speaking about.

The Hooks bubbled. "Work—we left off with how working is your drug of choice, your way to sedate yourself. Tell us, does your work also make you feel more worthy?"

I circled the Hooks. "Sort of, I think of teaching as a more noble profession."

The Hooks replied, "As if what we do makes us worthy, it's just another insidiously pervasive lie in our culture. What if we are simply worthy regardless of what we do, regardless of the color of our skin, regardless of our bank accounts? Tell me, do the longer hours that come with taking on more classes, committee work, and other responsibilities at school give you the sense of self you crave, the security you are after?"

I stopped circling as I spoke. "No. It turned out to be a false god I was following. I simply exhausted myself, over-scheduling and overcommitting myself. I told myself when the school year ended, I could rejuvenate myself. I would have more discretion on how I spent my time. Except the more I rested in June, the more tired I felt. I wasn't experiencing much renewal, just this pervasive heaviness I couldn't get out from under. I felt like I was slowly drowning."

The Hooks continued. "Yes, this is another theme for you, for us. A generation of hooks has grown out of committing yourself to something or someone else when you have yet to make and keep that commitment to yourself. Your capacity for self-sacrifice borders on martyrdom. With you, it is often all or nothing. You give, give, give till you can't give anymore, till the well is dry. The challenge is you don't see it coming, you never notice when you have over-extended until it is too late. Congratulations, you're not too sensitive anymore, you're completely insensitive to yourself. You've mastered ignoring your needs and wants at the most essential level, feeding your soul."

Sarcasm was a new twist coming from the Hooks. Even though the bubbles floated up towards the surface as the Hooks spoke, the effect of their words were anything but buoyant. The weight of their words was becoming unbearable, and I found it harder to breathe. I had no defense against the gravity nor accuracy of their assessment of me. I lacked the reflexes to dodge their rendition of my personal history. Instead I felt nailed down like a butterfly whose wings were pinned to a board for eternity. I kept my silence.

"When you realized slowing down your work didn't help, you ultimately took a sabbatical. Your year in Kauai marked the beginning of honoring your commitment to yourself. These were landmark choices, evidence that you have begun to listen from within. Relax, we haven't grown as much in size over these last years."

Turns out sarcasm was contagious. "That's a comfort." I'd grasped my opposite shoulder and started massaging it in a futile attempt to release the tension that was building. I hadn't realized I'd drifted closer to Forgiveness until I felt her hands on my shoulders. She lifted them slightly up then pulled them back—apparently I'd been hunching. I felt her hands take over massaging my trapezius muscles. She kneaded me with just the right pressure as I began to purr inside. I let my arms hang by my sides. The Hooks had been quiet. I asked, "How can I become better at listening to myself?"

The familiar wave of bubbles released. "Know that you are an extremely sensitive being, that you can know what you feel if you sit still long enough and give yourself permission to let those feelings flow, unjudged within you. However, you must be willing to listen openly and live with the consequences of what you perceive. When you realize that someone else may be hurt or not get what they want, you begin to tune out and then you become confused. You hate to disappoint other people because you haven't learned to live with disappointing yourself. You haven't accepted it as part of life. You would rather be confused or compliant than take a stand for what you want."

I was grateful for the massage, it kept me upright. "Ugh, I know this pattern. What follows is sadness or anger when I feel like others don't consider me as much as I consider them. It doesn't feel fair that I look out for their best interest but no one looks out for mine!" Just mentioning it made my neck tense and my jaw set. I was growling inside.

The Hooks continued, "This is an illusion, just another lie. You are not responsible for how another person feels, any more than they can take responsibility for how you may feel: hurt, happy, or otherwise. People feel what they feel. It is not up to you to help them avoid their painful feelings, nor ensure the environments or activities or foods that will make them happy. It doesn't work that way. People's feelings don't arise from what they do, where they are, who they are with, or what they eat. Feelings are an expression of a person's thought patterns, their history of trauma, what lives in their bodies unmetabolized. You think you have more control than you do. Tell me, when has someone ever changed your mind?"

I sensed this was a trick question. "Never?"

"Precisely, the only one who changes your mind is you. When feelings arise, it is entirely a matter of choice to react to all these stimuli in a certain way. Some people are less aware of their choices and thus are ruled by their conditioned reactions.

However, this too is their responsibility to slow down the reaction to the point of creative choice. There are no guarantees if you say or act a certain way that you can produce in someone the response that you desire." The Hooks were silent. The last of the bubbles drifted upward.

I waited. My attention returned to the massage Forgiveness was giving me, the pressure points she was working on my scapula. I rotated my head back and said, "Thank you, your hands are amazing."

Still no bubbles. The Hooks had just been talking about conditioned responses. *Can I be more patient, trust they will start up again? Am I being tested?*

The bubbles started to form again. "No, not tested, we were just making a point about reactivity and choice and where the locus of your ability to respond resides. Sure, you may increase the probability that someone may feel loving towards you if you hug them, yet it is ultimately their choice. You also know that a hug at the wrong time can feel smothering. We have ingrained in ourselves and witnessed in others habitual responses to certain stimuli: hugs, chocolate, rainy days, and harsh words all influence somewhat predictable responses. Knowing these probabilities, it is easy to forget that this is all they are, probabilities—not guarantees—of cause and effect. This is a slippery slope—the further we slide down it, the more we forget that we are ultimately the authors of our own lives. It's still our choice when we give the script to someone else to write."

Am I the author of my own life? I looked around at the current scene. *Clearly, I have a wild imagination.*

"It's true, you do have a wild imagination if you're willing to embrace it." A few bubbles trailed upward. "It's all about your relationship with yourself. Take now for instance, during your massage, no matter how masterful Forgiveness's hands are, she can't do it for you. You must be willing to receive her touch, to relax and let go of the tension. There is more going on here than her touch."

As if to punctuate the Hooks' speaking, Forgiveness withdrew her hands.

I did have a choice, what feelings I let dominate my experience. I was grateful for the gift of her touch and a bit disappointed it was over. The script was mine to write. *Will the leading lady be content or plagued by the feeling that nothing is ever enough?* I wanted to work on my character development.

A piece of seaweed was temporarily entangled on the Hooks till the current pulled it free. "The most precious choice we have is how we want to live our life. What is worth living for, dying for? For some, even torture will not cause them to betray who or what they love. Love and fear are powerful forces. Our history of torture, of slavery, of wars and colonization is all about control. Control over resources. Control over people. Control over the means of production. For what?" The bubbles stopped again.

I waited in silence with the Hooks' questions echoing in my mind. *For what? What is my life in service of? What is "success" for me? What is a good life?* I lay back down on the reef.

The Hooks continued, "More people are finally questioning their choices. How their choices have consequences for them and others. This is a potent time. The tides are turning on what is real and what is fantasy. You must decide what you choose to put faith in, what story you want to participate in."

The bubbles stopped again. I found myself appreciating this new rhythm of speaking, the quiet space to reflect, to let myself be influenced by what has been spoken without rushing to respond. I had time to check in with my body and my heart and bring these voices along with my quick mind to the conversation.

My body had settled. My hands rested open in my lap. My heart had a longing to inhabit a world where love was palpable between people, where authentic care and service were exchanged as the primary currency, not just in families but in whole communities and across the globe. The circle of care and compassion was so often tightly drawn around an individual looking out for their own best interest, or their family, or those who share their faith, or nationality or skin color. *When will I—we—be able to look beyond these false borders? When will I—we—let the pursuit of money, control, and power take a back seat? I'm not naive enough to think this will disappear entirely. When will I have the courage of my convictions to design my life this way?*

I wished I could have claimed that what the Hooks spoke of was new to me, but it wasn't, it was familiar territory. *I know this. I have even taught this. Yet despite knowing better, I can't seem to live it. I'm the one being incongruent! I need to direct my radar on me. What would it take to exercise my choice? Choice, easier said than done. React is more second nature, more often my modus operandi. Ugh.* I heard my father's admonishment when I was pointing out the hypocrisy of his life: "Don't concern yourself with me or anyone else—Sarah is a full-time job."

"So tell me," I asked the Hooks, "what is it that keeps me hooked into reacting instead of exercising my choice? What is the payoff?"

"We're glad you asked. We'll get to that question. First answer for us: Why wouldn't you want to be responsible for how other people feel?"

"Because I'd be limited by doing only what makes them happy, which may or may not be what I want. I'd wind up feeling trapped. Shit. Are these the invisible walls of my story?" I'd started to lean forward and had to resettle myself to maintain my balance.

Bubbles trailed up. "Good question. What does it feel like to take responsibility for how another person feels?"

"It depends. Sometimes I feel powerful and it's rewarding; at other times I feel more like a victim and burdened by it." I looked at Forgiveness, whose eyes were closed. *Is she napping? Are we boring her?* "I don't mind when I am able to bring more happiness to others, especially if it means doing something I enjoy. The catch is, when I feel responsible, I feel obligated to defer my happiness. This can mean making their wishes more of a priority than mine. I hate losing out and over time, it eats at me. Eventually, I can't stand it anymore and I have to get away. I know if I am by myself I can have what I want without anyone else's desires competing and winning. It gets tricky though, because I also don't really want to be alone all the time. I don't want to lose out on the relationship. Plus some things are only possible with collaborations. So it's a dilemma."

"So how do you get out of this dilemma?"

"Not particularly effectively. I can say I have to work because that feels like a legitimate excuse or I can find something to be angry about, pick a fight and isolate myself. Sometimes that anger is directed at the world, what's so fucked up about it. Sometimes it's directed at someone I love, when it appears that what they want counts more than what I want, when I see them as being inconsiderate. Then I feel justified in taking the attitude, *screw it, who needs them anyway?* and pretend I don't care and leave."

"How does that work for you?"

"Not so well, because I spend so much time brooding over how I left and if I will be able to mend the relationship that I lose energy for taking action towards what I want. I get sucked into a cycle of drama. I know I don't have the power to make anyone happy and yet I try anyway. I also don't want to upset anyone but inevitably something I say or do does. In the end I feel victim to their feelings and powerless to do anything about my own feelings." I was looking down, picking at the scales covering my lap. "This is pathetic and embarrassing to talk about." I looked directly at the Hooks; it was hard to focus on them all the time without any eyes to gaze into. "I hope you think we are getting somewhere here, because frankly I am just becoming depressed."

"Hang in there, we are getting somewhere very important. These hooks run deep. There are many layers. To learn from them you are going to have to be more patient instead of spiraling yourself into a dark mood."

"Yeah, sure, good reminder. I know those dark moods all too well." Once again, I laid my hands open in my lap, receiving. Clearly my hands had a mind of their own.

The Hooks continued. "Now we are back to your question of payoff. Why is it you don't choose what you want more often, even though you like where it leads? You must like the other alternative better because you choose to react."

I furrowed my brow in response. "That's rather astute of

you. I am choosing to react, aren't I?"

"Yes. Consciously or unconsciously. Why? I can sense that you know. You just don't want to say."

"It's true. The word that keeps coming to mind is *victim*. I hate to admit it, but from my behavior I can see I am a willing victim, all the while trying to exercise control over how others feel. It sounds a bit paradoxical. Am I making sense?"

"Right on target. Keep going. Why be the willing victim?"

"More paradox. Even though I feel trapped by their desires, I get to be free of taking responsibility for going after what I really want. Which means I can't disappoint myself by failing."

"Indulge me while I speak in extremes. What happens when you make everyone else responsible for your happiness while you are prisoner to theirs?"

"I may never disappoint myself, but everyone else eventually will. Especially if they aren't prey to this hook. They will set about doing what it is that makes them happy, unaware of what I want since I am often unclear about it. Or if we are at odds, they likely opt for what satisfies them."

"How do you feel when this happens?"

"Alone, neglected, and generally sorry for myself. The *poor me* syndrome kicks in. I hear the lines to that song 'Nobody loves me, everybody hates me, guess I'll go eat worms...' I feel like no one really understands me. Sometimes I can pull myself out of it with a sense of humor but most often I spiral down." My right index finger traced a falling spiral in the air towards the ground. "If I don't fall prey to the *poor me*, I usually fall back to being angry, typically at others because I feel like what I want doesn't count or matter enough to them." I put my hands up in fists in front of me, as if ready for a fight. *Ahh, I hate this.* I let my hands drop open again in my lap.

No bubbles were forming.

I continued. "In retrospect, I know who I'm really angry at: me. I am the one who's not valuing me enough to listen to what I want. *I* am the one who needs to care about what I want and make it count. My habit alternates between approach and avoidance. Sometimes I ask other people what they want first, hoping they will ask me in return. Often, I never even give voice to my desires; I just go along with others' requests. At other times I simply go about doing what I want without letting anyone know so I won't have to compromise again."

"What percentage of the time are you clear about what you want?"

"Maybe twenty or thirty percent. I know that's pretty low but it's true, kinda appalling when I say it out loud. I find answering the question, 'What do I want?' is one of the hardest for me to respond to. It makes sense, since I am so often paying attention to someone else's needs or wondering what is acceptable or what wouldn't be an inconvenience. Before I even start wondering what I want I have limited it, by my assumptions or actual input from others and the situation."

"Why don't you give what you want equal weight?"

"I think I recognized this hook from early childhood. Being an only child, if I wanted to play with other kids I felt like I had to go along with what they wanted to do. Fitting in was the price of belonging, a Faustian bargain if ever there was one. Having my opinion not count as much was my price of admission. I started discounting myself at an early age. This hook has stayed with me in my professional life. I feel like people don't listen to me as much or see me as credible. I'm still caught up on the message that I don't count as much." My voice started getting higher and louder. "I hate this hook. I hate not being listened to—or worse, having my ideas ignored until someone else says them and then everyone goes along with it. I particularly hate when I am talking with someone and offer an idea and later they think they came up with it themselves. I know this is being petty, but sometimes I want credit. I guess it's a way of proving myself."

"To whom?"

"I think I have to prove myself to everyone who doesn't see or listen to me. I hate not being understood." I'd started twisting my ring on my finger, pulling it over my knuckle and pushing it back on. "Yet I know, deep down, that the only person who really needs to see, listen, and understand me is me. I know it goes deeper than just seeing and hearing; it's about valuing myself, accepting myself and ultimately about self-love. Once again, intellectually I'm clear; it's just my actions don't reflect what I know. My knowing isn't embodied, there's this unholy gap. Crap. When will we be done talking about this? When can we start taking the damn hooks out?" I shook my hands in front of me in an attempt to release the agitation building up in my chest. I raised my voice as I said, "I want them out of me."

My shoulders were burning with tension again. That was a wasted massage. I scrunched them up to my ears and squeezed them tight then dropped them. My attempt to release the tension failed. I did it again and heard something crack. I rolled my shoulders back in circles, to no avail. It was like a vice grip was locked on my trapezius muscles. I rocked a bit from side to side, swaying, hoping to become more fluid like the seaweed that flowed past me.

The Hooks waited until I resettled from my outburst. "Patience is required. Even though we are making great progress, remember what we said when we started. These hooks took a long time to form. Layers of lies are being peeled back by eliciting their stories. We have misled you if you think we can just pull them out once we name them and hear their story. No. They have more staying power than that. Remember these lies aren't unique to you; some of these lies have become shared fantasies in our culture. To rid yourself of these lies requires more than honest disclosure. They have become part of the fabric of your life, in order to be free of them you will need a new narrative for your life. You'll need to weave in their replacements, embedding something else that displaces them or makes them obsolete. You'll need to act differently, address the gap you point out between what you know and how you act."

Good luck to me. "Say more, act differently how?"

"Have you forgotten how you arrived here in the first place?"

"No, this all started with me writing my blessing and speaking it each morning as I bowed."

"What's the essence of your blessing, what are you choosing?"

"I'm choosing what I want to believe, and how I want to live. It summoned Faith as my guide."

"How is it going so far?"

"There have been some challenging moments." *Understatement of the century.* "Surrendering isn't my strong suit. For that matter, neither is faith. I guess that's why she's my guide. Though I've noted she's currently absent." I looked around to see if it was still true, if she was lurking anywhere. "She said she wasn't my only guide." I turned towards Forgiveness, who smiled at me. "This whole journey is shattering my beliefs about what's possible, what's real, and what's fantasy. It's not every day one transits through a mirror or incarnates different aspects of oneself to talk to. One of my fears has been if I really let myself cry, feel the despair that haunts me it will be endless, swallow me whole. As it turned out my tears did become an ocean I could dive into and survive within as I explore them. It's all beyond my imagination. At least my worst nightmare of drowning hasn't come true." I flicked my fin and touched the scales that covered my former thighs. "It's been an odyssey of epic proportion."

A short burst of bubbles accompanied their question: "And now, how do you feel?"

I let my hands relax and fall open again. "Grateful. Now that the mermaid in me feels at home here, I wonder what it will be like to surface again? It has me questioning what of my former life do I still want?"

~⌒~

Ian had fallen asleep shortly after the plane left the gate. He'd had an unusually exhausting week of work. Their conversations about racism had been rougher than he expected. He heard the classic defensive move of folks claiming some of their friends and neighbors were Black, as if that absolved them from being racist. When the operations manager said "I don't see color" while looking at the only other Black person on the management team, his comment lit the match to a tinderbox that was waiting to catch fire. Another colleague called bullshit on his color blindness.

Ian knew then he had to abandon his agenda and unpack the conversation that wasn't being said. Even though folks had been assigned Kendi's book, it was clear most hadn't read or absorbed it. That in itself was an example of their privilege. Racism didn't force them to code switch—to modulate their tone, gestures, and speech to act white to be accepted. They weren't exhausted at the end of the day from side-stepping microaggressions or having to work twice as hard to prove their worth. They were already in white bodies and by definition already accepted as worthy, as better than simply by the fluke of their birth and color of their skin. Ian did his best to intervene, to explain why parading friendships or claiming to be color blind only made matters worse, but he felt he fumbled the opportunity.

He was tongue tied, normally more articulate, trying to choose his words carefully so as to not create greater offense; it made him self-conscious. He tried to gauge his effectiveness by the body language in the room; everyone was on edge, everyone was uncomfortable. Ian wasn't used to working with so much tension in his body, he was typically more at ease. He assuaged himself by remembering that comfort wasn't the standard of effectiveness, in fact being willing to be uncomfortable might even be a sign of progress. He hoped so.

The flight attendant's announcement to "prepare for landing, put away your tray tables, and bring your seat backs to the upright position" woke him. The pressure in his ears needed to be cleared. He was ready to be home in his own bed even if its only other resident was Per.

She was in good hands with Sam's care. A minimal task if there ever was one: feed her once a day and be sure she had fresh water. He sensed Sam appreciated the freedom to inhabit a new space and have it all to herself. Ian had given up on the kitty litter box; she never used it. Apparently it was beneath her. He left the bedroom window open, with no screen, so she could go in and out as she pleased. She always came home. He invented this method after several interrupted nights' sleep from her purring and pouncing to be let out. That and he was tired of cleaning up her shit or stepping in it barefoot at night when he went to use the bathroom.

Still, he was grateful for Per's presence, however erratic. She had a way of making her needs known. He'd be reading the paper on the porch in the morning and she'd come out to join him. A single meow announced her presence as she sat there eyeing him. Without any encouragement she'd leap into his lap, her body and tail blocking his ability to read. She wanted attention, now.

Sarah's pattern was uncannily similar. She didn't exactly meow but she would stand a moment and then plunk herself down in his lap, facing him, draping her long legs off the edge of his chair. She'd nuzzle his neck and chin if his face was freshly shaven and murmur, "Mmm, so smooth." Sometimes she would lead him back to their bedroom. He'd pretend he didn't know what was being asked and stand at the edge of the bed until she came up closer and playfully pushed him over on his back and crawled on top of him.

The plane's wheels bumped down on the runway and Ian's awareness jolted back to the present moment, where the only thing in his lap was his seatbelt.

~⟁~

"What happens when you are clear about what you want?" the Hooks asked.

"I tend to make progress towards it in pretty short order," I replied.

"How do you explain that?"

"I can't quite explain it. My clarity may give me confidence; I let myself believe it's possible and often it inexplicably starts to fall in place. Other times I find myself in a situation that begins to thread some of my aspirations together, yet not quite in a form I recognize, so I stay with the feeling that something is happening. I stay alert to what is emerging and how it aligns with what I'm wanting to create."

"Is it because of what other people do for you?"

"Sometimes, when I'm willing to ask for help and receive it. There is a kind of flow that sets up and things start to happen with more ease. Not always the way I expect them to but still in the same general direction. I persistently take actions, experimenting with what it would take to close the gap between where I am and where I want to go. I pay close attention to both where I am now with respect to what I want without making it worse or better, ignoring the cynic's voice who says it's not possible. When there's small progress I declare mini-victories, and when there are inevitable setbacks, I attempt to learn from them."

"What are the kinds of things you are wanting to create now?"

"I want to improve my relationship with Ian. I just got a recommendation for a therapist but I hadn't had a chance to ask him yet if he would go. I'd planned to pursue my artistic side more this summer, maybe learn how to make the silverware I dreamt about. I really miss horseback riding. I wanted to learn dressage but it's hard to find a well-trained horse that someone will let me ride. Horse women are notorious for not sharing. Not to mention lessons are expensive."

"Do you hear yourself explaining why it's hard to have what you want, to learn dressage?"

"Yeah. I don't want to make it any harder." *What if it were easy, what if there was grace?* "I need to find someone who has a horse but doesn't have the time to ride it every day and I can help them out."

"Maybe, be open to it. What else do you want?"

"I want to learn more about Egyptian symbolism and alchemy, to dive into the mystical traditions of my Celtic heritage."

"What would your life be like if you followed these interests?"

"I would be more creatively engaged with my life, following my curiosities and learning. Dare I say happy?"

"Why not go after them if they hold the promise of your fulfillment? And yes, this is a form of happiness."

"I will, when I have time, when school is out. I can pursue them more this summer. Aren't we on a bit of a tangent here? I thought we were here to listen to the story of my hooks and now our focus is on the future."

"It's all related—your inner beliefs, your outward actions, your true feelings and real desires. Trust me, one of the easiest ways to shed light on a hook is looking for the conflict between what you say you want and your current life."

"Right. Well, we are back in the territory of hooks. Trusting isn't so easy for me. I feel like I've done that before and been burned. I tend to ask plenty of questions, listening for people's ulterior motives."

"What do you find?"

"Sometimes they are clean and sometimes there are more than a few strings attached to people's actions or seemingly neutral questions."

"What kind of strings?"

"Often I've noticed when people ask me what I want when they are really looking to have their own needs satisfied. Ian and I went through this in our first six months of dating. One of our friends suggested we go on a 'questions diet,' no more questions. We had to just say what we wanted straight out. It was torture at first because of my reliance on questions. It revealed how often my questions were strategies to get information so I could get what I wanted without having to come out and say it."

"Why not say what you want straight up?"

"Well first I'd have to know what I wanted, second it makes me feel more vulnerable, and third, well it can be selfish to just be focused on what I want." My fingers were back to twisting my ring, pulling it up towards my knuckle and pushing it back down.

"So have you become better at only using questions when you're actually curious?"

"I'd give myself a B minus."

"What's stopping you from simply stating what you want more often besides what you mentioned so far?"

I stopped spinning my ring. I was reluctant to admit to the

unconscious beliefs I suspected influenced me. I felt Forgiveness's hand nudge my back. "Okay. Door number one is I don't believe it's possible to have what I want. Door number two..." I hesitated to say it out loud but the nudge was stronger this time. "...is that I don't believe I deserve it. Personally, I'd rather plead ignorance."

"Worthiness is a magnet for hooks. What about when you do know what you want, how does it feel to simply state it?"

"There's a bit of a rush of power. It's freeing, which is foreign, but I like it."

"What else prevents you from being straight up, saying what you want and letting the chips fall where they may?"

"I tend to hesitate or feign detachment if I think their agreement is critical or contingent on my achieving it."

"You mean you don't want to hear them say no to you so you ease in pretending it doesn't really matter to you either way."

I watched the bubbles rise as I nodded. "Yeah, it gets funky. That's when I can become more manipulative or covert with my requests, if I think others hold the power of permission or denial for what I want."

"Have you been stating what you want more often with Ian?"

"Yes, and no. I hear myself slip back into the old habit of asking questions or easing in."

"You are going to have to practice noticing your behavior more after the Hooks are removed. It is a very vulnerable time for you. The choice is yours to remove them permanently or to let them return. It will be much harder to remove them the next time, if you let them take up residence in you again. Let this be a warning to you: Go slow in making choices."

"Go slow, not my strong suit either. Okay. Duly noted." I started sculling my right hand in the water in figure eights, my fingers open, my wrist rotating.

"Remember to count to ten if you have to, instead of react-ing out of the old habits. Breathe. Pause. It's the second line in your blessing as we recall. It's your reactions that have kept the lies in place. You need to find the slow motion button for your life and take your hands off the fast forward. At any moment you have the choice to create your life anew. If you can learn this you will never have to fall prey to these or any other lies again. Are we being clear?"

"Yes. Once again it comes down to choice. How am I to recognize the truth from the lies?"

"By what your body, your instinctual nature tells you from inside. Which is why it's essential for you to slow down and check in with your body. You did this when Faith invited you to come with her. You checked in to how it would feel if she left without you and what it felt like to leave with her."

"I did. It was clear I wanted to go with her, at least while my eyes were closed. When I looked at Ian I started to sec-ond-guess myself."

"Your mind wants you to be rational. It may be deceived by lies that it's already accepted as if they were true. When these lies become habits, they become unquestionable and familiar. These are dangerous lies. They are the hardest to see, nearly invisible like the fish that swims in water can't see the water. It's what a fish has always known. These lies are held in place with an architecture of rationalizations."

"Can you give me an example?"

"We will give you two that branch from the same lie of false hierarchy. Race or being white for example—it's a construct, it's not real. It was made up so there could be a caste system of control that makes people with fair-colored skin better, more privileged than people with darker skin. When you see someone of color being treated with less dignity, unfairly, something arises in your body if you listen for it, if you don't dismiss it. However, being white you have the freedom to look away, to ignore it because you reside on the top of the hierarchy. False superiority is rampant in this culture of lies. Another variant that causes you more direct pain is that the mind, abstract thinking, is more valuable than the intelligence of our bodies and heart. Hence living with your sensitivities is disorienting because the prevailing culture doesn't value them, validate them and in turn you disregard them, at your peril."

"I'm following you. That feeling of something being wrong, I know it."

"That feeling of something being off, your dis-ease with it, you must learn to tune into this the same way you have tuned your radar to hidden agendas. If you create the time to be still, to be quiet and look *within* yourself, not *outside* yourself for the source of this illness, then you will discover the Hooks when they are still in their first layer or two. Don't ignore this feeling, or worse, start to make an excuse for it. When you place the locus of power outside yourself, thinking if only they would change or if only the circumstances were different, all would be well. That's a lie. Do not invest yourself in 'if only.'"

I knew this tendency in myself to wish others would change: Ian, my students, my parents.

"Be willing to feel what you feel, notice it. Don't dismiss it. Slow yourself down and listen to it. See what is actually unfolding before you, what is real and what is a lie disguised as a hook. Don't bite it even if it has the most alluring bait on its tip, because if you swallow it, you will be taken in again. The challenge is to witness it and name it for what it is. Remember you always have a choice to collude or to say no."

I folded my arms in front of myself, rubbing my palms along my upper arms. The bubbles had stopped again. I was hearing the last sentence over again: You always have a choice to collude or say no. *My power is in my choice.*

The bubbles started up again. "Breathe. Relax your arms, you are safe here. Lay your palms open on your lap, listen with your heart, listen to what is arising in your body. If you feel compelled to act, to react. Stop. There's a hidden trigger there for you, you're being hooked. The trigger may be something in your past, something unresolved that needs your attention. It is you that must be awake, alert to a lie about to take hold; it is you who is about to give your power away again. Remember the choice is always yours in the chess game: Will you be the queen or a pawn, the puppeteer or the puppet?"

"You keep talking about this power that I have and I sense what you say is real yet I don't understand it. Where does this power come from and why am I so ready to hand it over to someone else?"

"This is a good sign; the fact you are asking this question tells me you're only steps from the freedom you have longed for."

Suddenly a surge of energy moved from my fin into my chest. I rose and began to tread water, letting it ripple through me.

"Stay with the feeling, this too is part of your release into freedom."

"Is it finally time to take out the Hooks?" I looked down and my scales were glistening, more iridescent than before.

"Soon, not yet. You have more to learn."

"I want to move." The sensations coursing through my body were unfamiliar and powerful.

"Be still."

"This energy, it's like an electrical current. Where is it coming from?" The water around me started to glow in phosphorescence, to pulse with light that originated from me. Remaining still felt impossible. "I've never been good at being still. I always have this sense that if I stayed still, something would catch up to me and if it catches me I'll be trapped. Yet, I'm always looking for a place I can rest, a place I belong and can call home."

"This power you feel now, it scares you."

"Yes. It's unfamiliar."

"What is unfamiliar need not be scary. What is foreign to you,—the unknown—welcome it. Remember your blessing, be willing to be lost, to venture into the terra incognita, letting go of your need to know your need to figure it out, to be safe. You can trust in life."

"Mercy. You forget I'm not as faithful as I would like." *I hate it when my blessing is fed back to me. Whose bright idea was that anyway?*

The Hooks continued, "You have a choice to be faithful or fearful. Which will it be?"

"Right, I get to choose."

"You're tapping into your power, it comes from your connection to source, to what is divine in you and divine in all the world. You give your power away because you don't fully believe in it, it scares you to live with this knowledge. You cut yourself off. The price of your fear is your freedom, your life."

Their advice reminded me of the final sentence "I pay

with my life" that Faith admitted to sending me when I was younger.

"When you are ready to live within this awareness in every moment, you will have found the freedom you long for, the belonging that no one can take away from you regardless of where you are or whom you are with."

The bubbles stopped but the feeling of electricity coursing through me only increased. The luminosity prevented me from seeing the flash of the Hooks or even the reef; I couldn't see Forgiveness either. I lost my orientation.

CHAPTER 8

FIGHT FLIGHT FREEZE

A M I STILL *in water?* I felt suspended, almost weight-less. The luminosity of moments ago had vanished. It was pitch dark and impossible to get my bearings. A slight ripple of air flowed over my skin, creating the sensa-tion of movement. *What happened to the Hooks? Why did I leave so abruptly?*

My arms were outstretched, as if I was gliding or being carried along in a current. Something pervasive pushed against me. I tried to check if my scales were still on my legs. It took a deliberate effort to bring my arms to my sides, but before I reached them, I felt my direction shift precipitously down and my speed increased. When I instinctively stretched my arms again, I leveled off. I repeated a fraction of the movement and recognized the gesture. I was flapping, I was airborne. *Holy shit, I'm flying.*

I'd always envied seagulls, the way they can effortlessly ride wind currents. I learned to windsurf just to come close to the sensation of flying. A few minutes of having my rig completely dialed in, the right size sail for the wind speed, the correct heading, was heaven. I relished those moments of being able to lean back in my harness; my body weight levered against the force of the wind meant my meager arm strength didn't have to hold up the sail. My arms were relaxed, and I could even sail one-handed on the boom, sensing how to trim the sail. With my feet securely tucked under the foot straps on the back of my wave board, my bent knees absorbed the impact of the waves. I flew across the water with the wind at my face. A holy trinity of rolling waves, steady winds and me. Heaven.

Where are the winds carrying me? The Hooks never said goodbye or foretold where I would be going. No part of this journey had much warning, though at least I'd had a guide. I looked around and surmised I was alone. What had the Hooks said when I left? I was hardly following their advice to be still and pause, at least not in this moment. The electric energy I'd been feeling was still present. It had something to do with my ability to choose to be in relationship to the divine, to reconnect to source. Was that the source of light? If so, I'd disconnected; not even a hint of the luminescence I was experiencing remained. They said something about it being the source of freedom and sanctuary I long for. *Not helpful, too cryptic.*

As my eyes adjusted to the dark I noticed there was a periodic light coming from above me. A crescent moon slipped out from the clouds shining more brightly. *Are you waxing or waning?* It'd been so long since I'd seen the moon that I'd lost track of time and its cycles. This was the first time I found myself alone since I left my home with Faith. A sequence of questions paraded through my head. *Where is Faith now? Will I see Forgiveness again? What lies ahead on my journey?*

I flapped my wings and was impressed by the speed they carried me. In the distance was a flash of heat lightning. I was flying towards a storm. The next flash briefly lit up a mostly barren landscape below me. The ground was covered in black lava rock flows like the Kauai shoreline. Except there was no sign of water. The volcano's eruption annihilated everything in its path; no new life had grown up yet. One tree had been spared. Its branches were mostly bare, only a few leaves hung on, dangling in the wind. I aimed for an upper limb, extending my legs and talons in front as they securely gripped the branch. It took a moment for me to regain my balance on my perch. *Not bad for my first landing.*

The winds raged around me. I didn't care. I was warm. My attention was on my wings. My coloring was mottled brown with dark, complex markings. The skin on my legs was entirely obscured with feathers. The tightly nested feathers on my wings included longer ones below with shorter ones above. I rustled through them with my beak admiring their layers.

I'd never been a bird watcher. I knew the obvious difference between a duck, a pigeon, and a raptor but the finer distinctions, like their calls or names, were lost on me. Scanning the landscape I discovered my head rotated well over 180 degrees. A decisive clue. *I'm an owl, a powerful hunter in the darkness.*

Poking around with my beak, I accidentally plucked a feather from my chest. *Shit, was that one important?* I stopped. Losing essential feathers that may not have their replacements lined up felt ill advised. The feather descended in spirals as it disappeared. Another heat lightning strike illuminated below, revealing a structure of some sort near the base of the tree.

The sound of thunder instantaneously followed the flash

of lightning. *I'm at the heart of the storm.* My instinct for self-pres-
ervation had me questioning the wisdom that flew me here.
Again another lightning strike. I counted, *One, Mississipp—*
boom. That was too close and too loud for my sensitive ears.
God is truly bowling a strike now. Then I heard another sound that
wasn't thunder, but distinctly human.

"Goddamn it, enough already. Stop it. I've had it,
stooooop. This is enough, enough, let me the fuck out of here.
LET ME OUT OF HERE!"

Then silence followed until a deep-throated primal howl
began that went on and on. I wondered what creature was
accompanying this human. I launched off my branch to take
a closer look. Each lightning strike offered another glimpse.

The structure was a square cage, about three feet across
with a height of six feet, the kind you might drop down in the
ocean to be protected from sharks. But there were no predators in sight; just a woman, alone, inside the cage. She had to be
the source of the howling. I'd never heard a human utter such a
sound. I certainly had never managed to voice anything like it
myself. My Irish blood could be particularly wrathful at times
but when I unleashed it was typically in a torrent of scathing
words intended to wound. I'd never been a screamer. I tended
to argue or walk away. Experience taught me that if I continued to argue when I was pissed, eventually I'd spew some vit-
riolic criticism that never made me feel better in the long run.

Reluctant to descend any further, I opted to circle for
a while, observing her from a safe distance. Contrary to the
advice of the Hooks, when I got upset I'd get busy, not sit still.
As I flew, a montage of scenes from my childhood unfolded.
What they all had in common was a display of anger.

Being angry wasn't an acceptable emotion in my upbringing. How many times did I hear my mother say, "Don't take that tone with me"? Intelligence was valued. Emotional intelligence was underrated. For the longest time I didn't understand the point of being angry. I didn't believe anything good could ever come of it.

My dad always threatened my mum, "I can stay mad one day longer than you can." And he could. It wasn't until I began doing shadow work that I understood the value of anger, of being able to consciously inhabit my own inner warrior and set clear boundaries.

There were days when a screaming match between my parents created a dense tension in the air. No physical violence ever happened. Arguments ended almost as soon as they started with my father saying, "I don't need this shit, I'm out of here." The next sound I'd hear was a door slamming, followed by a car door and an engine starting. My bedroom was over the garage, down the hall from the kitchen. I'd hear my mum at the sink. I knew it was my mum who stayed behind because my dad never did dishes.

When literature spoke about the Berlin Wall coming down that divided East from West Germany or the politics of the Cold War, I couldn't help but think of my parents' marriage. I was no stranger to walls and freezing temperatures between distant parents. Eventually my mum would practice detente. She would always be the one to offer the olive branch even though I sensed it wasn't genuine. It was more like a concession.

As I grew older I'd ask her what was wrong. She'd share her frustrations, the injustices she felt, how he didn't consider her feelings, or how she had to do everything. It was easy to see my mum's side. She did everything around the house. He didn't lift a finger. He was rarely around. When he was home he just sat in his black leather reclining chair and watched TV or read.

My mum rarely sat down, unless she was at the hairdresser's or church. Occasionally, when a friend called she would plunk down in the kitchen chair. I never really heard my mum and dad talk about anything other than logistics, nothing meaningful. I used to think they did that when they went out to dinner. Dad would come home from a trip on a Friday. I would have made a welcome home sign that hung in the entryway at my mother's prompting. He would breeze in, shower, and change, coming downstairs smelling of Aramis aftershave and go fetch my babysitter.

Mum smelled of Estee Lauder. I enjoyed watching the ritual of her "putting her face on." That's what she called applying her makeup. It was a daily routine, often before I woke up. However, if she was going out for the night I'd catch the second showing. I had a front row seat on the toilet beside the counter, while she performed it in front of the sink. I studied her real face while she tended to her reflection in the mirror.

It began with foundation. She shook the bottle then poured it on her forefingers and generously dabbed it on her forehead, nose and chin, and her left cheek and then right. The gesture was remarkably similar to making the sign of the cross, after I dipped my right middle finger in holy water upon entering and exiting the church. For a moment she resembled a warrior from another culture, like the pictures in the golden yellow *National Geographic* magazine. Next, she smoothed the blotches all over until the shading was even, right to the edge of her hairline, under her jaw and into her neck area but not so low that it ruined the collar of her shirt.

She layered various shades of powder on her upper lids and with a black eyeliner traced along her lid's edges. After curling her lashes, she lengthened them with mascara. When she was done, her eyes announced themselves boldly from her face as if they grew in size.

She chose her lipstick to match her outfit and used the same color lipstick for blush. The finale was a square of toilet paper she would fold in half, and while rolling her lips over her teeth she would lightly bite the paper, leaving a print. She said it fixed her lipstick to her lips instead of coming off on a glass and lasted longer.

My mum worked at the Estee Lauder cosmetic counter going through college, selling and teaching women how to put on makeup. She was an artist and her face was her canvas. She typically put her face on while in her robe or her underwear to protect her clothes from stains. Her technique for pulling anything over her head while dressing was to place a black-and-white checkered silk scarf over her head and tie it below her chin. When she died and I cleared out her bathroom, I couldn't bring myself to throw out that makeup-smudged scarf.

No matter how much I watched this ritual as a child, I'd never been good at putting makeup on myself. I resisted wearing any daily cosmetics, other than lipstick as an adult. Subsequently, on special occasions when I actually wanted to wear it I was less than competent in putting it on. I tended to forget I was wearing it and when I invariably cried at weddings or funerals. I smeared it, wiping my tears. I was better off with my original face. I realized much later in life mum really did put a face on, at night and all day.

My parents' date nights always started at the bar and often ended at the bar; a solid meal was optional. I deduced from her refrain in arguments that he talked to everyone else, often total strangers or the bartender instead of her. Invariably one if not all of these lines would be yelled by my mother: "You don't care what's going on in my life or your daughter's life, you never ask about us!" or "Everyone is more important to you than your own family!" or "Why are you always so charming to the public and not to us?" His comeback was often, "I'm the one providing for this family, I can do whatever I damn well please. If you don't like it, leave." Nothing ever got resolved, it just simmered under the surface.

All the expressions related to drinking mystified me till I was older, till they made sense. "I could use a drink" or the irony of "happy hour" as if one could drink happiness, some days it was more the "forgetting hour." My mother never forgot and rarely forgave. Alcohol loosened her tongue. Her nickname was "the velvet hammer" because her statement might start out innocuously or even kindly but end by flattening you to the pavement.

Some nights, the bartender's last call at four a.m. was too soon for my father, so he'd invite his friends over for a nightcap. I think by then it should have been called a "dawn cap." More than a few Saturday mornings I'd wake to loud voices. When I came in blurry-eyed from sleep, it inspired the other couple to go home to their own kids.

My parents had an agreement with their friends. Whoever

was last to leave the bar would buy a half dozen donuts if Dunkin Donuts had opened by then. I loved finding freshly made donuts: jelly, chocolate, and cinnamon crullers on the kitchen counter. If the bag was missing, I'd run down to the mailbox in hopes of finding a drive-by delivery.

Just because my dad didn't do anything around the house didn't stop him from telling me what to do. My mum ran the house in his absence but she took the back seat when he was home. If I was around looking idle before he left for coffee or to go get his car washed, he would dole out my assignments to rake the lawn, clean out the cellar or the garage. They were never small tasks either like taking out the garbage or emptying the strainer. His assignments took hours and if I didn't do them, there would be hell to pay. I learned to get busy and be out of sight.

No, my dad never apologized and my mum rarely meant it when she did. Getting angry gets you nowhere. Mum always said, "What's the point of getting angry, there's nothing I can do about it." I knew apologizing pissed her off even more but she pretended it didn't matter. I'm sure she felt powerless; I know I felt it when I listened to her.

I think she actually thought she wasn't angry. I wished I could have held up a mirror so she could tell her face that, or a recording so she could hear her tone of voice. She wasn't just angry, she was molten. Even after he died my mum was still working out her unfinished business with me. She finally had her independence after years of taking care of my father but it was too late, she didn't know how to claim it. At times she was happy for me, at other times I could feel her comments laced with unspoken jealousy and bitterness. She had raised me to be independent, to not trust or rely on men, to not give my power away.

Yeah, the anger below me was all too familiar. What if I kept flying, put more than a little distance between us, more like the opposite coast or continent. *Maybe I can come back when she isn't so angry?* Then I started to laugh. *Who am I kidding, the longer I wait the worse it will be. It's probably been the waiting that has made it this bad now.*

With no further delay I tucked my wings by my side and dove directly for the cage, in pursuit of what would prove to be a very difficult catch.

～⌒～

Ian was fed up with lying for Sarah. He planned to tell Jocelyn and Jim the truth tonight over dinner. Jocelyn had pressured him to accept the invitation saying she hadn't seen him for forever. He looked in the refrigerator for lunch but its contents were predominantly condiments and beverages. He opted to eat out.

He texted Jim, *Court time before we become spectators? Join me for Wimbledon?* His and Sarah's favorite spot was Allie's Beach Street Cafe. He had a hankering for their Cubano sandwich. He'd not eaten there since she left. Coming at least partially clean later was freeing him to reclaim his life.

He missed chatting with Varga as a sommelier and hearing his reflections on his favorite wine finds. He checked to see if there was a wine tasting on Saturday night at Brix's South End location. *Just because Sarah is gone doesn't mean I have to sit home alone and wait for her.*

Jim texted back, *2:00 p.m. at courts and spectate later.*

Ian asked, *Tonight's menu?*

His phone buzzed again. *Paella.*

Ian was glad he asked; his cellar was shy on Spanish wines. He planned to ask Varga for his recommended pairing and stop by Helen's wine shop to purchase it. Even the thought of reconnecting with his community brought a smile to his face.

He walked into Allie's and Varga noticed him. "Well hello stranger, where's your better half?"

This is why I stayed away. More questions about Sarah. "Traveling, sadly."

Varga patted him on the shoulder. "Well it's summer. Her wings are clipped in the school year; you're always the one flying off."

Ian nodded. "It's true, just back last night and I leave again on Wednesday."

"When she returns, I've found a white she'll enjoy. Helen's featured it, it's a Picarana from Sierra de Gredos, near Madrid, Spain, the Bodega Marañones. Picarana is made from one hundred percent Albillo Real, a rare grape unique to the Sierra de Gredos. The flavor is crisp with stone fruit; I know Sarah isn't fond of Chardonnay."

"You've got her number. Hey I need a pairing for paella, what do you recommend?

"Hmm, paella can go equally well with white or red, but since you are a fan of red and Sarah's away I'd choose either a Rioja or medium-bodied Tempranillo, slightly chilled."

Ian predicted tonight would be a two-bottle night, so he would look for both and offer a bit of a taste test. He never read during lunch; instead Varga and he made small talk, something Sarah hated.

Next stop: Helen's Bottle Shop, named after the owner's two grandmothers, which sold small production craft cider, beer, and wines. Ian subscribed to the owner Alexis's monthly read, "Skin Contact" where she featured the wineries he might not ever have known about. He loved finding new wineries. Ian could happily spend the entire day talking about wine and Alexis indulged him, helping him find two great options to pair with paella. She was no fool; he left with a case of wine. By the time Ian had completed his errands he still had a small window to join Per for a quick nap before tennis with Jim.

He awoke feeling sluggish. Had he not made a date with Jim he would have rolled over and gone back to sleep. When he arrived late to the courts, Jim was practicing his serve.

"Hey Jim, do you mind if we just volley?"

"No problem. I can understand if I intimidated you with my blazing serve." Jim walked up to the net to retrieve a ball.

Ian fetched the other balls and tucked some in his pockets, pitching a few to Jim. He positioned himself behind the baseline, bouncing on his toes and swinging to hit an imaginary ball with his forehand and backhand strokes. "Okay, ready. Go ahead, see if you can ace me."

Ian returned the serve but it was out. The next ball he put in play. They volleyed their usual political views for the next half hour.

"The solution to the nation's divide is a third party—take the moderates from both and we may have a chance at common ground," Jim said.

"Unlikely to ever happen but a more centrist approach would serve the nation." Ian's game was off; he was hitting either into the net or beyond the baseline. They spent an inordinate amount of time chasing, not hitting, balls. "Hey Jim, I need to put myself out of my misery here. Today I will be a better spectator."

"I have to push back dinner tonight. Jocelyn reminded me she is at Authentic Movement today with the coven so I lost my sous chef."

"I can come over early and help. I've got a few bottles of wine for us to taste test."

"Deal. Let's catch some of the pros, I haven't seen any of Wimbledon yet."

They drove back to Ian's and popped a beer to watch. Later when Ian arrived in Jim's kitchen ready to chop he noted the new copper paella pan. "That's a beauty."

Jim had on a khaki apron with leather straps, and he handed Ian a denim one. "Yeah, we just acquired it. It inspired tonight's menu." A bag of Matiz España bomba paella rice, a jar of their sofrito along with Aneto broths was beside it on the counter. "The trick to authentic paella is authentic ingredients."

The kitchen already had the scent of simmering onions. Ian assumed his station at the cutting board after opening the first bottle of Javi Revert. As he poured them each a glass, he said, "This is his Sensal, from Valencia, Spain. It's a blend of Monastrell, Garnacha, and Alicante Bouschet; that last grape is from his grandfather's vines, the other two are newer vines."

By the time Jocelyn appeared, the paella was nearly done and more than half the first bottle was gone.

Ian asked, "What can I pour for you?" He was hoping to temporarily stave off the question he knew was coming. It didn't delay her for long.

"Whatever you're both drinking. I can't believe Sarah missed another day of Authentic Movement with us. What have you heard from her?"

Ian took a sip of wine and a deep breath, inhaling the hint of saffron. "Not a word and I don't expect to at this point. I've got to come clean here. She left abruptly, without her phone, and said she would be out of communication; she wanted to be on silent retreat. I thought she might be back in a week, a month on the outside but now, I'm not sure what's going on." The wine on an empty stomach had loosened his tongue. He was tired of lying for her. "We're both waiting for her to return, for any signal from her. Honestly, I'm struggling with not knowing any more than you. I've tried to cover up my clue- lessness by lying for her. I'm in the dark." He took another swallow of wine.

Jim stepped in diplomatically. "Women are like wine, brooding and mysterious at times and better with age, always worth the wait." He had walked up to Jocelyn and gave her a welcoming kiss. "Paella is ready when we are. I think I've got the crust on the bottom of the rice now. The kids made other plans, so as you can see, we will have leftovers."

Jocelyn didn't see this disclosure coming. She dropped the conversation about Sarah and refocused on dinner. "Let's eat outside, it's beautiful tonight. I'll set the table." She turned to Jim. "I love coming home to a meal that's ready. You spoil me." She gave Jim's shoulder a gentle pat of acknowledge- ment. She looked around the counters and sink, noting he had kept up on the dishes. "Such a clean kitchen. I'm a woman of leisure today."

Talk of Wimbledon dominated the first half of dinner. Jocelyn played doubles and was a strong competitor on the court; she had a serve that was difficult to return even for Ian. She had both spin and deep corner placement.

Jim asked Jocelyn, "How was Authentic Movement today?"

"Not the same without Sarah; three people is significantly different than four."

Ian could relate. *One is significantly different than two.*

Jocelyn had closed her eyes for a moment. "It gave me a chance to tap into just how overwhelmed I feel. I found myself resting, curled up around the standing drum as another mover played a steady beat. Its vibration penetrated my chest and belly as if it was rearranging the molecules in my body to create more space. After she stopped playing I could still feel this buzzing, pulsing in my skin that settled something amiss in me." She opened her eyes. The chattering of the birds filled the silence. She looked at her plate. "Jim, this paella is delicious. I appreciate it, I appreciate you." She leaned over and kissed him.

Ian witnessed their exchange and thought of his last night with Sarah. How it started out with a fuss over making dinner but they had recovered their connection in the bedroom before Rumored Woman appeared. He pushed it out of his mind and reached for another topic of conversation. "I'm halfway through *My Grandmother's Hands*. I can see why you and Sarah recommended it."

Jocelyn's fork stopped midair. She said, "Halfway already! Slow it down, Ian. Are you doing the practices he suggests with each chapter? They are the most important parts of the book."

Ian's plate was empty; he had been contemplating seconds even though he felt full. "I did blow past most of them telling myself I'd do them later."

Jocelyn replied, "Reading them doesn't count. You have to do them, over and over again. That's why they are called practices, it's the repetitions that make the difference. You're an athlete, so you know it's all about conditioning, retraining your body and unconscious responses."

"Okay, okay, I hear you, I'll double back. Speaking of which, now I'm going for seconds." The scrape of his wrought-iron chair on the stone patio was followed by a clap of thunder.

Later, as Ian drove home he clicked his windshield wipers on to a faster gear. He raced the storm home; he had left most of the windows open. Normally he would put the radio on but the steady swish of the wipers was accompanying his thoughts. The act of telling Jocelyn and Jim that he had no idea where Sarah had gone or when she would be back had lifted some of the weight of lying. He hadn't come completely clean, though. *Truth is stranger than fiction.* He didn't need them asking any more questions he couldn't answer. Living with the mystery was stressful enough.

On the way up the driveway, a huge wingspan flew over the car and caught Ian's eye. It had been months since he had seen the owl. *What do you portend?* He remembered the sacred owl, pueo, that visited them in Kauai during their sabbatical there. The pueo often appeared on nights when their conversations had been exploring more sacred questions, particularly how to live with a connection to the sense of reverence they more easily accessed on the island. Mainland living held the challenge of busyness, of distraction from what really mattered.

Their next vacation to Kauai wasn't until October. *Surely, Sarah will be back by then? If she isn't back in time, should I postpone the trip?* He hustled out of the car and into the house calling Sarah's name. Silence in return. *Why do I let myself get my hopes up? I should know better by now.*

The room lit up briefly with lightning and an immediate

clap of thunder. The storm was right over them now. "I hope you already went out, Per. Tonight the window is going to be closed." She rubbed up against his legs and meowed. He took it as a welcome.

He saw Sarah's engagement ring on their altar; he had put it there after she left. "Be back for our trip to Kauai, Sarah."

Later as he lay in bed he didn't bother to reach for his book. He closed his eyes and pictured the two of them walking on Lumaha'i Beach, where he planned to propose. He had done his research and knew that Venus would be visible alongside a slender crescent moon, offering a lovely celestial tableau in the dawn sky while they were there. He was a romantic at heart. It would be easy to lure her to the beach under the guise of searching for the elusive sunrise shells that washed up overnight on certain tides. Finding a whole one was indeed a treasure. Sarah was a treasure, where would she wash up?

He would say, "Look what I found."

When she looked to see what he held, he would drop to one knee and ask for her hand in marriage. He would have preferred to have her parents' blessing. However that was impossible, as they were both dead. He knew her parents hadn't approved of her first marriage. Her ex-husband had never asked for their blessing. Maybe from what Sarah had shared, blessings didn't matter much to him. Ian knew they mattered, to him, to Sarah, and to her parents.

He found himself talking to them lately, asking if they knew where she was. If he could talk to a cat, why not ancestors? The morning he placed their engagement ring on the altar he invoked them both by name. He asked them for their blessing after he lit the incense and candles. While he never heard their voices, he did pay attention to see if any unusual signs appeared. Later that morning he saw her father's name, Morgan, in an article he was reading in the paper. It wasn't much, but it was something.

That morning after his meditation he went in search of the shells they had brought back from Kauai. They were in a dish on the kitchen windowsill. He fished out the only whole sunrise shell he had found and put it on the altar, next to their engagement ring. The pinks and oranges really did look like a sunrise on the horizon. It made them distinctive and easier to spot from other shells. Lumaha'i was the same beach where the movie *South Pacific* was filmed, so tourists flocked there during the day even though it wasn't safe for swimming, as the undertow was fierce.

The lines of the song, "I'm going to wash that man right out of my hair..." played in his mind. He knew the words were misleading; it was a classic love story after all. Boy meets girl, girl resists boy and in the end, boy wins her over. *What if my life is no more complicated than that plot line? Wouldn't that be grand?*

Two weeks in Kauai was exactly what his soul craved right about now. He turned his bedside light out, fluffed his pillow, and rolled over to invite sleep.

CHAPTER 9

THE POINT

I LANDED ON THE upper right hand corner of the cage. My perch was temporary, it was within striking distance of the woman in the cage. The moment she caught sight of me she swung with her right hand, smashing her fist on the bars. I took flight instinctively. *Ouch, that must have hurt.*

I circled for a moment surveying where Rage lived. The lightning strikes continued to offer partial views of the landscape; it was a virtual wasteland. The solo tree I suspected was dead. The cage floor was compacted dirt. No hint of green anywhere, only lava fields. She looked ragged, her hair in knots, her clothing filthy. *What kind of hell is she condemned to?*

Her body contorted as she gripped the bars, her hands in fists. She rattled and rocked the cage. Her attempts to break free of its constraints were futile. It was well designed, showing no sign of giving way, despite her best efforts. While I was circling I heard her yelling at me. I needed to be closer to understand what she was saying; her words were being carried away in the wind between us. I returned to the corner of the cage, on guard to take flight if necessary. This time she kept her hands to herself, recognizing perhaps the limited place I could land. Instead I was met with demands disguised as questions.

She looked up at me yelling. "What do you want with me? Why come now?"

I didn't know where I found the wisdom to answer her. My mind had been blank before. What came out of my mouth surprised me as much as my changing into human form as I spoke. I still don't know what caught her off guard more, what I said or how I shapeshifted before her. In either event, it worked to get her attention and silence her for a minute or two. I was standing face to face with her, only bars between us.

My message was straightforward. However, the path to take me there would be anything but. "I am here to listen to you. I want to set you free." I knew I had better address my motives upfront. "I'm pretty sure you and I are one and the same."

"Bullshit. You just accidentally flew by me and felt somehow obligated to stop. I have had your attention before but you always fly off again, unwilling to listen, unwilling to acknowledge our relationship. Don't try and con me again, I'm wise to your act. It's old. Give it up and get your ass out of here. You won't suck me in again to believing things will be different the next time only to find it's the same old betrayal. I don't have time to listen to any more of your bullshit. Fuck off."

I asked, "What do you have time for?"

"Nothing that has anything to do with you or anyone else."

I could feel myself being pulled into her argument. "So just to confirm I'm hearing you right, you just want to be left alone to rage, is that it?"

"Yes, you are fucking brilliant. Now that you've figured me out, get lost."

"No," I said back firmly.

"What do you mean, no? You said you were here to listen to me. I told you what I wanted and now you ignore me?" Her tone was incredulous.

"I'm still listening. Just because I listen doesn't mean I have to agree with you, nor act on what you want. I'm here to set you free and if I leave now you'll remain locked up within your cage, no different than when I arrived."

"So unlock the goddamn door if you want to set me free, or are there conditions to my freedom that I have to abide by like being quiet or polite, not rocking the boat, not saying what I feel? Fuck that! I would rather live within these miserable visible bars than be asked to live within your invisible walls."

Although I didn't feel like we were getting anywhere in our verbal combat, I took the fact that she didn't physically strike out at me again as a small victory. I didn't know what to say to help her understand or believe I wanted a different outcome this time.

We stared in silence at each other for a long time; she was fuming inside. I opened my heart to witness her with no agenda, to let myself be moved by her. Her eyes said what her words would have conveyed: *Fuck you.* As I listened to the words behind her eyes, I also heard her rant: "Fuck you, you can't touch me, fuck you, you can't hurt me, you goddamn bastard, you'll never hurt me again, I don't feel a thing, it doesn't matter, I'm not here, you can't reach me, fuck you, I don't need you, I don't need anyone."

The same theme kept repeating as she recited the words over and over again. I could sense her walls going up even stronger, gaining reinforcement with each passing moment. She was making herself more and more impenetrable, feeling less and less, becoming less present. She was lost in her past, in a trauma that left her wanting to annihilate, not just fight, flight, or freeze. Her rage was all-consuming and the fire was burning in a blaze as strong as I'd ever felt. She was my defense system. *This woman is a walking volcano.*

For once I didn't take flight to my head; I stayed with her in my heart, in stillness and silence. I felt my spine straighten like one of the bars of the cage and my bare feet planted in the dusty earth. I settled in to witness this storm. She was anything but still. I watched her move about her three-foot cage. Her feet were bare; she couldn't pace so much as walk in circles, hands on her hips, her head looking down. She'd paused and circled in the opposite direction. My stomach felt nauseous and my mouth started to water as if I was about to throw up. I swallowed hard a few times and kept my focus on her.

She stopped. She reached across her body with her left hand to rub her right shoulder. The skin on the back of her hand was caked in dirt. *Did she hurt her arm when she struck the cage?* She moved her back up against the bars, lining up her left shoulder blade and slid it up and down a bit, leaning into the steel bars. My shoulders felt tense.

The way the lightning glinted off the metal bars reminded me of the Hooks. My ribcage was contracted, my breath shallow, my thigh muscles tense and my knees were locked. I felt compressed like a coiled spring. The longer I witnessed her, the more a pressure built inside me. *Where is the release valve?* I wanted to start yelling but I resisted it for a while. *What's the point?* I reached out to grip the bars of the cage with both hands. *Cold and solid.* A shiver went down my spine.

I felt trapped, even though I was outside the cage. I pushed and pulled as hard as I could on the bars, which didn't give a millimeter. I didn't let go. I continued to shake at the bars until my whole body was throwing my weight into it. Even though I felt the futility of my efforts, a part of me was deeply satisfied with letting the stopper off what was boiling inside of me. I heard an inner voice say, *What's the point of being angry? It doesn't get me anywhere.* I ignored it.

Right now, it's okay for me to be angry, really stark raving mad angry—it's necessary. I never let myself do this. What started as a groan swiftly broke into a scream, raging from depths that frightened me. After running out of breath I inhaled and started screaming again. A piercing pain lacerated the back of my throat. Rage placed her gritty hands on mine, closing over them, holding me as I held the bar. She was still for a change.

In that moment I realized I was the last person she wanted to fight with; of all the people she needed most to be heard by, she needed me to be on her side. She needed me to listen, to give voice to how we felt, not to betray myself by pretending what we felt didn't matter. Even though I'd let myself feel her anger and had begun to give voice to it, it wasn't enough to set her free; we were both still behind bars.

I asked her, "Do you have any idea where the key to this cage is hidden?"

Rage nodded.

"Well why don't you tell me so I can get us the hell outta here?"

"You're not going to like the answer."

"Try me. I really did come to set you, us, free."

"Okay then, I warned you. You'll find it inside a box marked PAIN. If you want to set me free, the price you will pay comes from opening up the boxes you've kept a tight lid on all these years."

That made sense. My quiet rage had been a defensive strategy from being vulnerable. My armor prevented me from feeling anything, I had become impenetrable.

"Why aren't you screaming at me anymore?"

She took a step closer, so our faces were only a bar's width apart. "Screaming is for when people aren't listening. You've heard me. This time you're not just giving me lip service to keep me quiet. I can trust there's space in you now to feel what it's like to be me. You have always had this ability; in fact, you offer your empathy to other people all the time. This is one of the things that pisses me off the most, how much attention and sensitivity you are willing to offer others and rarely offer yourself—me. I'm tired of being last on the list."

I felt her irritation building again at the thought of how many times I'd neglected myself for another's needs.

Her hands to this point had offered a steady pressure over mine, but now she started to tighten her grip. "I warn you, it will take all the strength we have to open the lid to pain."

What would my life be like if I tapped into her well of strength? How strong is she?

She replied, "Stronger than you can imagine."

As she spoke, she accented her words by turning her hands into a vice grip on mine. I thought she was going to crush my finger against the bar before she finished making her point. I was about to utter mercy when she relaxed her hold and let go.

I pulled back my hands and rubbed them. "If you aren't defending me from pain, what will you do?"

"Help you bear witness to it, not withstand it. Strength isn't always needed to resist, to fight or take flight. It takes more strength to be peaceful and present."

If she knows this, why is she still caged? Her gaze conveyed she wasn't finished with her point, but her mouth remained silent. I waited. There was a subtle shift happening within the core of my body—was there a new channel of communication opening up between us?

My insides often felt dark and cavernous but now I sensed a glowing chord that thickened and radiated as a beam of light spread beyond my spine out towards my limbs. The light seeped out pervasively, meeting my skin on the inside and resting there. The pressure I always felt on the outside of my skin for once wasn't stronger than the pressure I felt from within; there was a new sensation of equilibrium. In the past I'd oscillate between a hollowness in need of an outer shell or a surge of pressure in need of escape, more like a flat tire that occasionally became over-inflated and rock hard, ready to blow a gasket. Until that moment I hadn't realized how tired I'd grown of never being comfortable in my skin. I felt capable of anything. "So where do we find this box labeled PAIN?"

Rage retorted quickly, "Right where you hid it."

"What if I hid it so well I can't find it? Haven't you ever done that?"

With an edge of sarcasm to her tone she said, "Sure. Let me give you a clue. You'll find it right next to the taped-up boxes labeled FEAR and SHAME."

"That's a daunting cluster of well-sealed boxes." *Maybe I'll be lucky and find what I need in the box marked* PAIN *and I can leave the other boxes undisturbed.*

Rage said, "Wishful thinking. It's good to see you're keeping your sense of humor about you. You're going to need that."

I wasn't joking, I was hoping to get off easy. "So, I have a good guess. I bet it's in the deepest, darkest place I could find, figuring no one would be able to disturb it there."

"Sounds like you're warm. Where would we find that place?"

"Well it's not under my bed, it's not in my garage or attic. All those places are too close to home. No, my guess is it's in the woods somewhere where even the light of day doesn't penetrate because the understory is too thick. I find this is the one place in nature that panics me. I prefer a hike with a view; enclosures make me antsy. I need to see the horizon line and ideally be near water." I looked around—no water in sight.

Rage had returned to pacing. "Okay, so what are you waiting for? Go find that place, open those damn boxes, and get back here with the key."

"What about you, I thought you were coming with me?"

She retorted, "If I were free to go, you wouldn't need to get the key now would you?"

"I see your point, I'll be back. I promise."

Where to go from here? How to go from here? No more wings. Just my feet and a promise to go in search of the key. Who am I kidding, how am I going to find these well-hidden boxes? My head was beginning to throb. My skull felt tight. A shooting pain was striking behind my eyes, keeping its own beat. My sense of equilibrium had vanished. The only thing I wanted to do was go to bed and hide. *I could use a little guidance here!*

"I couldn't help hearing your disbelief, I thought it might be a good time for me to show my face. How about some company on your search?"

I'd recognized Faith's voice before I turned to see her behind me. "I was wondering if I had lost you."

"You can never lose me, you only think you do. I'm always around, albeit invisible most of the time."

"I like the thought of that: Faith, my one constant companion. If that's true then where have you been all those times I felt so alone?"

She linked arms with me. "As much as I like my nickname, Rumored Woman, I'm not just a rumor. I'm real if you choose to believe in me." She gently squeezed my arm. "You can sense my presence now because you see me, and now you must learn to feel me. I won't always be visible. Your senses are often directed at the outer world; you must learn to sense your inner worlds, too. This is where I reside. You can call upon me anytime. Just now you asked for a little guidance. You summoned me, as you have with your blessing. I sensed in this moment you might need to see me."

Without any hesitation, I replied, "I do. When don't I need your companionship?"

With her free hand she swept her hair over to one side; it rested over her right shoulder. "Well now, that is a great question. I would like to think the answer is never, but you need to answer that one for yourself."

"Yeah, I know there are times when I don't think I need anyone."

Without missing a beat Faith responded, "Even then you have a companion. You just met her."

I knew Faith was alluding to Rage. "She does have a tendency to show up to protect me. For a caged woman she's rather mobile."

Faith corrected me, "She doesn't come to you, you go to her. When you are with her, you too are caged. You're trapped in the past; something elicits an old childhood wound that you react to in the present. Think of it as a tripwire—you fall out of the present and into the cage of your reactions."

For a while there I had lost track of my headache, but it was suddenly back in full force. I reached my left hand to rub on my forehead, between my eyes.

Faith asked, "What is it telling you?"

"There is an escalating skirmish going on in there and no one is winning. My skull can't contain it anymore. It feels explosive in there."

Faith continued with her line of questioning, "What if you told your head to stop fighting it, that it's okay to accept whatever it is?"

Even her suggestion started to ease the throbbing, but then another voice showed up, a familiar one. "Don't be an idiot. What a stupid idea, don't listen to her, you know how easily everything turns to shit. Be vigilant."

Faith asked, "Whose voice is that?"

~⟲~

Jim slammed his first serve down the middle and caught Ian flat-footed for an ace. He called the score. "Fifteen–love. How's work going?" His next serve missed wide and he backed off on his second serve; it bounced high.

Ian returned the ball down the line. "I feel like I'm

constantly making missteps. I stuck my foot in my mouth recently using the phrase *grandfathered-in*."[20]

Jim returned it with a cross-court forehand. "Yeah, that's no good, definitely racist connotations there. Language is powerful. I make my living attempting to use it for the sake of justice. It's been eye-opening to learn the historical racist context for commonly used phrases like 'no comments from the peanut gallery' and 'being sold down the river.'"

Ian's backhand went into the net.

"Thirty–love." Jim's first serve grazed the net and landed in the service box.

"Let," called Ian.

Jim hit his next serve in.

Ian returned it to the baseline. "In the last few months I've learned more about the history of our country that was never taught in school. I consider myself an educated person and I'm ashamed to admit I didn't understand how our economy was built on the backs of slaves. I'd never heard of Juneteenth nor understood that it took two years after the Emancipation Proclamation was passed to free slaves for it to be enacted in Texas."[21]

Jim's backhand return was out. "Thirty–fifteen. They might have been freed but it wasn't long before Jim Crow laws were passed. Separate rarely meant equal." His serve was on the line.

Ian's forehand put it at Jim's feet. A cross-court rally

[20] Scottie Andrew and Harmeet Kaur, "Everyday words and phrases that have racist connotations", CNN, July 7,2020. https://www.cnn.com/2020/07/06/us/racism-words-phrases-slavery-trnd/index.html.
[21] Elizabeth Nix, "What is Juneteenth?", History, June 22, 2022. https://www.history.com/news/what-is-juneteenth.

ensued. "Jocelyn's recommendations for reading have been keeping me busy."

Jim said, "Yeah she's been after me too, you forget I'm married to her. She wept reading *Caste*, saying she could only read it in small doses. I finally picked it up to see what was troubling her so much."[22]

"Who wrote it?"

"Isabel Wilkerson, she also wrote the non-fiction historical recounting of the Great Migration, *The Warmth of Other Suns*, about the six million African Americans fleeing the South."

"Sarah read that too; it's on our shelves."

"Start with *Caste*. I think the subtitle is *The Origins of our Discontents*. I was horrified to learn the Nazis sent a delegation to the States to study our approach to race relations! Even they could see that our treatment of 'Negroes' went too far." Jim tapped the ball just barely over the net out of Ian's reach.[23]

"Damn. Seriously. The Nazis' playbook was modeled after us?"

"Yup. Forty–fifteen, game point."

"That's unbelievable." Ian bounced on his toes and unleashed his strength on the ball with his forehand. It went deep as planned and then he rushed the net. He took the full force of Jim's return and punched it back across the court, winning the point.

"Forty–thirty. She's made a brilliant analysis of the hidden caste system in the States, comparing it to India and Germany as the current that runs deeper than racism. I'm reading her chapter about the symbols of caste. She points out how Confederates

[22] Isabel Wilkerson, *Caste: The Origins of Our Discontent*, New York, NY, Random House 2020. https://www.isabelwilkerson.com/.
[23] Terry Gross, "It's More Than Racism: Isabel Wilkerson Explains America's 'Caste' System", NPR: Fresh Air, August 4, 2020. https://www.npr.org/2020/08/04/898574852/its-more-than-racism-isabel-wilkerson-explains-america-s-caste-system.

erected monuments to Robert E. Lee and continued flying their flags, as if they had won the Civil War. Displaying these symbols of power is a constant reminder to the atrocities committed against slaves, actions which at any other place or time in history would have been judged as crimes against humanity. She compares it to Germany, where the monuments are to the victims not the oppressors. Germany hasn't swept their history of World War II under the rug. Remembering their role in the Holocaust isn't contentious like critical race theory is in this country." His backhand went into the net.

Ian threw him two more balls.

"Forty–all. I know I'm unpopular in my party, but I support the taking down of these statues. How can we move on as a country if we can't even face our history?" He served another ace.

"We can't. Nice serve."

"My ad." His next serve was in. Ian returned it with a slice that dropped in the service box and then he rushed the net. Jim's forehand was aimed straight at Ian's chest. Ian attempted to volley it past Jim's wingspan but Jim lobbed it back, driving Ian to the baseline. His return backhand landed just wide.

Jim stood and watched it go out. "Game, good comeback. I need some water."

They walked to the bench, dropping their rackets in favor of their water bottles and sat side by side. Ian said, "'I win, you lose' is true in sports but this zero-sum game is being applied erroneously to society, as if being 'anti-racist' is being 'anti-white,' as if a gain for Blacks or any person of color is thought to be at the expense of whites, when the opposite is true."

Jim replied, "The more simple the argument, the better

the soundbite or tweet, the more it's repeated and believed, it doesn't matter if it's true."

Ian was screwing back on the top to his water bottle. "We need people to understand that a gain for the most vulnerable has often translated into a gain for everybody."

Jim shook his head. "People don't believe that, it sounds like a platitude."

"Trickle-down economics is more of a meaningless platitude, what I'm talking about is real; it's documented as the curb-cut effect."[24]

"You mean when cuts into curbs made sidewalks wheelchair accessible—"

Ian interrupted, "Yeah, it helped all the suitcase-traveling public." He raised his water bottle. "Or seatbelt legislation for children that saved lives or bike lanes that lead to an increase in retail sales."

Jim stood up. "Perception is everything. Your serve."

---

[24] Angela Glover Blackwell, "The Curb-Cut Effect", Stanford Social Innovation Review, Winter 2017. https://ssir.org/articles/entry/the_curb_cut_effect#.

CHAPTER 10

ARCHENEMIES

W HO ADMONISHES ME *not to believe in what Faith says?* "It sounds like fear to me. Yet, why doesn't Fear show herself like all the other women? Wait, don't answer that, I think I understand. If Fear showed herself, she wouldn't be afraid, now would she? She would be Courage."

Faith took a step. With our arms linked, I followed along as we circled Rage's cage. "What you say is true about Fear's nature: She is a professional at camouflage and hiding. She can make herself invisible on a whim. However, this isn't Fear speaking, although it's a close relative. Listen some more."

I listened but no one was saying anything, it was quiet. Not a comfortable silence though, one that was filled with something going unsaid; it had a kind of tension to it. Something wasn't right. She spoke again.

"Don't be an idiot, you're just being set up."

She sounded mistrusting, skeptical—more than skeptical,

she sounded cynical. I never thought of myself as a cynic. *But it fits. How did I get to be so cynical? What's a cynic anyway, if not someone who is afraid, so afraid to believe in what is good they would rather believe in what is awful? A perverse way of being right. Crap.*

Faith nodded. "You asked a question I was considering answering. I wasn't sure, though, if you were only talking to yourself?"

Hah, me talking to myself, Ian would like that. "Which question was that?"

Faith recounted, "How did I get to be cynical?" She paused for a moment and stopped walking so she could look directly at me. "Why don't you try answering that for yourself, I'll listen and add in what I'm thinking if you don't mention it."

I knew I wasn't born that way. I replied, "I don't remember being cynical when I was young, I remember being trusting."

Cynicism spoke again. "Perhaps too trusting."

"Stop it. Who asked you for your two cents?" I looked around, as she still hadn't shown her face.

"No one. I don't have to wait to speak. If I waited to be consulted I would never say anything. Whoever asks a cynic their opinion?"

I had dropped my arm from Faith and put my back to the bars of Rage's cage. "Well maybe there's a good reason for that, like no one wants to hear what you have to say because it's always so negative, predictably negative. But I'm willing to break with tradition and ask you when you became one of my voices? I don't remember you as a child."

Her disembodied voice continued, "No, I wasn't part of your childhood, although the seeds I grew out of were planted then, so to speak. When you were very young you were trusting and innocent, willing to be in a relationship with everybody and everything; you believed the world was a place filled with good things to be explored, filled with magic and love. There was no room for me in your life then. I came later after you had been disillusioned a few times."

"When are you referring to?" I expected her to show herself any second. Rage put her hand over my shoulder from behind.

"Around the time you were in high school, your bubble started bursting. You woke up to how unhappy the allegedly 'happy' home was that you were living in. Since then you've kept pretty busy so you didn't have to feel the anger, fear, and pain that lingered in you and your parents. This is a perfect breeding ground for me. However, you were still determined that you could keep yourself apart from all this. You kept telling yourself when you got married and started a family that it would be different. I've heard this before. Everyone thinks with them, it will be different. Except it isn't. It's the same old story wherever you look. You never really listened to me until after your marriage started to fall apart. Since your divorce we've been on better speaking terms. I was surprised you didn't know my name earlier."

I had to sit down before I fell down. I felt the gut punch of her words. Her recollection of my childhood, my failed marriage, took my breath away. The pounding in my head had returned. I pulled my thighs up tight against my stomach, wrapping my arms around my shins, my chin resting on my knees. The steel bar of the cage pained my lower back as I rounded into a tight ball. I ignored it. I felt Rage looking over me. She had moved her feet between the bars and wedged her toes under my butt. I closed my eyes trying to block everything out.

I spoke to the ground. "Ugh, is this true? Has my unwillingness to accept my own anger, fear, and pain left me vulnerable to becoming a cynic?" *Is this what has taken away my ability to believe in anything or anyone, including myself?* I lifted my head up and opened my eyes. I wanted to see the face of Cynicism, not just hear her voice in my head. I wanted to get better at recognizing her. I looked around. "Where are you? Why haven't you shown your face like all the others?"

With the direct invitation, Cynicism stepped out of the shadows as if she had been behind me the whole time. She towered above me, looking down at me. Her face was weather-worn and tough, like alligator skin but colorless. Her hair was cut short and blunt; it stuck out in jagged spikes. The effect was harsh. Her eyes were vacant—no life, no feeling. Her body was draped in dark, nondescript clothing, essentially cloaked.

I felt Rage's toes nudge my butt. I stood up and leaned against the bars for support. I felt the pressure of a hand on my shoulder. I turned to see Faith was still standing beside me in all her radiance. I exhaled. The contrast between them was night and day. When I looked upon Faith I felt a stirring of warmth. I wanted to lean towards her, to link arms again. When I turned towards Cynicism, my body recoiled. I felt the need for protection. I turned back towards Faith in search of answers. "How is it I am discovering my relationship with you now?"

Faith left my side and stepped into the narrow space between me and Cynicism. She faced me square on, her back to Cynicism. Her feet were solidly planted on the ground. "Cynicism is my archenemy."

Cynicism bristled and walked back into the shadows.

While I could no longer see her, her voice had lost its disguise. I knew our exchange wasn't over; she wouldn't be so easily dismissed.

Faith continued, ignoring Cynicism's reaction, "You have kept her voice at bay for many years so I've never felt like I had to step in. However, just as your world is unfolding as you may have hoped, you've become all too willing to listen to her. Instead of trusting what's going well, you keep expecting the other shoe to drop."

I nodded. "Yeah, I have thought at times, *This is too good to be true.* I keep waiting for the rug to get pulled out from underneath me as it often does. I don't trust it will last." I could still hear the voice of Cynicism; it had become my own.

Faith said, "Nothing lasts, the good times nor the bad. You've heard the expression, *this too shall pass.* It's true. It's the one thing you can count on, change."

"Cynicism has a way of robbing me of the good times."

"Yes, when you let her. She is gaining a stronger and stronger foothold in your life. I am not handing you over to her so easily, not when you have come so far and you are so close to creating the life you have longed for."

Faith placed her hand on my other shoulder. Rage hadn't let go from behind. It was an odd configuration to be between.

She continued, "I know it feels like you are never going to get there. This is when most people give up because they think it's too hard; they don't believe it's possible even when they are so close to their destination. Cynicism's cloak obscures its nearness."

My eyes were cast down to the ground. I felt Faith's touch on my forehead. Her fingers combed into my hairline towards the crown of my head. Her hand gently caressed the curve of my skull, and she paused, lightly pressuring the base of my neck. I looked back up at her. She let go of my shoulder and offered me her hand. I took it. "This is what people mean when they say they've lost faith. However, to feel me with you, you must be willing to call on me. If you won't summon me, regardless of my proximity, you will never know I am here."

My grasp tightened on her hand. Tears welled up in my eyes and rolled down my cheeks. What she said about being tested lately felt true. The tests were coming at me from all directions: my mum's death, the injury to my Achilles heel, even the tensions in my relationship with Ian.

Faith asked, "Would you be willing to give voice to some of the turmoil you've been in lately?"

"Sure." It was nearly impossible to object to Faith's requests. "I get the feeling you already know about it because it's really a matter of faith. It centers on the challenge to have faith in myself and an even harder challenge for me is to have faith in my relationship with Ian, in others, and ultimately in the world we live in. The expressions I heard growing up, *going to hell in a handbasket* or *being up shit's creek without a paddle* surface regularly in my mind."

Faith came alongside me again and we linked arms. We walked shoulder to shoulder around Rage's cage, while she stood in the center of it, pivoting to keep an eye on us, as if she held a lunge line and we were the horse going through our paces.

"I know that if I have more faith in myself, in my own instincts, trusting my relationship with Ian wouldn't be such an issue. That expression *can't get there from here* haunts me most days. Until I believe in myself, knowing that I am enough, just as I am, no amount of assurance from Ian or anyone else is going to out-weigh the fears I let take over inside me. I know all this—I just can't seem to live it, to embody it." I wanted to crumple again. I was tired of covering the same ground over and over and never arriving at a different destination. I wanted to be free of this end-less cycle.

We had made a few loops around the cage; Rage silently witnessed us. I wanted to deliver on my promise to Rage but my self-doubt was gaining a foothold. "Can we start walking some-where, towards the boxes? I know they aren't hidden here."

Faith looked at Rage and said, "See you later."

I watched Rage nod slightly in acknowledgement. I added, "I'll come back for you, to free you, I promise." I reached my hand through the bars of the cage but she didn't take a step towards me, and her hand stayed at her side. The distance between us spoke volumes. She held my gaze without blinking. I waved briefly before retracting my hand. She never said good-bye, but I felt her eyes on my back as we turned to go.

While I walked away with Faith, the distance between Rage and I continued to grow. The path between the lava flows was wide enough for us to stay side by side. "I feel like I live with this underlying doubt in myself, that if I am not careful, somehow I am going to do something wrong and my whole life will crumble around me. Everything feels so precarious. Ironically, I also walk around feeling like I'm so lucky to have such a wonderful life compared to so many other people. I don't understand what I have done to be so blessed. Why can't I shake the feeling that I don't deserve it or I can't count on it?"

"You tell me. I think you know," Faith said.

"I know the sensation, I don't know the cause."

"Start with what you know. What's the sensation?"

"It's like I'm walking on eggshells or living in a house of cards that will topple as soon as the big bad wolf gives it one strong huff and puff." The air was so dry my nostrils hurt when I inhaled and my lips were chapped. The terrain under my feet was slightly softer. I looked down to see it had changed from lava rock to just dirt. However, the random contact with a loose, sharp stone was surprisingly nasty. It sent a spike of pain up from the heel, making me want to buckle to ease the pressure. "I don't feel very grounded or resourceful. I've been questioning and doubting everything lately, just adrift. I can't access my old confidence or the faith I once had in myself or others. It's like I've come unmoored or I forgot to toss my anchor in."

Faith commented, "I've never thought of myself as an anchor."

"Oh, I have. I even bought a root carving in the shape of an anchor as an image for me to have in my bedroom for when I fall asleep and wake in the morning."

Faith nodded. "Ah yes, a root carving, it fits with your desire to feel more grounded as well. I missed that on my visit to your bedroom. Tell me, what would be different if you had more faith, if you felt that anchor within you instead of just gazing at it outside yourself in the form of a sculpture?"

"I would know that I could trust myself, count on myself no matter what happens with Ian or anything else. I would be at home inside myself. Like the equilibrium I briefly felt before with Rage, that the pressure inside my skin was equal to the pressure I feel outside myself. In my blessing, I've named it embodied presence. I've known it briefly at times.

I want to drop into my life, to more fully and consistently inhabit my skin. When I can feel myself on the inside, I feel solid, resourceful, safe even, that no matter what, I will be okay. I actually believe that all will be well." I stopped walking. A spark went off in my head, I felt a new connection being made between two historically separate places in myself. I paused so as not to interfere with the leap across the synapse. I had a premonition that this connection was essential. "If I had faith, I think it means I would finally be free to believe that love is real."

Faith had been attentively watching me. She smiled. "Oh, I assure you love is real, more real than anything else people tend to believe in. There are a lot of false gods out there, but love isn't one of them." She began walking again.

I mused. *What is the face of Love? How will I recognize her if she shows herself, like Faith and Cynicism?* I looked down in an attempt to avoid the sharper rocks. *Do Ian and I have the kind of relationship that can last, that can withstand the test of time?*

"Do you?" Faith asked.

I was startled, forgetting Faith could read my mind. "I don't know. We've been talking about our future together, about marriage and having a family. Sometimes I'd say we have a great relationship, better than most married couples. Yet I know that's not the yardstick. It's not about comparing. It's about whether we have the kind of relationship we want. If our relationship sustains us, on all levels." I couldn't help seeing the tarot card of the Tower, with all the figures tumbling out of the windows. "My sense is what matters most to us in the world is what we hold in common."

"What's your sense of your relationship with Ian, do you

trust it?" Faith asked.

"I don't think so, not yet. I still see discrepancies between what is said and what is acted upon. I know that to some degree, there is always a gap. What I attend to is the willingness to continually acknowledge the gap, to see it for what it is, not making it better or worse. We're different in how we tend to the gap, which makes it hard to resolve issues. I'm afraid of repeating my parents' marriage again, where they never resolved anything. They hoarded their resentments until there was no space for true reconciliation in our house."

"Yes, your history has influenced you. Let's look closer at your relationship with Ian. How do you tend to the gap differently?"

I kicked a stone in front of me which threw off my stride with Faith for a moment. "My compulsion is to bring up the disparities, to be sure we both notice them and are not kidding ourselves. Sometimes I feel like Ian would rather be in denial. He takes optimism to an extreme. Though he describes it as wanting to focus on what is going well as a starting point. It's just he never hangs in long enough to cover the territory that's not so grand." I side-stepped a jagged rock. "I'd like to be better at acknowledging what's right. It's true, it's not all bad and that's not the message I try to convey but he frequently hears it that way. If he occasionally initiated a conversation about what's not working between us, maybe I could be less vigilant. The role reversal where he is more responsible to step in the shadows means I can hold up the pole about what's going well and feel more satisfied."

The path ahead had narrowed. Faith let go of my arm to walk in front of me. She redirected the focus of our conversation. "Hmm, let's hone in on your relationship with me for now; it's interrelated to your relationship with Ian. What's hindering your having the kind of relationship with me that you long for?"

I watched her feet and tried to step where Faith walked. "I feel like I am tapping into an old fear that something can sneak up on me, waiting till I let my guard down and it will attack me."

Faith kept talking without looking back. "Does this fear have a name?"

I wanted to say no but I knew his name. I could tell Faith knew it too; her question was a mere formality. I had the sense she actually did have eyes in the back of her head. A claim my mother made. Unlike my mum, she didn't miss anything. I had the uncanny feeling she was always watching me. Her back being turned to me was an illusion, like the illusion she was walking before me. I looked up for a moment and missed the jagged lava edge that split my little toe off from the others, sending a shooting pain up my foot and causing me to stumble. "Mercy that hurt!"

She asked, "What's going on in your body?" but she didn't stop walking or turn around to check on me.

I paused to wiggle my small toe; it wasn't broken. I started walking again, head down. I inventoried my body. "Besides the pain in my little toe, my heart is racing." My breaths were shorter and shallow. "My ribcage is braced, the way I felt just before I screamed with Rage." I'd forgotten about him for years until I listened to the fury behind Rage's eyes. She excavated that buried memory.

Faith spoke like a mental tour guide. "I sense we're getting warmer, how about we start with that memory?"

CHAPTER 11

CIRCUITOUS TRAILS

I WASN'T READY TO go directly there so I gave voice to its most recent resurrection. "One morning after my husband and I started sleeping in separate bedrooms, he appeared by my bed. I don't know if he physically woke me or I just sensed his presence. I groggily opened my eyes to see him standing over me. He asked if he could come into bed. I didn't really want him to but I didn't say no. I slid over. When he came under the covers I started to panic. I could hardly breathe. I felt an undeniable, irrational, and disproportionate threat.

"He wasn't doing anything, he wasn't even touching me but I felt compelled to get away. I rolled over and immediately exited the bed on the other side and scurried to the bathroom. Safely behind the closed door I leaned against it, hugging myself, resisting my childhood memory of an unwanted guest in my bedroom. I pushed it away again. I didn't want to be defined by it, to give it any weight. I splashed water on my face and looked at myself in the mirror. I told myself I was fine and flushed the toilet before I left. When I came out of the bathroom, I claimed I was hungry and went down to the kitchen. I never mentioned it to him. Even now, I can feel the compulsion to run away."

A deep exhale escaped my body. Even though I was staring at the ground where I walked, I felt hollow inside. I noticed the path had widened again. The lava rocks were all but gone. I felt the pressure of Faith's arm slip into mine as she walked alongside me. Her pace had slowed down.

I listened to the birds' chatter. My voice was the first to pierce the silence. "My life, my happiness, my well-being—all feels so fragile and vulnerable to the unexpected. I know I have trust issues with men. My history of betrayals with men are preventing me from committing to Ian. How do I know he won't be like all the others?"

Faith asked, "What others, can you give me a few examples?"

"Oh mercy, where do I start?"

She squeezed my arm gently in assurance. "From the beginning is always helpful. There is no rush; take all the time you need."

The pace of our walking was slower than I was used to, it gave me more time to take in my surroundings. It was strewn with carcasses of downed bleached-out trees. Underneath them grew sporadic splashes of verdant green mosses and lichen reinhabiting what appeared to be an uninhabitable landscape.

"Growing up, we never spoke of my dad's drinking. He

wasn't violent or incapable of working, he was just absent. Even when he wasn't traveling he was never home, he was out at a bar or sleeping it off. We rarely did anything as a family other than dinner. I stopped expecting it to change. I didn't realize it could get worse. When I was in high school my Dad had a gallbladder attack and his emergency surgery gave the surgeons a look at his liver.

"I heard my mum screaming at him one night, 'You heard the doctors, your liver is shot. If you don't stop drinking they said at best you have another six months to live.'

"He didn't stop. Since I wasn't supposed to know, I never said anything. I went from feeling terrified by the news to feeling crushed. I reasoned he didn't stop because he didn't love us or me enough to want to stick around. I cried alone a lot in my bedroom that year.

"A few months later he had another health crisis and was diagnosed as a diabetic. He had to prick his finger several times throughout the day to measure his blood sugars and give himself a shot in the morning and before bed. He hated needles but being a diabetic forced his hand to shift his eating and drinking habits. Initially, he only had a glass of wine at dinner. Eventually we discovered his drinking patterns had never really changed. He was just better at hiding it, like the pack of cigarettes he tucked inside his sock even after he told us he quit. I could smell the smoke on him, I knew he was lying.

"One summer night while we were out to dinner, I took a sip of his Diet Coke without asking. He glared at me. This was a highly unusual behavior on my part, since I never drink Coke or anything with caffeine. I don't know what compelled me, maybe thirst. Maybe you?" I looked up at Faith but she didn't admit to it either way.

"Anyway, I discovered it wasn't just Coke. It was rum and Coke. I didn't keep his lie a secret. I announced it. We later learned he had an arrangement with the bartender that every other drink he ordered was to be a rum and Coke. At the table, we only heard him refer to his order as a Diet Coke or his famous, 'I'll have another.'"

Faith commented, "It sounds like the fear is about being deceived in relationships." She looked directly at me when she asked, "Tell me, how else do you think you have been deceived in your personal relationship?"

"Well, *deceived* isn't exactly the right word. I still think betrayal is more accurate." I felt uncomfortable correcting Faith. "Here's another example, you decide. After graduating college, I began a romantic relationship with a longtime friend of mine, Simon. Simon had a special place in my heart from the first day I met him freshman year of college. We were always able to talk honestly about our lives. We just clicked.

"It was with him that I first began to explore other forms of spirituality. I remember his talking about the *Seth* books he was reading and my fascination with their being channeled. We never dated, not because I wasn't attracted to him. He had started a relationship with an upperclassman so our relationship was relegated to just friends. Ironically, when he broke it off with her I was in a relationship. Later he got back together with her and their relationship oscillated between on and off even after she graduated. I never liked her or the way she toyed with his heart. I was the one who picked up the pieces after she shattered him again. He always went back to her like a moth to a flame despite my advice." Ferns were uncurling in the landscape at various heights.

"Men can be fools," said Faith.

"After our graduation he had broken up for what he claimed was the final time. He had a job teaching at a boarding school in New England. One weekend he drove to visit me at my parents' home on the Cape. We spent a heavenly day at the beach, talking about what was meaningful to us, sunning, laughing and swimming. While we were playing in the water, initially just roughhousing, the sexual current between us was undeniable. Finally our timing was in sync. We were both single." I closed my eyes, calling up the memory to briefly leave this arid landscape behind. My arm was still linked to Faith's, and with her as my trusted guide, I ventured into different territory.

"I remember surfacing right in front of him, our bodies so close they nearly touched. The water line was just above our belly buttons where we stood on a sandbar. I was wearing a bikini and was about to fuss with it but the playful connection between us had changed and I stayed still. Our height was similar enough that we were eye to eye. Simon's eyes were a gorgeous blue and I'd wanted to dive into them for years. When he took a step closer I felt the warmth of his stomach on mine.

"All I desired at that moment was more of him. He leaned in for a kiss without closing his eyes and I leaned towards him, our lips welcoming one another's, nesting naturally together. I didn't want it to ever end. I didn't want us to question this seismic shift in our relationship or pull back. I wanted to linger in our salty kiss forever.

"I didn't hesitate anymore. I jumped up, wrapping my legs around his waist, my arms over his shoulders, subduing any second thoughts. The water displaced my weight. He didn't pull back or falter, he just cupped my ass in his hands and pulled me even closer. Simon was as hungry for me as I was for him. When I finally slid off I felt his hardness in my crotch. We pressed up against one another and I said, 'To be continued.' We needed privacy. Something the beach at that hour, nor my parents' home could offer.

"We agreed to return later that night when the beach would be ours. We kept that promise. What started out as two beach blankets lying smooth and flat on the sand quickly became a tangle, like our bodies. The sand didn't matter. We rinsed it off later in a late-night naked swim. What mattered was having him deep inside me. That night we made love in the sand, and our passion for each other became the compass we followed for the next few months. My best friend had become my lover and I'd never been happier." I opened my eyes to purple patches of wildflowers; this new dimension to the landscape transformed the canvas that stretched out before us. I found myself appreciating the resilience, wondering what nature's paintbrush would add next.

Faith commented, "It is beautiful here. Nature has a way of rebounding even from the most extreme devastation. Let's come back to your story. What I hear is your connection with Simon met you on all levels: emotionally, spiritually, and physically."

I nodded in agreement. "Living in separate states, we

relied on the phone calls to maintain our connection between weekend visits. I remember the night I sat in bed and listened to him tell me he had just returned from visiting his old girl-friend. I'd been resting against the headboard and drew my knees up to my chest. I didn't know she was back in the picture. I was afraid he had slept with her so I asked directly if he had. I could barely breathe as I waited in the silence for his answer. He told me what I didn't want to hear.

"He said, 'Yes Sarah, I feel terrible about it, it was a mistake.'

"I almost dropped the phone. I couldn't feel my hand holding it, I went numb. I calmly replied, 'Thanks for not lying to me.' I didn't hear or say much of anything after that. I don't recall hanging up. I just stopped answering his calls. I'd lost more than my lover, I'd lost my best friend and the sin-gularly happiest time of my life." The verdant landscape now felt incongruent; my emotional body was back in the cage with Rage, reliving my devastation. My blood was simmering, about to boil just recounting the memories.

Faith asked, "Did you ever talk it through?"

"No, I didn't see the point. I couldn't ever trust him again. I felt like an idiot believing we had something special, that he loved me as I loved him. I was wrong. Not just about him."

"About who else?"

What the fuck, let's just unearth all these not-so-happy trails. "A mentor of mine who had moved away was back for a teaching conference. He was an older man with a distinguished profile, not unlike a bird of prey, the way his nose curved downward. He had gifted me my first set of Runes, a Nordic divination practice that I pulled regularly. I've always preferred to keep my own counsel. When he invited me to join him for dinner, I accepted. It wasn't unusual for us to share a meal when he lived nearby, although it was always lunch.

"During dinner he made an overture of putting his hand on mine. I didn't react by pulling it away but it made me uncomfortable. His conversation wasn't inappropriate so I figured I was imagining things. Simon had cautioned me about him. He insisted he was 'hot' for me. My retort was logical. The age difference was ridiculous. The man had grandkids for god's sake. How could he possibly think there would ever be anything between us? I had dismissed Simon's spidey sense until dinner when I began to believe him.

"That night when I dropped him back off at his hotel, he invited me to come up. He had brought his bag of Runes and wanted us to both pull and do a reading together. I ignored my own inner warning bells and Simon's prediction and agreed to his invitation." I took a deep breath and rolled my shoulders to try to release the tension in my neck.

"His hotel room had no desk or chair, so we both sat on the bed. I was near the pillows. He sat too close beside me. When he turned his shoulders towards me I thought he was reaching for the bag of Runes on his nightstand. He wasn't. He made a pass at me. His body weight suddenly came over me, forcing me back on the bed as his lips were flaccid on mine. I felt paralyzed. An inner voice kept repeating, *Oh my god, is this really happening?*

"Folds of his crepey skin hung down off his face towards me. I wasn't kissing back but I wasn't protesting either. It was surreal. All I felt was disgust. When he tried to put his tongue in my mouth it snapped me out of my paralysis. I closed my lips shut, rolling them over my teeth. My hands finally moved from my sides and pushed against him. He moved away enough for me to get out from underneath him. I lunged for my purse and darted for the door. My legs were like noodles as I ran down the emergency stairs, afraid to wait for the elevator. The outside door had the bar across it; I leaned in as if tackling it open. It was pitch dark out. I hadn't come in through this door so it took me a moment to figure out where I'd parked my car.

"By the time I'd run through the parking lot to my driver side door I dropped my purse searching for my keys. I kept muttering, 'Shit, shit, shit, shit.' I fumbled with the key; my hand was shaking too much to line it up with the narrow entry. I was terrified he was going to follow me. By the time I got in my car and locked the door, I was vibrating all over. A torrent of tears started to flow that didn't stop during the drive home, nor while I stood in the shower till the hot water ran out. When I crawled into bed, I wanted to hear Simon's voice, to tell him what happened, to tell him he was right but we weren't speaking. I called in sick the next day so I didn't have to face anyone. I never spoke to my mentor again."

I leaned my head on Faith's shoulder. She squeezed gently on my arm and leaned her cheek on my head. She said, "I know these are difficult memories. Go on. How did you cope?"

"On weekends I would drive down to the Cape, walking the beaches regardless of the weather, somehow the gray, blustery days were more inviting than blue skies. One day I went back to the beach where Simon and I had first kissed, where we made love. I was shattered inside and I couldn't figure out how the pieces went back together again. All my edges were raw, nothing fit anymore, everything hurt. I kept scouring my relationships—with Simon, my with my mentor, for clues. Was the love between Simon and I real? Why was his pull towards his old girlfriend stronger than his commitment to me? Why wasn't I enough for him? Did my mentor really believe in my talents as a teacher or was he just attracted to me and bided his time till he cultivated my trust? How many other young women had he gifted Runes? Why was I so stupid, such an idiot to believe he had my best interest at heart? He was a married man—did his vows to his wife mean nothing? Why do men cheat on the women they profess to love?"

"Those are difficult questions to ask and answer," Faith said.

One of the not so fun facts Ian retained was his father's birthday. It made no sense that he remembered it. He only had vague memories of him, given he left before he was six and none of them centered on celebrating his birthday. Maybe it was the repetition, eight, eight, August eighth. He was always hungry for information about his father, as if knowing something about him was the same as knowing him. What he craved to know was why he abandoned his family, but that question went unanswered.

Ian had agreed to a last-minute trip to facilitate a board meeting in Blaine, Minnesota. Scheduling it proved to be anything but easy. Sitting at his computer Monday night with a glass of red wine he attempted to make his flight and hotel arrangements. The flight he typically came home on was already booked which meant he had to spend an extra night there. Not that it mattered he had no one to come home to with Sarah gone. The hotel he usually stayed at was also sold out, as were most hotels nearby. He recalled the name of a bed and breakfast he had seen during his commute and they had one room left. The rental car agency had no economy or midsize cars and their rates, even with his Avis preferred discount, were nearly twice what he typically paid. *What's with the sudden attraction to Minneapolis?* It was early August and according to the forecast it was going to be sweltering. Luckily he spent most of his time indoors in air conditioning. His trips in the winter were often below freezing; they had overground walkways, like gerbil tunnels to protect you from the elements. At least the people were true to the stereotype, *Minnesota nice.*

His suitcase had a permanent place in the corner of their bedroom, near the altar. If Sarah had been home she would have complained. She didn't get to have an opinion now. She forfeited that when she left in May. His habits around the house had shifted in her absence. He left dishes in the sink after meals until the pile demanded his attention because he was out of bowls or plates. He would wash one and put the rest in the dishwasher. He hadn't vacuumed until he realized Per had fleas. He immediately purchased her a flea collar and hired a cleaning service to do a deep clean and return weekly. When he came home to a kitchen with clean counters, an empty sink, faucets that sparkled and a freshly made bed, he had to admit he preferred it that way; he simply didn't want to do it himself.

Leaving his dirty clothes on the bedroom floor and a sink full of dishes was his way of exercising his freedom. He knew it would have irked Sarah and even though she wasn't here to be irritated, it pleased him nonetheless. He was done lying for her to their friends and done with coming home to an empty house, an empty bed, waking and eating alone.

Ian couldn't pack tonight even though he was flying out tomorrow; the only clean clothes he had were at the dry cleaners. He flung his book on the bed and startled Per. "Sorry schmutt, that wasn't meant for you."

In the bathroom he stared at Sarah's toothbrush as he took his out of their shared cup. He picked it up and dropped it in the trash. Her face cream and cleanser had been crowding the side of the sink. He stashed them in the already over-crowded drawer. She could deal with it when she returned, *if* she returned.

He stared at himself in the mirror as he stood in front of their one sink. Regrettably, he didn't have to move to share it with her as they got ready for bed together. After he spit out his toothpaste, he yelled, "Damnit Sarah, enough already."

It wasn't easy to be angry at someone who wasn't there. It wasn't fair that she left that night, with no word, no commitment to returning. He had to wait for her and his patience had worn thin, threadbare. He took her towel off the hook by the shower and dumped it on the ground. He had left everything where she kept it for months as if when she returned they could go back to the way things were between them. What if there was no going back? Ian didn't want to entertain the thought; he was furious with her for jeopardizing their relationship.

He knew he needed to move on with his life, but how? He didn't want to imagine a future without Sarah in it but his memories of her were starting to fade and be replaced by a growing annoyance he couldn't tame. It leaked out when people asked about her and when she was coming back. His new favorite line was "She hasn't decided yet, she's keeping us all in the dark."

Ian switched off the bathroom light and walked past their shared altar, letting his toes graze the crumpled fox pelt below it. He bent to pick it up. Its silky fur left him longing to run his fingers through Sarah's long hair, to feel it land around his face and trail down his chest as she kissed him. The thought of her aroused him. He was tempted to drop her damn pelt but instead he placed it under the altar. It wasn't his hands he wanted to feel around him; that wasn't the relief he longed for.

The days passed in a blur, and facilitating the board meeting was blessedly uneventful. By Friday afternoon he finished early and had hours to kill before dinner. He put on his running shorts but when he emerged outside to the wall of heat he concluded it was too hot to exercise. He craved a cold, coconut ice cream cone and asked Siri where to find a homemade ice cream shop. The scent of sweet waffle cones greeted him on the sidewalk while he waited in line with everyone else who had the same idea. He suspected the refrigerators weren't keeping up because his scoop didn't hold its shape at all as the cashier packed it. When she handed it to him after paying, the cone had already begun to drip. His equanimity was all but gone as he fervently licked the sides to keep up with the meltdown.

There was a street with a few shops and an artist gallery he walked by. It was the kind of store he and Sarah would have wandered in together, an artist co-op, with handmade pottery, jewelry, weavings and painting. After tossing the last of his sticky mess in a garbage can he walked in, keeping his hands to himself.

He glanced in the jewelry case to see if anything might appeal to Sarah. She preferred curved lines and asymmetry. Instead his eye was drawn upwards, to a watercolor painting on the wall. The central figure was diving horizontally, an athlete of sorts from the outline of the tank top and shorts, reaching to catch something golden in front. The few brush strokes captured a sense of motion, of freedom or almost flying. The initials AG were in the corner. Ian didn't see a price anywhere.

He walked around and flipped through the prints but there was nothing else smaller or even remotely similar to it. Normally Sarah and he chose art for their living space together. He wondered if she would like it. The colors were bold, indigo blue for the clothing, greens for a field below and a golden disk. It wasn't their color palette but he didn't care, he was inexplicably drawn to it.

The woman behind the counter was an attractive blonde, her hair pulled back in a messy ponytail. He wondered how long it would be if she let it down. The arm holes of her top were cut wide, revealing the edges of her breast. Everyone was dressed to stay cool. The fan was aimed to blow directly on her, making the fabric ripple. Ian realized he was staring at her when she said, "Is there something you wanted to purchase that I can help you with?"

"Ah, yes I was wondering how much that painting is on the wall?" He turned and pointed to it where it hung opposite her.

She hesitated. "That's $1,500."

Ian turned back to face her. Her green eyes mesmerized him. "Ah, is there anything else by this artist, AG? I looked but couldn't find their work."

"No, not like this." She looked down and started shuffling papers.

Ian pivoted again, contemplating the pull the painting had on him. "Do you know what the subject matter is?"

"Yeah, it's a layout—when an ultimate frisbee player literally flies through the air to catch the disc. There's a tournament here now if you want to watch it yourself. They're remarkable athletes."

"I'll take it." He pulled out his wallet from his back pocket, his fingers still sticky from the ice cream. He had never bought a painting this expensive before. There were a lot of things happening lately that had never happened before. *If Sarah doesn't like it, tough.* He was starting to understand the concept of retail therapy. He handed her his credit card.

"I don't have a box for it, will bubble wrap do? "

"That's okay, I plan to carry it with me." It was long but not wide; it would fit in the first class overhead compartment or closet. As a platinum medallion Delta frequent flier he was sure they would accommodate him.

He signed his name to the receipt and asked, "Can you tell me about the artist and where I could find more of their work?"

She had turned to walk into the back room to fetch the stepladder. When she returned with it she came around to the other side of the counter. Her tank dress stopped above her knees; she was wearing flips and kicked them off to climb up. Ian stood close in case she lost her balance. Her crotch was at eye level and he doubted she had any underwear on. As she reached her arms up higher, the hem raised as well. His furtive glance confirmed his suspicion.

She hadn't answered his question about the artist. She unhooked the painting and handed it down to him. "You're staring at her, I'm the artist."

He took the painting in one hand and offered her his other hand to steady her descent. "A pleasure to meet you. You're very talented, it's beautiful." She let go of his hand and he added, "Like you." The act of buying the painting had unleashed something in him. He had been captivated by her as much as he had been admiring her painting. He knew he was flirting now; he wanted to get to know her, ask her out for coffee or dinner. After all, he had one night here and he often returned. "Where's the tournament? That explains the booked hotels and rental cars. I wondered what the draw was to Blaine at this time of year."

"The fields are about five minutes away, there are at least a dozen of them, you can't miss them." She took the painting back from him and walked in the back room, leaving her flips and the ladder behind. He closed up the ladder and carried it to where she was bubble wrapping his painting. "It's not so hot if you're used to it. Everyone just takes a dip in the lake to cool off."

"I'm not much of a swimmer but a dip sounds welcome at this point. Where do you go?"

She glanced up at the clock on the wall; it was 4:40. "It's slow here today, you're my one sale. I'll close early and take you there." She exchanged his painting for the ladder he was still holding and put it against the wall. She walked closely past him to the front door and locked it, turning the sign to CLOSED, and picked up her flips. "Let me put my suit on. I'll be back in a minute."

Ian's pulse raced at the thought of seeing her wet; he guessed she wore a string bikini. He wasn't wrong. When she walked back towards him he saw the dark outline of it under her dress and the red knot tied behind her neck. He occupied his mind with math equations to keep himself tame. She turned out the lights and clicked off the fan.

"I'm Ian. What does the A stand for?" He thought aside from his assessment that she was all aces.

"Ariel, it's nice to meet you Ian. You've been my best customer all summer. It's only fair I help you cool off. How long are you here for?" She unlocked the door briefly and motioned for him to go first.

He walked out into the heat wave. "I fly out tomorrow, but I'm often here for work." He waited while she locked up.

"So where is your car? You can drive us." She had a small purse she dropped her keys and phone in.

He led her to the red Lincoln Nautilus and placed her picture that was now his in the back seat. He expected her to provide towels or to drive, but nothing was going as expected so he let it ride. He started the car engine and his music blared; he turned it off and put down the windows while adjusting the air conditioning to full blast. He was sweating and it wasn't from the heat.

She instructed him one turn at a time until they arrived at a small park that abutted a lake. There were homes with docks lining the edges of it, kids playing in a swimming area that was cordoned off. He locked the car and followed her to a patch of grass. She kicked off her flips and pulled her dress off, revealing mostly skin. Her thong bikini left nothing to his imagination. Her shapely ass was tanned like her back and legs, seamlessly inviting his eyes to admire it. She turned and caught him staring again.

He shook his head slightly. "You're a work of art yourself, I'm sorry I'm staring."

She smiled. "I assume you're swimming in your shorts. How about you get naked on the upper half and follow me." She started walking away towards the lake's edge.

Ian unlaced his sneakers and hurriedly took them off with his socks. He pulled off his T-shirt and jogged to catch up with her, ignoring the little stones under his feet. She was wading in the water and dove in. He waded in behind her.

The cool water was indeed a welcomed relief. The kids were splashing each other and stray drops landed on his dry chest; they felt cooler and tickled him. He walked until his chest was submerged.

He heard the kids' call and response, "Marco, Polo, Marco, Polo" and turned briefly to spy their water game of hide and seek. The child who was "it," Marco, kept his eyes closed, trying to sense where the other kids were that he needed to tag from their "Polo" response. Everyone else kept their eyes open and were free to sink below the surface if they wanted to stay stealth.

He liked the ground under his feet. He turned his attention back to where Ariel surfaced and waved for him to join her before she ducked under the roped-off area and started swimming away. He followed her lead.

It's just an innocent swim on a hot summer day, he told himself. If it turned into more he could always curb it; for now he planned to be carefree. Maybe he wouldn't eat alone after all tonight.

When Ian boarded the plane the next day with his painting in hand, he had been right that it fit in the overhead compartment. He stowed it easily but he couldn't as easily compartmentalize his encounter with its artist. He felt guilty. He couldn't deny his attraction and flirtation. He was grateful for Ariel's companionship, for how alive he felt in her presence. *I'm a man, I can't stop noticing a beautiful woman, I'm not blind.* Had he lived in Europe, there would be nothing wrong with his behavior. Except he was flying home to Massachusetts, this much was clear. Would Sarah be waiting for him? He doubted it. *So why am I waiting for her?* He was already anticipating his next flight to Minneapolis and the chance to see Ariel again.

∽◯∽

"I spent a lot of time alone after that, mostly walking the beaches around Boston and the Cape, searching for answers. They weren't forthcoming. One day at that same beach where Simon and I had connected, a man in a slick black wetsuit approached me and asked if everything was okay. I had already strolled the shoreline for hours but I didn't want to leave. Nothing had resolved in my heart. I sat not far from the abandoned lifeguard stand, my knees drawn up, one arm around them, my back braced to the wind, my hair blowing in front of my face. I hadn't seen him coming so his voice startled me." I took a deep breath of release. *So much water under the bridge. Is this really necessary?*

"Continue, please."

"He held a white bag of Pepperidge Farms Mint Milano cookies and offered me one. I took it. I didn't really like it after the first bite but I was polite. I couldn't exactly spit it out in the sand so I finished it. His voice was warm and kind;

he seemed safe enough. He was over six feet; my neck tilted back looking at him until he squatted down, balancing on the balls of his feet. I was grateful he didn't sit and he kept his distance. We chatted for a few moments about the weather and windsurfing. As he stood to leave he told me he had tickets to a theater performance in Boston. He asked if I'd join him for the show and allow him to take me to dinner. It felt harmless. There wasn't any attraction between us, just the companionship. I'd been lonely. I told him to pick a restaurant and I would meet him there; that way I didn't have to give him my number, nor be dependent on him for a ride, or even let him know where I lived. By that point my motto with men was—*proceed with caution.*

"When I saw him again at the restaurant, I hardly recognized him. As the hostess led me to his table he stood up to pull out my chair. He was a gentleman. He looked far more attractive in his cashmere sports coat and khaki pants than when all 6'2" of him was plastered into a full body wetsuit, his little paunch on display. His hair was thinning, a bit bald. He looked a lot like the actor William Hurt.

"It was an enjoyable evening. I told him where I worked that night. The next day a dozen red roses were delivered to me in my classroom with a note, *Your not-so-secret admirer, thanks for a lovely evening.*

"He slowly wooed me. I liked feeling wanted and the attention he showered on me. We became playmates, we biked together and he taught me how to windsurf. Looking back now I can see I threw myself into my relationship with Arthur so I didn't have to deal with the pain of my relationship with Simon ending, the loneliness.

"Arthur and I were never really friends first; we started sleeping with each other on our second date. It was totally out of character for me to skip the friendship stage before moving into the next stage of intimacy. My finger had accidentally hit fast forward and I couldn't find the reverse gear. After about six months he suggested we move in with each other since we were spending so much time with one another. His argument was *Why should you be paying rent on your minimal salary?* Financially, it made sense. I agreed, not appreciating the cost of my freedom, my time alone in my own space and how essential that is for me to really know what and how I feel.

"Soon after moving in with him, a headhunter scouted him for a job on the Cape. He accepted. The moving walkway I stepped on kept accelerating in pace. We started looking at real estate on the Cape. He sold the house I'd been sharing with him and bought a beautiful contemporary craftsman a few miles from his office. I started looking for a new teaching position on the Cape to eliminate my two-hour commute each way. We nested; furnishing it, gardening, putting in an outside shower on the back deck. In less than a year he had proposed and I said yes.

"We got married much to my parents' dismay; they didn't like him. My father almost disowned me when I told him we were engaged. My mum smoothed it over between us. I convinced myself I was happy. Now I wonder how much of my sleeping with Arthur and later my marriage was a rebound from Simon's betrayal."

Faith had been quiet for the whole story. She stopped walking. "Hold up a minute, which betrayal are you referring to now?"

"Isn't it obvious? Simon slept with his old girlfriend when we were in an intimate relationship! But that's not the only betrayal. My mentor, a married man, made a pass at me, betraying the trust of our professional friendship, making it romantic. Long before either of those, my father wouldn't quit drinking, he wanted the company of a glass more than the chance to see his daughter grow up." I was incredulous she had to ask this question.

Faith persisted, "I'm aware of that, and I know how painful this must have been for you, which is exactly my point. You pretended it didn't matter; you denied your feelings to the point of covering them over with another relationship. It's important you see there is more than one betrayal here."

I stared at her blankly. *What other betrayal? What is she getting at?* My brows were furrowed. There was only one other person, one common denominator to all the stories. *Did I betray myself?*

"I've never looked at it that way before. In fact, now that I think of it, this was Rage's point. She was furious with me for all the times I have been the one who hasn't listened to me and how I'm feeling, all the times I don't take care of myself as well as I tend to others." I knew this wasn't the first nor the last time I'd done this to myself. It's one thing to be hurt by those we love, it's worse though to compound the pain by re-wounding myself by pretending it doesn't matter and negating my own feelings.

The nausea and headache were back in full force. I yearned to curl up and hide and forget about my life for a long while.

Ian's twenty-minute nap was insufficient for me. I needed a seasonal hibernation, except there was no cozy space in sight. We had been walking for some time and the landscape showed no sign of shelter.

Faith said, "It is not yet time to hole up and hide. Come on, you've got a key to find."

The war my head was waging had yet to subside and my capacity to ignore it was limited. I kept walking reluctantly; her arm linked in mine was almost pulling me along. "Where are we going?"

"Hunting," Faith said, in a whisper. I took a hint that this would be the end of the conversation for a while.

Faith had let go of my arm again and led the way as I followed. The mosses underfoot were a welcome change from the abrasive pumice stones. I hadn't noticed the transition till we were silent. The distance between Faith and I varied. If she sensed me nearing she picked up her pace again.

We walked past spiky towers of purple, white, and blue blooms. I recognized them as lupine from my garden at home. Their dried pods popped in the late summer heat. I wanted to convert our side yard to wildflowers but I'd yet to convince Ian it was a good idea. He wanted a lawn. I wanted to create more of a butterfly habitat with poppies and columbine. As if on cue I saw my first butterfly take flight, its coloring almost indistinguishable from the indigo blue of the lupine.

As I looked closer at the tops of the other lupine towers, I discovered they were filled with more butterflies. When their wings were outstretched, it allowed me to see the magnificence of nature's paintbrush.

Faith asked. "How's your headache?"

I scanned my head for any hint of it. "Actually, it's gone."

"Awe is nature's Advil."

CHAPTER 12

FOX HUNT

WE HAD BEEN walking for what felt like hours. Our pace had gratefully slowed as most of it was trudging up along a mountainside. I preferred the flat, wide-open fields of wildflowers to this winding path of switchbacks. I missed the full warmth of the sun and the vistas we left behind. At least it wasn't a dense evergreen forest. Less than half the leaves remained on the trees' branches, creating dappled light patterns on the path. My feet rustled loudly through the dried leaves. When I stopped for a moment and let Faith walk on ahead, my suspicion was confirmed: She was moving soundlessly through them. I didn't anticipate being able to imitate her, although I knew I could make vast improvements with some more focus.

I placed my feet more gently and deliberately on the ground, scuffing less. It only slowed me down. I experimented with minimizing my contact with the ground and walked on the balls of my feet, as if I was sneaking up on Faith. It worked.

I was far quieter. Next, I imagined a cushion of air below the balls of my feet, instead of stepping directly on the leaves themselves. As I became more adept, I stopped looking down while I walked. Faith turned back to look at me, she smiled as she glanced down at my feet. I felt her acknowledgment that I was barely making a noise myself. Maybe she looked back to be sure I was still with her.

When she stopped by a hole in the hillside, I joined her to look more closely. It had a few well-trodden trails branching out in different directions. I guessed it might be a den for an animal. I wanted to ask, *Hey, why are we stopping here?* but I held my tongue. I had forgotten that Faith didn't need words to hear me.

She simply said, "We've arrived."

I looked around to take in our surroundings. The hillside had a few trees and when I looked closer, a few more faint paths in the underbrush an animal had regularly traversed. We had stopped about a hundred yards from the rise of the hill along the mountain's slope. I was curious what the view was so I walked on a bit farther to look around, following one of the paths. Faith didn't follow me. There wasn't anything particularly noteworthy, just more of the same territory wherever I looked for miles. Why would the key be here?

I chose a different path to wander back down and discovered it led to a burrow on the hillside. The hole was edged by a boulder, only about a foot or so in diameter, maybe a fox den as a coyote wouldn't fit in it.

Faith wandered over to join me. She said, "So you've found the entrance. Good hunting. Now it's time to enter."

I couldn't detect any sarcasm in her voice. *There is no way I could fit inside that little opening.* "Do you mean reach in and grope for the key?"

She shook her head dismissively. She acted as if there was another obvious alternative. So far I had swum underwater as a mermaid and flown through the air as an owl. My heart started to race as I deduced I was at the threshold of another shapeshifting, earth this time. *Thank god we've skipped fire thus far. I'd rather leave that element out of this adventure. If I ever returned home, would this skill return with me? It would sure make life interesting with Ian. How would he feel waking next to a fox one morning?*

My affinity with foxes began during the year of my separation from my husband. Red foxes started showing themselves to me in broad daylight, while driving, biking, and walking in various towns of New England. A close friend planning her wedding requested I offer a reading from one of her favorite books, *The Little Prince*, by Antoine de Saint-Exupéry. I read the passage that contains the fox's famous line, "It is only with the heart that one can see rightly; what is essential is invisible to the eye."

On the day I was moving out of my home on the Cape, Ian drove me in his truck to gather the few belongings I planned to take: my clothes, books, and desk. My bike and windsurfing equipment were already at my parents' place on the Cape. We were driving south on Route 495 when I noticed a dead fox on the side of the road. I said, "Oh no, that's a bad sign."

Ian pulled off the highway at the next exit and doubled back. He said, "No, not necessarily. We need to check it out. There are no coincidences, don't disregard it; that's what would be disrespectful."

My response was, "Seriously, we're about to go pick up roadkill?"

He said. "If it isn't mangled, I know a taxidermist who can save the pelt. I have a friend with a hunting license we can use because it's illegal to pick up roadkill."

Who knew? This was not how I imagined my day unfolding; my life truly abhorred a plan. When we pulled over on the shoulder, traffic was light and we swiftly got out to see it up close. I was awestruck by her beauty. I don't know why I assumed she was female, it just felt right. She lay crumpled. I wanted her to still be breathing. I'd rather have brought her to a vet.

I approached slowly with Ian. The only blood we could see was coming from her mouth. I knelt beside her repeating aloud, "It's okay, it's okay," as much to calm myself as for her as I reached to stroke her. She was no longer warm to the touch but her body was still soft and pliant. She hadn't been dead long. I couldn't hold back my tears. She was a gorgeous animal. One less of them in the world felt like a huge loss.

I said, "Okay, let's take her, she didn't die in vain."

Her pelt rested under my altar by day and was on my lap most mornings or evenings when I meditated. Her fur was so inviting to stroke, I'd come to know her more intimately. I'd often imagine her prowling through the fields and pouncing in search of mice. I wasn't brave enough to ask the taxidermist to keep the head and paws.

Faith startled me out of my memories when I heard her say, "Precisely."

"Precisely, what? I need to be more brave?"

"No, it's time to become the fox. There's no better animal for hunting in dark places, other than perhaps an owl."

"So I'm conjuring myself into a fox now? I don't know how to turn myself into a fox, any more than I know how to disappear from my bedroom, or become a mermaid or an owl." *Although admittedly, I'd love to know how I do it.* She started to chuckle and then outright laugh, which I figured must be related to something other than what I said because I wasn't that funny. I started looking around. *I could use a good laugh.* She just kept laughing, the kind of laugh that was infectious. I found myself laughing with her although oblivious as to why.

The tension caused by concentrating on being more quiet as we walked through the forest drained away, revealing the real source of tension. My constant inner dialogue of *what the fuck* that I tried to keep at bay because all of this had been so bizarre. I had done my best not to be relentlessly asking questions about what was happening, to hold to my agreement to trust my guide. Faith.

Her laughter had subsided, as had mine. Her face transformed with a broad grin. I sensed she was ready to clue me in.

"Look down."

I looked down at her request as if the mystery would be revealed to me there, only to look back up with a blank stare on my face. I didn't know what I was supposed to see.

Faith said, "Look closer, move your feet."

When I looked down again to watch my feet come out from under their cover of leaves I was dumbfounded to see paws. *How come I didn't notice this before?* "When did you do this to me?"

Faith's laughter bubbled up again. "I didn't do it, *you* did." She punctuated her sentence with a smug smile.

"When? How?" I asked in disbelief.

Faith asked, "When you were concentrating on not

making any noise, what were you imagining?"

I replied, "Little cushions of air between my feet and the leaves, so I could be as quiet as you. We were hunting Fear; I'd thought we might need to sneak up on her so we didn't scare her away."

"Now look at the bottoms of your feet, I mean paws," Faith said.

I lifted my left paw in front of my right knee, twisting it to see the bottoms. Sure enough I had four oval tiny pads just under my black curled nails, with surprisingly long fur between them. My close examination ended as I lost my balance and fell over. Peals of laughter erupted from Faith again.

"These little paws might be quiet, but they sure aren't very stable," I said.

Faith replied, "That's because you're supposed to have four of them at a fourth the height. Now that you are down there, why not stay there on all fours, so to speak?"

I could tell she was ready to burst out again in laughter. I was torn between how amusing it all was and how ridiculous I felt. I ignored her request and knelt instead. I wanted an explanation. *If I am to turn myself into a fox I need more guidance than this comedy act.* Sitting back on what was once my heels I said, "Okay, I've always wanted to be a magician so help me out here and stop laughing for a while. Back when I was a mermaid, I remember my journal manifested out of thin air—or water, as it was. When I inquired then, I was told that it was your job to teach me. So here I am, a ready and willing pupil. Enlighten me."

Faith came and sat beside me. She was silent for a while and I opted to hold the silence with her. I had already asked my questions, made my requests. The next move was hers.

While we sat I listened to the sounds of the woods I hadn't heard before. Birds were singing to one another at a distance. There was a faint buzz of insects. I doubted it was a bee, as there weren't any flowers around. I heard the wind passing through the leaves on the trees and watched more golden leaves drop periodically to the forest floor. The ground was nearly completely covered with leaves, in shades of cranberry and browns, burnt oranges, and mustard yellows with a few brighter yellows mixed in. It hadn't rained recently, so everything was crisp. The dried leaves lightly rested on one another, easily swept up by a breeze to another location. The leaves were still damp underneath, near the ground. I smelled the faint rot of decomposing leaves after I disturbed them. Now that we were no longer moving, my body didn't generate enough heat to be naked. The idea of having fox fur on was more and more appealing; I knew how warm it was from having my pelt on my lap.

Ian woke from a dream where water had flooded the house; it was the third time water had figured strongly in his dreams and he missed being able to talk them over with Sarah over their breakfast together. She was always better at surfacing the deeper meaning in his dreams when they mystified him; she said it was the way of dreams. Come to think of it, her dreams were always more obvious to him, too.

Sarah was fond of Robert Johnson's approach to dream work, that every aspect of the dream was a symbol of oneself, that dreams were one way the subconscious has a conversation with us. Whenever Sarah dreamed of him and his character had done something irritating, it was especially confusing for her; she would get mad at him as if it was him in the dream. He did his best to maintain his sense of humor and gently remind her it wasn't really him, it was about her, that he hadn't done anything wrong. However, it was hard not to get defensive at times, especially if there was a kernel of truth in it that mirrored his daytime behavior. It was probably why her subconscious chose him as the symbol in the first place.

Now, if she dreamt about him with another woman, he would find it harder not to be defensive.

He told himself his swim and dinner with Ariel was completely innocent but even he didn't believe it. If he told Sarah about it, she would be hurt. She would conclude something was lacking in their relationship. She would lose her fragile trust in him.

Still, he found his mind replaying the moments of Ariel on the ladder retrieving the painting, their lake swim and their dinner together. They shared a pizza flavored with tandoori chicken and Indian spices which was as unexpectedly delightful as his time with her. Maybe his tastes were changing.

Ian rolled over and looked under Sarah's nightstand table to her bookshelf. He found, as suspected, her well-worn copy of *Inner Work: Using Dreams and Active Imagination for Personal Growth* by Robert Johnson.[25] He picked it up and flipped through it, seeing her underlines and comments in the margins. Reading her handwriting brought her closer to him.

On page nine she had drawn the infinity sign. He read the passage beside it. Johnson was speaking to the importance of a balanced life that kept the flow of energy and information

---

[25] Anja van Kralingen, "Inner Work (book review): Using Dreams and Active Imagination for Personal Growth", Center of Applied Jungian Studies, March 31, 2014. https://applied-jung.com/inner-work-book-review/.

open between the conscious and unconscious mind. As a Libra, Ian valued balance. Johnson referenced that the bridge between the conscious and unconscious arises in the form of dreams, visions, and rituals yet our modern, rational minds view these as primitive and superstitious. The result was we've divorced ourselves from sources of renewal, strength, and wisdom that live within us, cutting ourselves off from the source of our power.

Per kneaded the blankets and curled up against his legs. Her gentle weight was like an anchor to stay in bed. He surrendered to her and kept reading until his stomach voted him out with persistent growls. The last one was so loud she looked up at him. "I know, enemy number one. It's breakfast time." He left *Inner Work* on his nightstand.

After breakfast he sat with the morning paper. Per sauntered out of the bedroom just after he found the sports section and leapt directly into his lap.

He was envious of the cat; it had been too long since he had woken up with Sarah or had been able to go out in the living room to find her writing or reading. All he had to do was show up and she understood the signals. He too wanted a lap to curl up in and wake up the rest of the way in her arms. He never asked directly and she never refused him. He knew she enjoyed it as much as he did; it was one of those unspoken agreements they had.

Per didn't seem to understand the agreement; she didn't settle in for a few minutes with the intent of waking—she settled in for the duration. As long as the lap was there, she was content to rest in it.

Having finished the sports section he reached down to

find the business section, and Per looked up as if to check and see if this was a temporary disturbance. He said, "It's okay for now, but don't get too comfortable. I'm not here for much longer."

True to his word, he only skimmed the headlines, nothing interesting. There was a facilitation guide waiting for him to finish; he had a deadline with his client just around the corner. He needed to start rewriting the section, filling in the gaps that other people couldn't improvise. It wouldn't be difficult, it was all in his head, so he might as well get it finished. He dropped the paper by the chair and started to wiggle his legs to warn the cat of a change in residence. He spoke to her, "Okay, schmutt, time's up. Go hunt some birds or dragonflies or something. There's work to be done; we can't all lie around here like you."

Per took the hint and jumped down; she stretched and that reminded him he needed to stretch too. His run yesterday was longer than he was used to and he could feel it in his muscles this morning. He watched Per to see where she would find her next resting place and saw she went into the cat den he had bought her last week. It stood about two feet high, in the shape of a cylinder. It was carpeted on the outside so she could claw it up instead of the furniture. He should have bought it earlier. Sarah wasn't going to be happy when she saw how the cat had shredded the upholstery of their purple couch. He didn't mind, he never really liked that couch but it was comfortable enough and the right price at the secondhand store. He just couldn't get over the fact it was purple.

His gaze raised to where he had hung his new painting on the wall behind it. It didn't go with the decor. Maybe he would try it on the wall opposite their bed.

Last week when he walked into the pet store, the salesman resolved one of his dilemmas. Ian told him he didn't want to declaw Per but he couldn't let her keep tearing up the house and he didn't want to leave her outside the whole day. The salesman introduced him to a cat playground telling him it would solve his problems. *At least my problems with Per.* The man's sales pitch was brief as he pointed out the features of it. "She can claw, perch, and crawl in down here in this little hole."

Ian wasn't confident Per would consider this carpeted cylinder a playground, let alone a bed when she had his to choose from, but he bought it anyway because he was desperate. He wondered if that hole in the bottom would entice her. This was the first time he saw her go into it. Per was a classic cat: Just when he thought he had her figured out, she would surprise him.

~~⊙~~

Faith spoke, "So now you are ready to grow fur? I was waiting for your imagination to kick in again."

"Yes, fur sounds like a warm idea. Tell me how to begin."

"You've already begun, you have two paws, remember?" Faith was being evasive again.

"I know you say that you didn't give me paws, I did, but I don't believe you because I don't know how I did it, and I sure don't know how to do it again. So please stop with the cryptic clues and start giving me more instructions. I'm cold."

Faith ignored my direct plea and instead favored the Socratic method asking me to describe a fox to her. I closed my eyes and conjured my red fox pelt in my lap, as if I was meditating with it again.

"We call them red foxes but they are really more orange with black accents. The brightest orange is often the forehead between the ears. The fur along their back is a blend of orange on the surface and layers of gray or black nearest the skin; their bushy, long tail is almost the reverse, more black on the surface with auburn mixed in. Their chest and inside their legs is white, which often comes right up to their face, and inside their ears. Their legs have solid black stockings contrasting with their bright white underbelly. Their tail is long, full, and bushy, laced with a hue of black and a white tip. Their paws are often darker, shaded with black as well as the tips of the back of their ears." I paused to see what else she needed me to share.

"You're still missing the point." Faith said, "Stop trying to figure this out with your mind, Sarah, and give way to your imagination—it's more powerful than you ever give it credit. It's not a liability, it's an asset."

For the first time I sensed Faith becoming impatient with me. I asked, "Are you telling me if I simply imagine that I am a fox then I will become one?"

Faith said, "No, indeed it is not that simple; first you have to believe it and then it will become your reality. If you doubt it, you will never transform."

This is the surrendering part again isn't it? Faith just blinked slowly and nodded. "Damn, I hate this part, I'm not good at it." I caught a glimmer of something at the threshold of the fox den. The invitation was to enter. My mind said not in a million years.

What if I don't consult my mind? What if I take the advice of the Little

Prince's fox, "It is only with the heart that one can see rightly; what is essential is invisible to the eye"? What if I don't even use my eyes? I heard the line from my blessing, May I live in the inquiry of what if, maybe.

I closed my eyes. I didn't need them to see the world I was currently sitting in cold and naked; it was a distraction. The same world my mind defended against but clung to despite my desire to experience something to the contrary. I needed to offer myself up to a different world. I let my body's longing to be warm quiet my mind. This longing became palpable. I felt a heat rising from my feet, up my spine, tinglingly on the surface of my skin.

Becoming a fox would normally be beyond belief, beyond the confines of my rational mind, beyond my lived experience to date. Yet the fact that I had two paws as feet offered unde-niable evidence of the power of my imagination, to override my rational knowledge. What's true? I wasn't trying to become a fox before, I was experimenting with being quiet. I decided to let my body and desire lead for a change. I quieted the cynical voice that thought this was impossible. I ignored the voice that expected it to be difficult and complicated. What if it were as easy as following my desire to be warm?

I gave my full attention to this longing for warmth, to feel a heat wave blanketing my skin. I knelt before the den. The invitation to move underground beckoned. As I kept my eyes closed, I reached to the edge of the burrow, shifting my weight to my hands and knees.

I heard Faith say, "Crawl in."

I listened to her this time. Without opening my eyes I started crawling, letting my instinctive nature lead the way in the dark for a change. I crept through the opening ever so slowly without brushing the sides. I immediately felt warmer even though the air was dank with a pungent musky odor. I opened my eyes but it was too dark to see anything. There was a tickle in my left ear. I itched it, but instead of my hand reaching up, my hind paw gingerly scratched the back of it. Any doubt that still lingered regarding my current body was brushed away with my newly found flexibility. My feet had never bent to my ear before. I wished it was light enough to admire my new form.

My eyes had adjusted enough to glimpse the back wall of the den. I took a few hesitant steps towards it and stopped when I saw an intense green glow of an eye looking back at me. The fox was curled up in a ball, tail under her nose as she lay peering at me without lifting her face from her paws. When I continued another step towards her she picked up her head. I stopped. *Am I welcome here?* I wasn't sure what protocol to follow so I waited.

She tipped her nose into the air. I heard a faint sniffing, as if my scent would tell her whether she could trust me in her den. After a moment she got up. Her front paws outstretched, her butt in the air as her mouth opened into a big yawn. She leisurely walked over to smell me up close. I stayed still and waited. I witnessed animals do this before; in fact when greeting a horse I learned to breathe near its nostrils as a way of allowing us to get to know one another. She was reading my smells like a book I carried on me. *Do I smell human?* I hadn't tried to speak. *Could I? Is it even necessary or is she telepathic too?*

She had finished checking me out and returned to face me. "I know why you are here."

Her voice took me by surprise, it was soft and low. My

attention had been on shapeshifting and I'd lost track of why I was here.

She continued, "You have come in search of your pain."

What she said was true. I remembered my encounter with Rage and my intentions to find the key. "Who are you?" I asked, my voice unchanged by my transformation.

She replied, "I'm a fox, just like you."

"I can see that, I mean who are you in me? Everyone I have met so far is an aspect of myself. Besides, I'm not really a fox, I'm a woman."

"Your affinity to foxes is very strong or else you would not be here in my home. As for what part of you I represent, that is for you to discover, not for me to tell."

Whoever she is, she's wily. "Can you help me find my hidden pain?" I asked.

"Undoubtedly, there's no hiding place I can't find given some time. How much time do you have?" replied the Fox.

"As long as it takes," I said. *She's wily and confident.*

"Well, it's good to see that your patience has befriended you recently. Tell me, what will you do when you finally meet this hidden pain of yours? Aren't you afraid of uncovering it after all this time?"

I nodded. "The word that comes to mind is *terrified*. In fact, I am told that there is a box of fear nearby waiting for my attention as well."

The Fox tipped her nose again in the air. "Oh, that's helpful. I am particularly good at picking up on the scent of fear. Do you know what the fear is about?"

"I suspect it has to do with trusting myself and my judgment of men. I'm on the edge of becoming engaged after having been married before. My failed divorce still haunts me. Just the thought of it makes me want to curl up and sleep, could we nap first?" The tendency to want to nap under pressure was a trait I attributed to Ian. *Maybe we are becoming more alike over time.*

"Oh sure, no hurry. Curling up is one of my favorite pastimes; the only thing I enjoy more is hunting. I'll be here when you're ready to call on me. For now, rest, maybe even dream a little." She sauntered towards the back of the den and curled up again.

I followed her lead and lay on my side, imitating the way she tucked her nose by her haunches. I welcomed the escape and warmth my newly found fur coat provided. It had been awhile since I had rested, even longer since I had spooned in bed with Ian. *Does he miss me too?* The falling leaves we had walked through suggested it was already autumn. I left May first. Was he still waiting for me or had he found another relationship?

I dreamt of Ian. He was driving and we picked up two women hitchhikers. One of the women was very beautiful and he continued to look at her using the rearview mirror. When his eyes were on her, he inadvertently crossed the double yellow line into the other lane. There was a station wagon coming towards us in the opposite direction. I saw this and calmly said, "Pay attention to the road."

He said "I am!" indignantly, as he swerved the car to the right and we narrowly missed the other oncoming car.

I suggested, "Why not adjust the mirror so you can look at the beautiful woman *and* the road?"

He said, "You're upset."

I replied. "I understand." But inside I was upset even

though I didn't want to admit it. We arrived at our home in Kauai and walked in the side door from the garage to the kitchen.

When we were standing inside the kitchen, Ian said to the beautiful woman, "You must be hot, why not take off your sweater?"

When she began to lift her sweater up, Ian reached to help her. His hand brushed her stomach as he pushed it up. At first it didn't appear she had anything on underneath, until we noticed a knit bra. He said, "Follow me, I'll show you where I'll put your sweater." He walked her into our bedroom. I stood there with the other woman wondering how much I was supposed to tolerate.

I awoke angry at Ian. I looked to find him but it was dark and dank. *This is not my bedroom.* I saw my bushy tail and recalled shapeshifting into a fox. I rested my chin back on my paws and drew myself into a tighter curl. That was a dream. *A dream within a dream, perhaps, as nothing feels real.* Yet the feeling that he would find another woman more attractive than me and go off with her did feel like a very real fear.

Again, the feeling of betrayal was ever present. I sifted for the meaning of the dream but I couldn't shake the lingering anger and fear that it left in me, a dream hangover. I sensed I wasn't the only one who was awake now and looked over to see her alert green eyes kindly staring at me. I raised my head enough to speak. "I can't decide if you're my instincts or my intuition. Either way I know I need to listen to you more, to stop dismissing this way of knowing and communicating with my unconscious mind."

The Fox replied, "That is in part what your quest is about,

which requires slowing yourself down and paying attention."

"True, I'm recognizing a theme here. Yet I struggle with the distinctions between instinct and intuition. I especially find it difficult to discern between what my fear imagines and what my instinct and intuition tell me are real."

The Fox replied, "That's not surprising; instincts are highly misunderstood. I'm inclined to agree with Jung's interpretation, not Freud's. An overly simplified definition for now is that instincts are more a compulsive action or urge, the motivation is typically unconscious and intuition is more of a perception or apprehension.[26] Instinct and intuition are inextricably linked by archetypes, but I digress.[27] When you surface, and you will, do your research.

"Let's get back to your treasure hunt for the key. Oftentimes, it is the scent of fear that I travel. I hunt what fear imagines may be lurking in the shadows. I don't mind going into dark places, in fact I rather enjoy it. As you can see I'm quite at home in the dark. When I track down what fear is afraid of and it turns out to be worthy of the alarm, I too send you a signal but this signal comes in a different place in your body. You tend to miss it. Do you know what I am speaking of, do you feel differently when Fear is speaking to you than when you are listening to me now?"

"Well, yes, now I feel a sense of assurance."

The Fox asked, "Describe how it feels in your body."

"It starts in my throat area, by my clavicle and runs down the

---

[26] Gregg Boethin reading, "Carl Jung: Instincts and the Unconscious", (full audio), youtube July 25, 2022. 18:40. https://youtu.be/hrQjXYZQHag.
[27] Cary Dakin PhD. MFT, "The Connection Between Intuition, Instinct and Archetypes", Blog, March 2, 2018. https://www.carydakin.com/single-post/2018/03/02/the-connection-between-intuition-instinct-and-archetypes.

center of my body as if it was another spine. The sensation I have is one of feeling connected, strong and resilient, almost rooted."

"Now tell me what Fear feels like. How did you feel when you first awoke?"

"Rotten. There was a hot, roiling turmoil in my chest and in the pit of my stomach. I felt lost, disoriented and unsteady, even nauseous."

"How are you feeling now?" asked the Fox.

I replied, "Somewhere in between, it depends on what I think about. When I recall the dream, the awful feeling in the pit of my stomach grows."

"Hmm, intriguing. How are you interpreting the dream?"

"On the surface, as if it could be true, even though I know better. I know that everyone and everything in my dream is only an aspect of myself, a symbol of my unconscious that's meant to offer me a message. I know that Ian isn't Ian; rather, he represents some aspects of my masculine and all the women are an aspect of my feminine. For example, the beautiful woman is also a part of me that I am attracted to and want to get to know better, intimately. There's also another part of me in the back seat not getting any attention."

The Fox interrupted, "So despite knowing better, you persist in fearing what you already know isn't true. Why do you give the voice of fear so much unwarranted attention, ignoring me, your own intuition and instincts?"

She had me there. I replied honestly, "I don't know. I don't have any good excuse. I have certainly had enough of these dreams to know better, but they still panic me. They still tap into my fear that Ian will find another woman more attractive and pursue a relationship with her. Perhaps remnants of what happened with Simon. I also feel like this would be my karma for what I did to my former husband during our marriage, when I cultivated my friendship with Ian."

The Fox said, "I am starting to get the picture here—it sounds like you persist in believing in your worst fears because you feel like you deserve them, that it's punishment for what you perceive you have done wrong; that you have it coming to you, so to speak."

She paused, sniffing in the air like she did when I first entered her den. She continued, "I'm onto something now. So you don't ever fully trust yourself, me, or your relationships with others, even when I keep trying to tell you otherwise. I've been wondering who I was up against. I can see that fear and pain have another ally here we need to uncover. This is going to be a rewarding hunt." She was on her feet now, her ears perked up.

I was stuck on something the Fox had said. I needed more clarification before I went anywhere. "What did you mean when you said I didn't trust you even when you keep trying to tell me otherwise? How is it that you speak to me?"

She looked intently at me now, and walked closer before she sat back down. "I speak to you in all variety of ways, when you are awake with images, voices, feelings, sensations and even while you sleep in your dreams. I know you haven't been listening to this one. You've had a series of them because you persist in ignoring them. It's high time you deciphered them."

I sensed an edge of aggravation towards me. She was right. I had been trying to ignore these dreams of Ian with another woman.

The Fox said, "Sometimes I think you don't want to have a relationship with me. Despite what you say, your actions tell me otherwise."

I felt myself squirm. I didn't like how closely she tracked my behavior. I wondered if this was how others felt when I was hot on their trail. She sounded affronted, as if I wasn't being true to her or me as the case may be. *Could it be that I am the one who has betrayed myself all along by not listening to my instincts and intuition?* I had witnessed Simon return to his old girlfriend for years. I knew that dance by heart, by heartache. I ignored my sense that it was only a matter of time before he repeated those dance steps. I wanted to believe it would be different once we were together, but I knew better. I ignored my own inner knowing because I didn't want it to be true. *Ugh, wishful thinking.*

"It's true. I have ignored you when you tell me things that conflict with what I want. Sadly, you've been right. I've been wrong to dismiss you," I said. "The connection and assurance that comes from being in a relationship with you is what I crave. I want to become better at listening to your voice, discerning your message. Tell me how."

The Fox said, "Simply listen. It's not complicated despite your inclination to make it so. Pause and breathe, and in that stillness pay attention to all the other feelings that arise in your body as closely as you listen to your fear. Act on your hunches, like learning more about dreams. Remember, our own inner wisdom speaks through them *symbolically.*"

She placed special emphasis on the message of dreams being symbolic, Ian would have appreciated her gentle reprimand for taking my dream literally. I had been waking up lately with a dream hangover, all pissed off at him for going off with other women. Luckily he had a good sense of humor about it and he just laughed at me for missing the point. "Okay, I will. Now let's get started tracking my fear and pain." I stood up, ready to go.

The Fox didn't move. "We've already begun. Your dream is our starting place, so let's go back to the beginning. How does it start?"

CHAPTER 13

HITCHHIKERS

I PAUSED FOR A minute, feeling like I just had a fast one pulled on me. I had come into this den in search of boxes, hidden keys, a means to unlock Rage, to understand the way I imprisoned myself but now I was interpreting my dream. While I couldn't see the connection, I'd just promised to trust my instincts and intuition more. *Maybe if I do, my dreams will pick a new theme. This one is annoyingly redundant.*

"Okay, I'll start interpreting it; jump in with questions if you like. It begins with Ian driving. I'm the only passenger until he picks up two women hitchhikers. The masculine aspect of me prefers to drive and to know where I'm going, to be in control. It's also the part of me that rarely asks for help, even if I'm lost."

The Fox said, "There are three aspects of your feminine as passengers. Four is a powerful number; it's often symbolic of wholeness. What happens next?"

"We stop to pick up two women hitchhikers along the road, aspects of myself. It's time to integrate."

The Fox paused from licking her front right paw and asked, "What comes to mind when you think about hitchhikers?"

"They rely on the good will of others for transportation. They are not shy about asking for help, they frequently stick their thumb out. They are more *live in the moment* kind of people, unencumbered by tight schedules. The word *trusting* comes to mind. They never know when their next ride will show up so they live with mystery; they must have a good deal of patience or faith. Ah, that's a good sign, I'm slowing down to pick up the aspects of myself that are more patient, trusting, and who live with more faith." *That sounded exactly like the advice the Fox has just given me, to be still, to pause and listen to her, my instincts and intuition. No wonder she wanted to interpret the dream.* "So, are the hitchhikers symbolic of my instincts and intuition? Did I just pick you up?"

She tilted her head. "Perhaps. Let's stay with the dream and see where it takes us. What about crossing the line and the oncoming car?" She had switched to clean her other front paw.

"Hmm, yeah, that part is disturbing. My masculine, knowledgeable side that is typically in control is distracted by something behind me, and I've lost sight of where I'm going. I've become drawn to the beauty of the one who lives in the moment. But this is a hazardous amount of attention."

"And the double yellow line?" she asked.

"That represents something that is illegal to cross, typically because of unforeseen danger ahead. It reminds me of coloring at the kitchen table in the mornings as my dad left for work. He'd say, 'Stay inside the lines.' I was pretty obedient at that age. If I accidentally colored over a line, I'd scratch it away with my thumb-nail to make it less noticeable. I've abided by the lines most of my life, doing what's expected of me and not venturing into unknown territory until now. Huh, hitchhikers tend to live outside the lines, disregarding societal norms."

"What about the station wagon?"

"The station wagon is a suburban, family car, owned by people who live very much inside the lines. I actually drive one. The part of me that isn't driving sees the potential for collision with family life and she issues a calm warning to pay attention."

"How does the part of you that's typically in control, driving your life, react?"

"It says one thing and does another. I don't admit when I'm distracted or drifting, but still swerve to miss the accident. This is the side of me that has perfected denial and is commit-ted to the illusion of control."

"Is there an aspect of your life that has narrowly missed an accident that has to do with family?"

My stomach dropped as this symbol became obvious to me. I hesitated to speak it aloud and closed my eyes, trying to push the memories away. When I opened them again, she was staring right through me. I knew it was impossible to hide this from my instincts but I tried nonetheless. I surrendered to the feeling of being crushed and curled up in the fetal position. The silence was thick.

Finally, the Fox said, "Do you want to speak to this now or later? The dream has revealed a strong clue for what we are look-ing for."

"I'd rather wait. I'm not feeling up to it now and it's not like I'm going to forget it." *If only I could.*

She conceded. "Okay, remind me what happens next?"

"I suggest he adjust the rearview mirror so he can look at the beautiful woman *and* the road. I make it easier for him, for me, to safely do the very thing that is upsetting me all the while pretending it doesn't matter to me. *Shit.* I remember feeling irritated at this point, not so much about the potential accident, more about being ignored, passed over in favor of the beautiful woman. I'm no longer a willing passenger, I'm resentful but I don't give voice to any of this. I don't want to make myself vulnerable by revealing my true feelings, but my tone gives me away."

"Who is this passenger in you that is resentful, feeling passed over, that someone else is getting all the attention but she doesn't want to let on, she acts calm? It may be the part of you that keeps a tight lid on your emotions, showing one face on the surface while feeling something else inside. Is this familiar to you?"

I nodded. "Yes, when you put it that way. This is the part of me that feels deeply but never lets on how much the world affects me. I try to keep my distance, my objectivity. I try to keep my emotions out of it and just go along for the ride. I pretend everything's fine when it isn't. I pretend it doesn't matter but it does and I become resentful. I lie to myself and others with this mask I put on. It's just another form of control because I don't want the vulnerability that comes with these feelings." *Shit. Shit. Shit.* I curled tighter into a ball, tucking my nose into my tail. *This dream is too close to home.*

"Are you going to continue?" the Fox asked. "My sense is you have a longing you rarely give voice to, perhaps it's going unnoticed even to you. Why?"

"Maybe because I'm afraid to admit to wanting something I don't believe I can have or will ever happen?" I stayed tightly curled. "Eventually, I become numb, losing touch with what I long for and I'm left just going through the motions."

She asked, "Where did you learn this habit of not giving voice to how you really feel? Which of your parents pretended everything was fine when it wasn't?"

"My mum was masterful at feeling differently inside than what she showed to the public. Lately I've come to understand the double meaning of her expression, 'needing to put my face on.' I remember as a child sometimes being startled by my mum when she didn't have makeup on—it didn't look like her, yet it was her natural face. I never wanted to have to put a face on for the world or my family. I just wanted to look like me. Ironically, my mum never taught me how to apply cosmetics when I got older. I don't know if that's because I never asked her to or she didn't want to pass on that skill, literally or metaphorically. She knew the pain of inauthenticity. Yet even without the habit of using makeup, my dream is showing me I've learned to put a different face to the world than what I really feel.

"Whenever I was upset as a child, if I went to my mum for comfort she would try to talk me out of my feelings as if she could fix or change them. My disappointments, anger, jealousy, fear were unacceptable to her. She would point to what was good about my life, how fortunate I was or how what I thought was so painful wasn't so bad. She was fond of giving me books about young women who overcame severe obstacles like Helen Keller and *The Other Side of the Mountain*, when a US Olympic skier has a crippling accident at the trials and how she recovers. The general message being, it could be worse, you could be deaf, blind, or crippled, so buck up and move on. The Irish aren't known for coddling. Withstanding hardship is in our DNA." I couldn't curl up any tighter.

"Some days I'd wake in a funk and didn't want to get out of bed. She called them my dark Irish moods. Her advice was this is the day you wear your nicest clothes. She had a closet full of beautiful clothes and shoes. Her motto was to look the part until you can feel the part." *Essentially fake it till you make it.* "It actually worked at times. My mum was always well-dressed. She never let down and stayed in her robe all day. She had a strong influence on me and not just my wardrobe. My senior year of high school I won two awards: Best Dressed along with Ice Queen."

"What do you know about your mother's childhood?" the Fox asked.

"My mum didn't have an easy life growing up. She was part of a large Catholic family, one of seven children, although one died before her first birthday. She didn't get along with her mother. She told stories of how her mother screamed so loud at them, they would run around the house closing the windows so the neighbors wouldn't hear. I don't recall much of my grandmother. Before I turned eleven they were no longer on speaking terms. The Irish tend to write people out of their lives and never reconcile. Forgiveness might not be in my gene pool." I stretched my legs out and sat up. I thought of the people I'd written off already in my life: Simon, my mentor, my ex-husband.

The Fox had moved to cleaning her back paws. "Go on. Your ancestry matters, though most people disregard it, not understanding its untold influence on their lives."

"She spoke fondly of her father; she was closest to him. I never met my grandfather because he died when she was just eighteen. He had a fatal heart attack on the train ride home from work. She blamed her mother for breaking his heart. She told me she cried all night long, never even sleeping. That morning she vowed never to cry again. Their older brother, the priest, informed them there was to be no crying at church. I sense she never really recovered from the grief of his sudden death; a part of her died with him."

"What part was that?" asked the Fox.

"Her willingness to be vulnerable, to cry. She cut it all off. My father wasn't very comfortable with tears either. He was the first to say, 'Stop crying before I give you something to cry about.' When I was little, I'd let my whole body experience the emotions moving through me like big waves. For a time, my father's threats convinced me to contain them. Now I cry silently, letting the tears spill from my eyes. I've learned that if I ignore the impulse to weep, it always causes a wicked headache that aspirin can't ameliorate."

"What was your relationship with your mum like? She was the role model for your feminine side."

"She was my biggest cheerleader. Her sole focus was on me. She was determined to be nothing like her mother and encouraged me to follow my dreams. She believed I could do anything if I set my mind to it. By the time I was a senior in high school she started to follow her own dream of learning to fly. She declared she was done cooking and emphasized it by putting a Boston fern on the stove. She studied at night while I did my homework and took flying lessons while I was at school. She was more buoyant and happy than I'd ever seen her. Sadly, it was short-lived."

"What happened?"

"The day she was soloing to earn her pilot's license I was home with my dad. We lived on a corner lot of a four-cornered intersection that you could see from the living room window. My dad told me something was wrong, as he couldn't read the stop sign anymore from his chair. Foolishly, he opted to drive himself to the hospital instead of letting me call an ambulance. He made me stay home to tell my mum when she called with the news of her test. Their plan was she would call if she passed and he would drive to the hangar. She had made reservations at a restaurant in New Jersey; she was going to fly them both there for dinner to celebrate."

"Did she pass?"

"Yes, she was elated. Then I had to break the news that my father was in the hospital. I later learned that when he arrived at the ER, his blood sugars were so low, he should have been in a coma. It was a miracle he didn't pass out while driving. My dad's pure willpower got him there safely—that or his guardian angel. He stayed in the hospital a few days; the diagnosis was adult onset diabetes. My mum shifted her attention to taking care of my dad, learning how to manage his blood sugars. They never celebrated her becoming a pilot. Instead she never flew again." There were tears welling up in my eyes, and I let them fall. Her happiness was too good to be true.

"I kept encouraging her to continue flying. She gave up. Her argument was, 'What's the point, your father can't come with me now and I'm not going to go alone. His diabetes worsens with stress. We both know how stressful it would be for him to be in the co-pilot seat. What would I do if he had an episode while I'm flying?'

"She did have a point. Honestly, before he became a diabetic, I wondered how he would behave as a passenger, not in control. The only time I'd seen him in the passenger seat was when he was teaching me to drive or if my mum managed to convince him he was too drunk to be behind the wheel. My mum was also often a resentful passenger in her own life. Yikes, how have I become a resentful passenger in my own life?"

The Fox said, "By pretending your dreams don't matter to you. By not tending to your waking nor your sleeping dreams."

"Shit! I'm too skilled at disconnecting from what I want, what I'm attracted to. I tend to reason it away, pretend it doesn't matter. It's how I lose touch with my longings."

"There's an attraction in the dream, we'll explore it in a moment. First, how do you interpret the advice you are giving yourself about the rearview mirror adjustment?"

"It's a complicated symbol. On the one hand, rearview mirrors are essential for safe driving; it's not wise to change lanes on highways without checking so as to avoid a collision. Maybe looking behind myself is about seeing my history we've just spoken about, my ancestry. Maybe paying attention at times to my past can free me up to move forward, to travel in a different lane or direction."

"Is there something else in your past that needs your attention?" she asked.

"Probably. I watched this film, *The Wisdom of Trauma*, that spoke to how unprocessed trauma has a way of repeating itself until it can be integrated.[28] Earlier in my journey, I met Grief, my grief. Forgiveness became my guide as I dove into our collective tear pool. There are heartaches that weigh heavy on my chest that I've not tended, nor learned from or found a way to forgive myself. I guess that's why I'm here, looking for the key with you."

The Fox started to pace the perimeter of her den. "Sometimes it's not only *your* history that needs healing. Sometimes it's generational, reaching even further back in time."

I heard her emphasize the word *back*. "I've wondered to what extent my mum's unprocessed grief over her father's sudden death influenced her life and in turn influenced mine? We've both tried to push aside painful memories but they never really go away. I suspect they haunt me. Even when I'm happy, I can't shake the nagging feeling that the other shoe is going to drop, that the rug will be pulled out from underneath me. It makes me vigilant."

"Scanning your environment, keeping an eye out so to speak. Perhaps adjusting the rear view mirror is a kind of coping mechanism."

I nodded in consent. "Yeah, I'm always ready to solve things. But not so willing to feel them or give voice to them, I'm still behaving like an ice queen. I don't address my feelings or admit to being upset so I say, 'I understand.' Again meeting my emotions with a cool rational response. I think it's better to be calm and in control, not giving room to my emotions."

The Fox replied, "Both aspects of you in the front seat are in various forms of control and denial, about being distracted

---

[28] "The Wisdom of Trauma featuring Dr. Gabor Maté", directed by Maurizio Benazzo, Zaya Benazzo, Science and NonDuality (SAND) 1:28:00, 2021. https://thewisdomoftrauma.com/.

and upset. Perhaps these are the aspects of yourself more ruled by your mind, by abstract thinking. I'm curious what the difference is between the feminine aspects of yourself in the back seat, the hitchhikers?"

"Good question, I don't know." I was twisting the ring on my finger.

"Why not ask?"

I was about to say, *Because my dream is over. I can interpret all I want but I don't get to have a conversation with the characters in it*—but I knew better. I had already used Robert Johnson's technique of asking a dream character a question and writing with my non-dominant hand their answer. He called it "active imagination" as it opened up a dialogue between the unconscious and conscious mind. It was remarkably effective, like picking ripe fruit from a heavily-laden tree that everyone else just walks by. I held my tongue.

The Fox picked up on my unspoken analogy. "Yes, the trick is not ignoring the tree that is bearing fruit. Don't ignore your dreams and just walk by. Stop and engage—after all, they are all aspects of yourself."

I sat up on my haunches. "Yeah but active imagination is done by writing. I don't suppose you have pen and paper in your den and a way to give me my hands back?" I lifted a front paw as if to shake. "I can't exactly write with this."

"What if it was simpler than that?" the Fox used her hind leg to scratch her ear, letting her question hang in the air. "Once again you want to make things more complicated. Just ask her, yourself."

There was a certain elegance to her argument. Hesitantly, I tipped my nose in the air and said, "I would like to speak to the hitchhiker who was silent."

In no time we heard a response. "Which one? We were both silent."

I smiled at the Fox, who looked back smugly. I was surprised the voice was so clear and present. It was true, neither hitchhiker said anything. I hadn't thought of that. Not wanting to offend the one who wasn't as beautiful I asked, "Who is speaking now?"

"The one who's not so beautiful."

Once again I was reminded how transparent my thoughts were regardless of whether I gave voice to them. "What can I learn from you?" I asked.

Her voice was silky. "Something you'll have a hard time believing and accepting, yet as you already know, it is the key to your wholeness. You already recognize the other woman in you, but I am less familiar. You were right when you said we like to live in the moment, but that is where our similarities stop. She is the one who is sensual, sexual, and comfortable in her body. She naturally attracts attention from men. She reels them in without a word, without even trying. She is very powerful in her sexuality, a power you have recently discovered. She is willing to be picked up, to be undressed in front of others. She's not ashamed of her body."

I squirmed a bit. "You sound judgmental of her."

"No, that's not my voice that's being judgmental—that's another one of yours, the one in the front seat who still wants control, who resents her getting all the attention. You're even jealous of how much she enjoys herself. You think you can shame her but she doesn't respond to what others expect of her; she listens to her own desires. She's my good friend; we often travel together."

I asked, "Tell me more about yourself."

"I'm quiet by nature, enjoying time to myself. I relish the ordinary moments as well as the extraordinary ones. I have no need for control, nor to say anything. I'm not overcome with strong feelings of jealousy or possessiveness, nor am I afraid of the unknown. I help connect you to the place of peace, to what is numinous and sacred. Being still comes naturally to me. When you pay attention to me, you don't look for approval or appreciation outside yourself."

I couldn't help looking around the den for her presence, her voice was so clear. "I would like to get to know you better; you feel like a very unassuming presence. How can I experience you more in my life?"

"Be still. It will take some discipline to find where I live within you. When you head out for walks, stop, sit for a while. I'm the one who hears the buzz of the bees tending to the wildflowers, the one who brings your eye to their back legs laden with a growing seed of pollen. I'm the one who stops to watch the line of pelicans fly overhead, changing their formation and rippling like a wave in the sky. When you are with me, you too will be compelled to witness beauty, to tap into the correspondence of as above, so below." She paused, unhurried by the shared silence between us. "I disappear when you start to worry or get consumed by your doubts, when you start to plan out your day. I live in the transition time, the pause between all the doing. I'm with you in those early moments of waking, ready to help you retrieve your dreams from the night and help you live your dreams in the daylight hours. Bidden or unbidden, I'm there."

I was impressed with how easy it was to call up this other

aspect of myself. "I still can't see you; the image from my dream hasn't stayed with me. Will you show yourself to me?"

"Eventually you will recognize my face in the mirror, but now is not the time. You still have more polishing to do before you can see my reflection. I await that time."

"Thank you."

The Fox's eyebrows were raised. She asked, "Are you ready to continue with what happens next in your dream?"

I shook my head. "No. I need a moment to pause. That was incredible and so easy." I bowed in a long stretch and let my rump sink to the ground again, sitting more like a sphinx.

The Fox came and sat alongside me, her haunches snug to mine. "Excellent, you're already embracing your inner hitchhiker."

"Yeah, her peacefulness is something I rarely feel." I licked at my paws, admiring the whole transformation. I'd not paused to take in becoming a fox, how the world felt different in this skin, in contact with my instincts and intuition. The darkness of her den had no distractions; it invited me inward.

After enjoying the rest in our shared stillness, I returned to the end of the dream. "Next we arrived at our home in Kauai, coming in the door from the garage into the kitchen."

"What is your home in Kauai symbolic of?"

"It was the first home I felt like there was space for all of me."

"Go on, what's next?" She rested her chin on her two front paws.

"When we arrived inside, the masculine part of me that is attracted to my soft, sensual, feminine side is drawn together. Another aspect of me, the passenger, is now alarmed. She's afraid that the beautiful one will be naked under the sweater and I will completely lose the attention of the one who knows where she's going."

"Are you afraid of your passion?"

"Yeah, sometimes it feels out of control and becomes all-consuming. I lose my sense of balance and boundaries in knowing what's enough—not just in relationship to Ian, with work too."

The Fox recounted, "When she took off her sweater, she had something on underneath, a knit bra, just like the soft sweater. What does a bra symbolize for you? "

"It's a form of feminine support. Maybe it means I can support myself comfortably, softly. That I don't have to be hard or tough. It's just I'm afraid of being soft because at times I feel too vulnerable or exposed."

She continued to lean into me as she stretched on her side, revealing her belly. "Hmm, too vulnerable. What next?"

"The part of me that is grounded, in control has now partnered with the softer, beautiful aspect of myself and they are going to the bedroom, a private place for both rest and passion."

She wiggled on her back up against me for a moment. "You're tense."

"Yes." I bristled. "That's the part of me that feels left behind and intolerant. I don't realize I'm standing with an aspect of myself capable of the embodied presence I crave. My anger is cutting me off from her."

Her nose tipped in the air again. "Left standing in the kitchen, that triggers you. What does that mean to you?"

"This is a loaded symbol for me. The kitchen was my mum's domain; she fixed and cleaned up our meals, tended to the house, and parented me, whereas my dad had the freedom to go off pursuing his passions."

"So two aspects of you are left standing in the kitchen—one is at peace, the other one is resentful, afraid of being trapped. Where in your life are you afraid of being trapped like your mum?"

"If Ian and I marry and start a family. I'm afraid of relying on him for financial support, the way my mum was dependent on my father. I know we're different; she never worked after I was born. I also know I've already left a relationship that felt like a trap to me so I have evidence that I can leave. It's just that I don't want to do that again."

"Do what again?"

"Feel like I have to leave in order to live my life. I lost faith in my marriage as a place where I could learn and grow. What if I was wrong? Maybe I should have been more patient, I'll never know."

"It sounds like you are not only doubting yourself, you're shaming yourself: for your attraction to Ian, for losing faith in your marriage and not being patient enough, for divorcing."

I squirmed. "It's true."

"So we are back to the fear that if you make one wrong decision, one wrong move, then everything will fall down around you. Was that your experience, did everything 'turn to shit,' as you say, after your divorce?"

"Well, yes and no. Nothing terrible happened to me physically or professionally, but I couldn't shake my dark Irish mood, emotionally I was a basket case. At first I reacted by working nonstop so I wouldn't have to feel."

"How is it that working prevents you from feeling?"

"Good question, it doesn't really prevent my feelings

altogether, it just allows me to ignore them. I focus on my commitments to everyone else and ignore myself. I let my schedule get compressed with classes, grading, redesigning lessons, taking on committee work. You've already told me how powerful beliefs are. I have this belief that I can't be emotional and productive at the same time. Hence, I have become really good at shutting off whatever I am feeling so I can get my work done."

The Fox rolled over, turning her face towards me. "This is the part of you that's 'driven,' the driver in you."

I turned to look at her. "It could be. I was certainly headed for an accident with the pace I kept. I worked by day and fell apart by night or on weekends. After a while of this I realized I couldn't keep it up, that I needed more time and space to feel what was moving in me. Perhaps to look in the rearview mirror, in my past. Time to be still, like the other hitchhiker advised." I was suddenly really hot. I stood and stretched. "School vacations were never enough. I always filled them with errands or seeing friends; everything that had piled up while I was overworking during school finally spilled over, demanding my attention." I started to pace around the den, being in motion was comforting.

"I was on the West Coast, the day before a conference I was to present at. That night I dreamt my father and I were clinging to the wreckage of a sailboat. I saw my father start to slip under the water and swam to try to save him. He kept struggling and the weight of him was dragging me under-water with him. I'm a trained lifeguard and I knew that if I didn't let him go we were both going to die. I had to watch my father drown.

"I awoke in tears. It wasn't hard for me to interpret that my masculine side was going to kill me if I didn't let go. The dream hangover, however, was severe. I couldn't shake the underlying nausea and feeling of impending disaster. I told Ian briefly about the dream and said I needed to find a beach.

"As he was getting ready I noticed I missed a call from my mother. The message was short; she asked me to call her back. I didn't feel like talking then. The city's tall buildings and pavement were closing in on me. Only nature and open space would settle my nerves.

"We drove to Marin for a walk in the Tennessee Valley. We walked the mile long trail to the beach in silence. The smell of saltwater and the steady sound of the waves meeting the shore calmed my nerves.

"I leaned against a cluster of boulders near the water's edge and gave voice to the longing that had accompanied me along the trail. 'I just want to stop.' When Ian asked for clarity, I said again, 'I want to stop, stop working. I'm done. I want to take a sabbatical for a year.' The seaside was the one place where I always felt there was enough space for me to just be. All I wanted to do was sit by the ocean. It had been over a year since I had separated from my husband; the divorce was finally behind me and I was ready to stop. I wanted to take long beach walks and swim in warm waters. I wanted time to read and write, to listen to my dreams. I wanted to grow my hair, read my journals, and teach myself to play the saxophone. Ian asked what was stopping me. I told him I didn't want to leave my friends and family and I didn't want to walk away from what was budding between us. Without thinking about it, I asked him if he would consider coming with me. He didn't hesitate, he said yes..

"I knew at that moment it was going to happen. I didn't really believe that Ian would join me or if he did it might only be in the beginning. He is a raging extrovert; I expected island isolation to be a deterrent. I started to panic a bit about what it would be like to live together twenty-four-seven, and if I even wanted that given our relationship was so new. It all felt premature. I pushed my doubts aside about his coming and my need to be alone. I focused on how I would tell my parents.

"As we left the beach that day my resolve was tested when I returned my mum's call. She let me know my dad was in the hospital. He had a stroke the previous night and was paralyzed on his left side; his speech was slurred. He was in recovery and with rehab he could likely get back his motor function and speech. I didn't mention my dream of the wreckage or him drowning, nor my plans to stop working. I still believed my interpretation was also personal for me, to listen and be still or I would be forced to stop. So, in a way, I was paying attention to the advice of the other silent hitch-hiker." I kept pacing and the Fox watched me with her eyes, not turning her head.

"As my dad's health improved, I shared my plans. Meanwhile I was busy making arrangements, researching places to live, ending my lease, giving notice at school, selling my car and storing my belongings. After four months of planning, Ian and I flew to Kauai. I remember crying on the plane in sheer joy and relief before takeoff. I still couldn't believe he was with me, the tension of packing had us fussing at each other more than ever. I think both of us were panicking about spending the year together in a place we had never been before where the only other person we knew was each other."

The Fox just smiled at me. I knew what she was thinking; it took a lot of faith in myself and in my relationship with Ian to take that year off. I smiled back, she was right. In reality, nothing really turned to shit, it may have felt awful in the short term, but I wouldn't trade the life I had now for any second chance at my first marriage. *All of my mistakes, my humanness has been just perfect.*

I stopped pacing in front of her, facing her. "I'm feeling a pressing need to find that key I promised Rage, so I can set her free, set me free. I don't see how our dream interpretation is working. I know how hard she's been trying to protect me but I get the sense it's only isolated and imprisoned me. I'm still keyless."

She half smiled. "Your dreams occur in the darkest places, in the night. Reaching into the hidden meaning of their symbols is like opening up boxes to see what they reveal. If you are willing to reach deeper, even to the places you've wanted to avoid, your revelation awaits."

I heard her reference to the aspect of the dream I dodged about the oncoming car, the near accident. I was standing over her. I wanted to move on. "I think we've analyzed my dream at nauseum. We're just talking. I imagined we would go out hunting and actually track these boxes down that hold the key."

She didn't budge. "I hear you. You want to do something, to take control like the driver. Sometimes the most challenging and rewarding hunts are done from a still place. Your pain is nowhere to be found outside yourself; neither is your fear. We are not going to find them out there. Close your eyes and be still and tell me what you see. Inhabit this box you imagine we will find somewhere outside this den."

∼◦∼

Ian had moved his new painting of the layout from the living room to their bedroom. His eyes were continually drawn to AG's initials in the corner, and his memory of acquiring the artwork. The picture was symbolic of freedom for him, an elusive freedom.

The argument in his head still didn't have a clear winner. Sarah was the one who left him. How long was he supposed to wait? For all he knew, she may never come back and he was being an idiot putting his life on hold. He knew he was reframing the situation to justify his behavior.

If he continued to wait for Sarah, he was choosing to make himself miserable with no guarantee she would return. If he started dating in her absence, when she returned, *if* she returned, she would feel he had betrayed her. Either way he lost out. Not unlike the double bind he felt in conversations around racism; when white men were lumped together as if all white men were the same, it was racist. If he pointed it out he was seen as being defensive, unwilling to listen, yet the point was racial stereotypes were harmful. Just as he wouldn't expect a Black woman or man to speak for all Black women or men. He was tired of hearing how all white males wanted to hoard power, were colonizers, and only had their own best interests in mind.

If he spoke for too long he was taking up too much air time. He was supposed to step back and let other voices in the room. What happened to hearing from all voices? *Diversity is so much more than skin color, gender, or sexual preference. Being inclusive also means recognizing that extroverts don't know what they are thinking until they are saying it. I literally need to speak to think.* Silencing extroverts was like asking them to stop thinking. These invisible bars were imprisoning him and he was looking for a way out.

CHAPTER 14

BURIED MEMORIES

I SAT DOWN IN front of the Fox and remained quiet, but nothing came to mind. I listened for any instincts, combing my body for sensations, scanning for any random hints. I waited and listened until an uneasy feeling arose in my stomach.

"Follow that scent." She tipped her nose in the air. "What is happening in your body?"

"My gut's in turmoil. There's a burning in my chest, in my lungs, that makes it hard to breathe. I'm bracing myself but I don't know for what."

"How do you feel?" she asked as she sat up, so our eyes were equal to one another.

"Shaky. Weak. Lost."

"What else? Is there anything you're telling yourself?"

"That I can't win, that I'll never be enough," I replied.

She brought her nose to mine, and I could feel her breath as she asked, "So what do you do when you can't win, when you're never enough?"

261

I closed my eyes. "I get busy. I hide out."

"Where do you hide?" asked the Fox.

"In my work, under a mask of composure, of competency. It's the best way to keep my feelings private." I wanted to drop to the ground but I stayed seated.

"What doesn't she want revealed?" she asked.

I said, "Her shame. Her feelings of not being enough. She has struggled for so long with this feeling. Yet it always catches up to her regardless of where she runs or what she does." I paused and opened my eyes; she held my gaze. *Wait, why am I speaking in the third person?*

The Fox read my mind and replied, "I wanted to offer you another perspective on yourself. When you speak in the third person, sometimes an insight is more readily available than if I had put you on the spot and asked you directly. If I'd said, 'What don't *you* want revealed?' You would have wanted to keep it hidden. Paradoxically, for insight, to peer within, sometimes we need a little distance."

"Very clever. So we've surfaced Shame." I looked around. "Will I see her face?"

"I doubt it, it's not her way. She lurks in the shadows. It's enough that you can call her by name." Her hind leg briefly scratched her ear. "Tell me what you know about how she moves in your life?"

I kept an eye on the den walls to catch a glimpse of her shadow. I thought about pacing in the den, flushing her out, but I didn't have the energy for it. Instead, I lay down on my side and rested my nose on my back haunches. "She's insidious. No matter how competent I am, no matter how much money I earn, despite the recognition I'm offered, I can't escape this nagging feeling that something is wrong, wrong with me. There is no proving to myself that I'm good enough. The feeling I've done something unspeakably wrong haunts me. I'm exhausted from trying to outrun it."

"So where does that leave you?" The Fox sat down before me as a sphinx.

"Like I am now, curled up in a ball, hiding where no one can find me."

"Was there a place you went as a child where no one could find you?"

"Hmm, yeah. In my old bedroom closet. It wasn't built as a conventional rectangle. There was an extra sneaky space to the right, beyond the wall you can only find if you crawled into the closet. I discovered it one day playing hide and seek with my friends. No one ever found me when I hid there. It was over the staircase. The slant of the ceiling created a sloped forty-five-degree angle wall, a cubby that was about two feet wide. I would crouch in there with my butt on the slope, knees up against the wall, arms wrapped around my lower legs, my toes jammed on the slanted pitch, my chin on my knees. I made myself as compact as I could. I felt safe."

"You said your old bedroom, why did you move?" she asked.

"It wasn't my decision. I had slept upstairs down the hall from my parents. One day when I came home from grade school all my belongings were in the library downstairs, across from the guest bedroom. My mum wanted a place where she could permanently have the ironing board up that wouldn't be visible to guests. She ironed every day: my father's shirts, her own clothes and, around the holidays, napkins and tablecloths.

"Looking back I think she also wanted to commandeer

the extra closet space for her ever-expanding wardrobe and shoe collection. I still used it to hide, even when I didn't sleep there. Her pants and skirts were longer than mine, making the hiding place even more secure."

She asked, "How old were you?"

"I don't recall, maybe nine or ten. I preferred being upstairs where my parents slept. If I needed to call out at night from a bad dream, my mum would hear me and come in. When my dad traveled out of the country, she didn't mind if I came into her bed in the middle of the night." I sighed before continuing.

"My downstairs bedroom had ordinary closets, no crawl spaces. There was nowhere in my bedroom where I could hide that I couldn't be found. After the move I had trouble sleeping for the first time. I was convinced there were monsters in my bedroom. My parents assured me there weren't any but I still had a creepy feeling that kept me awake some nights." The queasy, nauseous feeling in my stomach was back. The memory I'd hid surfaced. I saw it even when I closed my eyes.

The Fox tipped her nose again in the air. I heard her sniffing. She said, "Let's look for the key there. Tell me her story." She set her chin back on her front paws.

I stood and looked around, scanning the den.

The Fox said, "It's okay, you are safe here." She sat up to look at me eye to eye. "Now is the time to give voice to this; you can't bury it any longer and still find the key."

I started to pace around the perimeter of the den, slowly at first while I reacquainted myself with the walls and the general shape of the cave. Once I had the lay of the land I picked up my pace. "A couple, friends of my parents, were visiting. They didn't have kids of their own. She worked full-time as an aesthetician; he had formerly been with the FBI and had some kind of private security job. The height differential between them was extreme, she was barely five feet and he towered over her at 6'2". As guests, they slept in the bedroom across from me. One night I awoke to him crawling into bed with me. I was disoriented seeing him there pulling off the covers.

"I told him, 'You're supposed to be across the hall, with your wife.'

"He said, 'She's sleeping. We need to be quiet so we don't wake her. Just move over, it will be our little secret. It will be fine. I'm tired. I just want to get warm and sleep. Roll over.' He spoke with a tone of authority.

"I felt unsettled. I was groggy. My eyes just wanted to close again and go back to sleep. The draft he created holding the covers up gave me a chill. My nightgown was all bunched up and my legs were bare. I wanted to be warm.

"He said, 'I'm just going to lie beside you. We can both sleep here. There's plenty of room. Come on, it's cold.'

"He didn't have any clothes on. I believed him that he would only lay down, that he was tired, that he was cold. It was how I felt. I didn't listen anymore to the creepy feeling inside, the part of me that knew he belonged across the hall. I let him talk me out of it. At the time, I didn't know people did anything but sleep, or read or talk in bed.

"He crawled in, all 6'2" of him. He didn't just lie beside me. He lied. He was everywhere at once, laying on top of my small frame. I could barely breathe. All I could smell was Courvoisier. He put his lips to mine; his tongue forced its way inside my mouth, touching my teeth and my tongue, which felt weird and gross. I couldn't talk. My voice was caught in my throat. My chest felt like it would be crushed under his weight, it was on fire. His mouth was smothering mine and I tried to brace myself so I could breathe. I didn't understand what was happening. I was scared and knew something was terribly wrong but I felt helpless to do anything about it. Everything within me was tense and then I went numb and everything went black. When I awoke in the morning he was gone." My pacing had sped up, I slowed down and exhaled.

"You're here in the den with me, you're okay; watch your paws as you pace, feel the dirt on your pads. The smell is dank, I know, but it's home to me; you're safe in the dark." The Fox lay down again. "What happened next? Did you tell your parents?"

"I heard my mum in the kitchen and went out to see her standing in her robe, still with last night's makeup on her face, black mascara smudges below her eyes. She had a roll of Pillsbury doughboy cinnamon buns she'd just rapped on the corner of the counter to split open and was peeling back the paper to put the buns in the circular pan.

"My mum looked up briefly and said, 'Mornin' pumpkin, how did you sleep?' She went back to arranging the buns.

"I sat down in the kitchen chair at the end of the table and started to tell her what happened. 'Jed came into my bed-room last night instead of the guest room. He woke me up and wanted me to roll over so he could get in bed with me. He was naked. He said he wanted to sleep with me.'

"I watched her freeze. She glared at me. I sensed every-thing shift in the air. She looked furious, like she did when I was in trouble or she was fuming at my father. I knew at that moment no matter what I said I was about to be into serious trouble. If it was really bad she would say, 'Wait till your father comes home,' which meant a spanking with his belt. But my dad was already home, he was sleeping upstairs. I remembered Jed saying it was our secret. Keeping secrets was often the price of being able to tag along with older kids in the neighborhood. I was good at it, I never told on anyone. When I paused, she used my full name, not my nickname.

"She shook the spatula at me. 'Sarah Ann O'Sullivan, tell me what happened next.'

"I finished telling her I couldn't get him to leave, I couldn't get him off of me, I couldn't breathe and I was scared. I told her he put his tongue in my mouth. She held the spatula up midair like she was going to strike the buns or me. I suspected she was about to yell at me so I stopped. I waited.

"Nothing happened. She went back to smoothing the frosting on the buns. I just watched her in silence. She swirled a white layer on top till there were no bare spots. She never said anything more about it and neither did I. She gave me the little plastic container to finger lick the frosting caught in the edges.

"The feeling that I'd done something wrong lingered, but I didn't know what it was and I didn't ask to find out. I had escaped the punishment I was sure was going to be severe. Our guests left early. Everything felt awkward, like the air was thick and heavy with silence. In a strange way I felt lucky, like I was off the hook for whatever it was. I didn't want to risk bringing it up again. I was sure if I did, I'd be in trouble.

"Later that day, my dad installed a lock on my bedroom door and told me to use it when visitors came. I could turn the knob on the inside. No one could get in while I slept unless they had the key or if I unlocked it. When we had guests, I locked my door so they wouldn't get confused and wake me instead of going to their room.

"Years later, as a freshman in college I was dating a senior. I wanted him to be my 'first' partner in making love. I expected it to hurt, to bleed. There was no sharp pain and no blood stains on the sheet. I knew from reading Victorian romance novels that virgins bleed. If this was a sign of my innocence, then I'd failed. I was guilty. Mine was lost and I didn't even know how, but I suspected when." I'd slowed my pace and came to a stop before her where she lay slightly curled on her side.

She asked, "What are you feeling in your body now?"

"Unsettled, numb. Empty."

She raised her head. "What else are you sensing, any thoughts or impressions?"

"That I'm mostly going through the motions, no real pleasure nor pain which is sadly familiar." I sat back on my haunches.

"Anything else underneath?" she asked, laying her head back down.

"I'm guarded, tense, on edge. I feel like it's not okay to rest, it's not safe, even though in my mind I know this was a long time ago and that there is no threat here. It's like an undertow I carry with me that I've kept contained or try to stay one step ahead of lest it pull me under. Maybe this is why I stay on the move." I looked around the den again to see if we were still alone.

"In your dream, you are encountering the more sensual, passionate side of yourself. Do you know her in your life?" the Fox asked.

"I started to get to know her with Simon, but I put all of that aside, afraid of being burned again. That is, until Ian came along. My marriage was one of comfort, of security, of having fun, not of passion or sensuousness nor the sacred." How long had I been walking through my life without really inhabiting it? *It's amazing how I can still be so highly productive and competent but disconnected and disembodied. I'd become adept at fooling everyone, even myself—right into marriage.*

She lifted her head to ask, "So what broke the spell?"

I stood back up and changed directions to pace counterclockwise around the den. "The summons for me to return to my body came after my husband and I tried to start a family. After six months of being off the pill, our lovemaking took on new meaning. For once I wasn't afraid of becoming pregnant. At least that was the fear I always thought I brought to the act.

"Now I actually wanted a child. When I discovered I was pregnant I was bursting to share the news with our friends and family. We had planned to tell everyone the night of my husband's birthday party. But that morning I started to bleed. Just a little, but enough to notice. I knew something was wrong. At first I thought, maybe I read the early pregnancy test wrong, maybe I wasn't pregnant. I used the second test. The urine strip changed color again, I was pregnant. Then I feared I was miscarrying. We didn't tell anyone that night. Instead I went for a series of blood tests that week.

"I was pregnant, but my hormone count was climbing too slowly. I went in for a sonogram and the image showed the fetus was in my fallopian tube. The diagnosis was that my pregnancy wasn't 'viable' and had to be terminated, immediately." I hung my head lower as I walked.

"The language the medical community uses is heartless. I was scheduled for surgery that day. They told me I was lucky that they had caught it in time. I didn't feel lucky, I was bereft. They said it was good I was paying such close attention because it could have killed me if it had ruptured; the hemorrhaging would have required immediate medical intervention. All I could focus on was that our little miracle of life, my baby would never be born. I wasn't going to be a mum." I paused.

She softly asked, "What did you tell yourself about the ectopic pregnancy?"

"The old feeling of not being good enough, that something was seriously wrong with me was back in full force. At first I was crushed that my body didn't know how to get pregnant the right way. I wasn't used to feeling incompetent. There was nothing I could do about it. No amount of willpower was going to create a different outcome.

"Later I concluded I was defective. I was ashamed that my body didn't know how to cultivate and incubate life. I took it as evidence that I probably wouldn't have been a good enough mum. I felt like a complete and utter failure."

"How did your husband cope with it?" the Fox asked.

"His sadness barely lasted a week; he got over it. I didn't. Even though our baby, the fetus, was only the size of an almond, she was real to me. I'd already bought her a baby blanket, the one I now use as a prayer mat. Being pregnant was the first time I felt like I was good enough. Being pregnant felt like it connected me with what was divine in life in a way I had never known before and can't even quite find words for even now. I finally believed I had something beautiful within me. Her death devastated me." I stopped pacing and stretched into a bow over my front paws to the side of the Fox. I let my butt sink to the ground.

"After surgery I sat alone, numb, on my back porch. The surgery only required a tiny incision. The physical scar has virtually disappeared, the emotional scar never healed. I couldn't explain to anyone how much pain I felt inside. My stomach hurt all the time, like something was stabbing me. I lost my voice for about ten days and with it my sense of worth. It's impossible to teach when you can't speak.

"Later I threw myself back into my classes to try to forget. It didn't work. Instead of feeling better, I exhausted myself and alienated myself from my husband. I carried this perpetual weight of sadness in my chest and an ache in my lower right back. I kept silent about it and pretended it wasn't there, until it became normal. I forgot what it was like to live without these pains pressuring me."

"Did you ever give voice to it?" the Fox asked.

"Many months later, at a community building workshop. During our circle time, stories of women miscarrying and aborting their children were told. My chin began to quiver and I couldn't hold my tears back as I listened to women who knew my pain. I finally grieved amidst these other women, the loss of being a mother who would never give birth to her child."

"Did anything change after sharing your grief in the circle?"

"Yes, a passion for life stirred in me, for being present, for experiencing the sacred in connection, in community with others. I'd felt held in the circle in ways I'd only ever felt when I was alone in nature. I started to sense something else was possible. There was an invisible realm that called to me, beyond the more visible world I inhabited. I started to understand how I belonged in both. The loss of my pregnancy forced me to admit I wasn't in control and no matter what I did I couldn't bring the seed of life within me to fruition. There was nothing to do but surrender.

"I began to see how life was unfolding all around me. How I had been closed off to it because I was so full of my plans. Ironically, the death of this new life brought me alive to the beauty that surrounded me. I can remember driving north on Highway 425 from the Cape that fall witnessing the explosion of color in the leaves along the roadside. The road became the aisle en route to the altar of life; I felt held in nature's sanctuary. I had made that same commute for over a year and never took notice of its profound beauty. I recognized there was so much more to life than what I was allowing myself to live and I wanted to open myself to this way of living. It wasn't lost on me that my fleeting pregnancy had actually given birth to something new in me. It woke me up to my inner life that I'd been missing and longing for all along."

"How did your husband respond to your 'rebirth,' if we can call it that?" asked the Fox.

"Unfazed. I did my best to explain my new outlook on life to him, to share it with him. I was always left with the feeling I spoke a different language. I had become a foreigner in my own home, in my own marriage. How could I be so utterly changed by the experience of losing our baby and he be so utterly the same as before? I sensed the gap growing between us but I gave it no real attention or concern, until it was too late."

Her nose was tipped in the air again. "Too late, how?"

CHAPTER 15

WAKING UP

J IM HAD COME to the threshold of the living room and raised his voice loud enough to be heard over the vacuum. "I'm ready to go." Jocelyn's back was turned to him as she attacked the corners of the dog's bed with the extension nozzle. He repeated himself but she didn't pause. He walked up behind her and debated turning off the canister or reaching for her; he opted for the latter.

She spun around and jokingly threatened to vacuum him.

He noticed the flash of white in her ears. She had her noise-canceling AirPods on. He tapped the off button with his foot. "Time to go, we're carpooling tonight, remember? Traffic on a Saturday night to Boston is never light. I'll drive us to Brix, and you drive back."

Jocelyn removed both AirPods and tucked them away in their case. She noted it wasn't a request. She countered with her own demand. "Okay, but on the way there we listen to either Esther Perel or *Your Undivided Attention.*"[29]

Jim would have preferred neither, but he had already appointed her their designated driver so he felt obliged. "Okay, let Ian decide, we'll wait to start it till we pick him up."

After Ian got settled into the back seat and before he and Jim had a chance to launch into a philosophical conversation about politics, Jocelyn offered up the choice of podcasts.

"For our commute we can either listen to *Where Should We Begin*, the episode 'It's Very Hard to Live with a Saint'—and before you bristle, remember it's not about you necessarily, it's about the archetypal pattern she names.[30] I've not finished it yet but I think you would both find it helpful in your relationships, hint, hint. "

"What's door number two?" Ian asked.

Jocelyn replied. "The Center for Humane Technology's podcast, *Your Undivided Attention.*"[31]

Ian said, "Given you're married to Jim Anderson and my partner is AWOL, unless she has one that addresses abandonment issues, I vote *Your Undivided Attention.* Which one did you have in mind? I've heard most of them."

Both podcasts talked about changing the quality of individuals' lives; Esther's method was via the quality of relationships; CHT was through the quality of attention. Jocelyn queued up episode 46. "Have you heard the one where their producer Stephanie interviews Tristan and Aza? It's a departure from their normal format of a guest speaker."

[29] Esther Perel, "*Where Should We Begin*", podcast. https://www.estherperel.com/podcast.
[30] Esther Perel, "*Where Should We Begin*", S4 episode 5, "It's Very Hard to Live with a Saint", podcast. https://www.estherperel.com/podcast.
[31] Tristan Harris and Aza Raskin, Center For Humane Technology, "*Your Undivided Attention*", podcast. https://www.humanetech.com/podcast.

"No," Ian replied, "I've missed that one, what's it called?"

"It flies in the face of *Father Knows Best* perennial wisdom; it's about the importance of doubt." She had it up on her phone now and read the title: "Here's Our Plan and We Don't Know." She pressed play.[32]

Jim was parallel parking as the episode came to a close, perfect timing. "I love the idea of a doubt club. When you think about it, my whole profession is predicated on the ability to create or remove doubt. Making room for doubt is an art."

"Yeah, and you're great at it. I hate arguing with you when you lawyer up." Jocelyn said, "I think the leverage is less about being open-minded, and more about being open-hearted. Really letting the impact of our action sink in."

They had exited the car and were walking along the sidewalk. Jim asked, "Did they ever start The Ledger of Harms?"

Jocelyn replied, "They did, thank god. It's near impossible to change what we can't perceive is happening, it's the boiled frog phenomenon."

"Boiled frog, that doesn't sound appetizing." Jim was holding the door open. "I hope it's not on the menu tonight with the tasting."

Jocelyn walked in first, commenting, "You're eating it every day...you know what it means. If you put a frog in boiling water it will jump out, but if you slowly turn up the heat, it lulls the frog to sleep and they die, hence boiled frog. Our technology addiction has rendered us boiled frogs and we don't even know it."

Ian followed. "Sad but true. The invisible harms that never show up on a company's ledger sheet. Good on them to

---

[32] Tristan Harris and Aza Raskin, Center for Humane Technology, "*Your Undivided Attention*", episode 46, "Here's our plan and we don't know", podcast. https://www.humanetech.com/podcast/46-heres-our-plan-and-we-dont-know.

try and make them more transparent. It's a compelling phrase, Ledger of Harms.[33] The question is, how can we make companies more accountable for the externalities they never pay for? There ought to be a law against it." Ian sat down and picked up the wine tasting menu. "Now, I need a drink."

～◯～

The Fox sat like a sphinx beside me awaiting my response.

"At first, I filled my longing for connection with other women, delving into the mysteries and the unanswerable questions with them. What I didn't see coming was how vulnerable I was to trying to fill this longing with another man. I continued to explore community building, particularly Scott Peck's approach which he also referred to as stages of spiritual development.[34] His framework is that groups move through pseudo-community, chaos, and emptiness before they reach true community." I laid my chin on my front paws and closed my eyes.

"It began the night I walked with Ian along the river after our group dinner. Unbeknownst to one another, we had both signed up for the same community building workshop. We had known each other for years from our volunteer work. We had been friends since before I met my husband; I'd never been attracted to him. I was interested to catch up on what was happening in his life. We talked and stumbled along the path navigating rocks, roots, and each other. We connected as we found our way in the dark, sharing what was important in our lives, for our futures. How were we to know then we were talking

[33] Center for Humane Technology, "Ledger of Harms", project. https://ledger.humanetech.com/.
[34] One Community, "The Four Stages to Achieving True Community", webpost. https://www.onecommunityglobal.org/stages-of-community-building/.

about our future together?

"The trail led us through a huge round metal drainage tunnel that was rippled instead of smooth. It was tall enough to walk through but tricky to walk side by side without bumping into one another because it curved up on the sides and wasn't really very wide nor flat. We hooked arms at the elbows to steady ourselves. As we came out of the tunnel, I went to release my arm from his but instead my hand gently slipped into his. It felt so natural at first, like I found home.

"A rush of warmth infused my body, followed by an immediate voice in my head yelling. *What are you doing holding another man's hand as a married woman? That's not okay!* I froze. I stopped. I asked him if it was okay, needing reassurance. When he said, 'Sure, I don't mind,' I was relieved, at least temporarily, giving myself permission to continue.

"At the end of our walk, we sat by the water, on separate, cold, cement steps. Neither of us wanted the night to end but we were afraid to touch each other again with anything but our words. There was so much heat burning inside me I was surprised that the concrete didn't sizzle with the contact of my body. I was dumbstruck by my sudden attraction to him. What had changed? How did this happen out of nowhere?

"It was clear he was attracted to me; he told me straight out, 'I find you so beautiful.' It melted me further. I believed him like I had never believed anyone before. I felt beautiful for who I was, I felt seen and heard and understood for the first time in a very long time. I let him inside my heart that night.

"A horrible guilt gripped me for being attracted to another man as a married woman. My connection with Ian felt both wrong and right at the same time. My husband and I had stopped—or maybe never started—speaking at this level of intimacy and I longed for it. I was resolved to offer my husband the kind of attention and listening I'd offered Ian. I wanted a shared inner life in my marriage, not just a shared outer life. When I returned home I confessed to Arthur about Ian, about holding his hand and how I felt seen and heard and how I wanted this in our marriage. I told him I wanted to start therapy to find a bridge to connect us again before the gap between us had grown too vast. I told him I felt alone even when I was with him. I don't think he heard anything other than I held another man's hand and was attracted to him.

"Arthur was ten years my senior and had been married before. His former wife betrayed him by having an affair with her boss. His life as he knew it blew up when she told him she was leaving him. I didn't want to do this to him again. I wanted us to find another way, which is why I was honest from the beginning. Arthur wanted me to stop seeing and speaking to Ian. At first I wouldn't. I didn't want to lose the connection I'd found. It felt like a lifeline.

"Later I agreed to end all communications because I needed to stop comparing Arthur to Ian. About a year later we divorced. I betrayed the love of a man I had promised to share my life with. He trusted me and I didn't prove worthy of that trust. Now I've found it hard to trust myself to be faithful and near impossible to trust anyone else. I know how quickly everything can change."

I opened my eyes to see the Fox was staring right at me. The themes of faithfulness, betrayal, and passion that had surfaced in my dreams were all woven into my story. I curled back up into a tight ball, nose to tail. Despite the darkness I felt exposed. Retelling my history flayed me open sharper than any knife can peel back one's skin. And for what? I was no closer in my search for the key. I just felt like shit. *I may never crawl out of here.*

The Fox nudged me with her nose. "This is not your home. If you listen to me however, you will find your way there."

"Promise?" I asked.

"Yes, you can count on me. I will not lead you astray. But you have to listen to me more often."

I lifted my head slightly and sighed. "I'm the first to admit ignoring you, my instincts and intuition, hasn't worked for me so far. So we're back in the territory of trust. What now?"

She asked, "Are you ready to revisit your dream symbol of nearly hitting the oncoming station wagon, your symbol for family life?"

"I don't really see what this has to do with finding the key." I was already resisting her guidance.

The Fox said, "If you are willing to give voice to all of it, the parts you want to believe aren't that important and the parts that you don't want anyone to know about you, my instincts tell me it will help locate the key. You can't stop now and keep your promise to free Rage."

I had hoped to avoid going here. Hadn't I shared enough of what I was ashamed of in my life? An oppressive weight flattened me low to the ground. I wanted an even darker place to hide, further underground. "Some secrets are meant to be kept, buried. Very few people know this about me and my inclination has been to keep it this way. I'll bet you already know where this is going. Can't I just stay silent, skip this part?"

She shook her head. "What's been your experience of staying silent so far, how's it working for you?"

"You're sly. You know it hasn't worked to keep the judgments at bay because I've been mercilessly judging myself all along. Shaming myself has been far worse than anything my friends could say or do. I know because the few people I've told have been nothing but supportive and compassionate about what we went through."

"So remind me, what's the point of staying silent and secretive?" the Fox asked.

"It's not just because I'm afraid of being judged. This wound runs so deep, I'm afraid no amount of scar tissue can isolate me from the pain if I touch on it again."

"Scar tissue forms to heal a wound," she said. "The way you are speaking it sounds like this wound has never healed. What if your secrecy prevents healing? My gut tells me it's time to break your vow of silence."

My body agreed with hers. I felt a chord, like a lifeline, straightening my spine. I came uncurled and sat up. "What's really at risk isn't so much the vulnerability that other people will reject me, or judge me. I have faced this before on other issues and it's been okay. It's different this time." I looked around the den. "Before, if they didn't accept me, I could still accept myself. This time I feel so much more at risk because the one that doesn't accept me is me. I haven't been able to forgive myself for what I did. I've not been able to come to terms with it, nor find any peace within myself."

She whispered, "Maybe now it will be different. I want to hear you give voice to this aspect of your story. I can see you've been dragging it around behind you; it's tied to your heart. See what's possible. If you retrieve it, if you face it and acknowledge it, you may be surprised to discover what your heart is capable of."

I stretched in a low bow then shook my body before I began to walk counterclockwise around the perimeter of the den. *I'd been on this path before, countless times, why would it be different now?* I looked down at the ground, tracking each paw as it made contact with the earth. The Fox sat near the center watching me. I peeled off the edge of the den towards her crossing the midline until I reached the opposite wall and reversed direction for a few steps and then turned back in towards the center, passing by her again and reversing direction when I reached the opposite wall. I walked a figure eight, an infinity sign. There was something about the rhythm of continuous movement, clockwise and counterclockwise that comforted me, winding and unwinding. Moving from the edges to the center. She waited and watched me. Eventually I spoke of this haunting memory.

"Ian was driving us home along the Mass Pike, after having spent our first Christmas holidays with my parents. Our time together was warm and relaxed, surprisingly enjoyable. All the time my former husband had spent with my family was tense. I had forgotten what it was like to interact without that tension. Yet, my stomach had been bothering me throughout the visit. On the ride home I still felt nauseous—actually, I had felt nauseous on the ride to my parents as well but I attributed it to nerves. On the ride home I had no such excuse.

"Steely Dan was playing, Ian was drumming the steering wheel with his hands as he sang along to 'Time out of Mind.'[35] I didn't know all the lyrics, just the refrain. When I sang along it struck me why I might still be having waves of nausea. I

---

[35] Steely Dan, "Time Out of Mind", Gaucho Album, MCA Records. youtube, 4:14, September 28, 2019. https://www.youtube.com/watch?v=YLqHjwpUTsk.

heard myself say, *Children*. It hit me like a bat. Was I pregnant? Was this morning sickness? I tried to recall when my last period was but couldn't. I didn't track it that closely. It tended to be around the full moon. I looked up in the sky for a hint but it was too cloudy. I thought I might be late. But just because I was late didn't mean I was pregnant. I found excuses—the stress of the holiday, finishing up school, it all could have thrown me off.

"While I brooded on the possibility of being pregnant, Ian had changed instruments to his imaginary bass—one hand on the frets at the neck, the other strumming, his mouth imitating the beat of the bass. He only occasionally touched the wheel. He wasn't paying any attention to me as I slipped my hands inside my coat to cup my breasts. They did feel a bit bigger and tender to the touch. I didn't want to give voice to it. I did want to know for sure.

"I needed an early pregnancy test. I confessed my suspicion to Ian and we detoured to Rite Aid. The place was deserted, the artificial light too bright and sterile. I found the aisle for feminine products and the shelf of options for EPT tests. The selection was overwhelming. He just stood like a sentinel while I read the labels of each box, bewildered by which was best. I finally selected one that contained two tests. Thankfully the cashier wasn't chatty. She must have surmised she was witnessing something other than hope; after all there was no ring on my finger.

"The air was thick between us for the last half hour of the drive. The music was off. I kept telling myself it wasn't possible, yet inside I was afraid I already knew the tests would confirm my suspicion. The last time I used an early pregnancy test I had wanted to be pregnant. I had prayed the strip would turn color. Now I dreaded it.

"I couldn't imagine Ian and me getting married yet, and the idea of becoming parents was absurd. I knew his mother had become pregnant before she was married to his father; they married under pressure and later divorced. I didn't want to repeat his history. Nor marry again only to have it end in divorce. I told myself I was getting ahead of myself, that it was just my overactive imagination. Except my mind wouldn't be quiet. I scoured our history for how this could have happened. We were so careful since I wasn't on the pill. *No condom, no sex* was my rule. Then I remembered the time the condom came off after we finished making love. We had rested together too long on the couch with him inside me and when he pulled out, it wasn't on him. I had to go fishing for it with my fingers and waddled to the bathroom to take it out. I didn't want to believe the odds were that stacked against me, that I was that fertile. I wondered what soul wanted to come through that it threaded such a narrow pass?

"The directions on the box suggested waiting until morning to use the test because the hCG hormone count was higher in morning urine to indicate pregnancy. There was no way I could wait until morning. First, I'd never sleep and second we might suffocate from tension in the air before then. Hardly a word has been spoken since we said goodnight to the cashier. I didn't even help Ian empty the car. I bolted up the thirteen steps to my apartment door and straight to the bathroom.

"After peeing on the strip, I brought the test out to the island counter in the kitchen where Ian was waiting and set it down. He set the timer on his watch for ten minutes. Within two minutes the positive sign had started to appear. We both stood there watching it in silence waiting for the timer to go off to be sure. My body was frozen in place as if I could suspend time. If I didn't move or say anything it wouldn't be happening.

"I started to cry as I stared at the test. I couldn't look Ian in the eye. I desperately wanted to have children, but not now, not like this. I felt defeated. I was uncertain about Ian as my potential husband let alone as a father. I had fallen in love with him but I didn't know if it was the kind of love that could endure. Plus, I didn't exactly trust my capacity to mate in an enduring way with anyone at this point. Hell, I wasn't even officially divorced yet. In Massachusetts it takes six months after you file jointly for it to be official. I wasn't even off my former husband's medical plan yet.

"When I finally looked up at Ian he looked at me tenderly. I could see he was suspended in time too, waiting for me to take the lead. I moved into his arms and wept on his shoulder. He guided me to the couch, the same couch where we had conceived only weeks before. I spilled out everything I had been feeling and thinking and Ian simply listened.

"That night began an inner turmoil for me about what I should do. Even though my heart and mind said *No, now is not the time*, I also felt deep inside that another miracle of life had been given to me. I didn't want to disrespect this gift by refusing it. I was torn. I knew in my bones I wanted to be a mother someday, if I could. What if I aborted our baby and never became pregnant again—it's a miracle, after all. Could I live without regrets?

"Ian was supportive of whatever my decision was; he

offered to marry me if I was willing. I wanted more time, no pressure to consider marriage again. I didn't want to become husband and wife under these conditions; it felt like repeating his family's history and I wanted to break that pattern.

"We held each other and wept. We lit candles and set up an altar on the living room coffee table. Whatever we decided, I wanted to name our child. I wanted to acknowledge that we had conceived a life together. My sense was of a girl. We named her Zoe, meaning *life* in Greek. That night we prayed together. I lay awake on my back most of the night, with my hands resting on my belly asking Zoe why had she come into my life, what was it she had to teach me?

"I have always known that my children would be my teachers. My first child brought me a life-changing lesson of surrender. It was easier to look back and understand why it all worked out for the best. Without faith it was impossible to surrender to the moment and trust that the right outcome will emerge. At the time I didn't appreciate what a blessing it was; however, later when our marriage was on the rocks, I realized it would be a completely different story if we had a child together."

"What was Zoe's lesson for you?" she asked.

I smiled because I sensed she already knew the answer— actually, so did I. However, knowing it didn't mean I knew how to live it. "She came into my life to offer me forgiveness. To have compassion for myself, my mistakes, for all the outcomes I had a hand in creating that worked out to be my worst nightmares. This is a lesson I am still needing to learn; for some reason, compassion and forgiveness escape me."

The Fox said, "That has been your story to date. Let your

story change. What happened next?"

"Being faced with the choice to have our child or have an abortion, I was bereft. Like a true Pisces I swam in both directions on it, I went back and forth, relentlessly debating my options. How could I ever forgive myself if I refused to bring her life into existence? Who am I to play God with life and death choices? So what if it wasn't what I thought was going to happen in my life? What was more important, my life's plan or another life? What if this was exactly what I was to do but would never have consciously allowed it to happen? How could I know what was right? How could I make a decision and live with it for the rest of my life? What if I made the wrong decision?"

"Did you ask for help in your discernment?"

"No, too many of my female friends were struggling to conceive. It felt insensitive given their experiences of multiple miscarriages and the futility of fertility drugs. Their elusive dream was my nightmare. How could I tell them?"

"Did you tell anyone?" she asked.

"No. We agreed it was my, *our* decision to make. Ian consistently reiterated he would be supportive of my choice, either way. He listened to various scenarios. What if I carried Zoe to full term and offered her for adoption or arranged a private adoption for one of my friends? We both agreed if I carried her full term and held her in my arms, it would be torture to give her up to anyone else to raise even if they were our friends. I didn't want to be a witness in our child's life rather than her parents. Besides, how could I choose among my friends who would be her parents? If we married and raised her as our daughter, would I start to feel trapped, resentful that I'd never taken the time to make the commitment to myself, the very commitment I left my marriage to begin? Would I become like my mother, a woman who lived her life through her child, not for herself? I was afraid to miss my life. Would I an feel trapped into marriage? Would our marriage even last if we started as parents and not had a chance to be husband and wife? If I had an abortion and was never able to become pregnant again could I live childless without regrets?

"I didn't sleep well. I was nauseous with morning sickness that lasted throughout the day. I heard this clock ticking every moment pressuring me to decide. I walked the beach accompanied by my unanswerable questions. I couldn't figure it out, I couldn't make it better.

"What I kept hearing inside was *No, now is not the time.* However, as much as I wanted to say no to being pregnant, I couldn't bring myself to say yes to having an abortion. I appreciated that abortion was an option available to me; I just couldn't see myself doing it. I prayed there was another option that I just hadn't thought of yet.

"I had an overwhelming compulsion to hide, to curl up in the dark, where no one could find me. I fantasized I'd awaken in the morning, as if from a dream and everything would be okay again just like in fairy tales. I wanted a time machine, a chance to go back and have a second chance. I wanted to escape from having to make such a life and death decision, where no option was a good option."

I stopped talking and kept pacing the path of infinity in the den. It wasn't lost on me that I was telling a story of being caught between life and death, the tension of opposites. The sentence *an equal and opposite force* came back to my mind. I just kept hearing it again and again.

I kept my head down and continued. "In the end, I decided to have an abortion. I bled for weeks after they said I should be fine. I didn't take any time off, I just worked through it all. I've been unable to forgive myself for taking Zoe's life. My decision haunts me. This weight I carry around in my chest, it's unbearable at times, like now, it makes it hard to breathe. This ache in my lower right back has persisted as well."

The Fox asked, "What do you do when you feel it?"

"Part of me just wants to lie down, to give in to it and another part tries to fight it, by staying in motion because I'm afraid if I give in to it I will never get up. Work is my primary drug of choice to avoid the pain. I distracted myself with teaching, hoping to feel better by making other people's lives better, being of service."

"Does it work, do you feel better?" she asked.

"Temporarily at times, but it's waiting for me when I slow down. This ache won't go away; it has a hold on me. I can't undo my decision. I know I brought this on myself, it's my own fault. Now I feel helpless to do anything about it, there's no going back."

The Fox asked, "Have you ever felt helpless before, like you did something wrong and there was no going back, you couldn't change the outcome?"

I stopped pacing in the center of the den and looked at her. "Yes, I felt that way about my first pregnancy."

"How do you feel about your first pregnancy now?"

I replied, "That it was a blessing, though at the time if you had said that to me I would have wanted to bite your head off."

She said, "Some things can only be experienced with time; no one can tell us. This feeling of being helpless, not being able to change the outcome, how familiar is it? My sense is it goes back even further, that you felt it in your family growing up."

CHAPTER 16

VULNERABLE

I STARTED PACING AGAIN, letting the motion of my feet on the ground be where I put my attention, not looking at the Fox. "Yes, I felt that way about my parents' marriage, that they were unhappy and I couldn't do anything about it. That the only reason my mum stayed was because of me. It made me feel responsible for her happiness. I felt helpless when it came to my dad's drinking. When he knew it was a death sentence and he still didn't stop. I concluded he cared more about drinking than being my father, that he didn't really love me. That's when I decided I didn't need him, I didn't need anyone. I would figure out how to be okay on my own. I vowed to never make myself vulnerable to anyone again. I kept that vow; my Ice Queen award reflected it."

The Fox said, "I recall the turmoil of those years. It's a hard lesson to learn that you can't be responsible for other people's emotions and their choices, especially when you are up against addictive behavior." She tipped her nose in the air.

"I'm picking up another scent that relates to finding your key. You also shared another physical example of helplessness, of not being able to breathe, of feeling trapped."

I kept my eyes to the ground. "I did. When our guest came into my bedroom, my bed, I couldn't escape or breathe."

"In that instance of sexual abuse, when you woke up he was gone, it was over. Later when you spoke to your mum, how did you feel?"

"Like I'd done something wrong, something to be ashamed of but I didn't know what."

"So what did you tell yourself back then?" she asked.

"That I'd better be really good to make up for it."

"If you weren't good enough, what would happen, what was at risk?"

I paused in front of her. "Love. I thought their love for me was at stake, that it was conditional on my actions."

The Fox asked, "Were you able to be good enough?"

I shook my head. "Maybe in their eyes, but not in my own. The secret of that night, what happened, that I'd never told my mum the whole story, that I didn't even know how it ended, it haunted me. It's influenced how I felt about myself, my self-worth, my ability to trust and set healthy boundaries. I tried doing hypnosis when I was in therapy, but I couldn't recall anything after not being able to breathe."

She held my gaze. "It's okay if you can't remember it all." The Fox said, "What happened to you was wrong but it wasn't your fault. You were not responsible for it, you were the victim. As an adult, looking back now, can you understand that? Can you acknowledge you are not to blame?"

"Yeah, intellectually it makes sense to me. I've not wanted

this incident to define me but ignoring it and pretending it didn't happen hasn't helped. I've learned more about trauma since that time. I started reading *The Body Keeps the Score*, by Bessel van der Kolk, but I never finished it.[36] I know it's less about what happened to me and more about how I processed what happened. I'm working on changing the conclusions I drew about myself and how I act when I'm triggered. I know now that putting a lock on my door, while well intended, isn't what keeps me safe."

The Fox said, "Pretending you're not hurting physically or emotionally never works. You need to tend to yourself, to listen from within."

"*Work* being the operative word in the sentence, work hasn't been a salve. It has been my default. I've become a slave to it, a workaholic, which is why I took the sabbatical for a year on Kauai."

The Fox said, "Effectively you went cold turkey. Being on sabbatical, you removed your favorite coping mechanism." She tipped her nose to the air. "How was that for you?"

"Rough. I didn't have any external validation or sense of productivity to prop up my self-worth. I had to reckon with my identity. Who was I if I wasn't teaching? My old excuses were busted: If only I wasn't working so much, or if only the weather was better, or as soon as I get through this semester or when summer is here, then I will feel better. I was living in paradise with nothing but time but my dark Irish mood still kept me in bed. The undertow of depression only got worse with no work to sedate me."

---

[36] Bessel van der Kolk, "What is Trauma, The author of "The Body Keeps the Score" explains", Big Think, youtube, September 17, 2021, 7:48. https://www.youtube.com/watch?v=BJfmfkDQb14.

"What did you conclude about your excuses?" the Fox asked.

"That they were a load of crap, just lies I told myself. I should have known better than to invest myself in them because those deadlines came and went, but my mood was still numb, just wishing my life away."

"A part of you did know better, your instincts and intuition, but you didn't listen to them."

I looked at the Fox. "You're right. Those inklings you send me, the intimations, I do pick up on them and I also ignore them, at my peril. Damn. All this time I've been looking for the source of the betrayal outside myself rather than within. Not following my gut is its own form of betrayal. So is this what makes it so difficult for me to believe in myself at times, to believe in others, to trust love?"

"Likely a contributing factor." She nodded then asked, "How well do you feel your defenses are working?"

"In a way, all too well: They are keeping me locked in, from the inside, like my bedroom door. As good as my defenses may have been at keeping further pain out, the consequence is it has kept everything else out too, like warmth and self-love and understanding. This locked door just leaves me feeling abandoned, alone with my fear and shame, unlovable. My perpetual productivity and armor aren't my best line of defense despite how well I have perfected them."

Sensing the opening, she followed up with another question. "What if you were a bit more defenseless, a bit more vulnerable instead of so untouchable?"

"I would open up the possibility for a lot more pain into my life and right now, as you can see, I have about all I can bear."

She continued, "Help me understand what you believe

about pain? Maybe it's something to be avoided? It sounds to me that pain is something that you accumulate over your lifetime. From what you just said I suspect you are beyond your pain limit. Am I on track here?"

"I'm sure you are. I'm just not sure where we are going with this." I could feel her leading me somewhere again and I was reluctant to go there. I was tired of pacing though, I wanted to be still. I sat down beside her.

She implored, "Maybe it's okay to not know where you're going right now and simply trust me with the questions, if I may be so bold as to ask you to follow your instincts for now."

I smiled. "Cheeky, but I'll go along with it." I curled up beside her and laid my head on her haunches.

She let me get settled then said, "Tell me what else you believe or know about pain, like how it accumulates or dissipates?"

"Well it's just a part of life. The longer you are alive, I guess the more pain you are bound to experience. Time has a way of bringing it your way and I guess it's time that has a hand in lessening it as well. I've never really thought much about what makes pain go away."

"Well if it is simply time that has a hand in it, I can see why you are in trouble. My guess is that pain accumulates faster than it disseminates. There is a lot of suffering in the world. According to your theory, I'm surprised you reached your early thirties before topping out on your pain limit. What do you do to cope with pain?"

"If I'm not working, I might look for comfort in carbohydrates: toast, pasta, baguettes, all with lots of butter. Everything's better with butter. Long walks on the beach work for me too, sometimes I just give my pain back to the sea."

"What about turning to your friends?"

"Sometimes, mostly I turn to my journal to write it out. If I can't get outside, I put on music."

"How well is it working overtime given you are at your pain limit?"

"What are you getting at?"

The Fox replied, "Your experience of pain has to do with choice. You have just shared with me all the choices you make about how to deal with your pain once you already have it. Forgive me for pointing this out, but I think you are a little late in exercising your options. There are different kinds of pain. The pain that is inflicted on us that we are helpless to stop and the self-inflicted pain that we must become conscious of so we can choose to stop it."

I lifted my head from her haunches.

She looked back towards me out of her right eye. "Your ectopic pregnancy was devastating, but your self-talk around it made it worse."

Why hadn't I thought of that? I'd become trapped in a cycle of self-inflicted pain; my judgments about myself were simply cruel. "I needed some explanation as to why it had happened, I couldn't just accept it, so I found fault in myself. I told myself I had done something wrong to deserve it, that I wouldn't be a very good mum which is why my body couldn't bring a child into the world. I felt defective. I'm sure that influenced my decision to not bring my second child into the world. I opted for an abortion, because I couldn't conceive of a way that I would be a good mother. After my divorce, it's been hard to believe I can be a 'good wife,' whatever that is, or trust my judgment in men. It is impossible for me to trust everything will be okay since I don't feel okay with myself." I laid my head down again, the warmth of her soothed me. *Is this the key?*

I continued, "If I could learn to distinguish between these two forms of pain and not compound the pain life hands me by making myself wrong, then shame wouldn't have a home in me and my rage wouldn't have to defend me, cutting me off from myself and everyone else."

"Say more. Talk me through it."

I lifted my head up. "When something unfolds differently from what I wanted to happen or planned for, I tend to think of it as going 'wrong.' I immediately look for what I or someone else did 'wrong' to explain this occurrence. What if no one did anything wrong? Why is blame even necessary?"

I sat up on my haunches. "In those moments, what I need is to let myself feel the disappointment, not affix blame. I even try to avoid feeling disappointment by not letting myself get excited about things before they happen. I tell myself to wait until it goes well. I rob myself of the joy of anticipation." I started to traverse the infinity sign again in the den.

"I have been holding pain as an indicator of something having gone wrong, whether it's physical or emotional. What if I could take the right, wrong judgments out of the picture and just get curious? See it as an opportunity to listen and feel, to give the pain my attention, to breathe through it and release it."

"That sounds like a worthy experiment."

I picked up my pace as if I was hot on the trail. "Who am I to know how things are supposed to unfold in the future? While it's okay to hope for certain outcomes, disappointment is a part of life, as is pain and suffering. It's not 'deserved' or indicative of worthiness. Bad things happen to good people.

My ectopic pregnancy, while crushing, was part of a larger mystery unfolding in life I'm meant to trust."

The Fox said, "I hear the line of your blessing, 'May I become patient with uncertainty, welcoming mystery into my life as my beloved dance partner, letting go of expectations, even with disappointment, to honor what is authentic in the moment.'"

I nodded. "Yes, I'm choosing this. It isn't always easy because I grow attached to my expectations."

Instincts asked, "Why do you think you look for explanations or to find blame, fault in yourself or others when things don't go as you expected?"

I immediately heard my father's voice, "What did you think was going to happen?" My reply was often "I don't know" and his response was, "That's right, you didn't think about it," implying if I only thought about it well enough or long enough I could eliminate the mistakes or missteps, eliminate his disapproval and anger at me. He wasn't very understanding or forgiving. I looked around the den, sensing another shadow. I turned towards the Fox and said, "I have misplaced my faith in planning, in being in control, in thinking things through, another false god. While some planning is wise, I can't know the future. It's impossible to avoid disappointments or things going differently than planned."

The Fox smiled. "True, you can't know the future, your best laid plans can go astray. We're not saying don't make plans, just hold them more loosely, bend your knees more—be fluid, not rigid. That way when a strong wind or wave comes your way, you can ride with it, not be knocked over. It's the aikido move to receive that energy, by going with it and redirecting it.

However, to do this, you need to be *in* your body, with strong roots, not a few feet from it."

I stopped in the center of the den, in front of the Fox. I was looking at myself staring back at me. I had four paws in contact with the ground. I felt more stable and centered than when I walked on two legs. "I do need to rediscover my relationship with the earth. When I bow, I feel the support of the earth, both held up and simply held."

"Let this energy rise up in your body, draw it up from the earth on your inbreath. Don't close yourself off from its pulse, trust it," the Fox said.

I felt my paws on the solid ground. "Trust. It comes back to this, my inner hitchhiker being able to be still in the moment, less concerned with plans or being in control."

She asked, "What prevents you from embracing this inner hitchhiker?"

"Fear. It drives my need for control, in the guise of plans. I've preferred a firm grip on the steering wheel rather than sticking my thumb out. It's paramount to me to keep everything running smoothly so no one gets hurt or disappointed. I grew up in a very orderly household. The unexpected was rarely a pleasant surprise. I associate the unexpected more with pain and disappointment than with pleasure or joy." I sat down on my haunches. My bushy tail rested near my left side, offering an added warmth.

The Fox's habit of tipping her nose in the air helped me sense her next question before she voiced it. *How's it working for me?*

Everything was becoming clearer, the unintended consequence of my behavior. As I spoke a dim light glowed along the left wall of the den. "Ironically, my need to figure out the future, to smooth out any wrinkles or hiccups where things could go wrong can also set me up for disappointment on a regular basis when things don't go as I anticipate. I think I should have more control or influence than I can, mostly because I don't trust the universe is working just as it should be."

Shit, my faith is not absent, it's very much present, just misplaced. I leaned towards the Fox and she leaned towards me as we touched noses. She smelled of grass and loamy dirt.

She nodded for me to continue. We were tuned in with an inner dialogue.

"My faith is invested in entropy, that things left to their own devices will devolve, not evolve. That if I'm not careful everything will turn to shit. Even when everything is going well, I'm waiting for the other shoe to drop."

The Fox asked, "Is that what you want to have faith in, entropy?"

I immediately responded, "No. In a universe ruled by entropy, control is essential. How can I not have a warped sense of responsibility if this is what I believe about the world—I think 'if only' I had done something differently, everything would have been okay—they both add up to an inflated sense of power. There is no space in me to let things fall apart. I want to keep it all together, make it all okay, at least according to my standards and if I can't, I get down on myself for doing something wrong. What it boils down to is I have a tremendous fear of the future, of the unknown and if the outer world isn't okay, I'm afraid I won't be okay. I'm really feeling helpless, not powerful, because I'm letting what is outside of me determine how I feel inside. Does that make sense?"

I had been on a roll. When I paused to catch my breath I felt a familiar fog descend. *Crap.* "Everything was so clear moments ago. The key I've been searching for was about to land in my palm, but now I fear it's slipped from my grasp." Like those mornings when in the midst of recalling my night dream my mind wandered to my plans for the day or to check the time and in that moment my dream vanished.

The Fox stood up and took the few steps that separated us before she sat beside me, shoulder to shoulder. She turned to me and said, "Relax, you're hot on the trail. It can be a bit circular, doubling back on itself. Don't expect it to be linear, don't try to get ahead of yourself." She sniffed near my front paws. "Keep your nose to the ground and trust, even if it is turning out differently than you expected. You just have to follow the scent before you, you can't smell ahead of yourself— that's your mind, not your body giving you direction. It can be helpful, but not always trustworthy." She brought her nose back towards mine, her whiskers tickled before her nose nuzzled me.

The Fox continued, "We were talking about how your faith is misplaced, your belief the world will fall apart if you're not shouldering it. More personally, how when things go wrong around you, you feel you should have done something different to have avoided it. There's not much room in you for mistakes, missteps, for circling back and trying again."

I nodded. "True, I'm not very forgiving, I take my mistakes personally. My father only signed my report card if it was all A's; if there was a B+, my mum signed it. It's ridiculous when I think about it but it has a foothold in me nonetheless. If I got something wrong, something was wrong with me, I wasn't worthy of his approval. I've withheld my approval of myself. Honestly, I struggle with knowing what is good enough, if I'm good enough. There's a tangle here between my actions, thoughts and who I am in the world that I need to tease apart."

The Fox asked, "What if things do fall apart? Your ectopic pregnancy, your divorce marked times in your life when it crumbled. Yet amidst that loss, you found a connection to the sacred, an appreciation of mystery and new eyes to see the world's beauty even amidst the destruction."

I nodded in agreement. "Yeah, I came through it. I proved more resilient than I thought possible. Ironically, in the end I was better off. Things aren't always what they seem."

"Imagine that." She winked. "While there is an intimate connection between the state of the outer world and our inner world, paying attention to the direction and strength of that influence is essential. Listen carefully. When you use the state of the outer world—let's call it *sunshine*—to determine if you are happy within, then you will always be subject to the weather and feeling unstable. When you source the sun and moon within yourself, there is room in you for a rainy day, a monsoon season or even a typhoon. Where you place your faith is essential. Let your inner world influence your outer world, more than the other way around. This is the forgotten intelligence. No one else can grade this kind of intelligence, only you decide."

The Fox paused. I heard her reference to my profession of teaching, what society measures in terms of IQ.

She continued, "The root of the word intelligence begins with 'inter,' meaning between. We have come to think of intelligence as information we gather from outside ourselves, while there is infinite information available to us, what is essential is the meaning we make of it and how from within ourselves we source what is true. Be careful to discern between what you are told from outside yourself and what you know to be true from within."

I settled into what she had said and a quiet fell on the cave. My sense of responsibility, my ability to respond, my beliefs about the world and my role in it were all swirling around, starting to reconfigure themselves; when things went wrong on the outside, I felt wrong on the inside. My father's drinking, the strife in my parents' marriage, the night of sexual assault in my bedroom—I internalized all of it as something I'd done wrong, that something was wrong with me.

The Fox asked, "When you are feeling shame, can you distinguish what it feels like in your body?"

"Sometimes it's a turmoil in my stomach, like I've eaten something that doesn't agree with me. Other times it's a searing heat in my chest that can flush up my neck into my cheeks. When it has a hold of me, that's when I want to curl up and hide. But I can't escape the voice inside that's berating me; she follows me wherever I go. I hear her admonishing me that I should have done something different, I should have known better, that I didn't think it through well enough."

"How do you silence her?"

"I turn my attention to something else. If it's during the school day it's easier to focus on my students and my lesson plan. If it's after hours, it's harder. That's when I dive into a good book or watch a movie or series. Huh, the way my mum turned to daytime dramas. It numbs me out. It's how I try to change the channel."

"When the show is over, do you feel better?" the Fox asked.

"Not really, I hear this voice in my head that says I just wasted my time, my life. I can't win. I head to bed for the night and pray I don't wake up with it. The next morning I try not to think about it, I just get busy with my day." I was looking down at the ground. The thought of sleep was inviting.

"When have you been successful at silencing shame's voice or releasing its hold on your body?"

"Sometimes when I write in my journal or pull a tarot card I can find another perspective. Sometimes yoga or a hot bath helps me change the channel. I get the sense though it never really goes away with time, even the smallest seeds of shame feel like they take hold and grow roots in me."

"When you look back at your ten-year-old self, the one who listened to Jed's authority instead of that sense in your body that he didn't belong in your bed, what can you tell her now? What do you want to say to the one who rolled over and experienced all that happened afterwards that has made it hard for you to breathe?"[37]

"That it wasn't her fault. She couldn't have known what was going to happen to her. She was the victim." I paused and exhaled. "She was where she belonged, in her own bed. He was the one who didn't belong there. She did nothing wrong, he did. There was and is nothing wrong with her."

The Fox leaned into me and I leaned back. A lump rose up in my throat; tears began to well up and fall from my eyes. I let myself slowly drop to the ground beside her and curl up. She stayed seated, like a sentinel over me.

The Fox said, "That she can trust her instincts, her own inner knowing in her body, she doesn't have to roll over anymore, she doesn't have to listen to any outer authority when her body is telling her something different." She paused. "Imagine

[37] saprea, "The Effects of Child Sexual Abuse: Shame and Child Sexual Abuse", https://youniquefoundation.org/resources-for-child-sexual-abuse-survivors/effects-of-child-sexual-abuse/shame-and-child-sexual-abuse/.

her here now. What does your body, beyond your words, want to offer her? What gesture lives in you now?"

I said, "I want to enfold her, to hold her and assure her with my warmth that she is okay. I'd breathe with her until she melted in my arms."

The Fox said, "I sense she is present now. Time and space is an illusion; it's not what it seems. You can reach back to her, hold her. She's been waiting for you."

I lingered in this embrace, my heart pouring forth love. "Let the soft animal of your body, love what it loves..." The line from Mary Oliver's poem came rushing and kept replaying in my head. The Fox lay down beside me, curling around me. I closed my eyes and exhaled. I may have fallen asleep.

Later when I opened my eyes, the light in the room was different. I saw our shadows cast on the walls before us, a round mound that was larger than we were in reality. I watched it for a while; it pulsed with our breath.

I said, "Our shadow, it's out of proportion, bigger than life."

The Fox replied, "Yes, it's been trying to get our attention. Now that you see it, what comes up?"

"The cave wall looks like a blackboard, a classroom," I said. "Perhaps there's something to learn here."

She asked, "What would it be?"

"I don't have to mistrust myself and life. I don't have to perpetually defend myself, to be vigilant and on guard, to put a lock on my door and close the world out. I don't have to stay one step ahead of everything. It's what's been robbing me of my presence, of my ability to be still. I don't have to figure everything out to be safe." I exhaled deeply.

The Fox nudged me with her nose. "I hear the words of your blessing."

May I be willing to be lost, to venture into the terra incognita, letting go of my need to know, my need to figure it out to be safe, trusting life and experiencing the wonder of renewal.

She continued, "You needn't fear the unknown. Let yourself rest, restore, listen to your dreams. They are gifts, treasures awaiting you in the darkness." She looked around. "Darkness is essential. Welcome it. I call this den my home."

I sat up and the shadows on the wall reshaped in response. "If there is something I'm afraid of, I need to face it, not bury it, not let it grow out of proportion and rule my life."

The Fox sat up beside me again, shoulder to shoulder. The shadow shapeshifted again; the outline of the tips of our ears resembled mountain tops. She stood up and walked towards the shadow on the wall; her image became smaller till she was just a molehill. "While you can't change the past, you can put it to rest, you can learn from it." She turned to face me. "There is more to this key. Now that you've discovered shame's power over you, it's time to set you free."

Freedom is what I longed for, to trust myself, to trust life and be open and present. I stood up and slowly approached my own shadow, watching it diminish. I wasn't scared, nor angry anymore. The need to defend myself had dissipated. I felt tenderness towards my ten-year-old self, towards these buried memories. I wanted to be gentle and kind with her. She didn't know, she couldn't have known. *The future, it's unknowable.* I reached the wall, swiped it with my paw. The dirt crumbled a bit under my nails. "I had no idea how much I have been keeping this pain alive all the while defending myself from it. It's exhausting and alienating."

She nodded.

The opposite wall had a tiny golden light, like a candle illuminating the wall in a semi-circle. I felt a warmth glowing inside me.

I'd found the key. Forgiveness. "It's so obvious now, not elusive at all. Tenderness, not steel, was what was called for; kindness so as not to inflict any additional pain with my self-criticism, judgments, or shame. I may do things wrong but *I'm* not wrong. I am not my actions. It's all so easy to talk about and so difficult to enact. Knowing it is not embodying it. I have so much to learn about forgiveness."

The Fox said, "Before, you said you would do anything to protect her. What if that meant learning more about Forgiveness, being more—not less—vulnerable?"

I turned towards her. "That would be a new move. A different kind of strength. Before, I thought my Rage had the power to protect me, defend me. She's a warrior, after all. Now I can see how my own defenses have only made matters worse." I tried to imagine a different future. *What if I made a different choice? Rather than steel myself with the help of my silent Rage, what if I relied on my heart and mind more, with compassion and curiosity to find another way, to find the path of forgiveness?* "That would require a transformation on Rage's part, to become a more peaceful warrior, capable of defense as the last resort. She could disarm another with compassionate inquiry. Her strength would come from being willing to feel, to be vulnerable." I felt drawn to explore this new chapter of my life, one led by Faith not Fear. One where I put my thumb out to hitchhike more often. One where plans weren't my armor to try and outpace or outwit life's pain. Armor, the protective metal body encasement of the knights—*amor*, Latin for love.

I'd confused the power of Rage to protect me with the power of Love. *My heart doesn't want walls, it's not meant to turn to stone. It's the place of infinite capacity, that can embrace all of life, the suffering and the joy.* Ironically, the more I relied on Rage for protection, as a defense, the more cut off I became from myself and others. I'd become isolated and disconnected. These walls of protection had become walls of isolation. "I can see what I am doing to myself, but I don't see how to change it. Where do I find the power to make it different, to make a difference in my own life?" I looked towards my instincts and intuition for guidance.

The Fox smiled. "Yes, look to me first. It has everything to do with where you turn for guidance. What do you know in your gut, in your bones? What voice you choose to listen to matters. You've met many tendencies within yourself on this journey. Much of your inner life has been revealed; these voices are no longer strangers to you. You can recognize them now, call them by name. They are often well-meaning, trying in their own way to keep you safe. Although some of the assumptions they operate from may be outdated, they forget that you're constantly changing; who you were at ten, at twenty, is not who you are now." She paused.

I was staring at the flame of the candle, watching it flicker and dance ever so slightly.

"The choice is yours—who do you want to call upon at any given moment: Faith, Compassion, Forgiveness, Curiosity, Judgment, Criticism, Shame, or Cynicism? They are all here. Who will you cast in the leading role? Who only has a few lines in their cameo appearance? Remember, you're the author of the script and producer of the screenplay. It's your life. Your mind is very sharp but it cannot find the way alone. It will never figure a way out of your confusion; you must rely on your body as well. Pay attention to both your mind and body, and when in doubt, listen to your heart; it will never lead you astray."

I had this overwhelming urge to start digging. I listened to it. At first, I only pawed lightly at the dirt but before I knew it, I was digging furiously with my nose to the ground. I felt her eyes upon me and looked to the Fox as if to say *Don't just sit there, help me dig.* From her seated position, she rose and pounced. Her nose landed first, on top of the spot where I had been digging. She swiftly clawed at the dirt with equal intensity. I was grateful she didn't ask what we were digging for because I had no idea. I was even more grateful the dirt was soft. It was freeing to just listen to my instincts and not to have to have an explanation or reason to follow it, to just follow it, to let it lead me into the unknown, something my mind resisted. Moments later I had uncovered a root. It glowed with luminosity.

When I touched it, my left front paw transformed back into my hand, sending a ripple up my arm across my chest. I lightly pinched the root with my index finger and thumb. It had a pulse. I looked from the root to the Fox, sensing my time with her was nearly over. I was careful to dig with my right paw around it but one swipe uncovered more of the root below and I accidentally touched it. Another ripple transformed my claws into fingers, and my fur became skin up my arm. As the energy rippled up to meet in my chest, an undulation of heat swept down along my spine into my legs. I didn't have to look to know what was happening, but I did. I was in downward dog pose now; the last vestige of my animal body to go was my bushy tail.

I turned back to the root and gripped it with both hands,

expecting to pull it out. I heard the Fox snarl. The root had a force that began to pull me underground. I leaned back, bending my knees, digging my heels into the earth. I tried bracing myself so as not to get sucked in. I wanted to dislodge it. *If this is the weed of shame I'm going to pull it out by its root.*

The harder I tried to hold my ground and pull, the more the root pulled me in. During this tug of war, the root didn't give an inch. It ran too deep. I was no match for it; I was losing my footing.

I turned to look at the Fox for help. She watched with amusement, her black gums turned up towards her ears. My hands were now adhered to the root. I couldn't let go, nor could I resist for much longer. I remembered my last struggle with Forgiveness when I wanted to swim back to the surface and she kept pulling me under. *Shit, fighting isn't the response that is called for here. I am meant to surrender.* I relaxed my muscles to the force of the root, diving headfirst into the earth as if it were water.

The pull of this root became my guide. Its glaring green glow was in stark contrast to the darkness around us. *I'm okay. I'm okay.* I took a quick inventory of my body and I felt intact. *I'm okay. Maybe I'm a little slow on learning to surrender, so it's still not my first reflex. Eventually, I'll learn to do this with more grace.*

I tuned in as best I could to my descent. I couldn't detect any turns either way. Wherever we were headed, we were beelining for it. I tried to imagine where I was going. I wasn't left guessing for long.

Ian was delivering extra dining room chairs to Jim and Jocelyn's house for their party celebrating Mad Hatter Day.

They did it every year regardless of what day of the week it fell. Everyone loved it. The ticket for admission was to come in a silly hat. One couldn't help but smile and laugh throughout the party. Even the kids invited their friends.

Ian had a chair under each arm when Jim answered the door. "Hey, how are preparations going?" Ian asked Jim as he handed off the chairs.

"Ask Jocelyn." Jim took the chairs. "She's got a list in her head I'm sure I'm not aware of."

Ian smiled as he walked back to the car for the other two chairs. Sarah and Jocelyn were similar that way, tending to all the invisible aspects of what made the party flow. Jim had left the door open. As he walked through it he asked Jocelyn, "Where do you want these?"

"Over there together next to the wall and that little make-shift side table I stole from Sam's bedroom. I think we're set for the seating now. You're bringing the case of red and extra glasses early, right? I want to set up the bar over here."

Ian nodded. "The glasses are already on the front stoop. I'll go get the wine from my car now."

Jocelyn followed Ian to the front door. "Excellent, that frees up my mind to worry about something else. Actually, except for the food, we're good—but that's Jim's department."

When Ian came in with the case of wine, he put it by the living room bar. He heard Jim chopping in the kitchen. "Hey old man, do you need any help in there?"

"I wouldn't refuse it. There's an apron on the back of that chair—or at least there was wherever that chair went." Jim was looking around for it.

Jocelyn handed it to Ian. "Nothing escapes my notice."

She reached for her water glass.

Ian slipped the loop to the denim apron over his head and tied it behind his back. Jocelyn started unpacking the wine glasses. "Jeremy asked me if it was okay to have a beer at the party."

Jim stopped chopping. "What did you tell him? The last thing we need is a lawsuit for serving minors. If he has one his friends will think it's okay."

"I told him if he still wanted one after the party he was welcome to it, but he was not to drink during the party or allow his friends to; it was too risky. We are in new territory now. I hope he can think through the unintended consequences of his behavior and not just see us as denying him. You know how the forbidden becomes the wanted."

"I'll have a talk with him," Jim said. "Let's separate the sodas from the bar; it might be easier to notice if someone underage is helping themselves. Maybe between the three of us we can keep an eye on foot traffic to the bar."

"Not exactly a leverage point but a worthy redesign in the system. I'll put the bucket of ice on the porch with different glasses." She continued unpacking and arranging the wine glasses. "Speaking of leverage points, after hearing Tristan and Aza reference Donella Meadows' approach to leverage during the podcast, I've been meaning to resurrect her article. I finally reread it yesterday."[38] Jocelyn held a wine glass up to the light and saw it still had lipstick marks on it. She set it aside. "She was so wise, I wish she were still alive. I would have loved to listen to her and Resmaa Menakem have a conversation. Her willingness

[38] Donella Meadows, "Leverage Points: Places to Intervene in a System", Sustainability Institute, 1999. http://www.donellameadows.org/wp-content/userfiles/Leverage_Points.pdf.

to revise her own thinking was evidenced in the way she wrote. Initially she thought the most effective place to intervene in a system was at the level of mindsets or paradigm that the system was designed from—the beliefs that inform the goals, rules, and rewards."

Ian poured himself a glass of water. "That's why they pay us the big bucks as consultants. Working at the level of culture means questioning long-held beliefs about how things are done."

"True, being anti-racist is another paradigm. It's challenging, though, to replace deeply rooted beliefs." She kept unpacking the glasses, looking more closely at the rim. "I'd forgotten when she revised the list, she added that the power to transcend paradigms as holding the most leverage, to realize that no paradigm is necessarily 'true.'"

Jim chimed in, "What an appropriate theme for Mad Hatter Day, that there is no certainty to any of it, we can let go of it all. Ian, do you have a themed wine for that?"

"Hmm, I'll have to think about that a bit." He had finished chopping the yellow onion. "Where do you want this?" He wiped the corner of his eye with the back of his hand as he had started to tear.

"In the pan, on low heat. I need to caramelize it." Jim pointed with his elbow. "Next I need sliced red onions for a Greek salad." He added, "Please."

"My pleasure. So, the question is how does one transcend paradigms?" Ian rinsed the knife and sharpened it.

"Exactly, what does?" Jocelyn said, thinking of Resmaa's reference that we are bodies of culture. "I think this is where the body comes in, because the body gives us a direct experience of something by passing the mind in ways that's irrefutable."

Ian was back in his bedroom the night Rumored Woman appeared and disappeared with Sarah. He barely heard what Jocelyn was saying.

"...the body also has limits whereas our minds don't. We resist limits; we think it curbs our freedom. What if it's just the opposite?" Jocelyn carried the empty box towards the garage.

Ian heard the onions sizzling in the pan. Jim stirred them and turned down the heat, and pressed on the fan. "One of our partners at the law firm was diagnosed with cancer last year, stage four. Faced with his mortality, he retired. He wanted to spend his remaining time with his grandchildren. I heard last week he is in remission. Maybe just removing himself from the stress of work gave him his life back."

Jocelyn walked back in. "I saw his wife, Becca, in the grocery store the other day. She said he's never felt better. Life's a mystery. Who would have guessed? She said she had been after him for years to slow down, take a vacation, but he was always taking work home with him." She glared at Jim, clearing her throat to have him look up at her. "His favorite excuse was 'after the next case.'"

"My wife is about as subtle as a brick bat at times. I hear you. Less is more."

Ian mindlessly sliced the onion, still preoccupied with thoughts of Sarah. He swept the slices into the bowl. "I'm ready for my next assignment, boss." He preferred to linger here, rather than return to his empty home. Anticipating tonight's party lifted his spirits.

CHAPTER 17

RE-LEASE

MY HANDS BROKE through the surface first and gripped the edge of the ground as if it were the side of a pool. I attempted to hoist myself up. My triceps vibrated and launched a protest at being asked to support my weight. *Shit, I'm not strong enough.* The best I could do for a moment was a chin up before my arms gave way. It was long enough for me to see the glint of the bars of the cage and Rage curled up in the corner, asleep. My legs were useless; they had no purchase on anything solid and my hands were cramping from holding on to the ledge. Letting go wasn't an option. I hoped Rage, unlike me, was a light sleeper and called out, "A little help here please."

I heard her stir and maybe roll. I attempted to bring my chin back to the edge but my arm muscles were toast. She wasn't that far from where I hung, maybe an arm's length.

"Hey, wake up! I need your help." *So much for my defense system at the ready. Who knew Rage slept on the job.* I feared she would wake cranky like me.

She rolled over and the weight of her shoulder landed directly on my fingers, crushing them into the ground.

I yelled, "Ow! Get off me."

That woke her. Rage sprung to her feet. "What the fuck." She wasted no time on questions before she stamped her foot across my fingers and started to twist.

I screamed in pain, "Nooooo, stop it's me." If she wanted to torture me in that moment she couldn't have devised a more effective measure. I was afraid the weight of her feet were the only thing anchoring me. I was sure she had broken all my fingers.

"Oh shit," was all I heard before I felt her vice grip over my wrists pulling me up. "I'm so sorry, I didn't know it was you."

When my hips had cleared the edge, I brought my right knee up onto the ground. "Okay, you can let go now. I need my hands." *What's left of them.* "You might have asked first and pounced second." My fingers were throbbing but miraculously they all bent back and forth at my first request. My skin was rubbed raw in places. I bent over, resting my palms on my knees to catch my breath. On my last visit I never appreciated just how small her living space was. There was hardly room for one let alone two.

I used the support of the bar to stand. She had taken a step back. Her mouth hung slightly open as if she was going to say something but couldn't find the words. She had already apologized. It was an understandable mistake, an unfortunate one but still understandable as reactivity was in her DNA.

I turned towards her and hugged her hello. We had always

had bars between us before. At first she stiffened to my touch; her arms remained by her sides like a board. It was a one-sided embrace, as if she had no idea how to respond. *Is this her first hug?* I softly said, "It's okay, I'm not angry at you. How could you know, you were woken from a sound sleep."

Slowly she melted in my arms. Her shoulders rounded towards me and her hands hesitantly touched my thighs. I kept holding her close. It became obvious she had been holding her breath as she exhaled and her chest softened. Her knees bent a bit as she sank more towards me. One of her hands left my thigh; she placed it on my lower back.

I breathed deeply again. "It's okay, I'm not going anywhere. I'm here, I came back for you."

Her other arm wrapped around my shoulder and she squeezed me closer to her, letting her body mold to mine. Her hips and mine were no longer apart. Her breaths were steady and slow. I'd been watching the bars of the cage bending as she gave herself over to our embrace. She couldn't see it. Her back was turned to the ever-expanding opening.

I whispered in her ear, "I found the key."

She squeezed me again and her hips wiggled a bit. "I knew you would. I was counting on you."

I wiggled in response just before I released her from my embrace. I put my hands on her upper arms and gently rotated her. She was more like putty in my hands now than the armor of moments ago. *Everything can change in an instant.*

I expected her to stride out as soon as she saw the freedom that awaited her. Instead she just stood there. Freedom beckoned but she met it with stillness and silence.

These were new moves in Rage's repertoire, not the reactivity, pacing, force of destruction, and annihilation I'd left behind and met just moments before. *Who is she becoming? How will she move in the world when she is no longer caged?* I waited alongside her to make the first move.

She pivoted back towards me to say, "I want to leave the way you came. Take me with you."

I looked down, behind my feet. The hole was gone. "Really? Why not just walk out, that would be infinitely easier. Especially since the portal that brought me here has closed."

Rage persisted, as she scuffled her feet over the surface. "How did you find it?"

"I'm not exactly sure. I had a compulsion to dig and I listened to it. But I had claws then, I was a fox."

She turned to look back at me, her eyes were wide, brows lifted. "A fox, an owl—how about you teach me how to shapeshift?"

"I think you just did, when we embraced. There's something different about you, softer. I can hear it in your tone of voice. Do you sense a change?"

She embraced herself, rubbing the palms of her hands down the outside of her arms and then rested them on the small of her back, her elbows out. Her chest opened as her shoulders moved back. "I do. It's subtle, but yes. I feel more settled, less vigilant. Still, I'd been keen to have wings or fins or hooves."

I squatted down. "Don't discount the subtle shifts. Sometimes that's all it takes to open up new worlds and perspectives for how to move differently in the same territory." I half heartedly tried to dig with my fingers but the top layer was far too tough to penetrate. "I'll admit, claws would be an advantage now." Even my feeble attempts at scratching the surface had pushed dirt up under my nails, sending needle-sharp spikes into the tender places. I winced at the pain and stopped. No more torture. I abandoned the effort and looked up.

Rage offered me a hand and pulled me to my feet. "I've tried to dig myself out, but it never worked."

I scanned the area for a sharp flat rock or a thick stick to scratch the earth with, but her cage was swept clean. Outside the cage were lava rock formations and the one tree. I walked through the opening and picked up a fallen branch. It was too dried out to withstand any pressure; it just snapped. The volcano was hidden from view. *How long ago did it erupt?*

Rage became defensive hearing my attribution. "It wasn't me, I inherited this landscape."

I walked about looking for loose lava rocks in the shape of a triangle. I handed one through the bars for Rage to use. A weariness descended on me as I yawned. I went to sit for a moment on the lava rocks but shot back up immediately as my bare ass touched cold water. Upon closer examination, a small pool was caught in a hollow; it was hard to see its perimeter. I grazed my fingers along the surface of the water, to find its edges, then tested again with my hand to be sure I'd found a dry spot to sit beside it. I plunked down and watched Rage crouched over, digging steadily.

A stray hair was tangled in my eyelashes, it tickled my forehead. My fingers searched for it to sweep it back behind my ear. My touch was gritty, my skin was covered in dirt and grime. This journey was offering me an intimate relationship with the element of earth. I'd never appreciated how solid the ground was under my feet when I walked, how the earth always supported me. I asked Rage, who was diligently digging, "Are you making any progress over there?"

317

She rebuked my question. "You mean while you sit there watching me? No not really, this would go better with the two of us."

I patted the rock next to me. "I'm ready to help, but let's take a different approach. Let's try softening the ground up by using this water. Come over here next to the source. There's not much, so we can't afford to waste it in transit."

Rage hadn't left her cage yet. I watched her hesitate for a moment and then plunge through the opening. Her first taste of freedom. I wanted to ask her how she felt, as if she wasn't me. I listened inside instead. I felt more spacious, less dense.

As she walked over and peered at the puddle she said, "I miss water. I've been so mud-encrusted for years, I've begun to confuse it for my skin. The only time I get to shower is when it rains."

Being mud-encrusted. The image rang a bell but I dismissed it to get to work. I straddled the rock that held the puddle and tightly pressed my cupped hands together as I dunked them in the cool water. I tried to eliminate any space between my fingers where the precious water could escape. Carefully I lifted the ladle of my hands then tipped it to the nearest ground, repeating the gesture several times. While the dirt darkened at first, the water formed a tiny rivulet and ran off until it was absorbed.

"It's been a long time since this hardpan has been culti-vated." I reached down to feel if the ground was softening at all. I rubbed it with my fingers. It had just barely penetrated the surface. "This is going to be slow going." I looked at the tiny pool wondering if there would be enough to make a difference. "Let's go more slowly so as not to waste any more water."

I scooped a single palm full and let it drizzle from my hand this time, not dumping it. Rage was crouched below, rubbing the drops into the parched ground. A clump of hair was dangling in front of my eyes, blocking my view of how the ground was drinking it in. As I reached up to tuck it back behind my ear, a single drop of water fell from my fingertips and landed on Rage's face. A streak ran down her left cheek, another tiny rivulet. I was struck by how similar she was to the landscape we were now tending, hoping to leave behind.

I paused to stare at her and she stopped, looking up at me. The image appealed to me. It was like reverse makeup. Instead of applying it to hide one's face I was revealing her. I lightly dipped my index finger onto the surface of the water this time and barely touched her opposite cheek, releasing a second drip. A mirror image appeared; streaks of her real skin emerged.

Rage asked, "Are we face painting now? I thought we were digging?" Her voice was laced with a hint of irritation. I heard the familiar part of me speak. When I settled into a job to do, even if I didn't like what I was doing, I resented any distractions, anything that delayed me from finishing it.

I tilted my head. "Yes, not so much face painting as uncovering, revealing. I'd become accustomed to your grime-tainted skin and I forgot how underneath you might look different. Do you mind if I continue?"

She paused again, her tone warming, "Honestly, it's unsettling to have this kind of attention paid to me, literally kind attention. Part of me wants to get back to digging, to be in motion doing something productive and another part of me wants to just be still here with you, let you really see me."

Her eyes were looking away and back at me as she spoke, sending mixed messages: *Come close, go away.* I waited for a congruent signal.

She continued. "Even though I think I know you so well, I also feel like I hardly know you. I want to be known by you and long to have you know me. Do you ever feel two conflicting pulls within you?"

I lifted my hair up off my neck and pulled it to my right side. "All the time."

Now as she steadily looked up at me she asked, "So what do you do?"

"I've tended to favor the stay in motion option. *My driver.* Being productive gives me a false sense of security that I know what's going on, that I'm in control. It's probably time to break this habit, to stop perpetuating the illusion of control it offers me when I'm consumed by what I'm supposed to do."

I went silent and just sat there, taking in our surroundings. I began to listen to my inner landscape; the settled spaciousness hadn't left me. I still felt weary, bone tired. Moving felt like it would be an effort. I wiggled my toes.

She bent at the waist, letting her head and arms hang down. I was looking at a curtain of hair as she spoke. "I'm not fond of being still. Even in this cage I tend to pace. It's not like I can get anywhere, but the perpetual motion keeps me occupied." She unfolded back to upright, her elbows bent in two triangles with her hands on her waist. She twisted from side to side.

I felt my own lower back in need of release. Her stillness of a moment ago was replaced by movement. "There was a time when I would hear this sentence in my head: *an equal and opposite force.* I was never really sure what it meant. Intellectually I know it's the tension between the opposites, like stillness and motion. Now I'm wondering if it's about something else?

What if it isn't about collapsing the tension to favor one side?"

Rage continued to twist slowly back and forth.

"I'm starting to sense a third option. What if I can honor both these conflicting signals? What if both can be true at the same time and I make space for them? I tend to ignore my body telling me I'm tired and push through it to keep working, or put off the pressure in my bladder that tells me it's time to pee. Sometimes I even resent that I have to stop what I'm doing to go to the bathroom. How crazy is that? When I get on a roll, my own bodily needs feel like an interruption, needs like sleep or hunger. I become deaf to them."

Rage nodded. "I know the feeling. Why do we do it?"

"I have an assumption I won't get my momentum back if I pause. My head wants to keep going, ignoring my body and tuning out my heart. The world of sensations and sensuality is lost on me when my head takes over, when fear takes over." *Fear lives in my head, not my heart. It's an imagined future, it's not real.* "My heart wants time to be still, to feel, to accept what's happening even when my mind doesn't 'like it.' But my head typically wins the argument. I stay in motion physically and mentally, taking too much on, feeling responsible and carrying an unrealistic burden on my shoulders, until eventually my body gives out. I hit a wall, a limit. I'm not paying attention anymore as I move through the world and I have an accident. I trip and fall, I stub and break a toe, or turn my ankle."

Break and brake, it's no accident these two words sound the same. "Finally I'm forced to be still, forced to come to terms with all that I've been holding at bay by being in motion. When I'm free to move again, I have to take it slower, test if I've mended." I looked directly into her eyes. "There's no need to rush. Let's take this slow, let's get to know one another."

Rage let her arms drop and nodded. She bent over and dipped her middle finger in the water. Her gesture took me back to walking in and out of church, the ritual of dipping my finger in the holy water and making the sign of the cross on my forehead, center of my chest, my left and then right shoulder.

She placed a drop on my forehead, between my eyebrows. It trickled down the ridge of my nose. She repeated the gesture, this time touching my throat above my clavicle. The drop tickled as it traveled on my chest between my breasts. As I looked down I could barely see the moistened path but I felt it. Her finger touched me again just below my belly button. Each sensation of the drop of water on top of my skin helped me drop into myself, reinhabiting my body, not just my mind.

She started stripping off her grimy top and pants, shedding them like a snake discards the sheath of its old skin. Her body still had the outline of her clothes. Except now she was wearing an outfit of pale creamy skin that met filth at the borders. Her neck and face were the dirtiest. I wanted to reveal more of her face and dipped both my left and right index fingers in the water, pressing them to the center of her forehead and drawing them away to her hairline, as if pushing the curtains open on a window. Next, I touched my wet forefingers just below her ears and traced them down along her jawline, meeting at the bottom of her chin. Last, I licked my own lips, moistening them, and took her face in my hands. I kissed her European style, first on her left cheek and then on the right. My lip prints were barely visible, yet she and I both felt them.

Who is she now? I cannot call her Rage. She stood before me, transformed into a centered warrior, one I loved and who I knew loved me. The hesitancy between us had fallen away, replaced with a peacefulness. I returned to scooping and slowly drizzling the water again, while she stirred it. Our movements were less mechanical, more ritualistic, as we prepared the ground before us. A bond continued to grow between us as we worked, one even stronger than the steel bars in the background.

I bent down to pick up the lava stone. Instead of digging, I started tracing tiny circles, mixing the water and dirt into a paste. We wordlessly switched roles as she began to drip the water. As I stirred, my hand moved counterclockwise in slightly widening circles. The top layer of mud grew with bottom layers giving way slowly. I paused to admire our progress. It looked like a slice of a tree before me, rings of ever-widening circles indicating the age of the tree. It was just barely wide enough for my feet to stand within.

A shudder of recognition from a former dream came rushing in, when I was balancing on a towering pole, not even the width of my feet, my toes curled around its edge. I struggled to steady myself on it as I tried not to look down. The ground was hundreds of feet below me. It was like a telephone pole but with no wires of connection. I was terrified of losing my balance, certain if I did I would fall to my death.

Slowly, I squatted to hold on to the base of the pole and realized my mistake. I wasn't any more stable crouching. There wasn't enough room to support me. Looking down made me dizzy. I was afraid to stand up again, convinced I'd lose my balance. Gradually I wrapped my legs around it, crossing my feet at the ankles and hugging the pole with my arms, my hands gripping my forearms. Temporarily, I felt far more safe and stable until the weight of me was too much for my strength to hold up. I started slipping down the pole.

The wood was rough and drove splinters into the inside of my arms and inner thighs as I slid; the sensation of being stabbed with a multitude of needles over and over again was too torturous. Reluctantly, I released my arms and legs from the pole, falling backwards in a rapidly accelerated descent. I knew the only hope I had of surviving was to slow down. I concentrated with all my being on the word *slow* and remarkably the pace of my descent lessened until I was nearly suspended— and then abruptly hit the ground. The impact startled me. I looked up to see Rage looking down at me.

She asked, "Where did you go?"

"It was a dream I'd had years ago. Honestly, it's hard to say these days what's a waking dream and what's a night dream. Something in the pattern of the mud brought it back and I slipped into it again."

"What was the dream trying to tell you?"

"That I'd lost my balance, my connection to the ground. That holding on so tightly in fear was only making matters worse. I need to let go and slow down if I want to live."

"Did you slow down?"

"Surprisingly yes, in the midst of a freefall, just by concentrating on it. Dreams have a way of defying the laws of physics. For that matter, my reality here has been defying them as well. So let's take that as a hint. Let's collectively concentrate on what we want: an opening, a way out of this arid, barren landscape."

"Agreed, I'm more than ready to alter my experience."

Alter and altar, same-sounding words, their meanings mingling in my mind. I bowed before my altar, and it altered my experience of my day, my life.

I continued stirring counterclockwise in slowly widening circles. When nothing changed for the next ten minutes I started to doubt our collective powers of concentration, until I scuffed over something solid. I released the stone to have direct contact with my fingers, touching something slimy that moved in response. My hand instinctively jerked back, afraid I'd touched a snake. I wasn't fond of snakes.

The surrounding ground was warmer. Holding the stone had insulated me from sensing the temperature change. When I touched it again to be sure, it was even warmer than the ground. It had a definite pulse. I kept two fingers on it and lay down on my stomach. Rage followed my lead, lying down across from me and placing her index finger beside mine. I moved my hand away so she could have direct contact.

I asked, "Can you feel its pulse?"

She nodded. It occurred to me this landscape would no longer be her home, our home. We'd found our way out.

She said, "Something's happening."

The ground was peeling away to reveal the root like the one that had brought me here. I reached back to touch it again, and this time I was able to wrap my fingers completely around it, feeling its pulse in the palm of my hand. Its pull was growing stronger.

There was no time to explain. "This is our opening, I hope you are ready to go." As I spoke, more of the ground surrounding the root was giving way. Instinctively I reached for the root with my other hand and she followed my lead again. Our four hands stacked one above the other, we rested on our elbows.

The heat of the ground warmed my belly and the tops of my thighs. I wished I'd told her more of the story of how I arrived.

I said, "Trust me, things are not what they seem; close your eyes and stay with me. Just don't resist this pull, let it guide us out of here. You will be okay."

Her face was remarkably calm, and in her eyes I recognized a glimmer of hope. I wanted to reach out to assure her but I didn't want to risk letting go. I bowed my forehead to touch her forehead. My hands began to disappear into the earth.

The pull was stronger than I remembered. The familiar sensation of being sloughed moved up my forearms as my elbows submerged. My face was less than an inch from being swallowed into solid ground. I took my own advice and closed my eyes, concentrating on the opening, on staying with this pulse. I prayed Rage could leave her inclination to fight behind and surrender gracefully. My shoulders and rib cage were swallowed next, followed by my hips, thighs, and calves. It felt like I was being dragged against sandpaper, with a single downward motion towards my ankles. It was bearable.

When the sensation changed to silk against my skin, I opened my eyes. I knew we were below ground; there was no horizon. It wasn't totally dark. There was a mix of colors emanating from the root, a vibrant blue and violet with a green hue surrounding it. The iridescence resembled a black pearl. The pull of our root held my hands like a magnetic force. Letting go wasn't even an option at the moment. Our speed increased as we descended along ever-narrowing turns of a spiral. It was eerily silent. The light pressure against my face felt like a cloth across my mouth, deterring me from trying to speak. I trusted she was with me, hoping she was as calm as when I last saw her.

My grip began to slip, though I didn't think I had loosened it. My body felt like I was bathing in rose petals. The colors that had emanated from the root were now the predominant colors surrounding us, the root itself nearly invisible. The only way I knew it was still there was the sensation of it slipping through my hands as it pulled me onward.

Up ahead I saw something familiar, a silver flash in the distance. We were heading straight for it. It grew brighter with each moment. *The Hooks.* I instinctively let go. Without the pull of the root, my movement slowed until I was knocked forward from something colliding with me from behind.

I heard, "Jesus Christ, what did you do that for?"

Well perhaps her name is still fitting. As she yelled at me, I recognized she didn't much like surprises; they had a way of ticking her off. When I moved to regain my balance I felt the propulsion that only a fin offers. I looked down to confirm my suspicion. I'd become a mermaid again, we were underwater.

Her shapeshifting wish was granted—we were both mermaids. I wondered how long it would take for her to notice. I mildly defended myself. "Letting go was a necessity, an instinct I listened to, besides would you have listened to me if I told you to let go?"

She replied, "I don't know, but I would have liked the chance to find out."

An undertow was carrying us towards the hooks. The flash caught Rage's eye and she asked, "What's that up ahead, that flickering light?"

"If my hunch is correct it's a hook. I was visiting it just before I met you the first time."

"A hook? What the hell are you talking about?"

"Like I said before we descended, things are not what they seem. There are more possibilities than what we've come to expect. Be open." I flicked my fin and swam in circles around her.

She noticed, "Holy shit, you did it again, you're a mermaid!"

I smiled knowingly. "Look down. You got your wish."

Her hands flew to her hips and former legs. She studied herself and looked up with her mouth hanging open.

"Are you ready to try out your new fin?"

"Absolutely, can't wait." She flicked her fin, swimming away swiftly. She was a natural. I caught up to her. Her arms were out in front, carving the water with her hands. She paused and spun in circles. The former filth outline of her clothes had disappeared; she had a luminosity about her skin that shimmered. She stroked her upper arm with the opposite hand saying, "I'm so smooth and silky and clean. I could get used to this. Is this our new home?"

My mind flashed to Ian and our home together. "As wonderful as it is, my hope is it's temporary, part of the journey." I swam alongside her. "There's so much of this story I've not shared with you. Let's pause a moment and let me catch you up."

We were swimming along the edge of a reef. I found a nook I could rest against, to stay still. She did the same. "Here are the headlines of a much longer story. When I first met Forgiveness, I was filled with grief. It was her guidance that finally allowed me to surrender to the depths of my feelings. She was a mermaid too. Did I mention her to you yet?"

She shook her head from side to side. "No, you have a

penchant for leaving out essential details."

"Well she is, with a little luck she is hanging around these reefs and we'll meet up with her again. She is the one who first introduced me to the Hooks."

"I still have no idea what you're talking about. How did you have a conversation with a hook?"

I said, "I don't blame you for being confused. It's disorienting to recognize everything outside is actually a part of me—even you and I, we are one. This hook represents the layers of lies I have chosen to believe in and live by. My addictive patterns of thought and actions have kept me caught up in a life that's not necessarily of my own choosing, my default life. I was starting to understand the power I've given these lies to derail me when I was catapulted from here to come pay you my first visit as an owl. When I left, to find the key, I had to hunt down buried memories. That's when I became a fox, to learn to listen to my instincts and intuition, to soften rather than constrict. Now that I'm back here with you, I gather there is something for both of us to hear if you are willing?"

Her brows were initially furrowed and then one raised upwards. I imagined the adjustments of being free from her cage would have been challenging enough without having to make sense of roots, shapeshifting, and conversations with hooks. Even the thrill of being a mermaid was a lot to take in.

With a bit of an edge on her voice she said, "I'm here aren't I?"

I reached for her shoulder and squeezed it gently. "Yes, you are and I'm grateful you wanted to come; I like your companionship. For now, all I expect you are going to have to do is listen, see if you can find a comfortable way to stretch out and relax."

Overall, I thought Rage was doing an impressive job keeping herself in check amidst this unknown territory. She did indeed find a reef of sorts nearby and lay down.

"I'm always on my feet, nearly always on guard until I drop from exhaustion." Her tone had softened. "I'd forgotten what it's like to simply rest, with no intention of sleeping. It feels like I'm laying down on the job. Maybe we've died and gone to heaven."

I hoped she was wrong, I had no intention of dying on this journey. I wanted to wake up soon in Ian's arms and discover that this was all just a wild dream. I turned my attention to the Hooks wondering if Forgiveness was anywhere nearby. I wasn't accustomed to being on this journey without my guides as companions. I had turned into the guide and I didn't feel qualified.

I traced my fingers lightly along the rounded surface of the metal. *Where did we leave off? Where will we pick up?* I didn't have to wait long.

Bubbles preceded the Hooks' deep voice. "Welcome back, we've been waiting for your return. Congratulations are in order as you found the key. We see you're not alone. A wise move to bring her with you. Introduce us, please."

What is her name now? I looked back to see her lift her head. I'd met her as Rage but sensed a series of transformations had taken place. Her presence, her voice, her strength had a different purpose. She still felt like a warrior to me albeit a more centered one. "Please meet my Peaceful Warrior."

She smiled and her eyes lit up at hearing her new name.

"We're here to listen, with our hearts and our minds."

CHAPTER 18

A-TENSION

THE HOOKS CONTINUED, "We left off speaking about the power you have to create your life just as you imagine. Do you remember how we spoke of how you give that power away?" A swell of bubbles streamed off the metal, revealing the direction of the current as they moved on an angle upwards.

Invisible forces made visible. I faintly recalled the conversation. Risking disapproval, I admitted to it. "Only vaguely, would you mind refreshing me before we go on? So much has happened since then." I picked under my nail at nothing and looked over at my Peaceful Warrior. She was watching a school of silver fish swim by.

The Hooks replied, "You'll want to remember regardless of what happens or risk repeating what you have forgotten. We don't wish to speak with you again in a few years. Pay close attention."

I felt sufficiently admonished and forewarned.

The Hooks continued, "When you get close to creating what you want, or when your life is going well, tell us what runs through your mind?"

"I start to doubt myself. I stop believing it's possible, that it's too good to be true. I begin to imagine all the things that can go wrong. I suspect there is something I haven't thought of that will cause everything to turn to shit."

"Precisely." A larger bubble emerged followed by a trail of smaller ones. "There comes a moment when your imagination stops serving you; it only distracts you and drains your energy with worry. Of course things will go wrong. The unexpected is inevitable. The future is not predictable, it demands you rise to the occasion, that you become resourceful and resilient."

I was running my fingers lengthwise along my scales. The sensation was hypnotic, smooth and slippery. I was tempted to count a row of them. "My worries gain momentum so quickly. I struggle to quiet this voice along with my fears. It's disabling; it's part of what causes me to lose faith in myself."

"You won't ever silence it, that's not the goal. We simply want you to stop believing it, because after all, it's about the future and worry doesn't have a crystal ball." The Hooks paused. A stingray flapped past us. "It's wise to listen at first. It's just looking out for your best interest. Sometimes fear helps you to be more prepared, to take in different perspectives. However, when you give it all your attention, it takes over, it takes center stage. It's not meant to be the leading actress in your life, more part of the ensemble."

I watched the patch of bubbles trail up. "Yes, if I listen to it too much it cripples me from taking action towards what I want. The cynic's voice takes over and I start believing I could never design the life I want to live."

"What is the life you want to live?" the Hooks asked.

I didn't hesitate. "One where Faith is my constant companion." My left hand went to gently rub the center space between my collar bones. "Not just called upon when things aren't going well, more an abiding presence." I looked around to see if she had returned. There was still no sign of her joining us.

The Hooks said, "It's a matter of choice, what voices you listen to and act upon. You'll need to remember your hands are on the dial of these voices. You get to decide whose voice matters, who you choose to believe. Why not dial down the voice of Worry and stop acting as if it's true? As we just said, it's not possible nor even desirable to silence your fears. There is good reason at times to be concerned. Just experiment for a while with dialing up the voice of Faith, from a whisper to your 'inside voice.' Offer it your undivided attention then act as if it's true."

I was trailing my hand through the water, making figure eights. "You make it sound so simple as if I could just decide and it would be so."

"What if it were that simple?" The bubbles naturally floated towards the surface. "What if it is all that simple? Why do you resist the elegance of life and wish to make it more complicated?"

"If it is this simple then why can't I do it? In my experience it's not this simple and I find it aggravating to hear you persist as if it were." I could see the warrior beside me rising to an alert position.

"The only reason you can't is because you don't believe

you can. Like I said, it's a matter of faith and faith is a matter of choice; it appears you're still more willing to be a victim."

That did it. Without even having to look I knew the heat wave behind me was coming from Rage. She felt like a volcano about to explode. I resisted the urge to duck and roll for cover; we were submerged in water after all. *What effect will this new element have on her? Air feeds flames, water douses it. Could she still be fiery now?*

My not-so-Peaceful Warrior blasted the Hooks. "Damn it, it's not true, she doesn't want to be a victim any more than me and I resent your accusations. You don't know what you're talking about so why don't you just shut the fuck up!"

Water didn't quell her fire. I was caught in the middle, witnessing Rage on the attack after we both agreed we were here to listen. I glared at her and she fell silent, but not still. She had risen up from the nook in the reef and was treading water beside me, ready to spring into action.

During their temporary truce I turned to her and asked, "What if it were true? What if the very act of you thinking you need to defend me arises from a belief of my being powerless, victimized? What if you *didn't* rush to my defense—at least if the threat isn't physical, only verbal?"

She treated it like a rhetorical question, giving me neither consent nor argument.

I continued. "In conversations, I'd like us to pause more often, slow things down. What if it is as easy as a choice I fail to make, to slow down long enough to discern whether a reaction is necessary? Without getting all pissed off again, are you willing to entertain the possibility? Will you slow down with me? After all, these are just words."

She settled back into her nook in the reef. I began to appreciate how hard it was for Rage to listen to anything that maligns me, it was as if she saw it as her job to defend me, against any potential threat, physical or verbal. *She has a hair trigger.*

I turned to the Hooks and said, "Okay, we are ready to listen again. You've touched a sore spot, but you knew that. In fact, I wonder if you weren't maybe goading us along a bit trying to provoke an outburst."

Silence was the only reply. Although if a hook could smile, I thought I sensed the hint of one. The Fox within me admired its wily ways. "You just proved your point—even reacting is a choice, just not a conscious one. Especially if my reptilian brain is activated by a perceived threat, whether it's real or imagined. When I let this take over, I become a victim of my own feelings or the feelings of those around me."

"Indeed." A single large bubble ascended. "Have you heard the quote by Eleanor Roosevelt, 'No one can make you feel inferior without your consent'?"

"No, but I like it." I looked back towards my Peaceful Warrior to see if she was paying attention. She didn't give me her eye.

"What we consent to is key. *Consensus reality* is another word for culture. Culture is a source of meaning in our lives...or not." Bubbles paused. "You may find the writings of Viktor Frankl helpful; he speaks to these questions you have about meaning and freedom. He wrote, 'Between stimulus and response there is a space. In that space is our power to choose our response. In our response lies our growth and our freedom.'"[39]

---

[39] Pursuit of Happiness, "Viktor Frankl", website. https://www.pursuit-of-happiness.org/history-of-happiness/viktor-frankl/.

Freedom is the magic word, it's what I crave. It hadn't occurred to me how I imprisoned myself until I met Rage in her cage.

~◎~

Ian booked his next client trip to Minneapolis with an extra night, giving himself the option to have another dinner with Ariel. He hadn't called her about it, and they never exchanged telephone numbers, although he knew the name of the shop and assumed if he rang it, she would answer. He hadn't decided yet if he wanted to pursue her and what it would mean for his relationship with Sarah—that was, if he even still had one.

On the one hand it was crazy: They lived in separate states, time zones even. However, on the other hand she was lovely, creative, and fun to be around. He'd enjoyed his time with her immensely when he wasn't feeling guilty about it. It was complicated. He hadn't asked if she was seeing anyone because he didn't want to lie about his circumstances. *I could just see her as friends.* Technically Sarah and he were separated at the moment. Ariel's initials in the corner of the painting pulled at him. She had signed it in red, the same color as her string bikini.

It was one of the many debates he was having lately in his head. His client wanted to book him during the time he had been protecting for their vacation to Kauai. It was paid work. He didn't want to go to Kauai alone. He did want a vacation, with Sarah.

He was standing in front of the painting now in his bedroom; he had hung it on the wall beside Sarah's side of the bed. The landscape scene that previously occupied the hook rested on the ground against the wall. He sensed it didn't belong here either, but he wasn't ready to move it.

～⊙～

Another single bubble escaped as the Hooks cleared their throat. "Ahhm." A stream of them followed. "You have a tremendous sensitivity to the world around you. You've developed a very strong defense mechanism for protection you believed you needed. She's lying behind you. She's forged a coat of armor that's nearly impossible to penetrate. However, your fix has backfired. Your attempt to avoid being vulnerable has insulated you from life's joy and not necessarily prevented the pain."

I nodded in agreement. "Go on, you have our attention."

"Without the ability to choose, your emotions tend to overwhelm you, even incapacitate you. It's not about stopping them or silencing them. On the contrary, it's about listening to yourself. Emotions are part of your energy body. Not feeling them causes stress. This energy needs a chance to move, it has information for you. It speaks to you in sensations and pulsations. You can communicate with your energy body through your breath and at times, visualizations of light. You need to take some time, some space, at least a breath or two to pause between feeling and acting. A pause that's long enough for choice to show up, otherwise you will be swept up in reactions, like we just witnessed."

I looked back at Rage to see if she was still paying attention. She caught my eye and nodded.

The Hooks continued, "Reactions have a way of compounding misunderstandings and hurt feelings, which can later justify the need for defense. It becomes its own self-sealing, self-fulfilling prophecy. The leverage here is with time, with a pause and in that space making a choice about what is real, what is needed."

"It's true, sometimes out of nowhere, for no good reason, I get hit with a wave of emotions that descend like heavy weather." I resettled myself on the reef.

The Hooks asked, "So what do you do when the storm comes?"

My hair was flowing with the current. I gathered it up and began to braid it. "Batten down the hatches, mostly by getting really busy. If I stay in motion, focused on tasks, engaged with other people, I can keep my feelings at bay."

"Ah, your second line of defense, busyness to keep your feelings from overwhelming you. It's another lie you tell yourself, sadly you are not alone. Work is the drug of choice of many, a way to distract and numb yourself from your feelings. Except one can never really quell the feelings that something is awry...forgive our pun that something isn't working."

Things are not what they seem.

The Hooks asked, "What's going on in your body now?"

"I feel restless, unsettled. My lower half is full of jitters. I wish I could shake them off."

"Try it. Listen to what your body is saying."

When I rose from the reef I stretched my arms and waved for my Peaceful Warrior to join me. We swam a short distance away. The reef beyond was completely different from my last visit; it had turned white.[40] Before it was teeming with life and

---

[40] Great Barrier Reef Foundation, "CORAL BLEACHING: What it is, how it happens and what we're doing to help.", website. https://www.barrierreef.org/the-reef/threats/coral-bleaching.

colorful fish but now the dark fish stood out in stark contrast as they swam past it. I noted there were less of them, either for lack of food or an inability to hide from their predators. We turned around and swam back towards the Hooks. I couldn't shake the feeling that I, humankind, was the perpetrator.

"When you have an uneasy feeling about something, what do you do with it?" The Hooks had been reading my mind.

I wasn't ready to be still so we both swam in wider circles around the Hooks. "I try to figure out the source of it, if it's me, if I've done something wrong. I attempt to find a way to resolve it or fix it."

"Feelings don't need to be figured out; we don't feel them with our mind. Only people who have no space for their feelings flee to their mind to escape them, or ask other people to justify them. Feelings are not rational. Again it's not complicated—your feelings are asking you to feel them. Pause and breathe through them, listen to them, move them, draw them, dance them. Mostly you name them and write about them. There are many options, the least effective being only to think about them. This tends to be very unsatisfying. They live on in your body as stress, uneasiness, as dis-ease. Left unattended, you become hyper vigilant, you never unwind. How often do you share your feelings with others?"

"Not that often, I don't think people are really interested. It's not exactly a conversation starter."

My Peaceful Warrior peeled off and chased the clouds of bubbles that were released whenever the Hooks spoke. "True, the most common question we hear in our culture is 'How are you doing?' It keeps us focused on what we are about to do or what we have done, as if productivity is a measure of our personal well-being, the way Gross National Product, GNP, allegedly measures a country's wealth. Busyness or business has become a kind of status, as if it's a reflection of your importance. The perception is if you have time on your hands you must either be a slacker or retired. You aren't the only one who focuses on *doing* to avoid *feeling*."

I stopped my swimming and sat down on the reef. "At the end of the day I reflect on what I accomplished, as if that was a measure of a good day. I don't recall the shape of the clouds or the sound of bird calls, mostly because I've not even noticed them. I've had my head down getting shit done. I've been busy."

My Peaceful Warrior came to sit beside me. A school of long silver fish was startled by the bubbles; they darted to the left and swiftly switched direction again.

The Hooks continued, "It's part of the invisible fabric of our culture. People ask us what we do for a living, implying what is most important to know about someone is their work. Why not ask: How is your heart today? How is your body today? What song is on your mind? What poetry have you read lately that you love? These are inwardly directed questions where we come to know a person by what they reveal about their inner state, not outward accomplishments or titles."

I cleared my throat. "What a different world that would be. I'd far prefer to be asked any of those questions instead of 'How are you doing?' Ironically, when I start to answer it, it forces me to think about what I was just doing—the past or what I plan to do next, the future—again not asking me to be present, to simply be in the conversation at that moment."

"Let us ask you now: How are you feeling? What are you paying attention to?"

"Ah, to know how I'm really feeling—not an easy question for me to answer. I often need to be alone or close my eyes to tune in."

"Go ahead, close your eyes if you like and check in. We are in no rush. You're safe here."

My Peaceful Warrior rested her hand on my shoulder. I closed my eyes. "My scalp feels tight in the back on my right side, not quite a headache but noticeable. The jitters in my legs are gone. I feel calmer in my chest." My right hand gently rubbed my chest. "More tender, softer."

"What about when you first wake in the morning—do you keep your eyes closed and tune into yourself as a way to start your day?"

"Sometimes. On weekends I may linger and fish for a dream. Over the last year I've been getting up earlier to bow, so I'm not rushing off to school. Before I bow I sense what I need to let go of to clear a space in me to speak my blessing."

"In a typical day, how much time feels spacious to you compared to compressed?" the Hooks asked.

My fingers were walking along the scales of my lap. "Ugh. Most of my days are overscheduled and pressured. I generally feel behind before the day's even begun. There's more to get done than I can possibly accomplish. I spend my days trying to tick off my never-ending to-do list, telling myself, *I just have to get to the end of a work project, finish grading my papers or reach the weekend, then I will have more time to relax.* But there's always something hanging over my head. I wake on the weekend seeing all the chores I've ignored during the week. I spend my Saturday and Sunday in catch-up mode in the garden or around the house. I'm on the move all day. Sadly though, no matter how much I accomplish, the feeling of accomplishment is fleeting; it gets overshadowed by everything that still needs my attention."

"It sounds exhausting." The Hooks continued, "When do you relax, on vacations?"

"No, it's the same pattern in a new place. Before leaving, I work extra hours so I depart exhausted. While we're on vacation there's a list of places we want to see, time spent figuring out routes, visiting hours, discovering great places to eat, packing and unpacking between hotels. We try to make the most of our time away."

"Your vacations don't sound very restful."

"They're not. I return to work behind again and have to put in extra hours to catch up. This is my life, and it's not working, to repeat your pun."

"No, sadly you are not alone. You're not the only one who is overscheduled, overcommitted, and short-changed on spare time."

"It's pathetic. On the weekend, if we make plans to host friends for dinner, I find I spend a good portion of the day cleaning the house, grocery shopping, planning the meal, setting the table and cooking. Even if I'm not doing those things, I'm anticipating when I will have to start and I feel squeezed."

"It sounds like you're not enjoying doing these tasks?"

"Not really, I'm wishing I was doing something else. I'm afraid I'm wishing my life away, missing it."

"You are. We are speaking to a core hook here. Who said vacuuming or planning a meal for friends can't be enjoyable? If you want to be somewhere else, doing something other than what you are doing, you are choosing not to be present, either consciously or unconsciously. Your attention is elsewhere.

Here's a little-known secret: Attention is the holy grail. It's an invisible holy grail you can drink from or discard, although we suggest you see it for the gold that it is. Drink from this cup and change your life."

I was leaning in now and my Peaceful Warrior had slipped her arm around my lower back. I was grateful she was paying attention. I needed her help to guard this holy grail. "Say more."

"By bringing your full attention to whatever you are doing at the moment, you make the simplest tasks remarkable. Time has a way of becoming spacious then, opening up. It's not about speed, it's about attention. Spacious time is available at any moment if we aren't rushing through the moment to get somewhere else, be with someone else, do something else. It's your measures of productivity and efficiency that have you objectifying and evaluating each moment to see if it is good enough."

"I know I should be more present. But I can't seem to land, to drop into the moment."

The Hooks said, "Stop measuring your moment and comparing it to a competing moment in your mind or the standard of your expectations. That's how your mind takes you elsewhere, telling you you're missing out on something or doing it wrong. What is actually happening is you are missing out on the moment in front of you. If you drop into that moment fully, I promise you: It will be spacious. Just feel the sensations in your body doing whatever tasks it is doing; give yourself over to them. It can be quite sensual. Look at the shapes before you with new eyes, as if you didn't know their names and are seeing them for the first time. How would you describe them to someone who is blind?"

My new eyes looked up to watch the circles bouncing into one another as ovals as triangles swam through them, dispersing these circular little worlds that flew higher and higher. *"Should" is a thief, robbing me of the present moment. It muscles in and grabs my attention, setting me up to be frustrated because it puts me at odds with whatever is happening in the moment. Attention is the holy grail.*

Ian's week of work in Minneapolis dragged on. Each night he debated with himself about calling the shop and decided it would be better to just show up on Friday night. Work ended at 4:20 p.m. and he jogged to his hotel room to change out of his professional attire in favor of a T-shirt and shorts. He wanted to appear casual even though inside he was a ball of nerves as he drove to see her.

He walked past the sweet smell of the ice cream parlor and glanced in the window of her shop. She was behind the cash register again, ringing up a customer. He kept walking. His heart was racing and his palms were sweating. He wiped them on his shorts and circled the block. It was 4:54 p.m. *Am I going in or walking by?* The time for procrastinating was over. Even though they might start out as friends, he knew when there was an attraction between two people, it wouldn't stop there. If he walked into that shop, he was making a choice to pursue another relationship.

When he smelled the waffle cones again, he stood still. *Nothing I eat nor buy is going to fill this emptiness I feel inside.* He admitted to himself that Ariel was no substitute for the longing he had for Sarah, maybe not even Sarah.

He returned to his rental car and drove in rush hour traffic to go eat dinner alone, again. The light ahead had turned yellow. He pulled up behind a long line of cars idling at the intersection and briefly rested his forehead on the top of the steering wheel. His heartbeat had returned to normal. The line had started to move; he wasn't sure if would make it. He didn't. It turned yellow and red again. He waited.

When Sarah chose to leave on her adventure he hadn't realized he would embark on his own. These last few months he had a taste of what it was like to live a lie as he withheld the truth about her sudden departure. Authenticity was a form of freedom he hadn't reflected on before he was forced to cover for her. The stress of maintaining a fabrication had invisibly taken a toll and caused him to initially isolate himself.

The light turned green and he lifted his foot off the brake.

∽◎∼

I asked, "But what about efficiency and productivity? There's gotta be a place for high standards."

The Hooks replied, "Yes, of course, when the goal is to be as efficient as possible to make something of the highest quality, by all means, reflect on your process and method and perfect it to the best of your ability. That is a quality of attention that is essential. It's just when we blanket this approach to everything, life becomes a transaction to be exchanged, controlled, and maximized. In that universe, the unexpected and the unplanned occurrence is a problem. Life isn't meant to be controlled, it can be trusted. The unexpected can also bring joy, surprise, wonder—depending on how we meet that moment. Even death can be a holy moment if we are present to it. You know this, you've been there. Resisting life is a death in itself, every moment."

My Peaceful Warrior spoke up. "I'm seeing a new role for me here. My vigilance has been in defense, in protection trying to keep her safe. Are you saying my job is to guard the holy grail, the quality of attention we bring, because this is what impacts the quality of our experience and our ability to respond?"

"Yes, the holy grail is attention, undivided attention, presence. When you are present, your time will be spacious. You will have to slow yourself down. By pausing there will be space to feel and time to choose your response. Multitasking is not about being present, it's about efficiency and about getting more things done in less time. This is how you squeeze yourself out, how you fragment your life into moments of compression. Tell us, what is essential for you to respond to? What do you see as your responsibilities?"

"I have a myriad of them: to my students, to my family and friends, to my community, and even to future generations—to leave our world a better place than I found it."

"What about your responsibilities to yourself?"

"You mean to take care that I eat and sleep well?"

"Yes, that's a start. I also mean the other dimensions of health. Like how your heart feels, listening to your longings? When do you make time for this deeper listening?"

"I'm honestly not very attentive to those," I admitted. "They tend to be last on the list."

The Hooks asked, "Why last priority, why not first? You are the instrument through which everything else is accomplished. If you are not well tuned, you will not play well. Our actions often speak volumes about our beliefs. It's telling that the first responsibility you list is to work, not to yourself. Why do these dimensions of your life not matter as much, nor count in importance?"

"Self-care is more of a concept, less a habit. My morning practice of bowing to the Great Mystery and saying my blessing is one way I tune myself."

"How long does that feeling last?"

"Maybe only a few minutes or maybe a few hours, rarely for the whole day. I've toyed with the idea of bowing several times a day like Muslims but at most I've added another bow at night. It's awkward to do if I'm not at home."

The bubbles released. "What if you just sat for a moment, with your palms resting open on top of one another in your lap? Simply take a moment to listen. You don't need to close your eyes, just soften your attention to the sensations in your body. This will bring you to the present moment."

Just thinking about it made me take a deep breath. Both of us let our hands rest in our lap. The iridescence of our scales glimmered. The current of the water was subtly pulling our fins and my thigh muscles tightened resisting it.

The Hooks continued. "This is a chance to push the reset button, to realign yourself. Why not listen *within* as much as you pay attention to the outer world?"

I found myself stretching, rolling my shoulders back, becoming more fluid. I'd been concentrating on what the Hooks were saying. I turned to look at my Peaceful Warrior.

She raised her eyebrows and said to me, "I like it. I'm ready to defend the Holy Grail of your attention." She ran her finger up my spine and I immediately sat up a bit straighter. The way

I centered myself when I rode a horse, shoulders back, elbows hanging loosely at my sides, calling upon my inner core to awaken, paying attention to my pelvis.

I smiled back. "It really isn't that complicated. We've got this."

She nodded.

The Hooks continued. "What about when you're sick or injured, how do you care for yourself?"

I immediately sagged a bit. "Those times are often tinged with disappointment. It feels like my body has let me down, preventing me from doing what I want. I'm impatient with the healing process."

"You don't want to spend time in the healing process, caring for yourself?"

I replied quickly. "Nope, does anybody?"

Bubbles started and dispersed and a yellow-and-black-striped fish tried to eat them. "Actually, some people are quite content to be home sick; it gives them the permission they need to shut the rest of the world out, a legitimate excuse. I gather this isn't true for you. What did you observe growing up?"

"I can't recall either of my parents ever being laid up in bed sick. Maybe they kept going during it given their unassailable work ethic. My dad's work revolved around extensive overseas travel so he was regularly gone for three to four weeks at a time. My mom stayed home and cared for me, our house, our friends and community. As far as I could tell, her job was never over; she had no vacation or time off. She did everything from mowing the lawn, to shoveling the snow and bailing out the basement when it rained. When I was older, I pitched in. I never saw my dad lift a finger, instead he readily handed out assignments. If he saw me coloring or reading when he left for work he would give me chores to do before he returned. It was best to be out of his sight."

The Hooks said, "You learned rest wasn't normal."

I nodded. "Sort of. When my dad was home, he rested. He sat in his black chair reading or watching TV, or sleeping off his hangover. The general attitude was he had deserved it but somehow neither my mum nor I hadn't earned the right to rest. Hmm."

There was a tap on my shoulder. My Peaceful Warrior's finger pointed towards a solo turtle, slowly flapping its front fins up and down as its back legs hung quietly behind. It cruised past us. The pattern around his head matched his fins; his oval eye looked briefly at us.

The Hooks asked, "What is one of your favorite childhood memories?"

"The summer I turned thirteen I learned that not all my father's trips were business trips. Apparently he was better at having fun than I knew. For years, during the last two weeks of August he had been going on an annual sailing vacation with 'the guys,' leaving my mum behind.

"When I became a teenager my mum put her foot down. She argued that I was old enough to tag along. I knew what that meant from hanging out with the older kids in the neighborhood. There was a price to pay, an unspoken rule. My admittance was contingent upon going along with what they wanted to do, not asserting my needs, essentially becoming invisible. Ironically that trip established a new definition of belonging I've been calling myself back to ever since."

A thin line of tiny bubbles arose. "Hmm, belonging, this

is a central longing. Tell us more."

"I'd never sailed before. My father taught me new nautical terms. He replaced the more familiar words of left and right with port and starboard; front and back became the bow and stern of the boat. Coming aboard was like entering a foreign land with new customs and language. However the lines of authority remained highly familiar. Clearly he was still captain, I was still crew. I literally swabbed the decks of footprints, spilled bits of food and drink after each sail. Whenever I hear halyards slapping against a mast it immediately brings me back to my V-bunk, as it was the last sound I heard before drifting off to sleep and the first upon waking.

"We docked near a restaurant where my parents spent most nights at the bar, so technically I was never that far away. My dad loved a crowd and often invited his favorite waiters, waitresses, and bartenders to join our 'family vacation' for a sail. We never knew who was coming until they walked down the dock. We would cast off each morning by ten a.m. with two dozen Dave's Donuts, twenty D'Angelos subs, and a well-stacked cooler of Michelob beer. The stern was a floating party."

"Did you join in on the party?"

"No, most of my time was spent at the bow, lying on my stomach, arms crossed in front with my chin resting on my hands. I'd scooch close to the edge, peering over so I could watch the waves break against the hull. The water, cleaved by the boat, would spray out in countless drops, arcing and returning to the ocean, over and over and over again. I mused on what it felt like to be the drops flying through the air. Is it thrilling or terrifying or perhaps a mix of both, like their version of a rollercoaster ride? Do they volunteer, wait in line or is it a random surprise who is swept up? I imagined some drops preferring the rush in the tumultuous white crests of the waves to the calmer, smooth blue expanse. Perhaps I was witnessing the lifetime of a drop of water, birthed on impact, fleetingly airborne and then dying with the return to the sea. Was it really that different from ours?

"On days with rougher seas, some of those drops would find me, forever separated from their companions. If the angle of the sun was just right, shimmering rainbows manifested in the mist tantalizingly within reach. I'd hold my hand out to catch myself a rainbow but it always slipped through my fingers. Periodically, someone would shout my way to be sure I was still awake. I was more than awake, I was rapt. I felt alive inside my skin. Maybe the sixty percent of me that was water was finally home. I never got seasick; on the contrary I'd fallen into sealove."

"You were having your own private party on the bow, with the elements." Bubbles danced upward.

"I was. I'd found my own separate haven. Few ventured forward to join me, and if they did, we rarely spoke. Some even napped, lulled to sleep by the rhythmic rise and fall of the bow. The sun-heated deck offered warmth below and a sunbeam blanket above.

"On particularly windy days, the conversation from the stern was drowned out by the rustle of the wind on the sails and the constant swish of the waves collapsing on one another. The absence of human voices invited a different kind of conversation with the ocean. I craved more fluency in this elemental communication the way others take an immersion course to study a foreign language. The water piqued my curiosity and invited me into a relationship I hadn't thought possible. I experienced the sea's infinite capacity to listen to whatever was on my mind without interruption all the while beckoning my imagination and offering me new perspectives. I never knew what a fabulous companion water could be and I've not forgotten it since. While my blood family inhabited the stern, I'd found a new sense of belonging on the bow." My hand traced the infinity sign in the water over and over again.

"My absence was dubbed as my 'bow time.' For more often than not I could be found there, either lying on my stomach or sitting on the boat's edge, my chest leaning against the lifelines for balance, my bare feet dangling off the rails, periodically kissed by rising waves. I was content to watch the mesmerizing patterns of the foam, to be swept up in my own engrossing conversation. Undoubtedly, our sailing vacation created a longing in me for being near, on, or in the ocean.

"What I couldn't know then is how the sailboat would become a metaphor for my life, navigating the constant tension between the social stern and the renewal of bow time. It's still not easy to choose between being with those I love and carving out the solo time to simply be with and reconnect to myself."

The Hooks were temporarily obscured by a school of white-and-black-striped fish with bright yellow lipstick swirling around us. Their top fins and tails were yellow, covered in a pattern of black polka dots. *How does nature paint each one with such perfection and uniqueness?* They swirled around us oblivious to our presence; one brushed up against my lap. I turned to see my Peaceful Warrior enthralled, her eyes light up, her fingers outstretched, not grasping as they swam around her arms as if they were just another branch of coral.

The Hooks waited until the clouds of yellow, black, and white receded. "Your bow time was an experience of presence within your being. You slipped into the seamlessness of life that is always available."

I nodded. "My bowing each morning is an invitation to this way of being. My blessing's opening line names it as 'embodied presence.'"

"When you live from this embodied knowing, there is a wordless intimacy; even your experience of self and 'other' disappears."

"True, it's just that I find it harder to access this in the presence of other people. At first I attributed it to being an introvert, but now I'm not so sure. When I was exposed to the Myers–Briggs Type indicator, it revealed how strong my preference for introversion is on the spectrum.[41] This came as a surprise to everyone but me. I'd developed a deceiving competence in extroversion as our family and societal culture tends to expect it. But it doesn't renew me, it drains me. Eventually I learned the cost for me of favoring the stern is this gradual, nearly imperceivable sensation that I'm no longer here, that I'm just 'tagging along' in my own life. That's when I hear, *Wish you were here*, my postcard moment." I felt a pressure run up my spine again and knew the touch came from my Peaceful Warrior. *Is she signaling that she will have my back and defend my bow time?*

The Hooks' voice hissed through a crack. "It is true, we have a culture that values extroversion over introversion, the exoteric outer world over the esoteric inner world. It's another

---

[41] The Myers Briggs Foundation, "MBTI Basics", website. https://www.myersbriggs.org/my-mbti-personality-type/mbti-basics/.

lie that one is more valuable than the other; beware of the false hierarchies. Your body, as an instrument, can tune to both. Be careful of the cultural messages that cause you to silence certain channels. We want you to remain connected."

"I'm starting to notice these hierarchies and symbols of them. I'm drawn to the infinity symbol, the inherent reciprocity of how opposing forces influence each other, and how differences can reside on a level playing field." I brought my palms towards each other without touching, to hold the invisible ball of energy between them. "I believe the energy between my hands is just as real as my hands. However, most of my life has been invested in the more tangible outer world that I can see with my eyes: earning my degrees, working, and socializing. I've kept my fascination with the unseen realms; the Egyptians' belief in the afterlife, the Celtics' Tír na n'Og, and the study of alchemy and mysticism under wraps. Even though I'm drawn to astrology, dream interpretation, and tarot, there's a part of me that has dismissed it as 'fringe.' I'm ready to trust the guidance these other ways of knowing offer me." After I finished speaking, another crink appeared on the curve of the Hooks.

The bubbles poured out of the crink faster as they spoke. "Living a more holistic life means retrieving those parts of ourselves that have been banished and marginalized to the periphery. We still value the mind over the body and spirit even though they are inextricably linked and interdependent. There are many other ways of knowing, the way symbols and archetypes convey meaning, how our intuition and instincts perceive the world and communicate with us. Ignore it at your peril."

I stretched upward, activating a fluid central cord that connected my gut to the crown of my head. "I'm wanting to be more inclusive of these diverse ways of knowing, trusting my intuition more, opening myself to a more sensual way of moving in the world where all my senses, inner and outer, inform my decision-making."

Most of the bubbles were pouring out of the crink now. "You get to decide. You do not have to accept what society says is important. Discern for yourself what is true, what living a good life means for you and how to really inhabit your life so you don't miss it, or have regrets on your deathbed."

I admitted, "I've not been making conscious choices, pausing to choose rather than react. It's disturbing to me how easily I've navigated the world on autopilot, giving it just enough attention to perform or be productive but not really giving anything my full attention because a part of me really wants to be somewhere else." A heaviness landed in my chest as I pondered how much of my life I may have missed. "These postcard moments trigger an instinct in me to retreat to my journal or a stroll on the beach to remember myself and inhabit my place in this world."

"Do you retreat to bow time after a postcard moment invites you back?"

I shook my head and looked down at my fin, gently rippling. "Sadly, not consistently. Following that impulse isn't always an option, especially in the midst of a myriad of commitments to other people. At least I tell myself it isn't. So instead, I tend to act like an old-fashioned switchboard operator. I answer the incoming calls from others as their lines light up on the panel in front of me and I connect them to their intended party. Yet, when I recognize the incoming call from myself, I say, 'Hold please,' anticipating that at the end of my shift, I'll have time to connect with myself. Except the shift is never really over, my sense of responsibility to others and what still needs to be done is endless. It didn't occur to me that by perpetually leaving myself on hold, my line would eventually disconnect."

A moray eel snaked past us.

"Are you still on hold?" asked the Hooks.

"Mostly yes. I'm still habitually telling myself, *When X is done, then I will take time to myself.* It means that whatever I'm doing is preventing me from my sacred bow time. It has bred an impatience in me if I'm engaged in something I'd rather not be doing or if something is taking longer than I expected I just get frustrated."

"It's good to hear you recognize how you set yourself up to be impatient, giving these voices more power." The bubbles flowed from the crink up above.

"Yes. I'm fed up with waiting, with putting myself on hold. It's not kind, it's cruel. It's a lie. It's never all going to get done. My to-do list is in a perpetual state of expansion, not contraction; it's seemingly infinite and my life isn't. For others this may seem obvious, for me it's an epiphany."

Another crink appeared further down the Hooks. Now streams of bubbles were escaping from both creases as they counseled me. "It's time for a new story, one that shifts your relationship to time and your ability to respond to yourself."

"Yeah, I'm ready. This belief in scarcity as it relates to time still snares me. It tells me there isn't enough time for me to do what I love. It keeps me from enjoying unstructured time, when the only commitment I have is to myself, to be still, to wander, to wonder. It tells me spending time simply following my curiosities isn't as worthy, it's indulgent, that it's 'doing nothing.' This internalized voice judges me as lazy or unproductive, because what do I really have to show for my time, what have I accomplished? I've learned to cloak my need to daydream into forms of exercise that are mindless like swimming laps, biking, or going for long walks along the beach." I shook my hands out in front of me as if I could shake this bad habit off. "It's time to rewrite the old formula, *When X is done I will tend to myself*, or that other people's needs and wants are more important than my desires."

The Hooks released two more waves of bubbles. When they dissipated, a new crack was revealed that spanned the distance between the two crinks. "So what happens the next time you hear the call, *Wish you were here?*" As they spoke a hissing sound emanated from the crack. Tiny bubbles lined up along it and peeled off.

"It's time I promptly answer it. I like the suggestion to just lay my hands in my lap, curled open and pause, take a breath. In that pause, I can give myself my full attention, sense how I'm feeling, if I am purring or growling inside."

My Peaceful Warrior spoke up. "More inward sensing, let the outer world fall away for a moment. I've got you covered."

I leaned over towards her. "Thank you, I want to drop into my skin, to reconnect."

~⌕~

When Ian drove home from lunch, he saw a poster in the window, BLACK LIVES MATTER. He understood the sentiment differently after his reading about the country's history and current treatment of Black people by the police, by the "justice" system that incarcerated disproportionately more Black men for the same crimes a white man committed.

He heard a siren go off behind him and saw the flashing light a few cars back in his rearview mirror. He pulled over to make way. He recalled the advice Black men give their sons and adhere to if pulled over by the cops, to keep their hands visible on the steering wheel at all times. Advice he had never been given nor had even known was necessary till recently. He read the CNN article "What Black People Are Doing to Protect Themselves at Traffic Stops."[42] Ian didn't fear he would be shot if he reached for his wallet or registration. He didn't drive with a GoPro camera on the dash so Sarah would know what happened to him if he had been stopped by the police. He had the freedom to go about his life, unafraid of unwarranted police interference, believing he would be treated justly by the law.

The siren passed and he slowly pulled back into the lane.

Racial profiling wasn't his reality but it was a reality. The unconscious and conscious bias of the police were on display now. *What about all the unconscious biases I have?* Ian wasn't sure how he would surface them. He arrived home and dropped his keys on the counter. Per knew what time it was—nap time. She followed him to the bedroom.

Ian awoke with Per's weight against his feet, facing Ariel's painting of the layout on their bedroom wall. It didn't belong there either. He sat up, turning his back to it and stretched. When he walked past their shared altar, the golden glint of Sarah's engagement ring caught his eye. It rested in front of the Queen, where he'd placed it. He knew waiting for her was

[42] Faith Karimi, "What Black drivers are doing to protect themselves during traffic stops", CNN, April 14, 2021. https://www.cnn.com/2021/04/14/us/driving-while-black-precautions-trnd/index.html.

a choice he made, not something foisted upon him.

He had finally put an end to the debate he'd been having with himself; his head was really the only one arguing with him. His heart and body knew what he wanted all along. He had tried to silence them, tried to protect himself from being hurt, from being vulnerable. He sat down cross-legged to meditate; it had been weeks since he had inhabited this place. He lit a new stick of incense and the candle and closed his eyes. The smell of sandalwood and jasmine accompanied his inbreath. His body softened as he exhaled. When he finished, the thought arose. *Being vulnerable isn't so bad, it's freeing.* He no longer felt as disconnected from himself or Sarah.

He looked at their engagement ring. "You are coming with me to Kauai." He had been picturing them there together, his proposal to her. He had an intuition she was going to return and he wanted to be available.

~⌒~

The Hooks continued, "Think of it as changing the channel. At times it's fine to be caught up in the future, imagining what's possible, or reflecting on the past, to learn from it. What we are asking you to pay attention to is how often your channel is dialed to the present moment."

My posture had been slumped until my Peaceful Warrior trailed her finger from my lower back up along my spine. Her touch felt like a chord of light that pulled me upward, centering and connecting me. "Not as often as I'd like. I know because I've come to associate a sense of resourcefulness when I'm present. If I'm anxious, it's probably because I've slipped into an imagined future that's not so pleasant. When I bow, I become more present and am flooded with a sense of connection." I noticed the sea floor moving again, an octopus skirted along, when it moved its flesh darkened to a deep purple. As it passed by the Hooks, a tentacle wrapped itself around it. I watched the white suction cups adhered to its edge, then a second tentacle coiled around it while it paused.

The Hooks' voice was muffled. "What hinders your ability to be present, to pay attention to the moment?"

The octopus settled, returning to the color of the sea floor, but I knew it was there. *Is it going to silence the Hooks? Should I do something?* I looked towards my Peaceful Warrior and she simply laid her palms open in her lap and kept them there.

I mimicked her. "Typically I'm in my head, literally ahead of myself in future scenarios of what might happen to ensure I'm prepared. I often feel overly responsible for everything I see, all that's not done or I think should be done. Parker Palmer describes this in his book, *Let Your Life Speak* as a shadow of leadership he calls 'functional atheism.' It's the unquestioned assumption that if anything is going to change, it's up to me to make it happen."

The Hooks' voice was still muffled. "Do you believe it? Is it all up to you? Are you that powerful?"

I kept my eye on the octopus as I spoke. "No, not when you put it that way, it's just an unconscious way of being in the world."

The octopus darted off and the Hooks' voice hissed, "What else hinders you?" as the bubbles streamed in tributaries from the crinks and crack.

I said, "Self-doubt. Whenever a peacefulness comes over me, I immediately start to doubt if it will last, if it's really true and if I deserve it." I moved off the reef to be upright.

The Hooks had become more like a river delta; streams of bubbles flowed forth as they spoke. "So you evaluate your own worth to have such a feeling. Tell me, who deserves to be peaceful, happy, or content? Again don't think about it too much, just say what comes to mind."

"People who have worked really hard, people who have had a life of pain and suffering deserve more happiness." I rubbed my fingers along the base of my neck and tipped my head back to stretch my spine as I watched the bubbles wend upward. I heard my answer and started to question it.

The Hooks persisted. "What about children? Do children have to earn the right to be happy or do they need to first work hard, experience pain and suffering?"

I knew they had laid a trap for me. "Don't be ridiculous. I spoke without thinking, you know I can't defend that train of thought."

"Nonetheless, you're hooked by it, unconsciously. You may not be able to justify it or 'defend it' as you say but now as an adult you appear to be living by it. You don't allow yourself happiness. How come?"

"I don't trust happiness."

"Why?" A singularly large bubble bounced out and then burst into many smaller ones.

"Because it always leaves without saying goodbye. One minute it's there and the next minute it's nowhere to be found. I feel like a fool when that happens. I hate the disappointment when it vanishes. It gets me every time."

My Peaceful Warrior asked, "What gets you?"

"Happiness dupes me. I start to think it's really here to

stay this time and I start believing in it. Just when I let my guard down, it flies off again."

"Huh, flies off again." My Peaceful Warrior spoke as she swam over to me, "It sounds like you could be talking about your father. Maybe he was around for a while and then the next day he was gone for weeks. When we're young, time doesn't make sense. We haven't grasped the future, how days become weeks become months—gone can just feel like forever." She came up behind me and put her hands on my hips, her front body against my spine. She spoke over my left shoulder. "You felt vulnerable. You counted on him being there and he wasn't. I've got your back now—you can count on me, I'm not going anywhere."

I laid my hands on top of hers, my spine elongated. "Maybe I did confuse his presence with happiness. Nonetheless, happiness is fleeting and it's still disappointing when it leaves."

The Hooks said, "Knowing that happiness is one of the many temporary feelings of your life, what if you were more willing to welcome it? Invite it in as a guest, instead of resisting with a closed, locked door. You'll never know what you are missing if you don't. Feelings come and go. Welcome each guest, even the uninvited ones. Have you ever allowed yourself to be happy for days?"

My right hand briefly rubbed the center of my chest. "I'm told I was a very happy child, I just don't remember much of my childhood. My mum said I was easily amused and delighted with the simplest pleasures."

The crack was spitting forth bubbles. "Children have a way of being happy, it's adults that make it more complicated."

I wrapped my arms around myself, holding my ribcage on either side. "I don't know, somewhere along the way I started paying attention to what was missing instead of what was present, or directed my attention to what would happen in the future."

"This is a central hook—how you relate to time and your feelings. Like we have said, you are an extremely sensitive person. This can be a blessing and a burden. Your gift in this world is your depth of feelings, your ability to sense and see past appearances. Your confusion to date has been what to do with those feelings and what you perceive that others may think they've concealed from you. Listen closely. All you have to do with your feelings is to feel them. Accept them and let them move without having to make sense of all of them. You don't need to resist them, nor do you need to act on them. Simply accept and feel them, ride them like a wave or a power-ful horse—stay in connection."

I still felt my Peaceful Warrior's pressure along my spine and took comfort in her presence. "This isn't new advice. Despite my knowing that feelings are meant to be felt, not nec-essarily explained away, I still try. I'm still trying to figure out why I feel the way I do and what I can do about it. It's agonizing when I get caught up in it. When I resist them, they only grow in magnitude, trying to get my attention. When I try to invalidate them—or, heaven forbid, someone else like Ian tells me I'm overreacting—it just makes me furious. I feel misunderstood, alone. Yet really all I need at that moment is for me to listen and understand me."

The Hooks asked, "When this is happening, are you feel-ing anything?"

"Yes, perhaps a little frightened, unsafe, and alone. My feelings can be overwhelming. I think if I can figure them out,

I won't feel so out of control. I'd rather make them go away and avoid ever having to feel them again, particularly if they are painful."

"Do they go away?"

"No, not until I listen to them."

"Hmm, you know if you listen to them, if you give them your attention, they will go away. Yet you resist them, suppress them, and it exhausts you. You're not alone. Our culture wants to avoid feeling anything unpleasant, labeling some feelings as negative: anger, frustration, disappointment, shame, guilt, and grief. It's another lie—these feelings are neither good nor bad, they are just feelings, a form of energy. The only reason they build up is because we ignore them. If the only time you let yourself feel them is when the dam finally breaks, you're left with the impression that they are overwhelming, that they can drown you. Yet we don't see how complicit we are in making them so powerful. It's our very act of ignoring them that makes them come on stronger to get our attention. At first, feeling them is more like taking a ride on a scooter. When we ignore them they grow to the size of an automobile, a van, or an eighteen-wheeler that hits us broadside to get our attention." The Hooks paused.

I leaned back into my Peaceful Warrior. I wanted to feel resourceful. I watched the bubbles ascend.

The Hooks continued, "We're not telling you not to reflect on your feelings. Please don't hear this as either/or. Your self-examination, your curiosity about repeating patterns and exploring underlying assumptions is laudable. It's simply no substitute for feeling what you are feeling at the moment. At times you use your mind to distract your heart. You're good at it. Until you're willing to create the space to simply feel what is arising, you won't be able to cultivate your connection to Compassion and Forgiveness. When these feelings have been genuinely welcomed within us, we are more able to extend them to others."

I let go of my sides and my Peaceful Warrior came alongside me. Her hands were facing palm up, in the curved gesture Forgiveness had taught me. We both found a spot on the reef to rest beside one another and laid our open hands in our lap.

The Hooks voice was consistently hissing now. "Forgiveness knows that not all emotions are created equal. Grief is a gateway to another world. It can break our hearts open and make us more capable of compassion and love. It can create a clearing if we are willing to surrender to the emptiness, the winter in ourselves that inevitably follows loss. Our time is limited; listen carefully. Tend to your own garden. One never plants a seed on top of an existing plant. We find a clear space to begin life, to nurture it."

I leaned forward. I heard the Hooks foreshadow an ending.

"You're an adult now, making choices for yourself. You don't need anyone's approval for the way you want to live your life. Similarly, you don't have to have a reason for your feelings to be valid. Your mind doesn't have to approve of your heart, nor your body's signals for you to feel them. Your mind is only engaged when you discern if you want to act on them. Your Peaceful Warrior here will protect the space for you to feel them. Let your mind be the servant of your heart, not the other way around."

I reached for my Peaceful Warrior's hand. She held mine.

"Remember, it's a lie that feelings have to be justified. You were taught this by people who were uncomfortable with their own feelings. Justification comes from the head, feelings arise in our body, and emotions are the language our heart speaks. Listen. Simply feel them. At times the feeling of sorrow you experience makes you more sensitive to the sadness in those around you. Beware, when you are around people who are unwilling to feel their own feelings, you needn't carry them for them. You unconsciously did this in your family and you do it for your friends and students at times. You must learn to distinguish between yourself and others. There's a difference between being sensitive to something and taking it in or on as if it is your responsibility."

"Hmm." I nodded. *Caring is not carrying.*

"If you don't design your life, society is all too happy to design it for you. It might not be the life you want. If you want spaciousness, you must create it, first inside and then it will become a reality outside. Our inner landscape has everything to do with our outer landscape."

I sat up. "Once again, you are telling me it's a choice. I'm the one who over-schedules myself. I just need to say no more often—a lot more often. I find people want to know what I'm doing. I'm not comfortable saying 'nothing.' I just want to be still and listen, which really isn't doing nothing. I simply want the freedom to be."

The Hooks asked, "What happens when you slow down, when you create the spaciousness you crave?"

"Invariably there's a disorientation period, where I keep questioning if there is something else I should be doing. It's hard to relax into it; I spoil it at times and fill it back up. Though I'm getting better at pausing. In that stillness I start to see the delicate web that connects my life to everything and everyone else, how interwoven we all are. I can sense that I'm not alone, that it's impossible to truly be alone. I feel a sense of connection in myself and how I really do belong and always have. My life starts to make a different kind of sense—not the 'intellectual' kind. I palpably feel a part of this fabric, not apart from it. I'd like to lean into this kind of 'sense making' more, the felt sense. When I do, it reveals all the other aspects of life that don't make any sense at all but I had come to think of as normal. My heart and body can't tolerate these incongruencies."

My Peaceful Warrior asked, "Like what?"

I turned to her. "Oh God, where do I start? How about the way we leave out the truth about the history of our country? How we settled this country by massacring the indigenous people, taking their lands, destroying their culture and language? We then built the wealth of the nation by purchasing African people as slaves, treating them as if they weren't human. How is it that some people have the right to kill other people, to use them with no regard for their well-being, giving them no choice in the matter? How was that acceptable? How did so many turn a blind eye? How am I still turning a blind eye?

"Our beloved Declaration of Independence states in its second paragraph: *We hold these truths to be self-evident, that all men are created equal, that they are endowed by their Creator with certain unalienable Rights, that among these are Life, Liberty, and the Pursuit of Happiness.* I don't believe we have held ourselves accountable to this. We are just pretending to believe it, giving it lip service. I don't know how to reconcile these irreconcilable differences. It's confusing. This confusion is familiar. If I'm confused, maybe I don't have to do anything; maybe that's how I absolve myself of responsibility, of taking action to address or speak to these glaring inconsistencies."

My shoulders caved. "Ugh. I sense and see too much and it hurts. It's overwhelming to the point of debilitation. I don't know what to do with all this pain and suffering I'm surrounded by that often goes unacknowledged. It's not just in society, it was closer to home too: My family life resembled a cold war at times. The silence was so thick it sucked the oxygen from the air; it was suffocating. I just wanted to be outside to escape it regardless of the weather."

The Hooks asked, "So what did you do?"

"I treated my parents differently. When my father was upset I'd stay out of sight, be quiet. When my mum was upset, I'd stay close, offer her a hug, offer to help with chores, tell her it was going to be okay, tell her I loved her. Except even when I wrapped her in a hug she felt like she was miles away. I felt powerless to change the dynamics I witnessed in my family. Eventually I decided to stop seeing it, just like I try to stop seeing homelessness."

A short burst of bubbles escaped. "Did that work?"

"No, it backfired. My feelings, as you know, didn't go away until they got my attention."

The Hooks said, "In your case, choosing not to see became a dis-ease for you; your vision was slowly deteriorating."

"Yeah, thankfully a routine eye exam caught it. As a child, when I wanted to block out the world, to stop seeing it, I literally put my hands up together in the stop gesture in front of my face." I demonstrated it, blocking out my view of the Hooks. "I thought that if I don't see you, then you don't exist. What I didn't know then was they existed separate from my ability to see them. As I grew older, I saw the limitations of my gesture and my assumption that I could make problems go away by ignoring them. But I still felt powerless to do anything so I tried not to see what was happening around me, even if it was in front of me. Denial is a powerful act." I rubbed my eyes.

"My body listened and my eyes developed a disease, tiny tears in the fabric that would lead to holes and the risk of my retina detaching. Detached retinas cause blindness, a true inability to see. It was a disease more prevalent in adults, occurring in their fifties. I was sixteen. I had surgery the next day. After the numbing drops, I watched them put a giant needle in my eye. I had to be perfectly still. The treatment was cryogenics, applying a freezing probe that creates scar tissue. My frozen feelings, unshed tears, were causing tiny tears, a rip, holes in the fabric of my eye. I remember journaling about it then, being struck that the spelling for the word tears as in the saltwater falling from our eyes is also spelled the same as tears, the pulling apart, ripping." *Can that be a coincidence?*

"I had to have both eyes, all four quadrants treated. It took months. The recovery was sitting still for weeks. Not using my eyes to read or watch TV. I couldn't do any activity that caused a rise in blood pressure—no bending down, no lifting, not even the weight of a newspaper. Essentially, doing nothing, being still was my prescription for healing. My body was trying to tell me it was okay to do nothing, to just feel, to let the tears fall. I wept plenty. It was healing. The tears have not come back, I think because my tears flow more freely now."

"Yes, we are fond of hearing your mantra, 'I am an ocean, I'm going with the flow.'"

A single reef manta ray cruised over our heads, moving with a majesty that captured our attention. Its underside was mostly white with black markings. I was sorry to see its skinny tail trailing behind. I wanted to swim alongside it.

The Hooks said, "Go, accompany it for a spell, listen to your longings. They will not lead you astray."

I didn't need any further encouragement. We both eagerly swam to catch up with it. Our view from behind revealed the graceful movements of its wings, the tips mostly white darkened in shade to solid black on the rest of its back. It flapped its triangular wings slowly up and down, a ripple moving across its body, creating the effect of elegantly flying through the water. Two narrow gray fish had attached themselves on top by its face, taking a free ride. When we came alongside it, it looked into our eyes, lifting it's wing so as not to touch us, allowing us to move closer: like the way I'd welcome a lover into my bed, lifting the sheets.

I swam upside down below it for another view. It surprised me and circled around me, a kind of somersault with me at the center. I arched backwards and swam in a circle, mimicking its gesture. The manta ray somersaulted again, keeping me in the center of its trajectory.[43] I felt the invitation to play, and motioned for my Peaceful Warrior to join us, not be a spectator. What followed was a game of follow the leader, each of us taking turns in the lead, an unchoreographed dance of synchronized swimming that filled me with tears of joy.

My heart swelled inside my chest to the point of breaking through the false boundary of my skin. I floated still on my side as it glided over me, just inches separating us. This time it didn't turn back and I watched its tail trail away, leaving me in awe.

---

[43] Louie Psihoyos, Racing Extinction, "The Breathtaking Mating Behavior of Manta Rays", Oceanic Preservation Society, June 5, 2015, 1:30, youtube. https://youtu.be/9qinG5a_26Y.

It was then that I noted we'd swum to shallower waters. The surface was within view, unlike the depths of where we had visited with the Hooks. Where were they? My instincts told me to return to them, rather than surface yet. Except I didn't know my way back. I'd been swimming in circles and was disoriented. The reef didn't have road signs. *A little guidance, please.* I looked in different directions and my Peaceful Warrior shrugged. We were lost. I couldn't see the familiar glint of the Hooks anywhere.

I recalled we had been swimming with the current when we followed the manta ray. My hair had floated out in front of me at times, blinding me. I hung still again to sense the direction the current was flowing and chose to swim against it. After a while I noticed another mermaid up ahead; she was gesturing for us to join her. As I came closer, I saw a glint of metal on her chest and recognized the face of Faith. I swam directly into her arms for an embrace. She spun me in circles that mirrored the joy of my body being entwined with hers. As I pulled back, her pendant took on new meaning; the infinity sign was implied, the lower curve in the shape of a hook. "Where are they now?" I asked.

"They are gone. They said they hoped to never see you again."

I'd seen them breaking down before my eyes, but I still expected to have to pull them out. "Huh, that surprises me, like seeing you now. I didn't think our conversation was over yet. I would have thanked them before I left."

"Was it an illuminating conversation?"

"Yes, in a paradoxical way. Their very existence was based on me believing in lies, adopting them as if they were true, lies I'd unquestionably bought—hook, line, and sinker. Our conversation offered me a vital perspective, leading me to doubt what I'd previously thought true. They encouraged me to question my beliefs rather than doubt myself."

"What was the last thing they said?" Faith asked.

"They encouraged me to follow my longing to swim with the manta ray. It was amazing, such a curious and gorgeous creature." I looked up again. "Is my journey about to end? The surface is nearer now than it's ever been before."

"Not quite. Let's swim, you have some composing to do." She swam off ahead into deeper waters, and we followed.

I relaxed with Faith in the lead, my Peaceful Warrior beside me. Part of me wasn't ready for this journey to end; I'd come to welcome the adventure of the unexpected.

Faith said, "Yes, you are more willing to be lost now, to venture into the terra incognita. This comes with having a relationship with faith."

"It's good to have you nearby."

"It's really up to you how near or far I am. When you are still and you listen, you will find me ready to guide you. You will not see me after this journey ends, but you can sense my presence if you pay attention."

I turned to my other side, wondering what was to become of my Peaceful Warrior. As I watched her swim beside me I heard Faith say, "She, too, will become invisible."

My Peaceful Warrior reached over and ran her hand from my tailbone up along my spine to the base of my neck. I remembered her promise to help guard my holy grail of attention, to help create space for me to pause. She smiled knowingly back at me.

Up ahead was the remains of a shipwreck. The vessel was broken in pieces, engulfed in corals and sea life, as fish from every color in the rainbow had made it their home.

"It is time for you to make a vow to yourself, where you will put your attention and what you commit to live by. Take your time—your vow is essential to living a life free of hooks. It will give you the ability to recognize lies, told to you by another, or whispered continually by societal culture. Claim and author your life. We will linger near here waiting to listen to you give voice to it."

The last line of Mary Oliver's poem, The Summer Day, came to mind asking me what I wanted to do with my one wild and precious life?[44] I swam around the wreckage. The way it teemed with life drew me in. Around its corner I came upon a turtle resting, its neck elongated as it looked to me. I tried to communicate that I was no threat, not wanting to disturb it. I wanted to imitate it.

I paused and stretched out sufficiently far away. I felt the importance of the task ahead of me and expected it might take me a while; it might be difficult—and then I caught myself. What if it flowed easily from me? I closed my eyes and the opening line offered itself as if on a silver platter.

"To grow wild by the sea." I smiled. *There's potential in that.* I opened my eyes and the turtle was still there.

"To slow down and listen to what I am sensing and feeling." I knew my Peaceful Warrior had been enlisted; she would help create the pause to choose, to not react in unnecessary defense. I wanted to feel the freedom of acting congruently from within.

"To act on it with authenticity and integrity." I closed my

---

[44] Mary Oliver, "Mary Oliver reads "The Summer Day", Beacon Press. 1990. 1:29, youtube, https://youtu.be/16CL6bKVbJQ.

eyes again, to check into my body, my heart. I was purring inside.

"To know if I am purring or growling inside and to let myself be known." I didn't have to have a reason to feel what I was feeling, nor a need to justify it, simply to let myself come to know myself. From here I would know what I wanted.

"To give voice to my longings and follow them to a place of belonging, be-longing." Just as the Hooks have said, trust my longings; they would not lead me astray. I opened my eyes again, taking in the surroundings of the creatures who had accepted my presence here, as equals. My left hand traced the infinity sign in the water. I wanted to give voice to what living with this awareness would mean.

"To be in reciprocity with all my relations." The draft had easily flowed from me and felt complete for now. *If I can remember it.* I closed my eyes again to recite it uninterrupted.

> *To grow wild by the sea.*

> *To slow down and listen to what I am sensing and feeling and to act on it with authenticity and integrity.*

I stalled, unsure of the next line. I listened inwardly and exhaled.

> *To know if I am purring or growling inside and to let myself be known.*

> *To give voice to my longings and follow them to a place of belonging, be-longing.*

> *To be in reciprocity with all my relations.*

I laid my hands open in my lap, and the glint of the gold ring on my right ring finger flashed back at me. I felt ready to speak my vow out loud for Faith and my Peaceful Warrior. I hadn't strayed far, and swam the rest of the way around the wreck to see Faith waiting for me.

"Where is she, my Peaceful Warrior? I'm ready to speak my vow."

Faith replied, "She never left you, nor will she. Your process of integration has already begun." She reached behind her neck and unclasped her pendant. She came behind me and fastened it around mine. "Your vow is beautiful. Speak it every day with your blessing."

I placed my left hand over the pendant, her gift of remembrance. I felt her hand gently cover my eyes. I closed them. The initial darkness soon became a mosaic of images: a galloping black horse with a long rippling mane, a circle of dark rocks in the blue waters near a shoreline, flames in a fireplace. She removed her hand from my eyes.

Next I felt the pressure of her finger on the center of my forehead and another finger at my navel with the slightest direction of up. The firelight grew luminous; no longer contained in a fireplace, it surrounded us in a golden light that penetrated my skin as if it seamlessly filled me. I wasn't burned by it, I felt buoyant and spacious as if my heart was overflowing with love.

She moved her hands to rest over my heart and her pendant. I laid my hands above hers and pressed gently, wanting to imprint her. Her presence, her touch, held me freely. She whispered in my ear. "It's time for you to begin your journey home.

Remember, if you choose, I'm always with you. You have the power to conjure me."

I slowly turned around to embrace Faith. Our chest and hips came together as I rested my cheek along hers. The smell of sandalwood and lavender surprised me. I inhaled more deeply, feeling her calm presence within, and said, "I'm grateful beyond words."

ACKNOWLEDGMENTS

T O THE MOON, that wakes me and reminds me, seen or unseen—a conversation is possible between us. To my beloved husband whose love has proved enduring, your willingness to question what is "enough" has helped us navigate our uncharted waters of a "good life." Thank you for our Sunday morning "handpakes" and countless hours of listening to Sarah and Ian's unfolding journey. To my son, who has always been my teacher, your integrity to your heart's longing gave me the courage to claim my love of writing.

To my circle sisters who've mid-wifed my becoming these last twenty-five years, encouraging me to break out of my "old shit story" and offered me new ways of being in the world by your example. To my dream group, our decades of tea and tarot have kept the channel to my dream world wide and flowing, helping me interpret its symbolic language.

To my teachers of Authentic Movement, Lee and Lynn Fuller, a deep bow of gratitude. My body is no longer a stranger to me because of your profound skills in witnessing—I know in my bones what is essential, how to see and hear myself. To my movement sisters, our shared commitment to

REFLECT

this collective practice has offered me the portal to a more authentic life.

To my spiritual coach, Sara Schley, who honors spirit and shadow, helping me to receive both more fully, bless you, may *Brainstorm* take the world by storm. To my colleagues, who understood when my "moonlighting job" needed to become my "day job," continue to step it up—the world is a better place for your leadership.

To my "alpha" reader Christie Lynk, who has read this series to its edge, more than once, and is as familiar with it as the forest trails we walk. Your accompaniment and abundance of support has been as delicious as our wild huckleberry feasts. My future readers thank you, as do I. To my editor, Kristen Hamilton, whose manuscript review and editing honed this book and set a clear path for me to learn the craft of writing. The shortcomings are mine; thanks for making fewer visible. To my beta readers, have no doubt you made this book better; I am in your debt. To my future beta readers, I know I need you now. Contact me via my website if this makes your heart sing.

To my illustrator, Connor Ryan, who knows how to break the frame, for your imagination and countless iterations of the symbolism until it captured the essence of the book, *mahalo*. To the Book Designers, Alan and Ian, for creating a beautiful visual invitation to this series.

To my readers, your relationship with the book brings it to life. May the very "real" organizations, musicians, poets, authors and places sprinkled throughout this "fiction" nourish your life as they have mine. Scan the QR code below for links to these resources. Stay tuned, the series has only just begun.

Visit RumoredWoman.com
for Readers Guide or to purchase and receive volume discounts.

*Read on for an excerpt of Return, the second book
in the Rumored Woman series.*

RUMORED WOMAN

RETURN

BOOK TWO

MORGAN MAGAURAN

CHAPTER I

SKIFF TO SHORE

I AWOKE TO THE sound of waves lapping and felt a gentle rocking motion as if I was in a giant cradle. My face was only inches from wooden slats. I lay in the fetal position on my left side; my head cradled in my bent arm, my feet tucked under a center bench. The vessel's side rails curved to a point. The itch on my lower leg was from my bedding, a bunched-up green-and-blue-plaid wool blanket. I recognized the cream long-sleeved linen shift, as a replica of the one I'd worn with Faith before I'd become a mermaid. *At least I'm not naked.*

I leaned up high enough to peer over the rail. The boat rocked precariously to one side until I centered my weight. I was drifting towards a small harbor, bordered by houses. In my underworld odyssey with Faith, I'd never seen a neighborhood, nor any other human that wasn't an aspect of myself. *Where am I?* I laid back down.

Pink and slate blossoming clouds blanketed the sky as rays of morning light snuck out to dance on the water. It looked biblical. *Why didn't I return home?* I thought I'd wake in my bedroom, returning through the mirror, the way I'd left.

My most recent memory was of being a mermaid, near the shipwreck. I'd composed my vow to myself and returned to share it with Faith, but she already knew it. I'd forgotten she had no need for the spoken word to know my inner landscape. The absence of my Peaceful Warrior had surprised me. She said my process of integration had already begun. When she fastened her pendant to my neck, she whispered in my ear that it was time to start my journey home. My hand immediately went to check if it was there. It was.

Pushing myself up to sit, the boat wobbled again, side to side. *Go slow, be still.* I twisted to look behind me; the sun had risen on the horizon with a distant land mass below it.

My throat was dry, and I looked in vain for drinking water. The absence of it and oars were disturbing. The skiff only had three simple wooden seats: one at the middle and two more spaced out towards the bow. It had an elegant craftsman design, a blend of wood and something that resembled hide. The visible latticework of its frame ran lengthwise from bow to stern and crosswise from side to side. The blanket offered a modest cushion from the bottom slats. If it were a fisherman's boat, thankfully it didn't smell of dead fish.

I inched towards the middle seat, now cautious about the stability, and gently hoisted myself up to sit on it. I pivoted, slowly lifting my right leg over to straddle the bench facing sideways. I paused to let the boat steady, then brought my other leg over to face the bow. The island before me couldn't be more than five miles long. As I sat exposed, a shiver sent my

elbows close into my body, and my shoulders rounded towards my ears. I pulled the linen hem down over my knees to cover more of my naked legs. Puffs of wind pressed against my back while tendrils of hair tickled the sides of my cheeks. I tucked them back behind my ears and gingerly retrieved the blanket from the stern to wrap myself up.

My hands clutched its edges as I crossed my arms in front; it became a welcome shield to the breeze that was blowing me towards shore. *I could convert it to a sail, if I outstretched my arms, offering more surface area for the wind to resist. Why bother hastening my arrival? Soon enough I will be blown there. Then what?*

The harbor was minimalist. It consisted of a simple pier and dock. There weren't any boats moored in the water, only a small row of similar-sized skiffs pulled up above the high tide line. A half dozen homes were set back from the shoreline on the right side of the pier. A stone bell tower announced itself midway up the island. The spacing of houses grew wider as I looked north. Scattered on the pastures were clumps of black and white sheep. The sun was casting my shadow in front of me, both in and beyond the boat; it would reach shore first.

The phrase *stranger in a strange land* echoed in my head. It took me a moment to recall the author of the sci-fi book by that title: Robert Heinlein. His protagonist's return was quite the adventure in challenging customs. This was not what I had in mind for mine. I dismissed the thought.

I hoped the inhabitants of this island spoke English. I wanted some aspects of my return to be easier. My stomach growled. *How will I eat with no money? Where will I sleep? I'm at the mercy of strangers. Homeless. No, I have resources—at a distance. My first priority is finding a phone. I can call Ian collect. I'll find a bank where he can wire me money.*

Church bells rang. I started counting: one, two, three, four, five, six, seven, then silence. *Seven a.m. is almost a civilized hour. No wonder no one is milling about.*

I leaned over to drag my fingers across the clear sea's surface. It was frigid, not the tropical waters I'd come from. Not for the faint of heart.

This was not the journey home I expected. The only thing I thought was up in the air was whether it would be day or night, or if Ian would be home or out. Clearly, I was wrong; there were many more variables in the equation. She didn't actually say go home, she said start my journey home. Being cast off in a boat with no oars, no money, no shoes and a shift of a dress felt more like a final test. *It could be worse. It could be raining or snowing with no civilization in sight. Remember Patience. I can do this.*

I heard the line of my blessing: *May I become patient with uncertainty, welcoming mystery into my life as my beloved dance partner, letting go of expectations, even with disappointment, to honor what is authentic in the moment.*

I wasn't feeling particularly patient. I lifted the blanket up over my shoulders and held it out with my hands for a makeshift sail. After a few minutes, my forearm muscles were burning and my shoulders were cramping. I wasn't moving any faster; in fact, my hair was no longer blowing at all. The wind had died down, only the current was carrying me now. I wrapped myself back up. *Patience. Surrender. Faith.* My hands were clutching the blanket tighter.

The church bell chimed once, marking the half hour. I'd be ashore before it rang again. I knew the time but not the day nor the month. *What if it's not the same year? What if time moved differently where I was and more than a few weeks or months have passed? How long could I expect Ian to wait for me without a word?*

As I glanced down into the water, the bottom had become visible. Barnacles covered the rocks. Not a welcome sight for bare feet.

It wasn't long before the waves had pushed me ashore and I heard the hull of the boat scraping against stones. When I stood up for the first time, my lower back complained of stiffness. The boat had halted in ankle-deep water. *Well, no worries about getting my nonexistent shoes wet.*

I shed the blanket in a heap to keep it dry. My feet found round stones, thankfully no barnacles. It wasn't sharp underfoot but it was still shockingly cold. I hauled the boat with both hands walking backwards till I'd secured it on the beach.

Leaving my security blanket behind, I walked across the cool damp sand. At the transition to a gravel road there were shards of broken glass I carefully avoided. Soon the smell of baking bread tormented me. My stomach grumbled again. Mercy, my mouth watered in anticipation. In front of the grocery store I spied a metal box with a glass window, the kind of thing that held newspapers. *I could find out the date without attracting attention to myself by asking.* When I reached it, my efforts were foiled—it was empty.

As I wandered the town, I spied an oval red sign with gold lettering indicating the POST OFFICE ISLE OF IONA. *So that's where I am, Scotland.* Its hours were 9:00 a.m. to 5:00 p.m. each day of the week, with an hour break for lunch. *How civilized.* It was only open Saturday from 9:00 a.m. to noon, closed Sunday. I had about an hour to wait, as long as it wasn't Sunday.

The smells of coffee and bacon wafting in the air tortured me. Still no people. *Does no one go for an early morning run or walk around here?* The rest of the road appeared to be private homes.

I returned to the main road and walked further north in search of a bank. The street narrowed, with no sidewalks and no more storefronts. The church bells started again: one, two, three, four, five, six, seven, eight. *At least I know the time.*

My return to town offered a different perspective, revealing a red telephone booth. *Thank god this relic still exists. I can call Ian.* The folding door creaked open and I prayed I didn't need change to access the operator. I lifted the receiver, heard a dial tone, and pressed the little white square labeled zero. It rang. I exhaled.

"Guid mornin', operator speakin', how kin ah hulp ye?"

I had a list of things I needed help with but knew she wasn't offering that kind of assistance. "I'd like to place a collect call please, from Sarah O'Sullivan, to the United States."

She asked, "Yer telephone batch, please. It mist be a landline, ye cannae place a collect ca' tae a mobile, thay cannae accept th' charges."

I recited our landline telephone number having no idea what time it was back home.

"Haud th' line."

I gripped the receiver like it was a personal flotation device. It rang and rang and rang. Then I heard my own voice

388

on the answering machine. The irony wasn't lost on me that I was listening to myself.

"Nae answer. Ye wull hae tae huv a go again. Guid day."

"Thanks."

Crap. I don't know anyone else's landline. I had a hard enough time remembering our own. For that matter I didn't know my friends cell numbers either; they were listed as favorites, no memory required. I couldn't reach out to anyone but Ian. *Okay, plan B, find a bank. Except I don't know my account number nor do I have any identification, and their security protocols won't look kindly on a barefoot woman. How can I prove I'm me?*

I turned back towards the coffee shop even though I knew I wouldn't be welcomed penniless and shoeless. *I can't exactly ask what day it is without raising suspicion about my sanity. No, the only question I could ask a local is "Can you tell me where the nearest bank is?"* It occurred to me it wasn't only the lack of people that was odd, it was the absence of any cars.

A young, red-haired woman in a T-shirt and jeans, with a white apron tied around her waist, exited the café. She was setting the outdoor tables with the metal holder for salt, pepper, and jam. I was so hungry even the tiny jam packets looked promising.

I said, "Good morning. Excuse me, can you tell me where the nearest bank is?"

"Guid mornin'. Ye wilnae be findin' a bank till ye git tae th' otherside o' Mull. Th' next ferry tae Mull is nae till mid-day. Thare ur nae mornin' runs oan Sunday."

I managed to say "Thanks so much" before I turned and walked back towards the beach. *No newspaper, no Ian, no bank, no post office opening today, and barely a common language. Crap. My plans had crumbled at my feet. My life abhors a plan.* I retreated to the boat to regroup and grabbed my only other possession, draping the blanket over my shoulders. *I may be sleeping on this again.* I didn't even have underwear on—talk about bare necessities.

The shoreline beckoned. I needed to create some distance between me and the odors of breakfast. I wasn't ready to beg for it and I couldn't think about anything else if I was smelling it. The tide line was strewn with washed-up seaweed the color of mustard greens and ripe apples. It oscillated like the sine curves on a heart monitor. My heart was racing. *Now what?* I steadied myself by examining the beach. I'd never seen these shades of cranberry seaweed. I couldn't help but wonder if it was edible. I followed its trail, even when it meant scrambling over the jetty of rocks to reach the other side of sand again. I startled a few black crabs, too tiny to have any decent meat in them.

Am I on my own now? Faith said I had the power to conjure her if I chose. I'd grown accustomed to seeing her. Now I needed to find a way to feel her. I'd love to ask her why she made my return home more complicated. *Hey, haven't I journeyed enough?* Silence. This felt more like a test of my resourcefulness. Well, it wasn't in my nature to fail.

My pulse settled as I walked. Up ahead a woman was traipsing down the grass hillside towards the beach. She came to the corner of the fence that had two steps beside it. *How convenient.* She walked up them and over the fence with ease. A towel hung over her shoulders. She wore a dark sweater and khaki shorts. Perhaps I didn't look so out of place. We could both be heading for a picnic of sorts. If only one of us had a food basket.

She entered the beach on the far side of another jetty of black rocks and disappeared. I kept walking and my pulse quickened again. My new plan was to nod good morning—to keep calm and carry on.

Continue reading Chapter One of Return on
RumoredWoman.com

About the Author

MORGAN MAGAURAN WAS born and educated on the East Coast. She now calls home an island in the Pacific Northwest, where she and her husband raised their son. Reflect is her debut novel and the first in the Rumored Series.

CPSIA information can be obtained
at www.ICGtesting.com
Printed in the USA
JSHW021952081122
32803JS00003B/8

9 798986 690308